BLOOD and GOLD

BLOOD and GOLD

or,

THE STORY OF MARIUS

THE VAMPIRE CHRONICLES

ANNE RICE

ALFRED A. KNOPF

New York · Toronto

2001

Title page art: *La Primavera: The Three Graces* (detail), by
Sandro Botticelli. Uffizi Gallery, Florence. Scala/Art
Resource, New York

Dedicated to my beloved husband, Stan Rice,
and my beloved sister Karen O'Brien

THE LISTENER

1

His name was THORNE. In the ancient language of the runes, it had been longer—Thornevald. But when he became a blood drinker, his name had been changed to Thorne. And Thorne he remained now, centuries later, as he lay in his cave in the ice, dreaming.

When he had first come to the frozen land, he had hoped he would sleep eternally. But now and then the thirst for blood awakened him, and using the Cloud Gift, he rose into the air, and went in search of the Snow Hunters.

He fed off them, careful never to take too much blood from any one so that none died on account of him. And when he needed furs and boots he took them as well, and returned to his hiding place.

These Snow Hunters were not his people. They were dark of skin and had slanted eyes, and they spoke a different tongue, but he had known them in the olden times when he had traveled with his uncle into the land to the East for trading. He had not liked trading. He had preferred war. But he'd learnt many things on those adventures.

In his sleep in the North, he dreamed. He could not help it. The Mind Gift let him hear the voices of other blood drinkers.

Unwillingly he saw through their eyes, and beheld the world as they beheld it. Sometimes he didn't mind. He liked it. Modern things amused him. He listened to far-away electric songs. With the Mind Gift he understood such things as steam engines and railroads; he even understood computers and automobiles. He felt he knew the cities he had left behind though it had been centuries since he'd forsaken them.

An awareness had come over him that he wasn't going to die. Loneliness in itself could not destroy him. Neglect was insufficient. And so he slept.

Then a strange thing happened. A catastrophe befell the world of the blood drinkers.

A young singer of sagas had come. His name was Lestat, and in his electric songs, Lestat broadcast old secrets, secrets which Thorne had never known.

Then a Queen had risen, an evil and ambitious being. She had claimed to have within her the Sacred Core of all blood drinkers, so that, should she die, all the race would perish with her.

Thorne had been amazed.

He had never heard these myths of his own kind. He did not know that he believed this thing.

But as he slept, as he dreamt, as he watched, this Queen began, with the Fire Gift, to destroy blood drinkers everywhere throughout the world. Thorne heard their cries as they tried to escape; he saw their deaths in so far as others saw such things.

As she roamed the earth, this Queen came close to Thorne but she passed over him. He was secretive and quiet in his cave. Perhaps she didn't sense his presence. But he had sensed hers and never had he encountered such age or strength except from the blood drinker who had given him the Blood.

And he found himself thinking of that one, the Maker, the red-haired witch with the bleeding eyes.

The catastrophe among his kind grew worse. More were slain; and out of hiding there came blood drinkers as old as the Queen herself, and Thorne saw these beings.

At last there came the red-haired one who had made him. He saw her as others saw her. And at first he could not believe that she still lived; it had been so long since he'd left her in the Far South that he hadn't dared to hope she was still alive. The eyes and ears of other blood drinkers gave him the infallible proof. And when he looked on her in his dreams, he was overwhelmed with a tender feeling and a rage.

She thrived, this creature who had given him the Blood, and she despised the Evil Queen and she wanted to stop her. Theirs was a hatred for each other which went back thousands of years.

At last there was a coming together of these beings—old ones from the First Brood of blood drinkers, and others whom the blood drinker Lestat loved and whom the Evil Queen did not choose to destroy.

Dimly, as he lay still in the ice, Thorne heard their strange talk, as round a table they sat, like so many powerful Knights, except that in this council, the women were equal to the men.

With the Queen they sought to reason, struggling to persuade her to end her reign of violence, to forsake her evil designs.

He listened, but he could not really understand all that was said among these blood drinkers. He knew only that the Queen must be stopped.

The Queen loved the blood drinker Lestat. But even he could not turn her from disasters, so reckless was her vision, so depraved her mind.

Did the Queen truly have the Sacred Core of all blood drinkers within herself? If so, how could she be destroyed?

Thorne wished the Mind Gift were stronger in him, or that he had used it more often. During his long centuries of sleep, his strength had grown, but now he felt his distance and that he was weak.

But as he watched, his eyes open, as though that might help him to see, there came into his vision another red-haired one, the twin sister of the woman who had loved him so long ago. It astonished him, as only a twin can do.

And Thorne came to understand that the Maker he had loved so much had lost this twin thousands of years ago.

The Evil Queen was the mistress of this disaster. She despised the red-haired twins. She had divided them. And the lost twin came now to fulfill an ancient curse she had laid on the Evil Queen.

As she drew closer and closer to the Queen, the lost twin thought only of destruction. She did not sit at the council table. She did not know reason or restraint.

"We shall all die," Thorne whispered in his sleep, drowsy in the snow and ice, the eternal arctic night coldly enclosing him. He did not move to join his immortal companions. But he watched. He listened. He would do so until the last moment. He could do no less.

Finally, the lost twin reached her destination. She rose against the Queen. The other blood drinkers around her looked on in horror. As the two female beings struggled, as they fought as two warriors upon a battlefield, a strange vision suddenly filled Thorne's mind utterly, as though he lay in the snow and he were looking at the heavens.

What he saw was a great intricate web stretching out in all directions, and caught within it many pulsing points of light. At the very center of this web was a single vibrant flame. He knew the flame was the Queen; and he knew that the other points of light were all the other blood drinkers. He himself was one of those tiny points of light. The tale of the Sacred Core was true. He could see it with his own eyes. And now came the moment for all to surrender to darkness and silence. Now came the end.

The far-flung complex web grew glistening and bright; the core appeared to explode; and then all went dim for a long moment, during which he felt a sweet vibration in his limbs as he often felt in simple sleep, and he thought to himself, Ah, so, now we are dying. And there is no pain.

Yet it was like Ragnarok for his old gods, when the great god, Heimdall, the World Brightener, would blow his horn summoning the gods of Aesir to their final battle.

"And we end with a war as well," Thorne whispered in his cave. But his thoughts did not end.

It seemed the best thing that he live no more, until he thought of her, his red-haired one, his Maker. He had wanted so badly to see her again.

Why had she never told him of her lost twin? Why had she never entrusted to him the myths of which the blood drinker Lestat sang? Surely she had known the secret of the Evil Queen with her Sacred Core.

He shifted; he stirred in his sleep. The great sprawling web had faded from his vision. But with uncommon clarity he could see the red-haired twins, spectacular women.

They stood side by side, these comely creatures, the one in rags, the other in splendor. And through the eyes of other blood drinkers he came to know that the stranger twin had slain the Queen, and had taken the Sacred Core within herself.

"Behold, the Queen of the Damned," said his Maker twin as she presented to the others her long-lost sister. Thorne understood her. Thorne saw the suffering in her face. But the face of the stranger twin, the Queen of the Damned, was blank.

In the nights that followed the survivors of the catastrophe remained together. They told their tales to one another. And their stories filled the air like so many songs from the bards of old, sung in the mead hall. And Lestat, leaving his electric instruments for music, became once more the chronicler, making a story of the battle that he would pass effortlessly into the mortal world.

Soon the red-haired sisters had moved away, seeking a hiding place where Thorne's distant eye could not find them.

Be still, he had told himself. Forget the things that you have seen. There is no reason for you to rise from the ice, any more than there ever was. Sleep is your friend. Dreams are your unwelcome guests.

Lie quiet and you will lapse back into peace again. Be like the god Heimdall before the battle call, so still that you can hear the wool grow on the backs of sheep, and the grass grow far away in the lands where the snow melts.

But more visions came to him.

The blood drinker Lestat brought about some new and confusing tumult in the mortal world. It was a marvelous secret from the Christian past that he bore, which he had entrusted to a mortal girl.

There would never be any peace for this one called Lestat. He was like one of Thorne's people, like one of the warriors of Thorne's time.

Thorne watched as once again, his red-haired one appeared, his lovely Maker, her eyes red with mortal blood as always, and finely glad and full of authority and power, and this time come to bind the unhappy blood drinker Lestat in chains.

Chains that could bind such a powerful one?

Thorne pondered it. What chains could accomplish this, he wondered. It seemed that he had to know the answer to this question. And he saw his red-haired one sitting patiently by while the blood drinker Lestat, bound and helpless, fought and raved but could not get free.

What were they made of, these seemingly soft shaped links that held such a being? The question left Thorne no peace. And why did his red-haired Maker love Lestat and allow him to live? Why was she so quiet as the young one raved? What was it like to be bound in her chains, and close to her?

Memories came back to Thorne; troubling visions of his Maker when he, a mortal warrior, had first come upon her in a cave in the North land that had been his home. It had been night and he had seen her with her distaff and her spindle and her bleeding eyes.

From her long red locks she had taken one hair after another and spun it into thread, working with silent speed as he approached her.

It had been bitter winter, and the fire behind her seemed magical in its brightness as he had stood in the snow watching her as she spun the thread as he had seen a hundred mortal women do.

"A witch," he had said aloud.

From his mind he banished this memory.

He saw her now as she guarded Lestat who had become strong like her. He saw the strange chains that bound Lestat who no longer struggled.

At last Lestat had been released.

Gathering up the magical chains, his red-haired Maker had abandoned him and his companions.

The others were visible but she had slipped out of their vision, and slipping from their vision, she slipped from the visions of Thorne.

Once again, he vowed to continue his slumber. He opened his mind to sleep. But the nights passed one by one in his icy cave. The noise of the world was deafening and formless.

And as time passed he could not forget the sight of his long-lost one; he could not forget that she was as vital and beautiful as she had ever been, and old thoughts came back to him with bitter sharpness.

Why had they quarreled? Had she really ever turned her back on him? Why had he hated so much her other companions? Why had he begrudged her the wanderer blood drinkers who, discovering her and her company, adored her as all talked together of their journeys in the Blood.

And the myths—of the Queen and the Sacred Core—would they have mattered to him? He didn't know. He had had no hunger for myths. It confused him. And he could not banish from his mind the picture of Lestat bound in those mysterious chains.

Memory wouldn't leave him alone.

It was the middle of winter when the sun doesn't shine at all over the ice, when he realized that sleep had left him. And he would have no further peace.

And so he rose from the cave, and began his long walk South through the snow, taking his time as he listened to the electric voices of the world below, not certain of where he would enter it again.

The wind blew his long thick red hair; he pulled up his fur-lined collar over his mouth, and he wiped the ice from his eyebrows. His boots were soon wet, and so he stretched out his arms, summoning the Cloud Gift without words, and began his ascent so that he might travel low over the land, listening for others of his kind, hoping to find an old one like himself, someone who might welcome him.

Weary of the Mind Gift and its random messages, he wanted to hear spoken words.

2

SEVERAL SUNLESS DAYS and nights of midwinter he traveled. But it didn't take him long to hear the cry of another. It was a blood drinker older than he, and in a city that Thorne had known centuries before.

In his nocturnal sleep he had never really forgotten this city. It had been a great market town with a fine cathedral. But on his long journey North so many years ago, he had found it suffering with the dreaded plague, and he had not believed it would endure.

Indeed, it had seemed to Thorne that all the peoples of the world would die in that awful plague, so terrible had it been, so merciless.

Once again, sharp memories tormented him.

He saw and smelled the time of the pestilence when children wandered aimlessly without parents, and bodies had lain in heaps. The smell of rotting flesh had been everywhere. How could he explain to anyone the sorrow he had felt for humankind that such a disaster had befallen them?

He didn't want to see the cities and the towns die, though he himself was not of them. When he fed upon the infected he knew no infection himself. But he could not cure anyone. He had gone on North, thinking perhaps that all the wondrous things that humankind had done would be covered in snow or vine or the soft earth itself in final oblivion.

But all had not died as he had then feared; indeed people of the town itself had survived, and their descendants lived still in the narrow cobbled medieval streets through which he walked, more soothed by the cleanliness here than he had ever dreamt he would be.

Yes, it was good to be in this vital and orderly place.

How solid and fine the old timber houses, yet the modern machines ticked and hummed within. He could feel and see the miracles that he had only glimpsed through the Mind Gift. The televisions were filled with colorful dreams. And people knew a safety from the snow and ice which his time had never given anyone.

He wanted to know more of these wonders for himself, and that surprised him. He wanted to see railroad trains and ships. He wanted to see airplanes and cars. He wanted to see computers and wireless telephones.

Maybe he could do it. Maybe he could take the time. He had not come to life again with any such goal, but then who said that he must hurry upon his errand? No one knew of his existence except perhaps this blood drinker who called to him, this blood drinker who so easily opened his own mind.

Where was the blood drinker—the one he had heard only hours ago? He gave a long silent call, not revealing his name, but pledging only that he offered friendship.

Quickly an answer came to him. With the Mind Gift he saw a blond-haired stranger. The creature sat in the back room of a special tavern, a place where blood drinkers often gathered.

Come join me here.

The direction was plain and Thorne hastened to go there. Over the last century he had heard the blood drinker voices speak of such havens. Vampire taverns, blood drinker bars, blood drinker clubs. They made up the Vampire Connection. Such a thing! It made him smile.

In his mind's eye, he saw the bright disturbing hallucination again of the great web with so many tiny pulsing lights caught within it. That vision had been of all the blood drinkers themselves connected to the Sacred Core of the Evil Queen. But this Vampire Connection was an echo of such a web, and it fascinated him.

Would they call to each other on computers, these modern blood drinkers, forsaking the Mind Gift altogether? He vowed that nothing must dangerously surprise him.

Yet he felt shivers through all his flesh remembering his vague dreams of the disaster.

He hoped and prayed that his newfound friend would confirm the things he'd seen. He hoped and prayed that the blood drinker would be truly old, not young and tender and bungling.

He prayed that this blood drinker would have the gift of words. For he wanted to hear words more than anything. He himself could seldom find the right words. And now, more than anything, he wanted to listen.

He was almost to the bottom of the steep street, the snow coming down lightly around him, when he saw the sign of the tavern: The Werewolf.

It made him laugh.

So these blood drinkers play their reckless games, he mused. In his time it had been wholly different. Who of his own people had not believed that a man could change into a wolf? Who of his own people would not have done anything to prevent this very evil from coming upon him?

But here it was, a plaything, the concept, with this painted sign swinging on its hinges in the cold wind, and the barred windows brightly lighted beneath it.

He pulled the handle of the heavy door and at once found himself in a crowded room, warm, and full of the smell of wine and beer and human blood.

The warmth alone was overwhelming. In truth, he had never felt anything quite like it. The warmth was everywhere. It was even and wondrous. And it crossed his mind that not a single mortal here realized how truly marvelous this warmth was.

For in olden times such warmth had been impossible, and bitter winter had been the common curse of all.

There was no time however for such thinking. He reminded himself, Do not be surprised.

But the inundating chatter of mortals paralyzed him. The blood around him paralyzed him. For one moment his thirst was crippling. In this noisy indifferent crowd he felt he would run rampant, taking hold of this one and that one, only to be discovered, the monster among the throng who would then be hounded to destruction.

He found a place against the wall and leant against it, his eyes closed.

He remembered those of his clan running up the mountain, searching for the red-haired witch whom they would never find. Thorne alone had seen her. Thorne had seen her take the eyes from the dead warrior and put them into her own sockets. Thorne had seen her return through the light snow to the cave where she lifted her distaff. Thorne had seen her winding the golden red thread on the spindle.

And the clan had wanted to destroy her, and wielding his ax he had been among them.

How foolish it all seemed now, because she had wanted Thorne to see her. She had come North for a warrior such as Thorne. She had chosen Thorne, and she had loved his youth and his strength and his pure courage.

He opened his eyes.

The mortals in this place took no notice of him, even though his clothes were badly worn. How long could he go unseen? He had no coins in his pockets to purchase a place at a table or a cup of wine.

But the voice of the blood drinker came again, coaxing him, reassuring him.

You must ignore the crowd. They know nothing of us, or why we keep this place. They are pawns. Come to the rear door. Push it with all your strength and it will give for you.

It seemed impossible that he could cross this room, that these mortals wouldn't know him for what he was.

But he must overcome this fear. He must reach the blood drinker who was summoning him.

Bowing his head, bringing his collar up over his mouth, he pushed through the soft bodies, trying not to meet the gaze of those who glanced at him. And when he saw the door without a handle, at once he pushed it as he'd been told to do.

It gave upon a large dimly lighted chamber with thick candles set upon each of its scattered wooden tables. The warmth was as solid and good as that of the outer room.

And the blood drinker was alone.

He was a tall fair creature whose yellow hair was almost white. He had hard blue eyes, and a delicate face, covered with a thin layer of blood and ash to make him look more human to the mortal eye. He wore a bright-red cloak with a hood, thrown back from his head, and his hair was finely combed and long.

He looked most handsome to Thorne, and well mannered, and rather like a creature of books than a man of the sword. He had large hands but they were slender and his fingers were fine.

It occurred to Thorne that he had seen this being with the Mind Gift, seated at the council table with the other blood drinkers before the Evil Queen had been brought down.

Yes, he had seen this very one. This one had tried so hard to reason with the Queen, though inside him there lurked a dreadful anger and an unreasonable hate.

Yes, Thorne had seen this very one struggling with words, finely chosen words, to save everyone.

The blood drinker gestured for him to take a seat to the right, against the wall.

He accepted this invitation, and found himself on a long leather cushion, the candle flame dancing wickedly before him, sending its playful light into the other blood drinker's eyes. He could smell blood now in the other blood drinker. He realized that the blood drinker's face was warm with it, and so were his long tapering hands.

Yes, I have hunted tonight, but I will hunt with you again. You need this.

"Yes," said Thorne. "It's been so long you can't imagine it. To suffer in the snow and ice was simple. But they're all around me now, these tender creatures."

"I understand," said the other blood drinker. "I know."

These were the first words Thorne had spoken aloud to anyone in years and years, and he closed his eyes so that he might treasure this moment. Memory was a curse, yes, he thought, but it was also the greatest gift. Because if you lost memory you lost everything.

A bit of his old religion came back to him—that for memory, the god Odin had given his eye, and hung upon the sacred tree for nine days. But it was more complex than that. It was not only memory which Odin gained, it was the mead which enabled him to sing poetry.

Once years ago Thorne had drunk that poet's mead, given him by the priests of the sacred grove, and he had stood in the middle of his father's house singing the poems about her, the red-haired one, the blood drinker, whom he had seen with his own eyes.

And those around him had laughed and mocked him. But when she began to slay the members of the clan they mocked him no more. Once they had seen the pale bodies with their eyes plucked out, they had made him their hero.

He shook himself all over. The snow fell from his hair and from his shoulders. With a careless hand he wiped the bits of ice from his eyebrows. He saw the ice melt on his fingers. He rubbed hard at the frost on his face.

Was there no fire in this room? He looked about. The heat came magically through small windows. But how good it was, how consuming. He wanted to strip off his clothes suddenly and bathe in this heat.

I have a fire in my house. I'll take you there.

As if from a trance, he woke to look at the blood drinker stranger. He cursed himself that he had been sitting here clumsy and mute.

The blood drinker spoke aloud: "It's only to be expected. Do you understand the tongue I speak?"

"It's the tongue of the Mind Gift," said Thorne. "Men all over the world speak it." He stared at the blood drinker again. "My name is Thorne," he said. "Thor was my god." Hastily he reached inside his worn leather coat and pulled out from the fur the amulet of gold which he wore on a chain. "Time can't rust such a thing," he said. "It's Thor's hammer."

The blood drinker nodded.

"And your gods?" Thorne asked. "Who were they? I don't speak of belief, you understand, I speak of what we lost, you and I. Do you catch my meaning?"

"The gods of old Rome, those are the gods I lost," said the stranger. "My name is Marius."

Thorne nodded. It was too marvelous to speak aloud and to hear the voice of another. For the moment, he forgot the blood he craved and wanted only a flood of words.

"Speak to me, Marius," he said. "Tell me wondrous things. Tell me all that you would have me know." He tried to stop himself but he couldn't do it.

"Once I stood speaking to the wind, telling the wind all things that were in my mind and in my heart. Yet when I went North into the ice, I had no language." He broke off, staring into Marius's eyes. "My soul is too hurt. I have no true thoughts."

"I understand you," said Marius. "Come with me to my house. You're welcome to the bath, and to the clothes you need. Then we'll hunt and you'll be restored, and then comes talk. I can tell you stories without end. I can tell you all the stories of my life that I want to share with another."

A long sigh escaped Thorne's lips. He couldn't prevent himself from smiling in gratitude, his eyes moist and his hands trembling. He searched the stranger's face. He could find no evidence of dishonesty or cunning. The stranger seemed wise, and simple.

"My friend," Thorne said and then he bent forward and offered the kiss of greeting. Biting deep into his tongue, he filled his mouth with blood, and opened his lips over those of Marius.

The kiss did not take Marius by surprise. It was his own custom. He received the blood and obviously savored it.

"Now we can't quarrel over any small thing," said Thorne. He settled back against the wall greatly confused suddenly. He wasn't alone. He feared that he might give way to tears. He feared that he hadn't the strength to go back out into the dreadful cold and accompany this one to his house, yet it was what he needed to do so terribly.

"Come," said Marius, "I'll help you."

They rose from the table together.

This time the agony of passing through the crowd of mortals was even greater. So many bright glistening eyes fastened on him, though it was only for a moment.

Then they were in the narrow street again, in the gentle swirling snow, and Marius had his arm tight around him.

Thorne was gasping for breath, because his heart had been so quickened. He found himself biting at the snow as it came in gusts into his face. He had to stop for a moment and gesture for his new friend to have patience.

"So many things I saw with the Mind Gift," he said. "I didn't understand them."

"I can explain, perhaps," said Marius. "I can explain all I know and you can do with it what you will. Knowledge has not been my salvation of late. I am lonesome."

"I'll stay with you," Thorne said. This sweet camaraderie was breaking his heart.

A long time they walked, Thorne becoming stronger again, forgetting the warmth of the tavern as if it had been a delusion.

At last they came to a handsome house, with a high peaked roof, and many windows. Marius put his key into the door, and they left the blowing snow behind, stepping into a broad hallway.

A soft light came from the rooms beyond. The walls and ceiling were of finely oiled wood, the same as the floor, with all corners neatly fitted.

"A genius of the modern world made this house for me," Marius explained. "I've lived in many houses, in many styles. This is but one way. Come inside with me."

The great room of the house had a rectangular stone fireplace built into its wooden wall. And there the fire was stacked waiting to be lighted. Through glass walls of remarkable size, Thorne saw the lights of the city. He realized that they were on the edge of the hill, and that a valley lay below them.

"Come," said Marius, "I must introduce you to the other who lives here with me."

This startled Thorne, because he had not detected the presence of anyone else, but he followed Marius through a doorway out of the great room into another chamber on the left, and there he saw a strange sight which mystified him.

Many tables filled the room, or perhaps it was one great broad table. But it was covered all over with a small landscape of hills and valleys, towns and cities. It was covered with little trees, and even little shrubbery, and here and there was snow, as if one town lay under winter and another lay under spring or summer.

Countless houses crowded the landscape, many with twinkling lights, and there were sparkling lakes made of some hard substance to imitate the gleam of water. There were tunnels through the mountains. And on curving iron tracks through this little wilderness there ran little railroad trains, seemingly made out of iron, like those of the great modern world.

Over this tiny world, there presided a blood drinker who didn't bother to look up at Thorne as he entered. The blood drinker had been a young male when he was made. He was tall, but very slight of build, with very delicate fingers. His hair was the faded blond more common among Englishmen than Norsemen.

He sat near the table, where before him was a cleared space devoted to his paintbrushes, and to several bottles of paint, while with his hands he painted the bark of a small tree, as if in readiness to put it into the world that stretched out all over the room, surrounding and almost enclosing him.

A rush of pleasure passed through Thorne as he looked over this little world. It struck him suddenly that he could have spent an hour inspecting all of the tiny buildings. It was not the harsh great world outside, but something precious and protected, and even slightly enchanting.

There was more than one small black train which ran along upon the wandering tracks, and a small droning noise came from these trains as if from bees in a hive. The trains had lights inside their tiny windows.

All the myriad details of this small wonderland seemed to be correct.

"I feel I'm the frost giant in this room," Thorne whispered reverently.

It was an offering of friendship to the youngish male who continued to apply the brown paint to the bark of the tiny tree which he held so delicately between his left fingers. But the youngish male blood drinker did not respond.

"These tiny cities and towns are full of pretty magic," Thorne said, his voice a little more timid.

The youngish male seemed to have no ears.

"Daniel?" said Marius gently to his friend, "do you want to greet Thorne who is our guest tonight?"

"Welcome, Thorne," said Daniel without looking up. And then as if neither Thorne nor Marius were there, Daniel stopped the painting of his tree, and dipping another brush into another bottle, he made a dampened spot for the tree in the great world before him. He set the tree down hard upon that spot and the tree stood firm as though rooted.

"This house is full of many rooms like this," said Marius in an even voice, his eyes looking at Thorne gently. "Look below. One can purchase thousands of little trees, and thousands of little houses." He pointed to stacks upon stacks of small containers on the floor beneath the table. "Daniel is very good at putting together the houses. See how intricate they are? This is all that Daniel does now."

Thorne sensed a judgment in Marius's voice but it was soft, and the youngish blood drinker paid no attention. He had taken up another small tree, and was examining the thick green portion which made up its leafy upper limbs. To this he soon applied his little paintbrush.

"Have you ever seen one of our kind under such a spell?" Marius asked.

Thorne shook his head, No, he had not. But he understood how such a thing could happen.

"It occurs sometimes," said Marius. "The blood drinker becomes enthralled. I remember centuries ago I heard the story of a blood drinker in a Southern land whose sole passion was for finding beautiful shells along the shore, and this she did all night long until near morning. She did hunt and she did drink, but it was only to return to the shells, and once she looked at each, she threw it aside and went on searching. No one could distract her from it.

"Daniel is enthralled in the same way. He makes these small cities.

He doesn't want to do anything else. It's as if the small cities have caught him. You might say I look after him."

Thorne was speechless, out of respect. He couldn't tell whether Marius's words affected the blood drinker who continued to work upon his world. Thorne felt a moment of confusion.

Then a low genial laugh came from the youngish blood drinker.

"Daniel will be this way for a while," said Marius, "and then his old faculties will come back to him."

"The ideas you have, Marius," Daniel said with another little easy laugh. It was hardly more than a murmur. Daniel dipped the brush again into the paste that would make his little tree stick to the green grass, and he pressed the tree down with appropriate force. Then out of a box beside him, he drew another.

All the while the small railroad trains moved on, winding their way noisily through hill and valley, past snow-covered church and house. Why, this tiny world even contained small detailed people!

"Might I kneel to look at this?" asked Thorne respectfully.

"Yes, please do," said Marius. "It would give him pleasure."

Thorne went down on both knees and drew himself up to the small village with its cluster of little buildings. He saw delicate signs on them but he didn't know the meaning of them.

He was struck dumb by the wonder of it—that rising and confronting the great world, he was to come here and stumble upon this little universe.

A finely made little train, its engine roaring, its cars loosely connected, came rattling past him on the track. He thought he glimpsed small figures inside it.

For a second, he forgot all else. He imagined this handmade world to be real, and understood the spell, though it frightened him.

"Beautiful," he said in thanks. He stood up.

The young blood drinker neither moved nor spoke in acknowledgment.

"Have you hunted, Daniel?" asked Marius.

"Not tonight, Marius," said the youngish one without looking up, but then suddenly his eyes flashed on Thorne, and Thorne was surprised by their violet color.

"Norseman," Daniel said with a little note of pleasant surprise. "Red hair like the hair of the twins." He laughed, a light laugh as if he were a little mad. "Made by Maharet. Strong one."

The words caught Thorne completely off guard. He reeled, scarcely able to keep his balance.

He wanted to strike the careless young one. He almost lifted his fist. But Marius held his arm firmly.

Images crowded into Thorne's mind. The twins—his beloved Maker and her lost sister. He saw them vividly. *The Queen of the Damned*. Once more he saw the helpless blood drinker Lestat with the chains around him. Chains of metal could never have held him. From what had his red-haired Maker created those chains?

He tried to banish these thoughts, and anchor himself within the moment.

Marius held tight to his arm, and went on speaking to the blood drinker Daniel:

"Let me guide you, if you want to hunt."

"I have no need," said Daniel. He had gone back to his work. He drew a large bundle from beneath the table, and he held it up for Marius to see. On the cover was painted, or printed, Thorne could not tell, the picture of a house with three stories and many windows. "I want to assemble this house," Daniel said. "It's more difficult than anything you see here, but with my vampiric blood it will be simple."

"We'll leave you now," said Marius, "but don't try to leave here without me."

"I would never do that," said Daniel. He was already tearing at the sheer wrapping of the bundle. Bits and pieces of wood were inside. "I'll hunt with you tomorrow night and you can treat me as though I am a child as you love to do."

Marius kept his friendly grip on Thorne's arm. He led him out of the room and closed the door.

"When he wanders by himself," said Marius, "he gets into trouble. He gets lost, or thirsty beyond the point where he can hunt on his own. I have to search for him. He was that way as a man before he was ever made a blood drinker. The blood didn't change him except for a little while. And now he's enslaved to these tiny worlds he creates. All he requires is space for them, and the packages of buildings and trees and such which he purchases through the computer."

"Ah, you have those strange engines of the mind," said Thorne.

"Yes, under this roof there are very fine computers. I have all I need," said Marius. "But you're tired. Your clothes are old. You need refreshment. We'll talk of all this later."

He led Thorne up a short echoing wooden staircase and into a large bedchamber. All the wood of the walls and the doors was painted here in colors of green and yellow, and the bed itself was fitted into a great carved cabinet with only one side open. It struck him as a safe and curious place without a surface untouched by human hands. Even the wooden floor was polished.

Through a broad door they entered an immense bath which was paneled in roughened wood with a floor of stone, and many candles for its illumination. The color of the wood was beautiful in the subtle light and Thorne felt himself becoming dizzy.

But it was the bath itself which amazed him. There before another glass wall stood a huge wooden tub of steaming hot water. Made like a great cask, the tub was easily big enough for several to bathe together. On a small stool beside the tub there stood a stack of what appeared to be towels. On other stools there stood bowls of dried flowers and herbs which Thorne could smell with his acute blood drinker senses. There were also bottles of oil and jars of what might have been ointments.

That Thorne might wash himself in this seemed to him a miracle.

"Take off the soiled clothes," said Marius. "Let me discard them. What else do you have that you would save other than your necklace?"

"Nothing," said Thorne. "How can I ever repay you for this?"

"But you already have," said Marius. He himself removed his leather coat, and then pulled off his wool tunic. His naked chest was without hair. He was pale as all old blood drinkers are pale. And his body was strong and naturally beautiful. He'd been taken in the prime of his life, that was plain. But his true age, either in mortal life long ago, or in blood drinker time now? Thorne could not guess it.

Marius took off his leather boots and his long wool pants, and not waiting for Thorne—only making a gesture that Thorne should follow—he stepped into the huge tub of hot water.

Thorne ripped at his fur-lined jacket. He tore it in his haste. His fingers trembled as he stripped away the pants that were almost ragged. In a moment he was as naked as the other, and in awkward haste he gathered the ruin of his clothes in a small bundle. He looked about.

"Don't worry about such things," said Marius. The steam was rising all around him. "Come into the tub with me. Be warm for now."

Thorne followed, first stepping into the tub and then sinking down in the hot water on his knees. He finally seated himself so that the water came to his neck. The shock of the heat was overwhelming and utterly blessed. He uttered a little prayer of thanks, something old and small which he had learnt as a child to say when something purely good happens.

Marius put his hand into the bowl of dried flowers and herbs, and gathering up quite a bit of this mixture he let it loose into the hot water.

It was a deep good perfume of the outdoors in summer.

Thorne closed his eyes. That he had risen, that he had come this far, that he had found this pure and luxurious bath seemed almost impossible to him. He would wake soon, a victim of the Mind Gift, back in his hopeless cave, prisoner of his own exile, only dreaming of others.

Slowly he bowed his head and lifted a double handful of the cleansing hot water to his face. He lifted more and more of the water, and then finally as if it required courage, he dipped his head into the tub completely.

When he rose again he was warm as if he'd never been cold, and the sight of the lights beyond the glass amazed him. Even through the steam, he could see the snow falling beyond, and he was deliciously conscious that he was so near and yet so far from it.

Suddenly he wished that he had not risen for such a dark purpose.

Why could he not serve only what was good? Why could he not live for what was pleasurable? But that had never been his way.

No matter, it was important to keep that secret to himself for now. Why trouble his friend with dark thoughts? Why trouble himself with guilty confessions?

He looked at his companion.

Marius sat back against the side of the wooden tub with his arms out resting upon the edge. His hair was wet and clinging to his neck and shoulders. He didn't stare at Thorne, but he was obviously conscious of him.

Thorne dipped his head again; he moved forward and lay down in the water, rising suddenly and turning over, letting the water run off him. He gave a little laugh of delight. He ran his fingers through the hair on his own chest. He dipped his head back until the water lapped at his face. He rolled over again and again to wash his full head of hair before he rose and sat back contented.

He took the same posture as Marius and the two looked at each other.

"And you live this way," said Thorne, "in the very midst of mortals, and you are safe from them?"

"They don't believe in us now," said Marius. "No matter what they see they don't believe. And wealth buys anything." His blue eyes seemed earnest and his face was calm as if he had no evil secrets inside, as though he had no hatred for anyone. But he did.

"Mortals clean this house," said Marius. "Mortals take the money I give them for all that's needed here. Do you understand enough of the modern world to grasp how such a place is heated and cooled and kept safe from intruders?"

"I understand," said Thorne. "But we're never safe as we dream, are we?"

A bitter smile came over Marius's face. "I have never been harmed by mortals," he said.

"You speak of the Evil Queen and all those she's slain, don't you?"

"Yes, I speak of that and other horrors," Marius answered.

Slowly without words Marius used the Mind Gift to let Thorne know that he himself hunted only the Evil Doer.

"That is my peace with the world," he said. "That is how I manage to go on. I use the Mind Gift to hunt those mortals who kill. In the big cities I can always find them."

"And mine is the Little Drink," said Thorne. "Be assured. I need no greedy feast. I take from many so that no one dies. For centuries I've lived this way among the Snow People. When I was first made I hadn't the skill. I would drink too fast and too recklessly. But then I learned. No one soul belongs to me. And I could go like the bee goes from flower to flower. It was my habit to enter into taverns where many are close together, and to take from one after another."

Marius nodded. "That's a good style," he said with a little smile. "For a child of Thor, you're merciful." His smile broadened. "That's merciful indeed."

"Do you despise my god?" asked Thorne politely.

"I don't think that I do," said Marius. "I told you that I lost the gods of Rome, but in truth I never had them. I was too cold of temperament to have gods. And not having had any true gods of my own, I speak of all gods as if they were poetry. The poetry of Thor was a poetry of war, was it not, a poetry of battles without cease, and of noise in Heaven?"

This delighted Thorne. He couldn't conceal his pleasure. The Mind Gift never brought this kind of keen communication with another, and the words that Marius spoke were not only impressing him, they were confusing him slightly, which was wonderful.

"Yes, that was Thor's poetry," he said, "but nothing was as clear and certain as the sound of the thunder in the mountains when he wielded his hammer. And alone at night when I went out of my father's house into the rain and wind, when I climbed the wet mountain fearlessly to hear that thunder, I knew the god was there, and I was far from poetry." He stopped. He saw his homeland in his mind. He saw his youth. "There were other gods I heard," he said quietly. He didn't look at Marius. "It was Odin leading the Wild Hunt through the skies that made the loudest noise; and I saw and heard those spirits pass. I never forgot them."

"Can you see them now?" asked Marius. It was not a challenge. He spoke only with curiosity. Indeed it had a bit of respect in it. "I hope you can," he hastened to add as if there might be some doubt as to the interpretation.

"I don't know," said Thorne. "It was so long ago. I never thought that I might recover those things."

But they were keen in his mind now. Though he sat in this warm bath, his blood soothed, all the cruel cold driven from his limbs, he could see the wintry valley. He could hear the storm, and see the phantoms flying high above, all those lost dead following the god Odin through the sky.

"Come," Thorne had said to his companions, the young ones, who'd crept out of the hall with him, "let's go to the grove, let's stand in the very grove as the thunder rolls on." They'd been frightened of the holy ground, but they couldn't show it.

"You were a Viking child," said Marius quietly.

"Oh, so the Britons called us," said Thorne. "I don't think we used that name for ourselves. We learnt it from our enemies. I remember their screams when we climbed their walls, when we stole the gold from the altars of the churches." He paused. He let his eyes rest calmly on Marius for a moment. "What a tolerant one you are. You truly want to listen."

Marius nodded. "I listen with my whole soul." He gave a little sigh and he looked out through the immense glass. "I'm weary of being alone, my friend," he said. "I cannot bear the company of those whom

I know most intimately. And they cannot bear mine on account of things I've done."

Thorne was surprised by this sudden confession. Thorne thought of the blood drinker Lestat and his songs. He thought of all those gathered at the council when the Evil Queen had come. He knew all had survived. And he knew that this blond one, Marius, had talked with reason more potently than any other.

"Go on with your story," Marius said. "I didn't mean to interrupt you. You meant to make a point."

"It was only that I slew many men before I ever became a blood drinker," said Thorne. "I swung Thor's hammer as well as my sword and my ax. I fought as a boy at my father's side. I fought after I buried him. And he died no straw death, I can assure you, but with his sword in his hand as he wanted it." Thorne paused. "And you, my friend?" he asked. "Were you a soldier?"

Marius shook his head. "A Senator," he said, "a maker of laws, something of a philosopher. I went to war, yes, for some time because my family wished it, and I had a high place in one of the legions, but my time wasn't very long and I was home and back in my library. I loved books. I still do. There are rooms of this house which are full of them, and I have houses elsewhere that are full of them. I never really knew battle."

Marius stopped. He leant forward and brought the water up to his face as Thorne had done before, and he let the water run down over his eyelids.

"Come," he said, "let's be done with this pleasure and go for another. Let's hunt. I can feel your hunger. I have new clothes for you here. I have all you need. Or would you stay longer in this warm water?"

"No, I'm ready," said Thorne. It had been so long since he had fed that he was ashamed to admit it. Once again he rinsed his face and hair. He ducked down into the water, and came up, pushing his wet hair back from his forehead.

Marius had already climbed out of the tub, and held out for Thorne a large white towel.

It was thick and roughened and perfect for mopping the water off his blood drinker skin which never absorbs anything. The air of the room seemed chilled for one moment as he stood on the stone floor, but very soon he was warm again, rubbing fiercely at his hair to press the last droplets out of it.

Marius had finished with the task and now took a fresh towel from the stack and began to rub Thorne's back and shoulders. This familiarity sent the chills through Thorne's limbs. Marius rubbed hard at Thorne's head, and then he began to comb the wet hair free of tangles.

"Why is there no red beard, my friend?" asked Marius, as the two faced each other. "I remember the Norsemen with their beards. I remember them when they came to Byzantium. Does that name mean anything to you?"

"Oh, yes," said Thorne. "I was taken to see that wondrous city." He turned around and accepted the towel from Marius's hands. "My beard was thick and long, even when I was very young, let me assure you, but it was shaved the night that I became a blood drinker. I was groomed for the magical blood. It was the will of the creature who made me."

Marius nodded. But he was far too polite to say her name, though the other young one had brashly spoken it.

"You know it was Maharet," said Thorne. "You didn't need to hear it from your young friend. You caught it from my thoughts, didn't you?" Thorne paused, then went on. "You know it was the vision of her that brought me out of the ice and snow. She stood against the Evil Queen. She bound the vampire, Lestat, in chains. But to speak of her just now takes the breath out of me. When will I ever be able to speak of her? I can't know now. Let's hunt, and then we can really talk to one another."

He was solemn, holding the towel against his chest. In his secret heart, he tried to feel love for the one who made him. He tried to draw from the centuries a wisdom that would quench anger. But he couldn't do it. All he could do was be silent, and hunt with Marius now.

3

I N A LARGE PAINTED WOODEN ROOM full of many painted cabinets and chests, Marius offered the clothes—fine leather jackets with small buttons of bone, many lined with silvery fur, and close-fitting pants of wool so soft Thorne couldn't see the weave of it.

Only the boots were a little too small, but Thorne felt he could endure this. How could such a thing matter? Not satisfied, Marius continued to search until he found a large pair, and these proved more than serviceable.

As for the costume of the times it wasn't so different from Thorne's old habit of dress—linen for the fine shirt next to the skin, wool and leather for the outer garments. The tiny buttons on the shirt intrigued Thorne, and though he knew that the stitching had been done by machines and was a common thing, nevertheless it delighted him.

He had a dawning sense of how much delight awaited him. Never mind his dark mission.

As Marius dressed, he chose red once more for his jacket and for his hooded cloak. It intrigued Thorne, though he had seen garments such as these on Marius in the vampire tavern. Nevertheless the colors seemed bright for hunting.

"It's my common way to wear red," Marius said to Thorne's unspoken interest. "You do as you like. Lestat, my sometime pupil, also loves it which annoys me mightily but I endure it. I think we appear to be Master and Apprentice when his shade of clear red comes so close to mine."

"And so you love him as well?" Thorne said.

Marius said nothing. He gestured to the clothes.

For Thorne, it was dark brown leather, more concealing, yet silken to the touch, and his feet went naked into the fur-lined boots on account of the size of them. He needed no cloak. He felt it would encumber him.

From a silver dish on a cabinet, Marius took ashes on his fingertips, and mingling these with blood from his mouth, he made the thin paste to cover his face entirely. It darkened him; it made the old lines of his face appear. It gave a graven character to his eyes. In fact, it rendered him entirely more visible to Thorne while no doubt disguising him for mortals.

Marius made a gesture that Thorne might do as well, but something prevented Thorne from accepting. Perhaps it was merely that he had never done this.

Marius offered him gloves, but these he refused as well. He did not like the feel of things through gloves. After so long in the ice, he wanted to touch everything.

"I like gloves," said Marius. "I'm never without them. Our hands frighten mortals when they take the time to look. And gloves feel warm which we never do."

Marius filled his pockets with paper money. He offered handfuls of this to Thorne, but Thorne refused, thinking it greedy to take this from his host.

Marius said, "It's all right. I'll take care of you. But if we become separated somehow, simply return here. Come round to the back of the house, and you'll find the door there open."

Separated? How might that happen? Thorne was dazed by all that was taking place. The smallest aspect of things gave him pleasure.

They were all but ready to take their leave when the young Daniel came in and stared at both of them.

"Do you want to join us?" Marius asked. He was pulling his gloves very tight so that they showed his very knuckles.

Daniel didn't answer. He appeared to be listening, but he said nothing. His youthful face was deceiving, but his violet eyes were truly wonderful.

"You know that you can come," said Marius.

The younger one turned and went back, presumably to his small kingdom.

Within minutes they were on their way in the falling snow, Marius's arm around Thorne as though Thorne needed the reassurance.

And I shall drink soon.

When they came at last to a large inn, it was into a cellar that they went where there were hundreds of mortals. Indeed the size of the room overwhelmed Thorne.

Not only did glittering noisy mortals eat and drink in this place, in dozens of little groups, they danced to the music of several diligent players. At big green tables with wheels they played at games of chance with loud raucous cries and easy laughter. The music was electric and loud; the flashing lights were horrid, the smell of food and blood was overpowering.

The two blood drinkers went utterly unnoticed, except for the tavern girl who accompanied them unquestioningly to a small table in the very midst of things. Here they could see the twisting dancers, who seemed one and all to be dancing alone rather than with anyone else, each moving to the music in a primitive way as though drunk on it.

The music hurt Thorne. He didn't think it beautiful. It was like so much confusion. And the flashing lights were ugly.

Marius leant over to whisper in Thorne's ear:

"Those lights are our friend, Thorne. They make it difficult to see what we are. Try to bear with them."

Marius gave an order for hot drinks. The little tavern girl turned her bright flirtatious eyes on Thorne. She made some quick remark as to his red hair and he smiled at her. He wouldn't drink from her, not if all the other mortals of the world were dried up and taken away from him.

He cast his eyes around the room, trying to ignore the din that pounded at his ears, and the overwhelming smells that almost sickened him.

"The women, see, near the far wall," said Marius. "They want to dance. That's why they're here. They're waiting to be asked. Can you do it as you dance?"

"I can," said Thorne almost solemnly, as if to say, Why do you ask me? "But how do I dance?" he asked, watching the couples who crowded the designated floor. He laughed for the first time since he'd ever gone North. He laughed, and in the din he could barely hear his own laughter. "I can drink, yes, without any mortal ever knowing it, even my victim, but how can I dance in this strange way?"

He saw Marius smile broadly. Marius had thrown his cloak back over the chair. He appeared so calm amid this awful unendurable combination of illumination and music.

"What do they do but move about clumsily together?" Thorne asked.

"Do the same," said Marius. "Move slowly as you drink. Let the music and the blood talk to you."

Thorne laughed again. Suddenly with a wild bit of nerve he rose and made his way around the edges of the crowded dance floor to the women who were already looking eagerly towards him. He chose the dark-haired of the three, because women with dark eyes and dark hair had always fascinated him. Also she was the eldest and least likely to be chosen by a man, and he did not mean to leave her harmed by his interest.

At once she rose, and he held her small limp hands in his and guided her out onto the polished floor, the relentless music suggesting nothing but an easy senseless rhythm, which she took up immediately and awkwardly, her fine delicate shoes clicking on the wood.

"Oh, but your hands are cold!" she said.

"I'm so sorry!" he declared. "You must forgive me. I've been in the snow too long."

Yea gods, he must be careful not to hurt her. What a simple trusting being she was, with her eyes and mouth sloppily painted, and her cheeks rouged, her breasts thrust forward and held in place by tight straps beneath her black silk dress.

Boldly she pressed against him. And he, enfolding her as gently as he could, bent down to sink his tiny fangs most secretively into her neck. *Dream, my precious one, dream of beautiful things. I forbid you to be afraid or to remember.*

Ah, the blood. After so long, it came, the blood pumped by her urgent little heart, her defenseless little heart! He lost the thread of her swoon and entered his own. He saw his red-haired Maker. And in a hushed moan he actually spoke aloud to the woman in his grip. *Give me all.* But this was wrong and he knew it.

Quickly he pulled away, only to find that Marius stood beside him with a hand on his shoulder.

As he let the woman go, she looked at him with glossy drowsy eyes, and he turned her in a rapid circle, laughing again, ignoring the course of blood through his veins, ignoring the weakness for more blood that overtook him. On and on they danced, as clumsy as the other couples. But he was so thirsty for more.

At last she wanted to return to her little table. She was sleepy. She couldn't think why. He must forgive her. He bowed and nodded, and he kissed her hand innocently.

Only one woman of the trio remained. Marius was now dancing with the other. Thorne offered his hand to that last of the three women, and vowed that this time he would need no guardian.

She was stronger than her friend. Her eyes were lined in black like an Egyptian, and she wore a deeper red on her lips, and her blond hair was full of silver.

"Are you the man of my dreams?" she asked him, raising her voice boldly over the music. She would have taken him with her upstairs in the inn at this moment.

"Perhaps so," he said, "if you let me kiss you," and caressing her tightly, he sank his teeth quickly into her neck, drinking hard and fast, and then letting her go, watching her drift and smile, cunning, yet sweet, unaware of what had happened to her.

There was no getting much blood from these three. They were too gentle. Round and round he turned her in the dance, wanting desperately to steal another drink but not daring to do it.

He felt the blood pounding inside him, but it wanted more blood. His hands and feet were now painfully cold.

He saw that Marius was seated again at their table and talking to a hulking heavily dressed mortal who sat beside him. Marius had his arm over the creature's shoulder.

Finally Thorne took the pretty woman back to her place. How tenderly she looked at him.

"Don't go," she said. "Can't you stay with me?"

"No, my dearest," he said. He felt the monster in him as he gazed down at her. And backing away, he turned and made his way to Marius.

The music made him wobbly on his feet. How dreary it was, how persistent.

Marius was drinking from the man as the man bent over near him as if listening to whispered secrets. At last Marius released him and righted him in his chair.

"It will take too many here," said Thorne.

His words were inaudible in the din of the electric music but he knew that Marius could hear him.

Marius nodded. "Then we seek the Evil Doer, friend, and we feast," said Marius. He sat still as he scanned the room, as if listening to each and every mind.

Thorne did the same, probing steadily with the Mind Gift, but all he could hear was the electric confusion of the music makers, and the desperate need of the pretty woman who still looked at him. How much he wanted her. But he could not take such an innocent creature, and his friend would forsake him if he did, and that was more important perhaps than his own conscience.

"Come," said Marius. "Another place."

Out into the night they went again. It was only a few short paces to a large gambling den, this one filled with the green tables on which men play the game of craps, and on which the wheels spun for the all-important winning numbers.

"There, you see," said Marius, pointing with his gloved finger at a tall gaunt black-haired young man who had withdrawn from the game, holding his cold glass of ale in his hand, only watching. "Take him into the corner. There are so many places along the wall."

Immediately Thorne went to it. With a hand on the young man's shoulder he looked into his eyes. He must be able now to use the old Spell Gift which so many blood drinkers were lacking. "You come with me," he said. "You've been waiting for me." It reminded him of old hunts and old battles.

He saw the mist in the young man's eyes, he saw the memory vanish. The young man went with him to the bench along the wall, and there they sat together. Thorne massaged the neck with thumb and fingers before he drank, thinking quietly within himself, Now your life will be mine, and then he sank his teeth deep and he drew easily and slowly with all his power.

The flood poured into his soul. He saw the dingy images of rampant crime, of other lives snuffed out by his victim with no thought of judgment or punishment. *Give me only your blood.* He felt the heart inside the man burst. And then he released the body, and let it lie back against the wall. He kissed the wound, letting a bit of his own blood heal it.

Waking from the dream of the feast, he gazed about the dim smoky room, so full of strangers. How alien all humans seemed, and how hopeless their plight. Cursed as he was, he could not die, but death was breathing on all of them.

Where was his Marius? He couldn't find him! He rose from the bench, eager to get away from the victim's soiled and ugly body, and he moved into the press again, stumbling full on a hard-faced, cruel man who took the nudge as an opportunity for a quarrel.

"You pushing me, man?" said the mortal with narrow hateful eyes as he gazed at Thorne.

"Come now," said Thorne, probing the mind, "have you killed men just for pushing you?"

"I have," said the other, his mouth in a cruel sneer. "I'll kill you too, if you don't get out of here."

"But let me give you my kiss," said Thorne, and clutching this one by the shoulders he bent to sink his teeth as the others around him, totally unaware of the secret fangs, laughed at this intimate and puzzling gesture. He drew a rich draught. Then licked the place artfully.

The hateful stranger was baffled and weakened, and tottered on his feet. His friends continued to laugh.

Quickly Thorne made his way out of the place and into the snow, and there he found Marius waiting for him. The wind was stronger than before, but the snow itself had stopped falling.

"The thirst is so strong now," said Thorne. "When I slept in the ice, I kept it like a beast chained up, but now it rules me. Once begun, I can't stop. I want more even now."

"Then more you'll have. But kill you can't. Not even in such a city as large as this. Come, follow me."

Thorne nodded. He had already killed. He looked at Marius, confessing this crime silently. Marius shrugged his shoulders. Then he put his arm around Thorne as they walked on.

"We've many places to visit."

It was almost dawn when they returned to the house.

Down into the wood-lined cellar they went, and there Marius showed Thorne to a chamber cut into the stone. The walls of it were cold, but a large sumptuous bed had been made inside the chamber, hung with brightly colored linen draperies, and heaped with intricately sewn covers. The mattress looked thick and so did the many pillows.

It was startling to Thorne that there was no crypt, no true hiding place. Anyone could find him here. It seemed as simple as his cave in the North, but far more inviting, far more luxurious. He was so tired in all his limbs that he could scarce speak. Yet he was anxious.

"Who is to disturb us here?" asked Marius. "Other blood drinkers go to their rest in this strange darkness just as we do. And there is no mortal who can enter here. But if you are afraid, I understand if we must seek some other shelter for you."

"Do you sleep in this way, unguarded?" Thorne asked.

"Even more so, in the bedroom above, like a mortal man, sprawled on my mattress in the cabinet bed among my comforts. The only enemy who has ever harmed me was a swarm of blood drinkers. They came when I was fully awake and aware as must needs be. If you like, I shall tell you that awful story."

Marius's face had gone dark, as though the mere mention of this disaster was evocative of terrible pain.

And Thorne understood something suddenly. It was that Marius wanted to tell this story. Marius needed to speak in a long flow of words as much as Thorne needed to hear words. Marius and Thorne had come upon each other in the proper moment.

But that would be tomorrow night. This night was ended.

Marius drew himself up and went on with his reassurance.

"The light won't come as you know, and no one will trouble you here. Sleep and dream as you must. And we'll talk on the morrow. Now let me take my leave. Daniel, my friend, is young. He falls on the floor by his little empire. I have to make him retire to a comfortable place, though I wonder sometimes if it matters."

"Will you tell me one thing before you go?" asked Thorne.

"If I can," said Marius gently, though suddenly he looked over-whelmingly hesitant. He looked as though he contained heavy secrets which he must tell and yet he feared to do it.

"The blood drinker who walked on the seashore," said Thorne, "looking at the pretty shells one by one, what became of her?"

Marius was relieved. He gave Thorne a long look and then in careful words he answered.

"They said that she gave herself up to the sun. She was not so old. They found her one evening in the moonlight. She'd drawn a great circle around herself of shells so they knew that her death was deliberate. There were only ashes there, and in fact, some had already been scattered by the wind. Those who loved her stood nearby and they watched as the wind took the rest. It was all finished by morning."

"Ah, what a dreadful thing," said Thorne. "Had she no pleasure in being one of us?"

Marius seemed struck by Thorne's words. Gently he asked:

"Do you take any pleasure in being one of us?"

"I think . . . I think I do again," said Thorne hesitantly.

4

HE WAS AWAKENED by the good smell of an oak fire. He turned over in the soft bed, not knowing where he was for the moment, but completely unafraid. He expected the ice and the loneliness. But he was someplace good, and someone was waiting for him. He had only to climb to his feet, to go up the steps.

Quite suddenly it all came clear. He was with Marius, his strange and hospitable friend. They were in a new city of promise and beauty built upon the ruins of the old. And good talk awaited him.

He stood up, stretching his limbs in the easy warmth of the room, and looked about himself, realizing that the illumination came from two old oil lamps, made of glass. How safe it seemed here. How pretty the painted wood of the walls.

There was a clean linen shirt for him on the chair. He put it on, having much difficulty with the tiny buttons. His pants were fine as they were. He wore woolen stockings but no shoes. The floors were smooth and polished and warm.

He let his tread announce him as he went up the stairs. It seemed very much the proper thing to do in this house, to let Marius know that he was coming, and not to be accused of boldness or stealth.

As he came to the door to the chamber where Daniel made his wondrous cities and towns, he paused, and very reticently glanced inside to see the boyish blond-haired Daniel at his work as though he had never retired for the day at all. Daniel looked up, and quite unexpectedly, gave Thorne an open smile as he greeted him.

"Thorne, our guest," he said. It had a faint tone of mockery, but Thorne sensed it was a weaker emotion.

"Daniel, my friend," said Thorne, glancing again over the tiny mountains and valleys, over the fast-running little trains with their lighted windows, over the thick forest of trees which seemed Daniel's present obsession.

Daniel turned his eyes back to his work as though they hadn't spoken. It was green paint now that he dabbed onto the small tree.

Quietly, Thorne moved to go but as he did so, Daniel spoke:

"Marius says it's a craft, not an art that I do." He held up the tiny tree.

Thorne didn't know what to say.

"I make the mountains with my own hands," said Daniel. "Marius says I should make the houses as well."

Again Thorne found himself unable to answer.

Daniel went on talking.

"I like the houses that come in the packages. It's difficult to assemble them, even for me. Besides, I would never think of so many different types of houses. I don't know why Marius has to say such disparaging things."

Thorne was perplexed. Finally he said simply,

"I have no answer."

Daniel went quiet.

Thorne waited for a respectful interval and then he went into the great room.

The fire was going on a blackened hearth within a rectangle of heavy stones, and Marius was seated beside it, slumped in his large leather chair, rather in the posture of a boy than a man, beckoning for Thorne to take his place on a big leather couch opposite.

"Sit there if you will, or here if you prefer," said Marius kindly. "If you mind the fire, I'll damp it down."

"And why would I mind it, friend?" asked Thorne, as he seated himself. The cushions were thick and soft.

As his eyes moved over the room, he saw that almost all the wood paneling was painted in gold or blue, and there were carvings on the ceiling beams above, and on the beams over the doorways. These carvings reminded him of his own times. But it was all new—as Marius had said, it was made by a modern man, this place, but it was made well and with much thought and care to it.

"Sometimes blood drinkers fear the fire," said Marius, looking at the flames, his serene white face full of light and shadow. "One never knows. I've always liked it, though once I suffered dreadfully on account of it, but then you know that story."

"I don't think I do know it," said Thorne. "No, I've never heard it. If you want to tell it, I want to hear."

"But first there are some questions you want answered," said Marius. "You want to know if the things you saw with the Mind Gift were entirely real."

"Yes," said Thorne. He remembered the net, the points of light, the Sacred Core. He thought of the Evil Queen. What had shaped his vision of her? It had been the thoughts of the blood drinkers who had gathered around her council table.

He realized he was looking directly into Marius's eyes, and that Marius knew his thoughts completely.

Marius looked away, and into the fire, and then he said offhandedly: "Put your feet up on the table. All that matters here is comfort."

Marius did this with his own feet, and Thorne stretched his legs out, crossing his feet at his ankles.

"Talk as you please," said Marius. "Tell me what you know, if you wish; tell me what you would know." There seemed a touch of anger in his voice but it wasn't anger for Thorne. "I have no secrets," Marius said. He studied Thorne's face thoughtfully, and then he continued: "There are the others—the ones you saw at that council table, and even more, scattered to the ends of the world."

He gave a little sigh and then a shake of his head, then he went on speaking.

"But I'm too alone now. I want to be with those I love but I cannot." He looked at the fire. "I come together with them for a short while and then I go away . . .

". . . I took Daniel with me because he needed me. I took Daniel because it's unendurable to me to be utterly alone. I sought the North countries because I was tired of the beautiful South lands, even tired of Italy where I was born. I used to think no mortal nor blood drinker could ever grow tired of bountiful Italy, but now I'm tired, and want to look on the pure whiteness of snow."

"I understand," said Thorne. The silence invited him to continue. "After I was made a blood drinker," he said, "I was taken South and it seemed Valhalla. In Rome I lived in a palace and looked out on the seven hills each night. It was a dream of soft breezes and fruit trees. I sat in a window high above the sea and watched it strike the rocks. I went down to the sea, and the sea was warm."

Marius smiled a truly kind and trusting smile. He nodded. "Italy, my Italy," he said softly.

Thorne thought the expression on his face was truly wondrous, and he wanted Marius to keep the smile but very quickly it was gone.

Marius had become sober and was looking into the flames again as though lost in his own sadness. In the light of the fire, his hair was almost entirely white.

"Talk to me, Marius," said Thorne. "My questions can wait. I want the sound of your voice. I want your words." He hesitated. "I know you have much to tell."

Marius looked at him as if startled, and warmed somewhat by this. Then he spoke.

"I'm old, my friend," he said. "I'm a true Child of the Millennia. It was in the years of Caesar Augustus that I became a blood drinker. It was a Druid priest who brought me to this peculiar death, a creature named Mael, mortal when he wronged me, but a blood drinker soon after, and one who still lives though he tried not long ago to sacrifice his life in a new religious fervor. What a fool.

"Time has made us companions more than once. How perfectly odd. It's a lie that I hold him high in my affections. My life is full of such lies. I don't know that I've ever forgiven him for what he did— taking me prisoner, dragging me out of my mortal life to a distant grove in Gaul, where an ancient blood drinker, badly burnt, yet still imagining himself to be a god of the Sacred Grove, gave me the Dark Blood."

Marius stopped. "Do you follow my meaning?"

"Yes," said Thorne. "I remember those groves and the whispers among us of gods who had lived in them. You are saying that a blood drinker lived within the Sacred Oak."

Marius nodded. He went on.

" 'Go to Egypt,' he charged me, this badly burnt god, this wounded god, 'and find the Mother. Find the reason for the terrible fire that has come from her, burning us far and wide.' "

"And this Mother," said Thorne. "She was the Evil Queen who carried within her the Sacred Core."

"Yes," said Marius, his steady blue eyes passing over Thorne gently. "She was the Evil Queen, friend, no doubt of it . . .

". . . But in that time, two thousand years ago, she was silent and still and seemed the most desperate of victims. Four thousand years old they were, the pair of them—she and her consort Enkil. And she did possess the Sacred Core, there was no doubt of it, for the terrible fire had come to all blood drinkers on the morning when an exhausted elder blood drinker had abandoned the King and Queen to the bright desert sun.

"Blood drinkers all over the world—gods, creatures of the night, lamias, whatever they called themselves—had suffered agony, some obliterated by terrible flames, others merely darkened and left with a meager pain. The very oldest suffered little, the youngest were ashes.

"As for the Sacred Parents—that is the kind thing to call them, I suppose—what had they done when the sun rose? Nothing. The Elder, severely burnt for all his efforts to make them wake or speak or run for shelter, found them as he had left them, unmovable, heedless, and so, fearing more suffering for himself he had returned them to a darkened chamber, which was no more than a miserable underground prison cell."

Marius stopped. He paused so completely it seemed that the memories were too hurtful to him. He was watching the flames as men do, and the flames did their reliable and eternal dance.

"Please tell me," said Thorne. "You found her, this Queen, you looked upon her with your own eyes that long ago?"

"Yes, I found her," Marius said softly. His voice was serious but not bitter. "I became her keeper. 'Take us out of Egypt, Marius,' that is what she said to me with the silent voice—what you call the Mind Gift, Thorne—never moving her lips.

"And I took her and her lover Enkil, and sheltered them for two thousand years as they remained still and silent as statues.

"I kept them hidden in a sacramental shrine. It was my life; it was my solemn commission.

"Flowers and incense I put before them. I tended to their clothes. I wiped the dust from their motionless faces. It was my sacred obligation to do these things, and all the while to keep the secret from vagrant blood drinkers who might seek to drink their powerful blood, or even take them captive."

His eyes remained on the fire, but the muscles in his throat tightened, and Thorne could see the veins for a moment against the smoothness of his temples.

"All the while," Marius went on, "I loved her, this seeming divinity whom you so rightly call our Evil Queen; that's perhaps the greatest lie I've ever lived. I loved her."

"How could you not love such a being?" Thorne asked. "Even in my sleep I saw her face. I felt her mystery. The Evil Queen. I felt her spell. And she had her silence to precede her. When she came to life it must have seemed as if a curse were broken, and she was at last released."

These words seemed to have a rather strong effect on Marius. His eyes moved over Thorne a bit coldly and then he looked back at the fire.

"If I said something wrong I am sorry for it," Thorne said. "I was only trying to understand."

"Yes, she was like a goddess," Marius resumed. "So I thought and so I dreamt, though I told myself and everyone else otherwise. It was part of my elaborate lie."

"Do we have to confess our loves to everyone?" asked Thorne softly. "Can we not keep some secrets?" With overwhelming pain he thought of his Maker. He did nothing to disguise these thoughts. He saw her again seated in the cave with the blazing fire behind her. He saw her taking the hairs from her own head and weaving them into thread with her distaff and her spindle. He saw her eyes rimmed in blood, and then he broke from these memories. He pushed them deep down inside his heart.

He looked at Marius.

Marius had not answered Thorne's question.

The silence made Thorne anxious. He felt he should fall silent and let Marius go on. Yet the question came to his lips.

"How did the disaster come to pass?" Thorne asked. "Why did the Evil Queen rise from her throne? Was it the Vampire Lestat with his electric songs who waked her? I saw him in human guise, dancing for humans, as if he were one of them. I smiled in my sleep, as I saw the modern world enfold him, unbelieving, amused, and dancing to his rhythms."

"That's what happened, my friend," said Marius, "at least with the modern world. As for her? Her rising from her throne? His songs had much to do with it.

"For we have to remind ourselves that for thousands of years she had existed in silence. Flowers and incense, yes, these things I gave her in abundance, but music? Never. Not until the modern world made such a thing possible, and then Lestat's music came into the very room where she sat shimmering in her raiment. And it did wake her, not once, but twice.

"The first time was as shocking to me as the later disaster, though it was mended soon enough. It was two hundred years ago—on an island in the Aegean Sea—this little surprise, and I should have taken a hard lesson from it, but this in my pride I failed to do."

"What took place?"

"Lestat was a new blood drinker and having heard of me, he sought me out, and with an honest heart. He wanted to know what I had to reveal. All over the world he'd sought me, and then there came a time when he was weak and broken by the very gift of immortality, a time of his going into the earth as you went into the ice of the Far North.

"I brought him to me; I talked with him as I'm talking to you now. But something curious happened with him which caught me quite off guard. I felt a sudden surge of pure devotion to him and this combined with an extraordinary trust.

"He was young but he wasn't innocent. And when I talked, he listened perfectly. When I played the teacher, there came no argument. I wanted to tell him my earliest secrets. I wanted to reveal the secret of our King and Queen.

"It had been a long, long time since I'd revealed that secret. I'd been alone for a century among mortals. And Lestat, so absolute in his devotion to me, seemed completely worthy of my trust.

"I took him down to the underground shrine. I opened the door upon the two seated figures.

"For the first few moments, he believed the Sacred Parents were statues, but quite suddenly he became aware that both were alive. He realized in fact that they were blood drinkers, and that they were greatly advanced in age, and that in them, he could see his destiny were he to endure for so many thousands of years.

"This is a terrifying realization. Even to the young who look on me, it is a difficult realization that they might become as pale and hard as I am. With the Mother and Father, it was horrifying, and Lestat was overcome with fear.

"Nevertheless, he managed to bridle his fear and approach the Queen, and even to kiss her on the lips. It was a bold thing to do, but as I watched him I realized it was quite natural to him, and as he withdrew from her, he confessed to me that he knew her name.

"Akasha. It was as if she'd spoken it. And I could not deny that she had given it to him through his mind. Out of her centuries of silence had come her voice once more with this seductive confession.

"Understand how young he was. Given the blood at twenty, he had been a blood drinker for perhaps ten years, no more than that.

"What was I to make of this kiss and this secret revelation?

"I denied my love and my jealousy completely. I denied my crushing disappointment. I told myself, 'You are too wise for such. Learn from what's happened. Maybe this young one will bring something magnificent from her. Is she not a goddess?'

"I took Lestat to my salon, a room as comfortable as this, though in another style, and there we talked until early morn. I told him the tale of my making, of my journey to Egypt. I played the teacher with great earnestness and generosity, and something of pure self-indulgence. Was it for Lestat or for me that I wanted him to know everything? I don't know. But those were splendid hours for me, I know that much.

"The following night, however, while I was about tending to the mortals who lived on my island and believed me to be their lord, Lestat did a dreadful thing.

"Taking from his own luggage a violin which was most precious to him—a musical instrument of uncanny power—he went down into the shrine.

"Now it is plain to me, as it was then, that he could not have done this without the aid of the Queen, who with the Mind Gift opened the many doors for him that lay between him and her.

"Indeed as Lestat tells it, she may have even put the very idea of playing the instrument into his mind. I don't think so. I think she opened the doors and summoned him, but it was he who brought the violin.

"Calculating that it would make a sound totally unfamiliar and quite wonderful to her, he set out to mimic those he'd seen playing the instrument, because in fact he didn't know how to play it.

"Within moments, my beautiful Queen had risen from the throne and was moving towards him. And he in his terror had dropped the violin which she crushed with her foot. No matter. She took him in her arms. She offered her blood to him, and then there happened something so remarkable that it's painful for me to reveal it. Not only did she allow him to drink from her, *she also drank from him.*

"It seems a simple thing, but it is not. For in all my centuries of coming to her, of taking blood from her, I had never felt the press of her teeth against me.

"Indeed, I know of no supplicant whose blood she ever drank. Once there was a sacrifice, and yes, she drank from that victim, and that victim was destroyed. But from her supplicants? Never. She was the fount, the giver, the healer of blood gods, and burnt children, but she did not drink from them.

"Yet she drank from Lestat.

"What did she see in those moments? I cannot imagine, yet it must have been a glimpse into the years of that time. It must have been a glimpse into Lestat's soul. Whatever it was, it was momentary, for her consort Enkil soon rose and moved to stop it, and by this time, I had arrived, and was trying desperately and successfully to prevent Lestat from being destroyed by Enkil who seemed to have no other purpose.

"The King and Queen returned to their throne, besmirched and bloody and finally silent. But for the rest of the night Enkil was restless, destroying the vases and braziers of the shrine.

"It was a terrifying display of power. And I realized that for his safety, indeed, even for my own, I must say farewell at once to Lestat, which caused me excruciating pain, and so we parted the following night."

Marius fell silent again, and Thorne waited patiently. Then Marius began to speak once more.

"I don't know what caused me the worst pain—the loss of Lestat, or my jealousy that she had *given and taken* with him. I'm unable to know my own mind. You understand I felt I possessed her. I felt she was my Queen." His voice dropped to a whisper. "When I revealed her to him, I was displaying a possession! You see what a liar I was?" he asked. "And then to lose him, to lose this young one with whom I felt such utter communion. Ah, that was such rich pain. Rather like the music of the violin, I think, just as deeply colored, such terrible pain."

"What can I do to ease your sorrow now?" asked Thorne. "For you carry it, as if she were here still."

Marius looked up, and suddenly an expression of pure surprise brightened his face. "You're right," he said. "I carry the obligation, as if she were still with me, as if even now I had to go and spend my hours in her shrine."

"Can't you be glad that it's over?" asked Thorne. "It seemed when I lay in my cave of ice, when I saw these things in dreams that there were others who were at peace when it was finished. Even the red-haired twins whom I saw standing before everyone seemed to have a sense that it was done."

Marius nodded. "They do all share this," said Marius, "except perhaps for Lestat." He looked wondering at Thorne.

"Tell me now how she was wakened finally," said Thorne, "how she became the slayer of her children. I felt her pass me, close and with a searching eye, yet somehow I was not found."

"Others as well escaped her," said Marius, "though how many no one knows. She tired of her slaughter and she came to us. I think she thought that she had time to finish. But her end came swiftly enough.

"As for the second resurrection, it was Lestat again, but I am as much to blame myself.

"This is what I believe happened. I brought the inventions of the modern world to her as offerings. At first it was the machines that played music, and then came those which would show moving pictures. At last, I brought the most powerful of all, the television that would play constantly. I set it in her shrine as though it were a sacrifice."

"And she fed upon this thing," said Thorne, "as gods are wont to do when they come down to their altars."

"Yes, she fed upon it. She fed upon its terrible electric violence. Lurid colors flashed over her face, and images accosted her. It might have wakened her with the sheer clamor. And I wonder sometimes if the endless public talk of the great world could not have in itself inspired an imitation of a mind in her."

"An imitation of a mind?"

"She awoke with a simple ugly sense of purpose. She would rule this world."

Marius shook his head. His attitude was one of profound sadness.

"She would outwit its finest human minds," he said sorrowfully. "She would destroy the vast majority of this world's male children. In a female paradise, she could create and enforce peace. It was nonsense—a concept drenched in violence and blood.

"And those of us who tried to reason with her had to take great care with our words not to insult her. Where could she have gotten these notions, except from the bits and pieces of electric dreams that she watched on the giant screen I'd provided for her? Fictions of all kinds, and what the world calls News, all this had inundated her. I had loosed the flood."

Marius's gaze flashed on Thorne as he continued:

"Of course she saw the vivid video songs of The Vampire Lestat." Marius smiled again, but it was a sad smile, and it brightened his face as sad songs brighten a face. "And Lestat presented in his video films the very image of her on her throne as he had seen her centuries ago. Breaking faith with me, he told the secrets I had confided to him."

"Why didn't you destroy him for this!" said Thorne, before he could stop himself. "I would have done so."

Marius only shook his head.

"I think I've chosen to destroy myself instead," he said. "I've chosen to let my heart break inside me."

"Why, explain this thing to me."

"I can't, I can't explain it to myself," said Marius. "Perhaps I understand Lestat only too well. He couldn't endure the vow of silence he'd given me. Not in this world you see around you with all its wonders. He felt driven to reveal our history." The heat danced in Marius's face. His fingers gripped the arms of his chair with only a little restlessness. "He tore loose from all bonds that connected us," he said, "friend and friend, teacher and student, old and young, watcher and searching one."

"Outrage," said Thorne, "what else could you feel but fury?"

"Yes, in my heart I did. But you see, I lied to them, the other blood drinkers, our brothers, our sisters. Because once the Queen had risen, they needed me. . . ."

"Yes," said Thorne, "I saw it."

"They needed the wise one to reason with her, and deflect her from her course. There was no time for quarreling. Lestat's songs had brought her forth a monster. I told the others there was no wound. I took Lestat in my arms. And as for my Queen, ah, my Queen, how I denied that I had ever loved her. And all this for the company of a small band of immortals. And I tell the truth to you."

"Does it feel good to you to say it?"

"Oh, yes, it feels good," Marius answered.

"How was she destroyed?"

"Thousands of years ago a curse had been put on her by one whom she had treated with cruelty and that one came to settle the score. A single blow decapitated our beautiful Queen, and then from her body the Sacred Core of the blood drinkers was promptly taken into the avenger, either from brain or heart, I know not which, for during those fatal moments I was as blind as all the others.

"I know only the one who slew the Queen now carries the Sacred Core within her and where she's gone or how I can't tell you."

"I saw the red-haired twins," said Thorne. "They stood beside her body. 'The Queen of the Damned,' said my Maharet. I heard those words. I saw Maharet with her arm around her sister."

Marius said nothing.

Again Thorne felt himself become agitated. He felt the beginnings of pain inside. In memory, he saw his Maker coming towards him in the snow. What fear did he have then, a mortal warrior facing a lone witch whom he could destroy with sword or ax? How frail and beautiful she had seemed, a tall being in a dress of dark-purple wool, her arms out as if welcoming him.

But I have come here for you. It is for you that I linger.

He wouldn't fall under her spell. They wouldn't find his body in the snow, the eyes torn out of his face, as they had found so many others.

He wanted the memory to go away. He spoke.

"She is my Maker, the red-haired one," he said, "Maharet, the sister of the one who took within herself the Sacred Core."

He paused. He could scarcely breathe he felt such pain.

Marius stared at him intently.

"She had come North to find a lover among our people," Thorne said. He paused, his conviction wavering. But then he continued. "She hunted our clan and the others who lived in our valley. She stole the eyes from those whom she slew."

"The eyes and the blood," said Marius to him softly. "And when she made you a blood drinker, you learnt why she needed the eyes."

"Yes, but not the true story—not the tale of the one who had taken her mortal eyes. And of her twin, I knew not an inkling. I loved her completely. I asked few questions. I could not share her company with others. It made me mad."

"It was the Evil Queen who took her eyes," said Marius, "when she was still human; and from her twin sister, the tongue. That was a cruel injustice, that. And one who also possessed the Blood could not endure it, and so he made them both blood drinkers before the Evil Queen divided them and sent each twin to a different side of the world."

Thorne gasped as he thought of it. He tried to feel love inside himself. He saw his Maker again in the brightly lighted cave with her thread and her spindle. He saw her long red hair.

"And so it was finished," said Thorne, "the catastrophe I beheld as I slept in the ice. The Evil Queen is gone, punished forever, and the twins took the Sacred Core, yes, but when I search the world for the visions or the voices of our kind I can't find the twins. I hear nothing of them, though I want to know where they are."

"They have retreated," said Marius. "They know they must hide. They know that someone may try to take the Sacred Core from them.

They know that someone, bitter and finished with this world, may seek to destroy us all."

"Ah, yes," said Thorne. He felt a chill come over his limbs. He wished suddenly that he had more blood in his veins. That he could go out and hunt—but then he didn't want to leave this warm place and these flowing words, not just now. It was too soon.

He felt guilty that he had not told the whole truth of his suffering and his purpose to Marius. He didn't know if he could, and it seemed a terrible thing now to be under this roof, yet he remained there.

"I know your truth," said Marius gently. "You've come forth with one vow and that is to find Maharet and do harm to her."

Thorne winced as though he'd been struck hard in the chest. He made no answer.

"Such a thing," said Marius, "is impossible. You knew it when you left her centuries ago for your sleep in the ice. She is powerful beyond our imagining. And I can tell you, without doubt, that her sister never leaves her."

Thorne could find no words. At last he spoke in a tense whisper.

"Why do I hate her for the form of life she gave me, when I never hated my mortal mother and father?"

Marius nodded and gave a bitter smile.

"It's a wise question," Marius said. "Abandon your hope of harming her. Stop dreaming of those chains in which she once bound Lestat unless you truly wish for her to bind you in them."

It was Thorne's turn to nod.

"But what were those chains?" he asked, his voice tense and bitter as before, "and why do I want to be her hateful prisoner? So that she can know my wrath every night as she keeps me close to her?"

"Chains made of her red hair?" Marius suggested, with a slight shrug of his shoulders, "bound with steel and with her blood?" he mused. "Bound with steel and with her blood and gold, perhaps. I never saw them. I only knew of them, and that they kept Lestat helpless in all his anger."

"I want to know what they were," said Thorne. "I want to find her."

"Forswear that purpose, Thorne," said Marius. "I can't take you to her. And what if she beckoned for you as she did so long ago, and then she destroyed you when she discovered your hatred?"

"She knew of it when I left her," said Thorne.

"And why did you go?" Marius asked. "Was it the simple jealousy of others which your thoughts reveal to me?"

"She took them in favor one at a time. I couldn't endure it. You speak of a Druid priest who became a blood drinker. I know of such a one. Mael was his name, the very name you've spoken. She brought him into her small circle, a welcome lover. He was old in the Blood and had tales to tell, and she longed for this more than anything. I turned away from her then. I scarce think she saw me retreat. I scarce think she felt my hatred."

Marius was listening intently. Then he spoke.

"Mael," he said, his words gentle and patient. "Tall and gaunt always, with a high bridged nose and deep-set blue eyes and long blond hair from his servitude in the Sacred Grove. That's the Mael who lured your sweet Maharet from you?"

"Yes," said Thorne. He felt the pain in his chest slacken. "And she was sweet, that I can't deny, and she never spurned me. It was I who wandered away, towards the North land. It was I who hated him for his flattery of her and his clever stories."

"Don't seek a quarrel with her," Marius said. "Stay here with me, and by and by, she may come to know that you're here, and she may send you her welcome. Be wise then, I beg you."

Thorne nodded again. It was as if the terrible battle was over. He had confessed his wrath and it was gone, and he sat still and simple near the fire, the warrior no longer. Such was the magic of words, he thought.

Then memory came again. Six centuries ago. He was in the cave, and could see the flicker of the firelight. He was bound and couldn't move. She lay beside him, peering down into his eyes and whispering to him. He couldn't remember those words, because they were part of something larger and more terrible, something as strong as the threads that bound him.

He could break those threads now. He could cut loose of the memories and lodge himself firmly in this room. He could look at Marius.

He gave a long slow sigh.

"But return to your tale, if you will," he asked. "Why after the Queen was destroyed, and after the twins were gone, why then didn't you reveal your rage to the blood drinker Lestat, why didn't you take your vengeance? You'd been betrayed! And disaster had followed upon it."

"Because I wanted to love him still," said Marius, as though he had long known the answer, "and I wanted to be loved, and I could not forfeit my place as the wise and patient one, as I've said. Anger is too painful for me. Anger is too pathetic. I cannot bear it. I cannot act upon it."

"Wait for one moment," said Thorne. "Say this again?"

"Anger is too pathetic," Marius repeated. "It's too much at a disadvantage always. I can't act upon it. I can't make it mine."

Thorne gestured for quiet. He sat back considering, and it seemed a cold air settled on him in spite of the fire.

"Anger is weak," Thorne whispered. It was a new idea to him. In his mind anger and rage had always been akin. And rage had seemed something akin to Wodin's fury. One summoned rage before going into battle. One welcomed rage into one's heart. And in the ice cave, he had let an old rage awaken him.

"Anger is as weak as fear," said Marius. "Can either of us endure fear?"

"No," said Thorne. "But you're speaking of something inside you that's heated and strong."

"Yes, there is something brutal and hurt inside of me, and I wander alone, refusing the cup of anger, choosing silence rather than angry words. And I come upon you in the North land, and you're a stranger to me, and I can bare my soul to you."

"Yes, that you can do," said Thorne. "For the hospitality you have given me, you can tell me anything. I will never break your trust, that I promise. No common words or songs will ever come from me. Nothing can make such a thing happen." He felt his voice grow strong as he spoke. It was because he was honest in what he said. "What has become of Lestat? Why is he silent now? I hear no more songs or sagas from him."

"Sagas, ah yes, that's what he wrote, sagas of our kind," said Marius and again he smiled, almost brightly. "He suffers his own terrible wounds," said Marius. "He's been with angels, or with those beings who claim to be such and they have taken him to Hell and to Heaven."

"You believe these things?"

"I don't know. I can tell you only he wasn't on this Earth while these creatures claim to have had him. And he brought back with him a bloody Veil with the Face of Christ quite beautifully blazoned upon it."

"Ah, and this you saw?"

"I did," said Marius, "as I have seen other relics. It was to see this Veil and to go into the sun and die that our Druid priest Mael was nearly taken from us."

"Why didn't Mael die," asked Thorne. He couldn't conceal his own emotion when he said this name.

"He was too old for such a thing," said Marius. "He was badly burnt and brought low, as can happen with those of us who are very old, and after one day in the sun, he hadn't the courage for more suffering. Back to his companions he went and there he remains."

"And you? Will you tell me now with your full heart; do you truly despise him for what he did to you? Or is it your distaste for anger which makes you turn away from this thing?"

"I don't know. There are times when I can't look on Mael's face. There are times when I want to be in his company. There are times when I can't seek out any of them. I've come here with Daniel alone. Daniel always needs someone to look after him. It suits me to be near Daniel. Daniel doesn't have to speak. That he is here is sufficient."

"I understand you," said Thorne.

"Understand this as well," said Marius. "I want to continue. I am not one who wishes to go into the sun or seek some other form of obliteration. If you have truly come out of the ice to destroy Maharet, to anger her twin—."

Thorne lifted his right hand, gesturing for patience and silence.

Then he spoke:

"I have not," he said. "Those were dreams. They've died in this very place. It will take longer for memory to die—."

"Then remember her beauty and her power," Marius said. "I asked her once why she had never taken a blood drinker's eyes for her own. Why always the weak and bleeding eyes of a mortal victim? She told me she had never come upon a blood drinker whom she would destroy or even hurt, save for the Evil Queen herself and the Queen's eyes she couldn't take. Pure hatred prevented it."

Thorne thought on this for a long time without replying.

"Always mortal eyes," he whispered.

"And with each pair, as they endure, she sees more than you and I can see," said Marius.

"Yes," said Thorne, "I understand you."

"I want the strength to grow older," Marius said. "I want to find wonders around me as I always have. If I don't, I'll lose the strength to continue and that is what bites into me now. Death has put its hand on my shoulder. Death has come in the form of disappointment and fear of scorn."

"Ah, these things I understand, almost perfectly," said Thorne. "When I went up into the snow, I wanted to flee from these things. I wanted to die and not die, as so many mortals do. I don't think I thought I would endure in the ice or snow. I thought it would devour me, freeze me solid as it would a mortal man. But no such thing ever happened. And as for the pain of the cold I grew used to it, as if it were my daily portion, as if I had no right to anything else. But it was pain that drove me there, and so I understand you. You would fight pain now rather than retreat."

"Yes, I would," said Marius. "When the Queen rose from her underground shrine, she left me buried in ice and indifference. Others came to rescue me and bring me to the council table where we sought to reason with her. Before this happened, I could not have imagined such contempt from the Queen or such injury. I could not have imagined my own patience and seeming forgiveness.

"But at that council table, Akasha met her destruction. The insult to me was avenged with utter finality. This creature whom I had guarded for two thousand years was gone from me. My Queen, gone from me . . .

"And so I can see now the larger story of my own life, of which my beautiful Queen was only a part, even in her cruelty to me. I can see all the stories of my life. I can pick and choose from among them."

"Let me hear these stories," said Thorne. "Your words flow over me like warm water. They bring me comfort. I hunger for your images. I hunger for all you might say."

Marius pondered this.

"Let me try to tell my stories," Marius said. "Let my stories do what stories always do. Let them keep you from your darker dreams and from your darker journey. Let them keep you here."

Thorne smiled.

"Yes," he said, "I trust in you. Go on."

THE STORY

5

As I have told you, I was born in the Roman times, in the age of Augustus when the Roman Empire was immense and powerful, though the Northern tribes of barbarians who would eventually overrun it had long been fighting on its Northern frontiers.

Europe was a world of big and powerful cities just as it is now.

As for me, as I've said I was a bookish individual, and it had been my bad luck to be stolen from my world, taken into Druid precincts and there delivered to a blood drinker who believed himself to be a sacred God of the Grove and gave me nothing but superstition along with the Dark Blood.

My journey to Egypt to find the Mother was for myself. What if this fire described by the blackened and suffering god should come again?

Well, I found the Divine Pair and I stole them from those who had long been their guardians. I did it not only to possess the Sacred Core of the Divine Queen but because of my love of Akasha, my belief that she had spoken to me and commanded me to rescue her, and because she had given me her Precious Blood.

Understand there was nothing as strong as that primal fount. The blood rendered me a formidable blood drinker who could fight off any of the old burnt gods who came after me in the years to come.

But you must also understand: no religious impulse guided me. I had thought the "god" of the Druid woods to be a monster. And I understood that in her own way Akasha was a monster. I was a monster as well. I had no intention of creating a devotion for her. She was a secret. And from the moment she came into my hands she and her consort were most truly Those Who Must Be Kept.

This did not stop me from adoring her in my heart, and creating the most lavish shrine for her, and dreaming that, having spoken to me once with the Mind Gift, she would speak to me again.

The first city to which I took the mysterious pair was Antioch, a most marvelous and interesting place. It was in the East as we said in those days, yet it was a Roman city and had been shaped by the tremendous influence of Hellenism—that is, the philosophy and ideas of the Greeks. It was a city of new and splendid Roman buildings, and it was a city of great libraries and schools of philosophy, and though I haunted it by night, the ghost of my former self, there were brilliant men to be spied upon and wondrous things to be heard.

Nevertheless my first years as the keeper of the Mother and the Father were bitter in my loneliness, and the silence of the Divine Parents struck me often as particularly cruel. I was pitifully ignorant as to my own nature, and perpetually brooding on my eternal fate.

Akasha's silence struck me as terrifying and confusing. After all, why was I asked by Akasha to take her out of Egypt if she meant only to sit upon her throne in eternal stillness? It seemed sometimes that self-destruction was preferable to the existence I endured.

Then came the exquisite Pandora into my midst, a woman I'd known since her girlhood in Rome. Indeed, I'd once gone to her father to seek her hand in marriage when she'd been only a precocious child. And here she was in Antioch, as lovely in the prime of life as she'd been in her youth, flooding my thoughts with impossible desire.

Our lives became fatally intertwined. Indeed the speed and violence with which Pandora was made a blood drinker left me weak with guilt and confusion. But Pandora believed that Akasha had willed our union; Akasha had hearkened to my loneliness; Akasha had drawn Pandora to me.

If you saw our council table, round which we sat when Akasha rose, then you have seen Pandora, the tall white-skinned beauty with the distinct rippling brown hair, one who is now a powerful Child of the Millennia just as you are and just as I am.

Why am I not with her now, you may ask? What is it in me that will not acknowledge my admiration for her mind, her beauty, her exquisite understanding of all things?

Why can't I go to her!

I don't know. I know only that a terrible anger and pain divides us just as it did so many years ago. I cannot admit how much I have wronged her. I cannot admit how much I have lied about my love of her and my need of her. And this need, perhaps this need is the thing which keeps me at a distance, where I am safe from the scrutiny of her soft and wise brown eyes.

It's also true that she judges me harshly for things I have lately done. But this is too difficult to explain.

In those ancient times, when it was scarce two centuries that we lived together, it was I who destroyed our union in a foolish and dreadful way. We had spent almost every night of our lives quarreling, and I could not admit her advantages, and her victories, and it was as the result of my weakness that I foolishly and impetuously left her when I did.

This was the single worst mistake of all my long years.

But let me tell quickly the little tale of how we came to be divided by my bitterness and pride.

Now as we kept the Mother and the Father, the old gods of the dark groves of the North woods died out. Nevertheless an occasional blood drinker would discover us and come to press his suit for the blood of Those Who Must Be Kept.

Most often such a monster was violent and easily dispatched in the heat of anger, and we would return to our civilized life.

One evening, however, there appeared in our villa outside Antioch a band of newly made blood drinkers, some five in number, all dressed in simple robes.

I was soon amazed to discover that they perceived themselves as serving Satan within a Divine Plan that held the Devil to be equal in power to the Christian God.

They did not know of the Mother and the Father, and understand, the shrine was in that very house, down, beneath the floor. Yet they could hear no inkling of the Divine Parents. They were far too young and too innocent. Indeed, their zeal and sincerity was enough to break one's heart.

But though deeply touched by their mishmash of Christian and Persian ideas, of their wild notions, and by their curious appearance of innocence, I was also horrified by the fact that this was a new religion among the blood drinkers, and they spoke of other adherents. They spoke of a cult.

The human in me was revolted; and the rational Roman was more confused and alarmed than I can express.

It was Pandora who quickly brought me to my senses and gave me to know that we must slaughter the whole band. Were we to let them go, others would come to us, and soon the Mother and Father might fall into their hands.

I, who had slain old pagan blood drinkers with ease, seemed somehow unable to obey her, perhaps because I realized for the first time that if we remained in Antioch, if we maintained our household and our lives, more and more blood drinkers would come and there would be no end to killing them in order to protect our fine secret. And my soul suddenly could not endure this possibility. Indeed I thought once more of death for myself and even for Those Who Must Be Kept.

We slaughtered the zealots. It was a simple thing to do for they were so young. It took only moments with torches and with our swords. We burnt them to ashes and then scattered those ashes as, I'm sure you know, must be done.

But after it was over, I lapsed into a terrible silence and for months would not leave the shrine. I abandoned Pandora for my own suffering. I couldn't explain to her that I had foreseen a grim future, and when she had gone out to hunt the city or to do whatever amused her, I went to Akasha.

I went to my Queen. I knelt before her and I asked her what she meant for me to do.

"After all," I said, "these are your children, are they not? They come in new battalions and they don't know your name. They likened their fangs to those of serpents. They spoke of the Hebrew prophet Moses, holding up the serpent staff in the desert. They spoke of others who might come."

No answer came from Akasha. No real answer was to come from Akasha for two thousand years.

But I was only beginning my awful journey then. And all I knew in those anxious moments was that I had to conceal my prayers from Pandora, that I couldn't let her see me—Marius, the philosopher—on bended knee. I went on with my praying, I went on with my feverish worship. And as always happens when one prays to an immobile thing, the light played upon the face of Akasha; the light gave some semblance of life.

Meantime, Pandora, as embittered by my silence as I was by Akasha's silence, became utterly distraught.

And one night she hurled at me a simple household insult, "Would that I were rid of them and rid of you."

She left the house and she did not return the next night or the night after that.

As you can see, she was merely playing the same game with me that I had played with her. She refused to be a witness to my hardness. But she could not understand how desperately I needed her presence, and even her vain pleas.

Oh, it was so shamefully selfish of me. It was such a needless disaster, but powerfully angry with her, I took the irrevocable step of arranging for my departure from Antioch by day.

Indeed, by the light of the dim lamp, so as not to arouse my mortal agents, I gave orders for myself and Those Who Must Be Kept to be transported in three immense sarcophaghi to Rome by sea. I abandoned my Pandora. I took with me all that was mine and left her only the empty villa, with her own possessions strewn rather carelessly and insultingly around it. I left the only creature in the world who could have patience with me, who could give me understanding, and who had done so, no matter how often or how hard we had fought.

I left the only being who knew what I was!

Of course I didn't know the consequences. I didn't realize that I would not find Pandora for hundreds of years. I didn't know that she would become a goddess in my mind, a being as powerful in my memory as Akasha was to me night after night.

You see, it was another lie, like unto the lie I've told about Akasha. I loved Pandora and I needed her. But in our verbal combat, I had always, no matter how emotional, played the role of the superior mind who was in no need of her seemingly irrational discourse and always evident affection. I remember the very night that I gave her the Dark Blood how she had argued with me.

She said, "Don't make a religion of reason and logic. Because in the passage of time reason may fail you and when it does, you may find yourself taking refuge in madness." I was so offended by these words coming from the mouth of this beautiful woman whose eyes so entranced me that I could scarce follow her thoughts.

Yet in those months of silence, after we had slain the New Believers, this was precisely what had happened. I had lapsed into a form of madness and refused to speak a word.

And only now can I admit the full folly of it, that my own weakness was unsupportable to me, and that I could not endure having her as the witness of the melancholy which shrouded my soul.

Even now, I cannot have her as a witness to my suffering. I live here alone, with Daniel. I speak to you because you are a new friend and can take from me fresh impressions and fresh suggestions. You don't look at me with old knowledge and old fear.

But let me go on with my tale.

Our ship arrived at the port of Ostia in good order, and once we had been transported in three sarcophaghi to the city of Rome, I rose from my "grave," made arrangements for an expensive villa just outside the city walls, and arranged an underground shrine for Those Who Must Be Kept in the hills well away from the house.

A great guilt weighed me down that I had placed them at such a distance from the place in which I lived, read my books, and took to my crypt at night. After all, they had been within my very house in Antioch, though safely beneath it, and now they were some miles away.

But I wanted to live close to the great city, and indeed within a few short years, the walls of Rome were built out and around my house so that Rome enclosed it. I had a country villa in town.

It was no safe place for Those Who Must Be Kept. So it proved most wise that I had created their shrine well away from the burgeoning city, and settling into my villa, I played "a Roman gentleman" to those around me, the loving master of several simple-minded and gullible slaves.

Now understand that I had been away from Rome for over two hundred years.

Glorying in the cultural riches of Antioch, a Roman city, yes, but an Eastern city, listening to her poets and teachers in the Forum, roaming her libraries by torchlight, I had been horrified by descriptions of the latest Roman Emperors who had disgraced the title altogether by their antics and inevitably been murdered by their bodyguards or their troops.

But I was far wrong that the Eternal City had fallen into degradation. Great Emperors of the past hundred years there had been such as Hadrian and Marcus Aurelius, and Septimius Severus, and there had been an enormous number of monumental buildings added to the capital as well as a great increase of population. Not even a blood drinker such as myself could have inspected all of Rome's temples, amphitheaters and baths.

Indeed Rome was more than likely the largest and most impressive city in the world. Some two million people made up the populace, many of the plebs, as the poor were called, receiving a daily ration of corn and wine.

I yielded to the spell of the city immediately. And shutting out the horrors of the Imperial quarrels and continuous war along the frontiers, I diverted myself by studying the intellectual and aesthetic handiwork of mankind as I've always done.

Of course I went immediately to play the hovering ghost about the town houses of my descendants, for I had kept some track of them, though never admitting it to Pandora, and I found them to be good members of the old Senatorial class, striving desperately to maintain some order in government, while the army elevated Emperor after Emperor in a desperate attempt to secure power for this or that faction in this or that far-flung place.

It broke my heart actually to see these young men and women whom I knew to have come down from my uncles and aunts, from my nieces and nephews, and it was during this period that I broke my record of them forever, though why precisely I cannot say.

It was a time for me of breaking all ties. I had abandoned Pandora. I had put Those Who Must Be Kept at some remove from me, and now I came home one night, from spying upon a supper party at the house of one of my many descendants, and I took out of a wooden chest all the scrolls in which I had written the names of these young people, gleaned from letters to various agents, and I burnt them, feeling rather wise in my monstrosity, as though this would prevent me from further vanity and pain.

After that, I haunted the precincts of strangers to gain knowledge. With vampiric dexterity I slipped into shadowy gardens and listened at the open doorways of the dimly lighted villas as those inside talked softly over dinner or listened to the delicate music of a young boy accompanying himself with a lyre.

I found the old conservative Romans very touching, and though the libraries were not as good here as they had become in Antioch, I found much to read. There were of course schools of philosophy in Rome, and though they too were not as impressive as those in Antioch, I was interested in listening to what I could.

But understand, I did not really enter into the mortal world. I made no friendships with mortals. I did not converse with them. I only watched them, as I had always done in Antioch. I did not believe then that I could penetrate with any true success into their natural realm.

As for my blood thirst, I hunted furiously in Rome. I kept to the Evil Doer always, which was a simple matter, I can assure you, but I fed my hunger far more than I needed to feed it. I bared my fangs cruelly to those I killed. The huge population never left me hungry. I was more the blood drinker than ever in my existence up to that time.

It was a challenge to me to do it properly, to sink my teeth but once and cleanly, and to spill not a drop as I took the death along with the blood.

There was no need in such a place as Rome of those times to hide the bodies for fear of discovery. Sometimes I threw them in the Tiber. Sometimes I did nothing but leave them in the street. I loved particularly to kill in taverns which is something I like even now, as you know.

There is nothing like the long passage through the damp dark night, and then the sudden opening of the door of the tavern upon an entire little universe of light and warmth and singing and laughing humans. I found taverns very enticing indeed.

Of course, all this ravening, this endless killing—it was on account of my grief for Pandora, and it was because I was alone. Who was there to restrain me? Who was there to outdo me? No one at all.

And understand, during the first few months, I might have written to her! There was surely a chance that she had remained in Antioch, in our house, waiting for me to come to my senses, but I did no such thing.

A fierce anger, the very anger I fight now, welled up in me, and it made me weak, as I've already told you. I couldn't do what I had to do—bring her back to me. And sometimes my loneliness pushed me to take three and four victims in a night, until I was spilling blood I couldn't drink.

Sometimes in the early hours of the morning my rage was quieted, and I went back to my historical writing, something which I had begun in Antioch and never revealed to a single soul.

I described what I saw in Rome of progress or failure. I described the buildings in ponderous detail. But then there came nights when I thought that everything I'd written was useless. After all, what was the purpose? I could not enter these descriptions, these observations, these poems, these essays, into the mortal world!

They were contaminated in that they came from a blood drinker, a monster who slew humans for his own survival. There was no place for the poetry or history which had come from a greedy mind and heart.

And so I began to destroy not only my fresh writings, but even the old essays which I had written in Antioch in the past. I took the scrolls out of the chests one by one and burnt them as I had burnt the records of my family. Or I merely kept them, locked up tight, and away from my eyes, so that nothing I'd written could spark in me anything new.

It was a great crisis of the soul.

Then something happened which was totally unforeseen.

I came upon another blood drinker—indeed I came upon two of them in dark streets of the late night city as I was coming down a hill.

The moon had gone behind the clouds at that moment, but naturally I could see quite perfectly with my preternatural eyes.

The two creatures were approaching me rapidly with no knowledge that I stood against the wall, trying not to block their path.

At last the first of the pair lifted his head and I recognized the face at once. I knew the hawk nose and deep-set eyes. I knew the gaunt cheeks. In fact I recognized everything about him, the slope of his shoulders, his long blond hair, and even the hand that held the cloak at his throat.

This was Mael, the Druid priest who had long ago captured me and taken me prisoner, and fed me alive to the burnt and dying God of the Grove. This was Mael who had kept me in captivity for months as he prepared me for the Dark Magic. This was Mael, the pure of heart, and the fearless one, whom I had come to know so very well.

Who had made Mael a blood drinker? In what grove had Mael been consecrated to his old religion? Why was he not shut up in some oak tree in Gaul, there to preside over the feasts of his fellow Druids?

Our eyes met, but I experienced no alarm. In fact, I had assessed his strength and found it wanting. He was as old as I was, yes, that was plain, but he had not drunk as I had from Akasha. I was by far the stronger. There was nothing he could do to me.

And so at this moment, I looked away and to the other blood drinker who was much taller, and infinitely stronger, and whose skin was a dark-brown color, surely from having been burnt in the Terrible Fire.

This one had a large face of rather agreeable and open features, with large questioning black eyes, a thick and well-proportioned mouth, and a head of wavy black hair.

I looked back to this blond-headed one who had taken my mortal life with such religious conviction.

It occurred to me that I could destroy him by ripping his head from his body, and by keeping possession of his head and then placing it somewhere in my garden where the sun would inevitably find it and burn it black. It occurred to me that I ought to do this, that this creature deserved no better. Yet there were other thoughts working in my mind.

I wanted to talk to this being. I wanted to know him. I wanted to know the other being with him, this brown-skinned blood drinker who stared at me with such a mixture of innocence and warmth. This blood drinker was much older. This blood drinker was like no being who had ever come at me in Antioch, crying for the Mother and Father. This being was an entirely new thing.

It was in this moment that I understood perhaps for the first time that anger was weak. Anger had robbed me of Pandora over a sentence of less than twenty words. Anger would rob me of Mael if I destroyed him. Also, I thought, I can always delay the murder. I can talk with Mael now. I can let my mind have this company it craves and I can always kill him later on.

But I'm sure you know such reasoning is false, because once we grow to love a person we are not likely to want that person's death.

As these thoughts raced through my mind, words suddenly spilled from my lips.

"I'm Marius, don't you remember me?" I said. "You took me to the Grove of the Old God, you gave me to him, and I escaped." I was appalled at the hostility with which I'd spoken.

He cloaked his thoughts completely, and I couldn't tell whether he had known me by my appearance or not. He spoke quickly in Latin.

"Yes, you abandoned the grove. You abandoned all those who worshiped you. You took the power given you, and what did you leave for the Faithful of the Forest? What did you give back?"

"And you, my precious Druid priest," I said, "do you serve your old gods? Is that what has brought you to Rome?" My voice was quaking with anger, and I felt the weakness of it. I struggled to regain clarity and strength. "When I knew you, you were pure of heart. Seldom have I ever known any creature more deluded, more given over to comforts and illusions of religion as you were." I stopped. I had to check myself, and I did.

"The old religion is gone," he said furiously. "The Romans have taken even our most secret places. Their cities are everywhere. And thieving barbarians swoop down upon us from across the Danube. And the Christians, the Christians come into places where the Romans are not. There is no stopping the Christians."

His voice grew louder, even though it had taken on the tone of a whisper.

"But it was you, Marius," he said, "you, who corrupted me. It was you, Marius, who poisoned me, it was you who divided me from the Faithful of the Forest, you who gave me dreams of greater things!"

He was as angry as I was. He was trembling. And as often happens with two people who are quarreling, this anger produced a good calm in me. I was able to sink my enmity down into myself with that little resolve, You can always kill him later, and so I went on.

The other creature looked quite surprised by all this and fascinated with an almost childlike expression on his face.

"What you're saying is nonsense," I answered. "I ought to destroy you. It would be an easy thing for me to do."

"Very well then, try," he answered.

The other one reached from behind and put his hand on that of Mael.

"No, listen to me, both of you," he said in a kindly rather deep voice. "Don't go on with this quarrel. However we came to the Dark Blood, either through lies or violence, it has made us immortal. Are we to be so ungrateful?"

"I'm not ungrateful," I said, "but I owe my debt to fate, not to Mael. Nevertheless, I'm lonely for your company. That's the truth of it. Come to my house. I'll never harm anyone who comes as a guest under my roof."

I had quite surprised myself by this little speech but it was the truth.

"You have a house in this city?" asked Mael. "What do you mean by a house?"

"I have a house, a comfortable house. I bid you to come and talk to me. I have a pleasant garden with beautiful fountains. I have slaves. They are simple-minded. The light is pleasant. The garden is full of night-blooming flowers. Come."

The one with the black hair was openly surprised as he had been before.

"I want to come," he said, glancing at Mael, though he still stood behind him. His voice had an authority to it, a pure strength, though it was soft.

Mael was rigid and helpless in his anger. With his hawk nose and frightful eyes, he reminded me of a wild bird. Men with such noses always do. But in truth, he possessed a rather unusual beauty. His forehead was high and clear, and his mouth was strong.

But to go on with my tale, it was only now that I noticed that both men wore rags like beggars. They were barefoot, and though blood drinkers are never truly soiled, for no soil clings to them, they were unkempt.

Well, I could soon remedy that if they would allow. I had trunks of garments as always. Whether I went out to hunt or to study some fresco in a deserted house, I was a well-dressed Roman, and often carried dagger and sword.

At last they agreed to come, and with a great act of will, I went ahead, turning my back on them to lead them, using the Mind Gift to maximum effect to watch over them that neither tried to strike out at me.

Of course I was profoundly grateful that Those Who Must Be Kept were not in the house where either of these two might have detected their powerful heartbeats, but I could not allow myself to visualize these beings. On we walked.

Finally, they came into my house, looking about themselves as though they were among miracles when all that I possessed were the simple furnishings of a rich man. They gazed hungrily at the bronze oil lamps that filled the marble-floored rooms with brilliant light, and the couches and chairs they hesitated to touch.

I cannot tell you how often this has happened me over the centuries, that some wandering blood drinker, bereft of all human attachments, has come into my house to marvel at simple things.

This is why I had a bed for you when you came here. That is why I had clothes.

"Sit down," I said to them, "there's nothing here that can't be cleaned or thrown away. I insist that you be comfortable. I wish we had some gesture that I might give, equal to that which mortals make when they offer guests a cup of wine."

The larger taller man was the first to be seated in a chair, rather than a couch. Then I followed taking a chair as well, and bidding Mael please to be seated to my right.

I could see now quite clearly that the bigger blood drinker possessed infinitely more power than Mael. Indeed he was much older. He was older than me. That was why he had healed after the Terrible Fire, though that had been two hundred years ago, I had to admit. But I sensed no menace from this creature, and then quite unexpectedly, indeed, silently, he gave me his name.

"Avicus."

Mael gazed at me with the most venomous expression. He did not sit back as he might have done, but kept himself bitterly erect and ready as if for a brawl.

I sought to read his mind but this was useless.

As for me, I considered myself the consummate master of my hatred and my rage, but when I saw the anxious look on the face of Avicus I thought perhaps I was wrong.

Suddenly, this blood drinker spoke.

"Lay down your hatred, each for the other," he said in Latin, though he spoke with an accent, "and perhaps a battle of words will put all to right."

Mael didn't wait for my agreement to this plan.

"We brought you to the grove," he told me, "because our god told us we must do this. He was burnt and dying, but he would not tell us why. He wanted you to go to Egypt, but he wouldn't tell us why. There must be a new god, he said, but he didn't tell us why."

"Calm yourself," said Avicus softly, "so that your words truly speak for your heart." Even in his rags he looked rather dignified and curious as to what would be said.

Mael gripped the arms of the chair and glared at me, his long blond hair hanging over his face.

"Bring a perfect human for the old god's magic, we were told. And that our legends told us was true. When an old god is weak there must be a new one. And only a perfect man can be given over to the dying god for his magic in the oak."

"And so you found a Roman," I said, "in the prime of life, happy and rich, and dragged him off against his will. Were there no men among you who were fit and right for your own religion? Why come to me with your wretched beliefs?"

Mael wasn't slowed in the slightest. At once he continued.

" 'Bring me one who is fit,' said the god, 'one who who knows the languages of all kingdoms!' That was his admonition. Do you know how long we had to search for such a man as you?"

"Am I to feel sorry for you?" I said sharply and foolishly.

He went on.

"We brought you to the oak as we were told to do. Then when you came out of the oak, to preside over our great sacrifice, we saw that you had been made into a gleaming god of shimmering hair and eyes that frightened us.

"And without a word of protest, you raised your arms so that the

Great Feast of Sanhaim could begin. You drank the blood of the victims given you. We saw you do it! The magic was restored in you. We felt we would prosper, and it was time to burn the old god as our legends told us we must do.

"It was then that you fled." He sat back in his chair as though this long speech had taken the strength out of him. "You didn't return," he said disgustedly. "You knew our secrets. But you didn't return."

A silence fell.

They didn't know of the Mother and the Father. They knew nothing of the old Egyptian lore. I was too relieved for a long moment to say anything. I felt more calm and controlled than ever. Indeed, it seemed rather absurd that we were having this argument, for as Avicus had said, we were immortal.

But we were human still, each in his own way.

Finally I realized that Mael was looking at me, and his eyes were as charged with rage as before. He looked pale, hungry, wild as I've said.

But both of these creatures were waiting upon me to speak or do something, and it did seem the burden lay with me. At last, I made a decision which seemed to me to be its own form of reckoning, and its own form of triumph.

"No, I didn't come back," I said to Mael squarely. "I didn't want to be the God of the Grove. I cared nothing for the Faithful of the Forest. I made my choice to wander through time. I have no belief in your gods or your sacrifices. What did you expect of me?"

"You took the magic of our god with you."

"I had no choice," I said. "If I had left the old burnt god without taking his magic, you would have destroyed me, and I didn't want to die. Why should I have died? Yes, I took the magic that he gave me and yes, I presided over your sacrifices and then I fled as anyone of my nature would do."

He looked at me for a long time, as if trying to decide whether or not I wanted to quarrel further.

"And what do I see now in you?" I demanded. "Haven't you fled your Faithful of the Forest? Why do I come upon you in Rome?"

He waited a long moment.

"Our god," he said, "our old burnt god. He spoke of Egypt. He spoke of our bringing him one who could go down into Egypt. Did you go to Egypt? Did you seek there the Good Mother?"

I cloaked my mind as best I could. I made my face severe, and I tried to figure how much I should confess and why.

"Yes, I went to Egypt," I said. "I went to find the cause of the fire that had burnt the gods all through the North lands."

"And what did you find?" he demanded.

I glanced from him to Avicus and I saw that he too waited upon my answer.

"I found nothing," I responded. "Nothing but burnt ones who pondered the same mystery. The old legend of the Good Mother. Nothing further. It is finished. There is no more to tell."

Did they believe me? I couldn't tell. Both seemed to harbor their own secrets, their own choices made long ago.

Avicus looked ever so slightly alarmed for his companion.

Mael looked up slowly and said with anger,

"Oh, that I had never laid eyes upon you. You wicked Roman, you rich Roman with all your splendor and fine words." He looked about the house, at its wall paintings, at its couches and tables, at the marble floors.

"Why do you say this?" I asked.

I tried not to despise him but to see him, and understand him, but my hatred was too great.

"When I took you prisoner," he said, "when I sought to teach you our poetry and our songs, do you remember how you tried to bribe me? You spoke of your beautiful villa on the Bay of Naples. You said that you would take me there if only I would help you escape. Do you remember these awful things?"

"Yes, I remember," I said coldly. "I was your prisoner! You had taken me deep into the forest against my will. What did you expect of me? And had you let me escape, I would have taken you to my house on the Bay of Naples. I would have paid my own ransom. My family would have paid it. Oh, it's too foolish to speak of these things."

I shook my head. I grew too agitated. My old loneliness beckoned to me. I wanted silence in these rooms again. What need had I of these two?

But the one called Avicus appealed to me silently with his expression. And I wondered who he might be.

"Please, keep your temper," said Avicus. "I'm the cause of his suffering."

"No," said Mael quickly. He glanced at his companion. "That can't be."

"Oh, but it is," declared Avicus, "and always has been, ever since I gave you the Dark Blood. Gain the strength either to remain with me or to leave me. Things cannot remain as they are."

He reached out and put his hand on his companion's arm.

"You've found this strange being, Marius," he said, "and you've told Marius of the last years of your strong belief. You've relived that awful misery. But don't be so foolish as to hate him for what happened. He was right to seek his freedom. As for us, the old faith died. The Terrible Fire destroyed it, and nothing more could be done."

Mael looked as dejected as any creature I've ever seen.

Meantime my heart was fast catching up with my mind. I was thinking: Here are two immortals but we cannot solace one another; we cannot have friendship. We can only part after bitter words. And then I'll be alone again. I'll be proud Marius who left Pandora. I shall have my beautiful house and all my fine possessions to myself.

I realized Avicus was staring at me, trying to probe my mind, but failing though his Mind Gift was quite terrifically strong.

"Why do you live as vagabonds?" I asked.

"We don't know how to live as anything else," said Avicus. "We've never tried. We shy away from mortals, except when we hunt. We fear discovery. We fear fire."

I nodded.

"What do you seek other than blood?"

A miserable expression passed over his face. He was in pain. He tried to hide it. Or perhaps he tried to make the pain go away.

"I'm not sure that we seek anything," he said. "We don't know how."

"Do you want to stay with me," I asked, "and learn?"

I felt the boldness, the presumptuousness of this question, but the words had already been said.

"I can show you the Temples of Rome; I can show you the big palaces, the houses that make this villa appear quite humble indeed. I can show you how to play the shadows so that mortals never see you; how to climb walls swiftly and silently; how to walk the roofs at night all over the city, never touching the ground."

Avicus was amazed. He looked to Mael.

Mael sat slumped, saying nothing.

Then he pulled himself up.

In a weak voice he continued his condemnation.

"I would have been stronger if you hadn't told me all those marvelous things," he said, "and now you ask if we want to enjoy the same pleasures, the pleasures of a Roman."

"It's what I have to offer," I said. "Do what you wish."

Mael shook his head. He began to speak again, for the benefit of whom I don't know.

"When it was plain that you wouldn't return," he said, "they chose me. I was to become the god. But for this to happen we had to find a God of the Grove who had not been burnt to death by the Terrible Fire. After all, we had destroyed our own gentle god foolishly! A creature who had had the magic to make you."

I gestured as if to say, It was indeed a shame.

"We sent word far and wide," he said. "At last an answer came from Britain. A god survived there, a god who was most ancient and most strong."

I looked to Avicus, but there was no change in his expression.

"However we were warned not to go to him. We were told that it was perhaps not something we should do. We were confused by these messages, and at last we set out for we felt that we must try."

"And how did you feel," I asked cruelly, "now that you had been chosen, and you knew that you would be shut up in the oak, never to see the sun again, and only to drink blood during the great feasts and during the full moon?"

He looked straight ahead as if he couldn't give me a decent answer to this, and then he replied.

"You had corrupted me as I told you."

"Ah," I said, "so you were afraid. The Faithful of the Forest couldn't comfort you. And I was to blame."

"Not afraid," he said furiously, clenching his teeth. "Corrupted as I said." He flashed his small deep-set eyes on me. "Do you know what it means to believe absolutely nothing, to have no god, no truth!"

"Yes, of course I know," I answered. "I believe nothing. I consider it wise. I believed nothing when I was mortal. I believe nothing now."

I think I saw Avicus flinch.

I might have said more brutal things, but I saw that Mael meant to go on.

Staring forward in the same manner he told his tale:

"We made our journey," he said. "We crossed the narrow sea to Britain and went North to a land of green woods and there we came upon a band of priests who sang our hymns and knew our poetry and our law. They were Druids as we were Druids, they were the Faithful of the Forest as were we. We fell into each other's arms."

Avicus was watching Mael keenly. My eyes were more patient and cold, I was sure. Nevertheless the simple narrative drew me, I have to confess.

"I went into the grove," said Mael. "How huge the trees were. How ancient. Any one of them might have been the Great Tree. At last I was led to it. And I saw the door with its many iron locks. I knew the god was inside."

Suddenly Mael glanced anxiously to Avicus, but Avicus gestured for him to go on.

"Tell Marius," he said gently, "and in telling Marius, you tell me."

It had such a soft sound to it, this utterance. I felt a shiver on the surface of my skin, my lonely and perfect skin.

"But these priests," said Mael, "they warned me. 'Mael, if there is any lie or imperfection in you, the god will know it. He will merely kill you and you will be a sacrifice and nothing more than that. Think deep because the god sees deep. The god is strong but the god would be feared rather than adored and takes his vengeance, when aroused, with great pleasure.'

"The words shook me. Was I truly prepared for this strange miracle to come upon me?"

He glared savagely at me.

"I thought over everything. Your word pictures came back to me! The beautiful villa on the Bay of Naples. How you had described your rich rooms. How you had described the warm breezes and the sound of the water on the rocky shore. How you had described your gardens. You had spoken of gardens. Ah, could I endure the darkness of the oak, I thought, the drinking of blood, the starvation between sacrifices, for what would this be?"

He paused as if he couldn't continue. Again he glanced at Avicus.

"Go on," said Avicus calmly in his deep voice.

Mael continued:

"Then one of these priests accosted me and took me aside and he said, 'Mael, this is an angry god. This is a god who begs for blood when he shouldn't want it. Do you have the strength to present yourself to him?'

"I had no chance to answer him. The sun had just gone down. The grove was full of lighted torches. The Faithful of the Forest had assembled. All my fellow priests who had come with me surrounded me. They were pushing me towards the oak.

"When I reached it, I insisted that they free me. I put my hands upon the bark, and I closed my eyes and in the silent voice, as I had prayed in my home grove, I prayed to this god. I said 'I am of the Faithful of the Forest. Will you give me the Sacred Blood so that I might return home and do what my people wish me to do?' "

Again he stopped speaking. It was as if he was staring at something dreadful that I could not see.

Avicus spoke up again.

"Continue," he said.

Mael sighed.

"There came a silent laugh from inside the oak, a silent laugh and an angry voice! It went inside my head, and I was shaken by it. And the god said to me, 'Bring me a blood sacrifice first. Then and only then will I have the strength to make you a god.' "

Again Mael broke off. Then, "Surely you know, Marius," he said, "how gentle our god was. When he made you, when he spoke to you there was nothing of anger or hate in him, but this god was full of wrath."

I nodded.

"I told the priests what the god had said to me. They drew back in a group, all afraid and disapproving.

" 'No,' they said, 'he has been asking for blood too much. It is not fitting that he should have it. He is to starve now as always between each full moon and until the yearly rituals so that he comes from the oak thin and ravenous, like the dead fields, ready to drink the blood of sacrifice and become plump with it, like the bounty of the coming spring.'

"What was I to say?" asked Mael. "Finally I tried to reason with some of them. 'To make a god, surely he needs strength,' I explained. 'And he himself is burned from the Terrible Fire, and perhaps the blood helps him and heals him. Why not give him sacrifice? Surely you have a condemned man in one of the villages or settlements who can be brought to the oak?'

"They drew back altogether, and they stared at the tree and its door and its locks. And I realized they were afraid.

"Then a dreadful thing occurred, which changed me utterly. There came from the oak a stream of enmity that I could feel as though some-one full of rancor were staring at me!

"I could feel it as though the being looked upon me with all his rage, his sword raised to destroy me. Of course it was the power of the god, using his mind to flood mine with his hatred. But so strong was it that I could not think of what it was, or what to do.

"The other priests ran. They had felt this anger and hatred as well. I couldn't run. I couldn't move. I stared at the oak. I think the old magic had caught me. God, poems, songs, sacrifice—those things did not matter to me suddenly. But I knew a powerful creature was inside the oak. And I didn't run from it. And at that moment my evil plotting soul was born!"

Mael gave another very dramatic sigh. He was silent, his eyes fixed on me.

"How so?" I asked. "What did you plot? You had spoken through the mind with the gentle god of your own grove. You had seen him at the full moon take sacrifice, both before and after the Terrible Fire. You saw me when I was changed. You've just said so. What struck you so about this god?"

He looked overwhelmed for a moment.

Finally, gazing ahead of him again as if he had to, he continued.

"This god was more than angry, Marius. This god meant to have his way!"

"Then why weren't you afraid?"

A silence fell in the room. I was truly a bit perplexed.

I looked at Avicus. I wanted to confirm: Avicus was this god, no? But to ask such a question was crude. It had been said earlier that Avicus gave the Dark Blood to Mael. I waited, as it was proper for me to do.

Finally Mael looked at me in the most sly and strange fashion.

His voice dropped, and he smiled venomously.

"The god wanted to get out of that oak," he said, glaring at me, "and I knew that if I helped him, he would give me the Magic Blood!"

"So," I said smiling, because I couldn't help it. "He wanted to escape the oak. But of course."

"I remembered you when you escaped," Mael said, "the mighty Marius, blooming from blood sacrifice, running so speedily from us! Well, I would run like you! Yes, and yes, and as I thought these things, as I plotted, as I thought, I heard the voice from the oak again, directed soft and secretive, only to me:

" 'Come closer,' it commanded me, and then as I pressed my forehead to the tree it spoke. 'Tell me of this Marius, tell me of his escape,' it said. 'Tell me and I will give you the Dark Blood and we will flee this place together, you and I.' "

Mael was trembling. But Avicus looked resigned to these truths as though he had pondered them many times.

"It does become clearer," I said.

"There is nothing that is not connected with you," Mael said. He shook his fist at me. It reminded me of a child.

"Your own doing," I said. "From the moment you stole me from the tavern in Gaul. You brought us together. Remember that. You kept me prisoner. But your unfolding story calms you. You need to tell us. Tell more."

It seemed for a moment he would fly at me, desperate in his rage, but then there came a change in him. And shaking his head a little, he grew calm, scowling and then went on:

"When this confirmation came to me from the god's own mind," he said, "I was fatally set upon my course. I told the other priests immediately that they were to bring a sacrifice. We had no time for quarreling, and that I should see that the condemned man was given to the god. I should go into the tree with the condemned man. I had no fear to do it. And they must hasten with all things, as the god and I might need the night for our magic to be done.

"It seemed an hour passed before they found the wretched man who was to die in the tree, but at last they brought him forward, bound and weeping, and very fearfully they unlocked the mighty door.

"I could feel the mounting rage of the god inside. I could feel his hunger. And pushing this poor condemned wretch before me, I entered, torch in hand to stand inside the hollowed chamber of the tree."

I nodded with a small smile to say only I know.

Meantime Mael's eyes had shifted to Avicus.

"There stood Avicus much as you see him now," Mael said, still looking at his companion. "And at once, he fell upon the condemned man. He drank the blood of this piteous victim with merciful speed, and then he cast the body away.

"Then Avicus fell upon me, taking the torch from me, hanging it up on the wall so that it seemed dangerously near the wood, and grasping me tight by the shoulders he said,

" 'Tell me of Marius, tell me how he escaped the Sacred Oak. Tell me the story or I'll kill you now.' "

Avicus listened to all this with a calm face. He nodded as if to say, That was how it took place.

Mael turned away from him and looked forward again.

"He was hurting me," Mael said. "If I hadn't said something quickly he would have broken my shoulder, so I spoke up, knowing how well he might search my thoughts, and I said, 'Give me the Dark Blood and we shall escape together as you have promised. There is no great secret to what I know. It is a matter of strength and speed. We take to the tree limbs, which they cannot do so easily who follow us, and then we move through the trees.'

" 'But you know the world,' he said to me. 'I know nothing. I have been imprisoned for hundreds of years. I only dimly remember Egypt. I only dimly remember the Great Mother. You must guide me. And so I'll give you the magic and do it well.'

"He was true to his promise. I was made strong from the start. Then together, we listened with minds and ears for the gathered Faithful of the Forest and the Druid priests, and finding them quite unprepared for our departure, we forced the door with our united strength.

"At once we took to the treetops, as you had done, Marius. We put our pursuers far behind us, and before dawn we were hunting a settlement many many miles away."

He sat back as though exhausted by his confession.

And as I sat there, still too patient and too proud to destroy him, I saw how he had woven me into all of it, and I wondered at it, and I looked to Avicus, the god who for so long had lived in the tree.

Avicus looked calmly at me.

"We have been together since that time," Mael said in a more subdued voice. "We hunt the great cities because it is simpler for us, and what do we think of Romans who came as conquerors? We hunt Rome because it is the greatest city of all."

I said nothing.

"Sometimes we meet others," Mael continued. His eyes shot towards me suddenly. "And sometimes we are forced to fight them, for they will not leave us in peace."

"How so?" I asked.

"They are Gods of the Grove, the same as Avicus, and they are badly burnt and weak and they want our strong blood. Surely you've seen them. They must have found you out. You cannot have been hiding all these years."

I didn't answer.

"But we can defend ourselves," he went on. "We have our hiding places, and with mortals we have our sport, our games. What more is there for me to say?"

He had indeed finished.

I thought of my own existence, my life crowded with so much reading and wandering and with so many questions, and I felt utter pity for him along with my contempt.

Meanwhile the expression on the face of Avicus touched me.

Avicus looked thoughtful and compassionate when he looked at Mael; but then his eyes fell on me and his face quickened.

"And how does the world seem to you, Avicus?" I asked.

At once Mael shot me a glance and then he rose from his chair and came towards me, bending over me, his hand out as if he would strike me.

"This is what you have to say to my story?" he demanded. "You ask of *him* how he sees the world?"

I didn't answer. I saw my blunder, and had to admit to myself that it wasn't deliberate. But I did wish to hurt him, there was no doubt of it. And this I had done.

Avicus had risen to his feet.

He came to Mael and guided him back, away from me.

"Quiet, my beloved one," he said gently to Mael. He drew Mael back to his chair. "Let us talk some more before we part with Marius. We have till morning. Please, be calm."

I realized then what had so infuriated Mael. It was not that he thought I had ignored him. He knew better. It was jealousy. He thought that I was trying to woo away from him his friend.

As soon as Mael had taken his chair again, Avicus looked to me almost warmly.

"The world is marvelous, Marius," he said placidly. "I come to it as a blind man after a miracle. I remember nothing of my mortal life except that it was in Egypt. And that I was not myself from Egypt. I am afraid now to go there. I am afraid old gods linger there. We travel the cities of the Empire, except for the cities of Egypt. And there is much for us to see."

Mael was still suspicious. He drew his ragged and filthy cloak up around him as though he might at any moment take his leave.

As for Avicus he looked more than ever comfortable, though he was barefoot and as dirty as Mael.

"Whenever we have come upon blood drinkers," said Avicus,

"which isn't often, I have feared them, that they would know me for a renegade god."

He said this with considerable strength and confidence so it surprised me.

"But this is never the case," he continued. "And sometimes they speak of the Good Mother and the old worship when the gods would drink the blood of the Evil Doer, but they know less of it than me."

"What *do* you know, Avicus?" I asked boldly.

He considered as if he weren't quite sure that he wanted to answer me with truth. Then he spoke.

"I think I was brought before her," he said, his dark eyes rather open and honest.

Mael turned to him sharply, as if he meant to strike him for his frankness, but Avicus went on.

"She was very beautiful. But my gaze was lowered. I couldn't really see her. And they were saying words, and the chanting was frightening to me. I was a grown man, that much I know, and they humiliated me. They spoke of honors that were curses. I may have dreamt the rest."

"We've been here long enough," said Mael suddenly. "I want to go."

He rose to his feet and quite reluctantly Avicus followed.

There passed between us, Avicus and me, something silent and secretive, which Mael could not interrupt. Mael knew it, I think, and he was in a sustained fury, but he couldn't prevent it. It was done.

"Thank you for your hospitality," said Avicus, reaching out to take my hand. He looked almost cheerful for a moment. "Sometimes I remember little mortal customs. I remember touching hands in this way."

Mael was in a pale rage.

Of course there was much I wanted to say to Avicus but I knew now that such was very simply impossible.

"Remember," I said to both of them, "I live as a mortal man lives, with the same comforts. And I have my studies always, my books here, you see. Eventually I will travel the Empire, but for now Rome, the city of my birth, is my home. What I learn is what matters to me. What I see with these eyes."

I looked from one to the other of them.

"You can live in this way if you like," I said. "Surely you must take fresh garments from me now. I can so easily provide them. And fine sandals for your feet. If you would have a house, a fine dwelling in which to enjoy your leisure hours, I can assist you in obtaining it. Please take this from me."

Mael's eyes were blazing with hatred.

"Oh, yes," he whispered at me, too angry for a full voice. "And why not offer us a villa on the Bay of Naples, with marble balustrades overlooking the blue sea!"

Avicus looked directly at me. He appeared quiet in his heart and genuinely moved by my words.

But what was the use?

I said no more.

My proud calm was suddenly broken. The anger returned along with its weakness. I remembered the hymns of the grove, and I wanted to move against Mael, for all the ugliness of it, to quite literally tear him limb from limb.

Would Avicus move to save him? It was likely. But what if he did not? And what if I proved stronger than both of them, I who had drunk from the Queen?

I looked at Mael. He wasn't afraid of me, which I found interesting.

And my pride returned. I could not stoop to a common physical battle, especially one which might become hideously awkward and ugly, one which I might not win.

No, I was too wise for it. I was too good of heart. I was Marius, who slew the Evil Doer, and this was Mael, a fool.

They made to walk away through the garden and I could find no words to say to them, but Avicus turned to me and said quickly, "Farewell, Marius. I thank you and I will remember you."

And I found myself struck by the words.

"Farewell, Avicus," I answered. And I listened as they disappeared into the night.

I sat there, feeling a crushing loneliness.

I looked at my many bookcases, and at my writing table. I looked at my inkstand. I looked at the paintings on the walls.

I should have tried to make peace with Mael, surely, to have Avicus as my friend.

I should go after them both. I should implore them to remain with me. We had so much more to say to one another. I needed them as they needed each other. As I needed Pandora.

But I lived the lie. I lived it out of anger. This is what I'm trying to tell you. I have lived lies. I have done it again and again. I live lies because I cannot endure the weakness of anger, and I cannot admit the irrationality of love.

Oh, the lies that I have told myself and others. I knew it yet I didn't know.

6

FOR A FULL MONTH, I didn't dare to go to the shrine of Those Who Must Be Kept.

I knew that Mael and Avicus still hunted Rome. I caught glimpses of them with the Mind Gift and occasionally I even spied upon their very thoughts. Sometimes I heard their steps.

Indeed it seemed to me that Mael was actually tormenting me with his presence, attempting to ruin my tenure in the great city, and this made me bitter. I contemplated attempting to drive him and his companion away.

I also suffered considerable preoccupation with Avicus, whose face I could not forget. What was the disposition of this strange being, I thought. What would it mean for him to be my companion? I feared I would never know.

Meantime, other blood drinkers occasionally hunted the city. I felt their presence immediately, and there was no doubt on one particular night that a skirmish occurred between a powerful and hostile blood drinker and Avicus and Mael. With the Mind Gift I knew all that took place. Avicus and Mael so frightened the visitor that he was gone before morning, and had even given word in a lowly voice that he would never come to Rome again.

This put me to pondering. Would Avicus and Mael keep the city clean of others, while leaving me alone?

As the months passed this seemed to be the case.

A small band of Christian blood drinkers tried to infest our hunting ground. Indeed they came from the same tribe of snake worshipers who had come to me in Antioch insisting that I had old truths. With the Mind Gift I saw them fervently setting up their temple where they meant to sacrifice mortals. I was deeply repelled.

But once again Avicus and Mael put them to rout, apparently without being contaminated by their extravagant ideas about us serving Satan—a personage for whom Avicus and Mael would have had no use as they were pagans. And the city was ours again.

I did note in watching these activities from afar, however, that neither Mael nor Avicus seemed to know his own strength. They might have escaped the Druids of Britain by using their supernatural skills, but they were unaware of a secret which I had already learnt—that their powers increased with time.

Now I had drunk the blood of the Mother so I fancied myself much stronger than either of them on that account. But quite apart from that, my strength had increased with the centuries. I could now reach the top of a four-story tenement—of which there were many in Rome—with comparative ease. And no band of mortal soldiers could have ever taken me prisoner. My speed was far too great for that.

Indeed when I took my victims, I already faced the problem of the old ones, to restrain my powerful hands from crushing out the life that pumped the blood into my mouth. And oh, was I ever still thirsty for that blood!

But as I spied upon these various activities—the routing of the Satanic vampires—I stayed away from the shrine of Akasha and Enkil for too long.

Finally one early evening, using my skills at their most powerful to cloak my presence, I did go out into the hills and to the shrine.

I felt that I had to make this visit. Never had I left the Great Pair alone for such a period, and I did not know whether or not there might be consequences for such neglect.

Now I realize such a fear was utterly ridiculous. As the years passed I could neglect the shrine for centuries. It was of no consequence whatsoever. But then I had only begun to learn.

And so I came to the new and barren chapel. I brought with me the requisite flowers and incense, and several bottles of scent with which to sprinkle Akasha's garments, and once I had lighted the lamps and set the incense to burning, once the flowers were in their vases, I felt an overall weakness and went down on my knees.

Let me remind you again that during my years with Pandora, I almost never prayed in this manner. But now Akasha belonged only to me.

I looked up at the unchanged couple, with their long black plaited hair, seated on the throne as I had left them, both freshly dressed in their Egyptian clothes of fine linen, Akasha in her pleated gown, the King in his kilt. Akasha's eyes still wore the imperishable black paint which Pandora had so carefully applied. And around Akasha's head was the glistening gold diadem with its rubies which Pandora had placed there with loving hands. Even the gold snake bracelets on her graceful upper arms had been the gift of Pandora. And on the feet of the two were the sandals which Pandora had fastened with care.

It seemed in the wealth of light that they had grown paler in complexion and I know now, centuries later, that I was right. They were healing rapidly from the Terrible Fire.

On this particular visit, I also paid keen attention to the expression of Enkil. I was too aware of the fact that he did not and had never incited my devotion, and I thought this was unwise.

In Egypt when I had first come to find them—a zealous new blood drinker, inflamed by Akasha's plea to take them out of Egypt—he had moved to block my path to the Queen.

Only with difficulty had he been made to return to his posture of seated King. Akasha had cooperated in that all-important moment, but the movements of both of them had been sluggish and unearthly and dreadful to behold.

That had been three hundred years ago, and the only gesture from either of them since had been the open arm of Akasha to welcome Pandora to herself.

Oh, how Pandora had been blessed in that gesture from Akasha! I would never forget it all my long years.

What were Enkil's thoughts, I asked myself. Was he ever jealous that I addressed my prayers to Akasha? Did he even know?

Whatever the case, I told him in a silent voice that I was devoted to him, that I would always protect him and his Queen.

At last, reason left me as I gazed on them.

I let Akasha know how much I revered her and how dangerous it had been for me to come. Only out of caution had I remained away. I would never on my own have left the shrine deserted. Indeed, I should have been here, using my vampiric skill to create paintings for the walls or to make for them mosaics—for though I never thought of myself as having possessed any skill in this regard—I had used my powers to make passable decorations for the shrine in Antioch, indeed very good ones, whiling away the lonely hours of the night.

But here the walls were simply whitewashed and the abundant flowers I'd brought seemed welcome color indeed.

"My Queen, help me," I prayed. And then as I meant to explain how miserable I was over the nearness of these two fellow blood drinkers, a dreadful and obvious thought came to my mind.

I could never have Avicus for a companion. I could never have anyone. For any blood drinker of even passable skill could learn from my mind the secret of Those Who Must Be Kept.

It had been vain and foolish for me to offer clothing and lodging to Avicus and Mael. I was doomed to be alone.

I felt sickened and cold in my misery. I looked up to the Queen and I could form no prayers with words.

Then quite helplessly I begged: "Bring Pandora back to me. If ever you brought her to me in the first place, bring her back, I beg you, I'll never quarrel with her again. I'll never abuse her again. This is unendurable, this loneliness. I need to hear the sound of her voice. I need to see her."

On and on I went in this manner, until suddenly I became alarmed that Avicus and Mael might be near to me, and I rose to my feet, straightened out my garments and made to take my leave.

"I'll return," I told the Mother and Father. "I'll make this shrine beautiful like the one in Antioch. Only let us wait until they've gone."

I was about to go out when abruptly the thought occurred to me—I needed more of Akasha's powerful blood. I needed it to be stronger than my foes. I needed it to endure what I had to endure.

Now understand, never since the first night that I had drunk from Akasha, had I taken more of her blood. That first night had been in Egypt when she told me with the Mind Gift to take her out of the land. Then and only then had I experienced the blood.

Even when Pandora was made a blood drinker, and she drank from Akasha, I had not dared to approach the Mother. In fact, I knew well how the Mother might strike down those who came by force to steal the Sacred Blood from her, for I'd witnessed such an aborted crime.

Now as I stood before the small dais with its seated royalty, the idea obsessed me. I must again take the Mother's blood.

In silence I begged permission. I waited for a sign. When Pandora had been made, Akasha had lifted her arm to beckon. I had seen it and marveled at it. I wanted such a thing to happen now.

No such sign came to me, however, and yet the obsession raged within me, until I moved forward, quite determined to drink the Divine Blood or die. I found myself suddenly embracing my cold and lovely Akasha with one arm behind her and the other lifted so that my hand held her head.

Closer and closer I came to her neck.

At last my lips were pressed against her cool unresponsive flesh and she had made no move to destroy me. I felt no fatal clasp on the back of my head. Silent as ever she remained in my arms.

Finally my teeth broke the surface of her skin and the thick blood, blood like that of no other among us, came into my mouth. At once I found myself dreamy and cast adrift in an impossible paradise of sunshine and green grass and flowering trees. What a comfort it was, what a balm. It seemed a garden of old Roman myth, one somehow familiar to me, protected forever from winter, and full of the most blessed blooms.

Yes, familiar and forever safe, this verdant place.

The blood ravaged me, and I could feel it hardening me, as it had the very first time it had come into my veins. The sun of the familiar garden grew brighter and brighter until the flowering trees began to disappear in the light. Part of me, some very small and weak part of me was afraid of it, this sun, but the larger part relished it, relished the warmth that was passing into me, and the comfort of what I beheld, and then all at once, as quickly as it had begun, this dream was ended.

I lay on the cold hard floor of the shrine, several yards away from the foot of the dais. I was on my back.

For a moment I was uncertain of what had happened. Was I injured? Was there to be some terrible justice in store? But within seconds, I realized I was as sound of limb as ever, and that the blood had greatly invigorated me just as I'd supposed.

I rose to my knees, and made certain with quick eyes that the Royal Pair remained as before. Why had I been thrown away from Akasha with such violence? Nothing was changed.

Then for a long time I gave my silent thanks for what had taken place. Only when I was certain that nothing further was to happen, I rose to my feet, and declaring that I would be back soon to begin my decorations of the shrine, I left.

I was enormously excited as I returned to my house. My increased agility, and keenness of mind were more than welcome. I determined to test myself, and taking my dagger, I plunged it all the way through my left hand, and then withdrew it, watching the wound as it immediately healed.

At once I spread out a scroll of the finest parchment and I began to write in my personal code which no other could read, of what had taken place. I didn't know why, after taking the Sacred Blood, I had found myself on the floor of the chapel.

"The Queen has allowed me to drink again from her, and if this is to happen often, if I can take nourishment from our mysterious majesty, I can attain enormous strength. Even the blood drinker Avicus will be no match for me, though this might have been the case before this night."

Indeed, as it turned out I was precisely right about the implications of this incident, and during all the centuries to come, I approached Akasha again and again.

I did this not only when severely injured—a tale I mean to tell you—but I did it at times when the fancy caught hold of me as if she had put it in my mind. But never, never, as I have confessed with bitterness, did she ever press her teeth to my throat and take from me my own blood.

No, that distinction was left for the blood drinker Lestat, as I have said.

In the following months, this new blood served me well. I found that the Mind Gift was stronger in me. I could well detect the presence of Mael and Avicus when they were quite far away, and though such spying opens a mental passage as it were by which they could see me as their observer, I was able, after seeing them, to quickly close myself off.

I was also able to tell quite easily when they were searching for my presence, and of course I heard, positively heard, their footsteps when they were in the precincts of my house.

I also opened my house to humans!

The decision came to me one evening as I lay on the grass in my own garden dreaming. I would have regular banquets. I would invite the notorious and the slandered. I would have music and dim lamps.

I considered the matter from every perspective! I knew that I could arrange it. I knew that I could fool mortals as to my nature; and how their company would soothe my lonely heart! I did not go to my daily rest in my house, but in a hiding place far from it, so what danger could there be in this new decision? None whatsoever!

It could easily be done.

Naturally, I would never feed upon these guests. They would enjoy complete safety and hospitality under my roof, always. I would hunt in far precincts and under cover of darkness. But my house, my house would be full of warmth and music and life.

Well, I went about it, and it proved far simpler than I had ever dreamt.

Having my sweet and good-natured old slaves lay out tables rich with food and drink, I brought in the disreputable philosophers to talk away the night to me, and I listened to them in their rambling, as I did to the old and neglected soldiers who had tales of war to tell which their own children did not want to hear.

Oh, this was a miracle, the admission of mortals to my very rooms, mortals who thought me to be alive as I nodded and coaxed them in their wine-fed stories. I was warmed by it, and I wished that Pandora were here with me to enjoy it for it was precisely the sort of thing which she would have wanted us to do.

Soon my house was never empty, and I made the amazing discovery that should I become bored in the midst of this heated and drunken company it was a simple matter for me to get up and go into my library and begin writing, for all the drunken guests simply went on with each other, hardly noticing what I did and only rousing themselves to greet me when I returned.

Understand, I did not become a friend to any of these dishonorable or disgraced creatures. I was only a warm-hearted host and spectator who listened without criticism and never—until dawn—turned anyone away.

But it was a far cry from my former solitude, and without the strengthening blood of Akasha, and perhaps without my quarrel with Avicus and Mael, I would never have taken this step.

And so my house became crowded and noisy, and wine sellers sought me out to offer their new vintages, and young men came to me, begging me to listen to their songs.

Even a few fashionable philosophers appeared at my door from time to time, and once in a while a great teacher, and these I enjoyed immensely, making very certain that the lamps were very dim and that the rooms were most shadowy, so frightened was I that the sharp-minded might discover that I was not what I pretended to be.

As for my trips to the shrine and Those Who Must Be Kept, I knew that I traveled in total secrecy for my mind was more securely cloaked than before.

And on certain nights—when the banquet in my house could well do without me—and I held myself to be entirely safe from all intrusion, I went to the shrine and did the work which I supposed would comfort my poor Akasha and Enkil.

During these years, rather than undertake mosaics which had proved very difficult for me in Antioch, though I had succeeded, I made murals on the walls of the common kind seen in so many Roman houses, of frolicking gods and goddesses in gardens of eternal springtime and bounteous flowers and fruit.

I was hard at work one evening, singing to myself, happy among all the pots of paint when I suddenly realized that the garden I was faithfully rendering was in fact the garden I had seen when I drank Akasha's blood.

I stopped, sat still on the floor of the shrine, as if I were a child, with crossed legs, and looked up at the venerable Parents. Was it meant to be?

I had no idea. The garden looked vaguely familiar. Had I seen such a garden long before I had drunk Akasha's blood? I couldn't remember. And I, Marius, prided myself upon my memory. I went on with my work. I covered over a wall and started all over again to render it more nearly perfect. I made better trees and shrubbery. I painted the sunlight and the effects of it upon green leaves.

When inspiration left me, I would use my blood drinker delicacy to creep into some fashionable villa outside the walls of the enormous and ever expanding city, and by the faintest light peruse the inevitably lush murals for new figures, new dances, new attitudes and smiles.

Of course I could do this easily without waking anyone in the house, and sometimes I need have no worry of waking anyone, for no one was there.

Rome was immense, busy as ever, but with all the wars, with all the shifting politics and scheming plotters and passing Emperors, people were being banished and recalled regularly, and great houses were often empty for me to quietly wander and enjoy.

Meanwhile, in my house, my banquets had become so famous that my rooms were always full. And no matter what my goal for any night, I commenced it among the warm company of drunkards who'd begun their feasting and quarreling before I ever arrived.

"Ah, Marius, welcome!" they would cry out as I came into the room.

How I smiled at them all, my treasured company.

Never did anyone suspect me of anything, and I did grow to love some of these delightful creatures, but always I remembered that I was a predator of men, and could not therefore be loved by them, and so I kept my heart covered as it were.

And so with this mortal comfort, the years passed, whilst I kept myself busy with the energy of a madman, either writing in my journals and subsequently burning them, or painting on the walls of the shrine.

Meantime, the wretched serpent worshiping blood drinkers came again, attempting to establish their absurd temple within one of the neglected catacombs where mortal Christians no longer gathered, and once again, Avicus and Mael drove them away.

I observed all this, immensely relieved that I had not been called upon to do anything, and painfully remembering when I had slaughtered such a band in Antioch and subsequently fallen into the piteous madness that had cost me the love of Pandora apparently for all time.

But no, not for all time; surely she would come to me, I thought. I wrote about it in my journals.

I put down my pen; I closed my eyes. I longed for her. I prayed that she would come to me. I envisioned her with her rippling brown hair and melancholy oval face. I tried to remember with exactitude the shape and the fine color of her dark eyes.

How she had argued with me. How she had known the poets and philosophers. How she had been able to reason. And I, I had mocked her all too much.

I cannot tell you how many years passed in this fashion.

I was aware that even though we did not speak to one another, or even face each other in the street, Avicus and Mael had become companions to me by their very presence. And as for their keeping Rome clean of other blood drinkers, I was in their debt.

Now, I didn't pay much attention to what was happening with the government of the Empire as I think you can ascertain from all I've said.

But in truth I cared passionately about the fate of the Empire. For the Empire to me was the civilized world. And though I was a secret hunter by night, a filthy killer of humans, nevertheless I was a Roman, and I lived in all other ways a civilized life.

I suppose that I assumed, much like many an old Senator of the time, that sooner or later the endless battles of the Emperors would sort themselves out. A great man, with the strength of Octavian, would rise to unite the entire world once again.

Meantime the armies would patrol the borders, endlessly driving back the barbarian menace, and if the responsibility fell, over and over again to the armies to choose an Emperor, so be it, as long as the Empire remained intact.

As for the Christians who existed everywhere, I did not know what to make of them at all. It was a great mystery to me that this little cult, which had begun in Jerusalem of all places, could have grown to such tremendous size.

Before I'd left Antioch, I'd been amazed by the success of Christianity, of how it was becoming organized, and how it seemed to thrive on division and dissent.

But Antioch was the East as I have said. That Rome was capitulating to the Christians was beyond my wildest dreams. Slaves had everywhere gone over to the new religion, but so had men and women of high position. And persecutions had no effect at all.

Before I continue, however, allow me to point out what other historians have also pointed out, that before Christianity, the entire ancient world lived in a kind of religious harmony. No one persecuted anyone else for religion.

Even the Jews who would associate with no one else were easily infolded by Greeks and Romans and allowed to practice their extremely anti-social beliefs. It was they who rebelled against Rome, not Rome which sought to enslave them. And so this harmony was worldwide.

Of course all of this led me to believe, when I first heard Christians preaching, that there was no chance of this religion gaining ground. It placed far too much responsibility upon the new members to avoid all contact with the revered gods of Greece and Rome, and so I thought the sect would soon die out.

Also there was the constant strife among the Christians as to what they really believed. Surely they would destroy one another, I thought, and the whole body of ideas, or whatever it could be called, would dissolve.

But no such thing happened, and the Rome in which I lived in the three hundreds was thronged with Christians, as I've said. For their apparently magical ceremonies, they met in the catacombs and also in private homes.

Now as I went along, watching all this, and yet ignoring it, there came a couple of events which stunned me out of my dreams.

Let me explain.

As I have said, the Emperors of Rome were constantly at war. No sooner had the old Roman Senate ratified the appointment of one than he was murdered by another. And troops were always marching across the far-flung provinces of the Empire to establish a new Caesar where another had been put to rout.

In the year of 305, there were two of these sovereigns known as Augusti, and two known as Caesars, and I myself did not know precisely what these titles meant. Or shall I say, I had too much contempt for all involved to know what they meant.

Indeed these so-called "Emperors" more often than I liked were invading Italy and one by the name of Severus in the year 307 had come all the way to the gates of Rome.

Now I, with little more than the greatness of Rome to keep me company, did not want to see my native city sacked!

It soon became clear to me when I started to pay attention that all of Italy as well as Sicily, Corsica, Sardinia and North Africa were all under the rule of the "Emperor" Maxentius, and it was he who had repelled Severus and was now repelling yet another invader, Galerius, whom he chased away in defeat.

This Maxentius who lived only six miles from the city walls was himself a beast. At one extremely unhappy event, he allowed the praetorians, that is, his personal guards, to massacre the people of Rome. And he was very against the Christians whom he persecuted needlessly and cruelly; and the gossip had it that he debauched the wives of outstanding citizens, thereby giving the greater offense. In fact, the Senators suffered a great deal of abuse at his hands, while he let his soldiers run riot in Rome.

None of this meant much to me, however, until I heard that one of the other Emperors—Constantine—was marching on Rome. This was the third threat in recent years to my beloved city; and I was much relieved when Maxentius went out to fight the important battle a great safe distance from the walls. Of course he did this because he knew the Romans would not support him.

But who could have known that this was to be one of the most decisive battles in the history of the Western world?

Of course the battle occurred in the day so that I could know nothing of it until I waked with the setting sun. At once, I rushed up the stairs from my underground hiding place and, coming to my house, I found all my regular philosopher guests drunk, and I went out into the streets to learn what I could from the citizenry of what had taken place.

Constantine was completely the victor. He had massacred the troops of Maxentius and the latter had fallen into the Tiber and drowned. But what was most significant to those congregating everywhere was the rumor that before Constantine went into battle he had seen a sign in the sky which had come from Jesus Christ.

Indeed the sign had been made manifest right after noon when Constantine had looked up and beheld just above the declining sun, the sign of the cross with the inscription "Conquer with This."

My reaction was incredulity. Could a Roman Emperor possibly have seen a Christian vision? I went rushing back to my desk, wrote down all these particulars in my precarious journal of events and waited to see what history would reveal.

As for the company in my banquet room they were now all awake and arguing about the whole matter. None of us believed it. Constantine a Christian? More wine, please.

At once, to everyone's amazement, but without doubt, Constantine revealed himself to be a Christian man.

Instead of endowing temples to celebrate his great victory, as was the custom, he endowed Christian churches, and sent out word to his governors that they should behave in the same manner as he had done.

Then he presented the Pope of the Christians with a palace on the Coelian Hill. And let me point out that this palace was to remain in the hands of the Popes of Rome for a thousand years. I had once known those who lived in it, and I went myself to see the Vicar of Christ ensconced in it, and speculated as to what all this would mean.

Soon laws were passed which forbade crucifixion as a form of execution, and also forbade the popular gladiatorial games. Sunday became a holiday. And the Emperor extended other benefits to the Christians, and very soon we heard that Christians were petitioning him to take part in their doctrinal disputes!

Indeed, their arguing over matters of doctrine became so serious in African cities that riots broke out in which Christians murdered each other. People wanted the Emperor to intervene.

I think this is a very important thing to understand about Christianity. It was from its very beginnings, it seems, a religion of great quarrels and wars, and it wooed the power of temporal authorities, and made them part of itself in the hope of resolving through sheer force its many arguments.

All this I watched with amazed eyes. Of course my guests argued furiously about it. It seemed some who were dining at my table were Christians and had been all along. Now it was out in the open, yet the wine flowed and the music went on.

Understand, I had no real fear of or inherent distaste for Christianity. As I have said, I witnessed its growth with amazement.

And now—as ten years or more passed during which Constantine shared the Empire uneasily with Lacinius, I saw changes that I did not believe would ever take place. Obviously the old persecutions had been utter failures. Christianity was a marvelous success.

There seemed to me to be a blending of Roman thinking with Christian ideas. Perhaps one should say it was a blending of styles, and ways of looking at the world.

Finally—when Lacinius was gone, Constantine became the sole ruler of the Empire and we saw all of its provinces united once more. He became obviously more concerned with the disunity of the Christians and we heard word in Rome of huge Christian councils in the East. The first took place at Antioch where I had lived with Pandora and which was still a great city, perhaps in many respects more lively and interesting at this point than Rome.

The Arian heresy was the cause of Constantine's discontent. And the whole thing had to do with something extremely small in the Scriptures which seemed to Constantine to be hardly worth the dispute. Nevertheless certain Bishops were excommunicated from the growing Church, and another more important council was held in Nicaea only two months later, where Constantine presided again.

There the Nicene Creed was adopted, which is recited by Christians even in the present time. The Bishops who signed this Creed effectively again condemned and excommunicated the theorist and Christian writer Arius as a heretic and doomed his writings to be burnt. He himself was to be shut out of his native Alexandria. The judgment was absolute.

But it is worth noting, and I did, that Arius continued his struggle for recognition, even though the council had cast him out.

The other great affair of this council, and a matter which is still rather confusing in Christianity, was the question of the true date of

Easter, or the anniversary of the resurrection of Christ. A determination was made as to how this date would be calculated, and it was based upon a Western system. And then the council came to an end.

Now the Bishops who had come to the council were asked to stay and help the Emperor celebrate his twenty years on the throne, and of course they did so, for how could they refuse?

But as soon as word reached Rome of these elaborate festivities, there was much jealousy and discontent. Rome felt ignored in all these goings-on. And so there was considerable relief and happiness when in January of 326, the Emperor headed for our city once again.

Before his arrival, however, terrible deeds became attached to Constantine's name. For reasons nobody could discover, he stopped along the way to put to death both his son Crispus and his stepson, Licinianus, and his own wife, the Empress Fausta. Historians can speculate forever as to why all this happened. The truth is, nobody knows why Constantine committed these acts. There may have been a plot against him. Perhaps there was not.

Let me say here that it cast a cloud over his arrival among the Romans, and that when he did come, it was no great consolation to the old ruling class, because he dressed very much in the extravagant Eastern style, with silk and damask, and would not be part of the important procession to the Temple of Jupiter, as the people had expected him to do.

Of course the Christians adored him. Rich and poor they flocked to see him in his Eastern robes and jewels. They were overwhelmed with his generosity as he laid the ground for more churches.

And though he had spent almost no time in Rome, he had over the years allowed for the completion of secular buildings begun by Maxentius, and he built a large public bath under his own name.

Then came appalling rumors. Constantine had plans for an entirely new city. Constantine found Rome old and decayed and lacking as a capital. Constantine meant to make a new city for the Empire; he meant to make it in the East, and it would honor his name!

Imagine it, if you can.

Of course the Emperors of the last century had moved all over the provinces of the Empire. They had fought each other, breaking into pairs and tetrarchies, and meeting here and murdering one another there.

But to give up Rome as the capital? To create another great city to be the center of the Empire?

It was unthinkable to me.

I brooded in hatred. I knew despair.

All of my nightly guests shared my misery. The elderly soldiers were broken by the news and one of the old philosophers wept bitterly. Another city to be the capital of the Roman Empire? The younger men were furious, but they could not hide their bitter curiosity, or their grudging guesses as to where this new city might be.

I could not dare weep as I wanted to for my tears would have been full of blood.

I asked the musicians to play old songs, songs I had to teach them for they had never heard them, and there came a strange moment when we sang together—my mortal guests and me—a slow mournful song about Rome's tarnished glory which we would not forget.

The air was cool on that evening. I went out into the garden and looked down over the side of the hill. I could see lights here and there in the darkness. I could hear laughter and conversation from other houses.

"This is Rome!" I whispered.

How could Constantine abandon the city which had been the capital of the Empire for a thousand years of struggle, triumph, defeat, glory? Couldn't someone reason with him? This simply could not come to pass.

But the more I roamed the city, the more I listened to talk both far and wide, the more I roamed outside the walls and into the towns thereabout, I came to see what had motivated the Emperor.

Constantine wanted to begin his Christian Empire in a place of incredible advantage, and could not retreat to the Italian peninsula when so much of the culture of his people lay to the East. Also he had to defend his Eastern borders. The Persian Empire of the East was always a threat. And Rome was not a fit place for a man in supreme power to reside.

Thus Constantine had chosen the distant Greek city of Byzantium to be the site of Constantinople, his new home.

And I should see my home, my sacred city, become now a castoff of a man whom I, as a Roman, could not accept.

There were rumors of the incredible if not miraculous speed with which Constantinople had been mapped out, and with which building was being done.

At once many Romans followed Constantine to the burgeoning new city. At his invitation perhaps, or simply on their own impulse

Senators decamped with their families and their wealth to live in this new and shining place, a subject on everyone's lips.

Soon I heard that Senators from all the cities of the Empire were being drawn to Constantinople, and indeed, as baths and meeting halls and circuses were erected in the new capital, beautiful statues were being looted from cities throughout Greece and Asia to adorn the new architectural works.

Rome, my Rome, what will become of you, I thought.

Of course my evening feasts were not really deeply affected. Those who came to dine with Marius were poor teachers and historians who had no means of moving to Constantinople, or curious and reckless young men who had not made the clever choice as yet.

I had plenty of mortal company as always, and indeed, I had inherited a few very quick-witted Greek philosophers who had been left behind by families who had gone to Constantinople where they would no doubt find more brilliant men to tutor their sons.

But this, the company in my house was a small matter.

In truth, as the years passed, my soul was crushed.

And it struck me as more than ever dreadful that I had no other immortal companion who might understand what I felt. I wondered if Mael or Avicus could possibly comprehend what was going on. I knew they still haunted the same streets as I did. I heard them.

And my need of Pandora became so terrible that I could not envision her or think of her anymore.

But still, I thought desperately, if this man Constantine can preserve the Empire, if Christianity can bind it and prevent it from breaking apart, if its disparate provinces can be united, if Constantine can keep back the barbarians who forever pillage without building or preserving anything, who am I to judge him, I, who am outside of life?

I went back to my scribbling on the nights when my mind was feverish. And on those when I was certain that Mael and Avicus were nowhere in the vicinity I went out into the country to visit the shrine.

My work on the walls of the shrine was continuous. As soon as I finished painting the walls of the entire chapel, I covered over a wall and began painting again. I could not make my nymphs and goddesses to suit my standards. Their figures were not slender enough for me, and the arms not graceful enough. Their hair was not right. And as for the gardens I rendered, there were not enough kinds of flowers for me to include.

Always, there was that sense of familiarity—that I had seen this garden, that I had known it long before I was allowed by Akasha to drink her blood. I had seen the stone benches in it, I had seen the fountains.

I couldn't shake the sensations of being in it as I painted, so strong was the feeling. I'm not sure it aided me in my work. Perhaps it hurt.

But as I gained skill as a painter, and I did indeed gain skill, other aspects of the work disturbed me.

I was convinced that there was something unnatural in it, something inherently ghastly in the manner with which I drew human figures so nearly perfectly, something unnatural in the way I made the colors so unusually bright, and added so many fierce little details. I was particularly repelled by my penchant for decorative details.

As much as I was driven to do this work, I hated it. I composed whole gardens of lovely mythic creatures only to rub them out. Sometimes I painted so fast that I exhausted myself, and fell down on the floor of the shrine, spending the paralytic sleep of the whole day there, helpless, rather than going to my secret resting place—my coffin—which was hidden not far from my house.

We are monsters, that is what I thought whenever I painted or looked on my own painting, and that's what I think now. Never mind that I want to go on existing. We are unnatural. We are witnesses with both too much and too little feeling. And as I thought these things, I had before me the mute witnesses, Akasha and Enkil.

What did it matter to them what I did?

Perhaps twice a year I changed their fancy garments, arranging Akasha's gown with fastidious care. I brought new bracelets for her more often and put these on her cold sluggish arms with slow tender movements so as not to insult her by what I did. I fussed with the gold in the black plaited hair of both Parents. I arranged a handsome necklace around the naked shoulders of the King.

I never spoke to either of them idly. They were too grand for that. I addressed them only in prayer.

I was silent in the shrine as I worked, with my paint pots and brushes. I was silent as I sat there peering in frank disgust at what I'd done.

Then one night, after many years of diligence in the shrine, I stood back and tried to see the whole as never before. My head was swimming. I went to the entrance to take the stance of a man who was new to the place, and forgetting utterly the Divine Pair, I merely looked at the walls.

A truth came clear to me in painful clarity. I had painted Pandora. I had painted her everywhere. Each nymph, each goddess, was Pandora. Why hadn't I known?

I was amazed and defeated. My eyes are playing tricks on me, I thought. I wiped them, actually wiped them as a mortal might do, to see all the better and looked again. No. It was Pandora, rendered beautifully everywhere that I looked. Dresses changed and style of hair, yes, and other adornments but these creatures were all Pandora, and I had not seen it until now.

Of course the never ending garden looked familiar. Never mind that. Pandora had little or nothing to do with those feelings. Pandora was inescapable and came from some different fount of sensations. Pandora would never leave me. That was the curse.

I concealed all my paints and brushes behind the Divine Parents as I always did—it would have been an insult to the Father and Mother to leave them—and I went back to Rome.

I had before me several hours before dawn in which to suffer, in which to think of Pandora as never before.

The drunken party was winding down a bit as it always did in the small hours, with a few guests asleep in the grass outside, and others singing together in a small group, and no one took notice of me as I went into my library, and sat at my desk.

Through the open doors I looked out at the dark trees and wished that my life were at an end.

It seemed I lacked the courage to go on in the existence which I'd made for myself, and then I turned and decided—simply out of desperation—to look at the paintings on the walls of the room. I had of course approved these paintings and paid to have them refreshed and changed many a time.

But now I took stock of them from my point of view not as Marius the rich man who can have whatever he wishes, but as Marius the monster painter who had rendered Pandora twenty-one times on the four walls of Akasha's shrine.

I saw suddenly how inferior were these paintings, how rigid and pallid the goddesses and nymphs who peopled this world of my study, and quickly I woke my day slaves and told them that they must have everything covered over with fresh paint the following day. Also an entire supply of the best paints must be purchased and brought to the house. Never mind how the walls were to be redecorated. Leave that to me. Cover up all that was there.

They were used to my eccentricities, and after making certain that they understood me, they went back to their sleep.

I didn't know what I meant to do, except I felt driven to make pictures, and I felt if I can cling to that, if I can do that, then I can go on.

My misery deepened.

I laid out vellum for an entry in my erstwhile journal and began to describe the experience of discovering my beloved everywhere around me, and how it seemed to contain an element of sorcery when suddenly I heard an unmistakable sound.

Avicus was at my gate. Indeed he was asking me with a strong current of the Mind Gift whether or not he might come over the wall and in to visit me.

He was leery of the mortals in my banquet room and in my garden. But might he come in?

At once I gave my silent answer that he could.

It had been years since I had so much as glimpsed him in the back streets, and I was not entirely surprised to see him dressed as a Roman soldier, and to see that he had taken to carrying a dagger and a sword.

He glanced fretfully at the door to the banquet room, but I gestured that he must pay the guests no attention at all.

His rich curling dark hair was well groomed and clean and he had about him an attitude of prosperity and well-being, except that his clothes were dreadfully stained with blood. It was not human blood. I would have smelled human blood. He soon gave me to know by a simple facial expression that he was in dire distress.

"What is it? What can I do for you?" I asked. I tried to cloak my pure loneliness, my pure need to touch his hand.

You are a creature like me, I wanted to say. We are monsters and we can put our arms around each other. What are they, my guests, but tender things? But I said nothing at all.

It was Avicus who spoke.

"Something dreadful has happened. I don't know how to correct it, or even if it can be corrected. I beg you to come."

"Come where, tell me," I said sympathetically.

"It's Mael. He's been grievously wounded and I don't know if the damage can be repaired."

We went out at once.

I followed him into a very crowded quarter of Rome where the newer buildings faced one another sometimes with no more than two feet in between. At last we came to a substantial new house on the outskirts, a rich dwelling, with a heavy gate, and he took me inside, through the entranceway and into the broad beautiful atrium or courtyard within the house.

Let me note here that he was not using his full strength during this little journey, but I did not want to point this out to him, and so at his slow pace, I had followed his lead.

Now, through the atrium, we passed into the main room of the house, the room where mortals would have dined, and there by the light of one lamp, I saw Mael lying in seeming helplessness on the tiled floor.

The light was glinting in his eyes.

I knelt beside him at once.

His head was twisted awkwardly to one side, and one of his arms was turned as though the shoulder were out of joint. His entire body was hideously gaunt, and his skin had a dreadful pallor to it. Yet his eyes fixed on me with neither malice nor supplication.

His clothes, very much like those of Avicus, hung loose on his starved frame, and were deeply soaked with blood. As for his long blond hair it was clotted with blood also, and his lips shivered as if he were trying to speak but could not.

Avicus gestured to me helplessly with both hands.

I bent closer to have a better look at Mael, while Avicus brought the oil lamp near and held it so that it cast a warm bright light.

Mael made a low, harsh sound, and I saw gradually that there were horrid red wounds on his throat, and on his naked shoulder where the cloth of his tunic had been pushed out of the way. His arm was at the wrong angle to his body, most definitely, and his neck had been horribly twisted so that his head was not right.

In a moment of exquisite horror, I realized that these parts of him—head and arm—had been shifted from their natural place.

"How did this happen?" I asked. I looked up at Avicus. "Do you know?"

"They cut off his head and his arm," said Avicus. "It was a band of soldiers, drunk and looking for trouble. We made to go around them, but they turned on us. We should have gone up over the roofs. We were too sure of ourselves. We thought ourselves so superior, so invincibly strong."

"I see," I answered. I clasped the hand of Mael's good arm. At once, he pressed my hand in return. In truth I was deeply shocked. But I could not let either of them see this, for it would only have made them more afraid.

I had often wondered if we could be destroyed by dismemberment, and now the awful truth was plain to me. It was not sufficient alone to release our souls from this world.

"They surrounded him before I knew what to do," said Avicus. "I fought off those who tried to harm me, but look what they have done to him."

"And you brought him back here," I said, "and you tried to replace both head and arm."

"He was still living!" said Avicus. "They had run off, drunken, stumbling miscreants. And I saw at once that he was still alive. There in the street, though the blood poured out of him, he was looking at me! Why, he was reaching with his good arm for his own head."

He looked at me as though begging me to understand him, or perhaps forgive him.

"He was alive," he repeated. "The blood poured out of his neck, and it poured out of his head. In the street, I put the head on the neck. It was here that I joined the arm to the shoulder. And look what I have done."

Mael's fingers tightened on my hand.

"Can you answer me?" I said to Mael. "Make only a sound if you cannot."

There came that harsh noise again but this time I fancied I heard the syllable Yes.

"Do you want to live?" I asked.

"Oh, don't ask him such a thing," Avicus begged. "He may lack courage just now. Only help me if you know what to do." He knelt down beside Mael and he bent over, carefully holding the lamp to one side, and he pressed his lips to Mael's forehead.

From Mael there had come that same answer again: Yes.

"Bring me more light," I said to Avicus, "but understand before you do. I possess no extraordinary magic in this matter. I think I know what has happened and I know how to undo it. But that is all."

At once Avicus gathered up from about the house a number of oil lamps and lighted them and set them down in an oval around Mael. It looked strangely like the work of a sorcerer marking off a place for magic, but I didn't let my thoughts become distracted by that annoying fact, and when I could finally see with the very best advantage I knelt down and looked at all the wounds, and I looked at the sunken, blood-less and skeletal figure of Mael.

Finally I sat back on my heels. I looked at Avicus who sat opposite me on the other side of his friend.

"Tell me precisely how you accomplished this," I said.

"I fixed the head to the neck as best I could do it, but I was wrong, you see, I did it wrong. How can we know how to do it right?" he demanded. "Do you know?"

"And the arm," I said, "it's badly joined as well."

"What shall we do?"

"Did you force the joining?" I asked.

He reflected before answering me. And then he said, "Yes, I think I did. I see your meaning. I did it with force. I meant these parts to adhere once more. I used too much force."

"Ah, well, we have one chance to repair this, I think, but understand again I possess no secret knowledge. I take my lead from the fact that he is still living. I think we must pull off both head and arm and see if these parts, when placed in correct proximity to the body, will not join at the right angles as they should."

His face brightened only as he slowly understood what I had said.

"Yes," he said. "Perhaps they will join as they are meant to join! If they can join so poorly, they can join in a way that is perfect and right."

"Yes," I said, "but you must do this act. You are the one he trusts."

He looked down at his friend and I could see that this task would be no easy thing. Then slowly he looked up at me.

"We must give him our blood first to strengthen him," he said.

"No, after it's done," I said, "he'll need it for healing. That's when we'll give it." I disliked that I had given my word in this, but I realized quite abruptly that I didn't want to see Mael die. Indeed, so much did I not want to see it that I thought perhaps I ought to take over the entire operation myself.

But I could not step in. It was up to Avicus how the matter went forward.

Quite abruptly, he placed his left hand firmly on Mael's shoulder and pulled Mael's badly joined arm with all his strength. At once the arm was free of the body with bloody ligaments trembling from it rather like the roots of a tree.

"Now, place it close to him, there, yes, and see if it does not seek its own place."

He obeyed me, but my hand was out to guide the arm quickly, not letting it get too close, but waiting for it to begin to move on its own. Abruptly I felt the spasm in the arm and then let go of it, and saw it quickly joined to the shoulder, the flying ligaments moving as so many little serpents into the body until the rupture was no more.

Alas, I had been right in my suspicions. The body followed its own supernatural rules.

At once, I cut my wrist with my teeth and I let my blood pour down on the wound. I saw it heal before my eyes.

Avicus seemed rather amazed by this simple trick, though surely he must have known it, for this limited curative property of our blood is almost universally known among our kind.

In a moment, I had given all that I wanted to give and the wound had all but disappeared.

I sat back to see Mael's eyes fixed on me as before. His head looked pathetic and grotesque at its incorrect angle. And his expression was hideously empty.

I felt his hand again, and the pressure was returned.

"Are you prepared to do it?" I asked Avicus.

"Hold him well by the shoulders," Avicus answered. "For the love of Heaven, use all your strength."

I put my hands up, and caught Mael as firmly as I could. I would have rested my knees on his chest but he was far too weakened for such a weight and so I kept to one side.

Finally with a loud moan, Avicus pulled on Mael's head with both his hands.

The gush of blood was appalling, and I could swear that I heard the ripping of preternatural flesh. Avicus fell back with the gesture, and toppled to one side, holding the helpless head in his hands.

"At once, place it near to the body!" I cried. I held the shoulders still, though the body had suddenly given a dreadful lurch. Indeed the arms flew up as if in search of the head.

Avicus laid the head down in the gushing blood, pushing it ever closer to the gaping neck, until suddenly the head seemed to move of its own volition, the ligaments once more like so many little snakes as they made to meet with those of the trunk, and the whole body gave another lurch and the head was firmly fixed as it should have been.

I saw Mael's eyes fluttering, and I saw his mouth open, and he cried out,

"Avicus," with all his strength.

Avicus bent over him, cutting his wrist with his teeth as I had done before, only this time it was to let the stream come down into Mael's mouth.

Mael reached for the arm above him, and he brought it down to him, drinking fiercely as his back arched, and his thin miserable legs quivered and went straight.

I drew away from the pair, out of the circle of light. I sat still for a long while in the shadows, my eyes fixed on them, and then when I could see that Avicus was exhausted, that his heart was tired from giving so much blood, I crept to join the two, and I asked if I might give Mael to drink from me as well.

Oh, how my soul revolted against this gesture. Why ever did I feel compelled to do it? I can give no answer. I don't know any more now than I knew at the time.

Mael was able to sit up. His figure was more robust, but the expression on his face was too dreadful to behold. The blood on the floor was dried and glittering as our blood always is. It would have to be scraped up and burnt.

Mael leant forward and put his arms around me in a terrible intimacy and kissed me on the neck. He didn't dare to sink his teeth.

"Very well, do it," I said, though I was dreadfully hesitant, and I put in my mind images of Rome for him to see as he drank, images of beautiful new temples, Constantine's amazing triumphal arch, and all the wondrous churches which were now erected far and wide. I thought of Christians and their magical ceremonies. I thought of anything to disguise and obliterate all the secrets of my entire life.

A miserable revulsion continued in me as I felt the pull of his hunger and his need. I refused to see anything of his soul with the Mind Gift, and I think my eyes met those of Avicus at one moment, and I was struck by the grave, complex expression on his face.

Finally, it was all finished. I could give no more. It was almost dawn and I needed what strength I had to move quickly towards my hiding place. I rose to my feet.

Avicus spoke up.

"Can we not be friends now?" he asked. "We have been enemies for so many, many years."

Mael was still wretchedly afflicted from what had befallen him, and in no state perhaps to declare on the matter one way or the other, but he looked up at me with his accusing eyes, and said:

"In Egypt you saw the Great Mother, I saw her in your heart when I drank your blood."

I went rigid with shock and fury.

I thought I should kill him. He has been good only for learning—how to put together again blood drinkers who had been dismembered—and it was time now to finish what the drunkards only started earlier this night. But I said and did nothing.

Oh, how cold was my heart.

Avicus was dreadfully disappointed and disapproving.

"Marius, I thank you," he said, sad and weary as he walked me to the gate. "What could I have done if you had refused to come to us? I owe you an immense debt."

"There is no Good Mother," I told him. "I bid you farewell."

As I hurried back over the rooftops of Rome, towards my own house, I resolved in my soul that I'd told them the truth.

7

I was very surprised the next night to find the walls of my library completely painted over. I had forgotten that I'd given such a command to my slaves. As soon as I saw all the pots of fresh paint in any number of colors, I then remembered what I had told them to do.

Indeed, I couldn't think of anything but Mael and Avicus and must confess I was more than fascinated by the mixture of civilized manners and quiet dignity which I found in Avicus and not at all in Mael.

Mael would always be for me a barbarian, unlettered, unrefined, and above all fanatical, for it was due to his fanatic belief in the Gods of the Grove that he had taken my life.

And realizing that the only way I could escape my thoughts of the pair was to paint the newly prepared walls, I set to work at once.

I took no notice of my guests who were already dining of course, and of those going and coming through the garden and the open gate.

Realize, if you will, that by this time I did not have to hunt for blood that often, and though I was still much too much the savage in this respect, I often left it till late in the evening or early in the morning, or did not hunt at all.

So to the painting, I went. I didn't stand back and take stock of what I meant to do. Rather I went at it fiercely, covering the wall in great glaring patches, making the usual garden which obsessed me, and the nymphs and goddesses whose forms were so familiar to my mind.

These creatures had no names for me. They might have come from any verse in Ovid, or from the writing of Lucretius, or indeed from the blind poet, Homer. It was no matter to me. I lost myself in depicting uplifted arms and graceful throats, in painting oval faces and garments blowing gently in the breeze.

One wall I divided with painted columns, and around these I painted vines. Another wall, I worked with stiff borders of stylized greenery. And the third wall I allotted into small panels in which I would feature various gods.

Meantime, the house grew crowded with the ever noisy party, and some of my favorite drunkards drifted inevitably into the library and watched me at work.

I knew enough to slow my pace somewhat so as not to scare them with my unnatural speed. But otherwise, I took no notice, and only when one of the lyre players came in to sing for me did I realize how mad the house must seem.

For there were people dining and drinking everywhere now, and the master of the house in his long tunic stood painting a wall, the proper work for craftsmen or artists, not Patricians you understand, and there seemed no decent boundary of any kind.

I began to laugh at the absurdity of it.

One of the young guests marveled at my talent.

"Marius, you never told us. We never imagined."

"Neither did I," I said dully, going on with my work, watching the white paint disappear beneath my brush.

For months I went on with my painting, even moving into the banquet room where the guests cheered me on as I worked. Whatever I accomplished it did not please me and it certainly did not amaze them.

They thought it amusing and eccentric that a rich man should decorate his own walls. And all the drunken advice I received did not amount to very much. The learned men knew the mythic tales I depicted and they enjoyed them, and the young men tried to get me in arguments which I refused.

It was the spacious garden I loved to paint above all, with no painted frame to set it apart from our world with its dancing figures and bending laurels. It was the familiar garden. For I imagined that I could escape into it with my mind.

And during that time I did not risk attending to the chapel. Rather I painted all the rooms of my house.

Meantime, the old gods whom I painted were fast disappearing from the Temples of Rome.

At some point or other, Constantine had made Christianity the legal religion of the Empire, and now it was the pagans who couldn't worship as they chose.

I don't think Constantine himself was ever in favor of forcing anybody in religious matters. But that's what had come about.

So I painted poor old Bacchus, the god of wine, with his cheerful followers, and the brilliant Apollo chasing the desperate and lovely Daphne who turned into a laurel tree rather than allow the godly rape.

On and on I worked, happy with mortal company, thinking, Mael and Avicus, please do not search my mind for secrets.

But in truth all during this time I could hear them very near me. My mortal banquet parties puzzled them and frightened them. I could hear them approach my house and then go away every night.

Finally the inevitable night came.

They stood at my gate.

Mael was for coming in without permission, and Avicus kept him back, begging me with the Mind Gift to admit them once more.

I was in my library, painting it over for the third time, and the dinner party that night, thank the gods, had not spilled over into the room.

I put down my brush. I stared at my unfinished work. It seemed another Pandora had emerged in the unfinished Daphne and it struck a tragic chord in my heart that Daphne had eluded her lover. What a fool I'd been to escape mine.

But for a long self-indulgent moment I looked at what I had painted—this unearthly creature with her rippling brown hair.

You understood my soul, I thought, and now others are coming only to sack my heart of all its riches. What am I to do? We argued, yes, you and I, but it was with loving respect, was it not? I cannot endure without you. Please come to me, from wherever you are.

But there was no time for my solitude. It suddenly seemed rather precious, no matter how much of it I had had in the past years.

I closed off my happy human guests from the library, and then silently, I told the blood drinkers that they might come in.

Both were richly dressed, and their swords and daggers were encrusted with jewels. Their cloaks were fixed at the shoulder with rich clasps and even their sandals were ornamented. They might have been preparing to join the opulently clad citizens of the new capital, Constantinople, where great dreams were still being realized though Constantine was now dead.

It was with mixed feelings that I gestured for them to sit down.

However much I wished that I had allowed Mael to perish, I was drawn to Avicus—to his keen expression and the friendly way in which he regarded me. I had time to observe now that his skin was a lighter brown than it had been, and that its dark tone gave a rather sculpted quality to his strong features, especially his mouth. As for his eyes they were clear and held no cunning or lie.

Both remained standing. They looked anxiously in the direction of the mortal banquet room. Once again, I urged them to be seated.

Mael stood, quite literally looking down his hawk nose at me, but Avicus took the chair.

Mael was still weak and his body emaciated. Quite obviously, it would take many nights of drinking from his victims before the damage done him would be completely healed.

"How have things been with you?" I asked, out of courtesy.

And then out of private desperation I let my mind envision Pandora. I let my mind completely recall her in all her splendid details. I hoped thereby to send the message of her to both of them, so that she, wherever she was, might receive this message somehow, a message which I, on account of the blood I had given her in her making, could not send on my own.

I don't know that either received any impression of my lost love.

Avicus answered my question politely but Mael said not one word.

"Things are better for us," said Avicus. "Mael heals well."

"I want to tell you certain things," I commenced without asking whether or not they wanted such knowledge. "I don't believe from what happened that either of you know your own strength. I know from my own experience that power increases with age, as I am now more agile and strong than I was when I was made. You too are quite strong, and this incident with the drunken mortals need not have ever taken place. You could have gone up the wall when you were surrounded."

"Oh, leave off with this!" said Mael suddenly.

I was aghast at this rudeness. I merely shrugged.

"I saw things," said Mael in a small hard voice, as though the confidential manner of it would make his words all the more important. "I saw things when I drank from you which you could not prevent me from seeing. I saw a Queen upon a throne."

I sighed.

His tone was not as venomous as it had been before. He wanted the truth and knew he could not get it by hostile means.

As for me I was so fearful that I dared not move or speak. Naturally I was defeated by this news from him, dreadfully defeated, and I didn't know what chance I had of preventing everything from becoming known. I stared at my paintings. I wished I had painted a better garden. I might have mentally transported myself into a garden. Vaguely I came to thinking, But you have a beautiful garden right outside through the doors.

"Will you not tell me what you found in Egypt?" Mael asked. "I know that you went there. I know that the God of the Grove wanted to send you there. Will you not have that much mercy as to tell me what you found?"

"And why would I have mercy?" I asked politely. "Even if I had found miracles or mysteries in Egypt. Why would I tell you? You won't even be seated under my roof like a proper guest. What is there between us? Hatred and miracles?" I stopped. I had become too heated. It was anger. It was weakness. You know my theme.

At this, he took a chair beside Avicus and he stared before him as he had done on that night when he told me how he'd been made.

I saw now as I looked at him more closely that his throat was still bruised from his ordeal. As for his shoulder, his cloak covered it but I imagined it to be the same.

My eyes moved to Avicus and I was surprised to see his eyebrows knit in a strange little frown.

Suddenly he looked to Mael and he spoke.

"The fact is, Marius can't tell us what he discovered," he said, his voice calm. "And we mustn't ask him again. Marius bears some terrible burden. Marius has a secret which has to do with all of us and how long we can endure."

I was dreadfully aggrieved. I'd failed to keep my mind veiled and they had discovered all but everything. I had little hope of preventing their penetration into the sanctum itself.

I didn't know precisely what to do. I couldn't even consider things in their presence. It was too dangerous. Yes, dangerous as it was, I had an impulse to tell them all.

Mael was alarmed and excited by what Avicus had said.

"Are you certain of this?" he asked Avicus.

"Yes," Avicus answered. "Over the years my mind had grown stronger. Prompted by what I've seen of Marius, I've tested my powers. I can penetrate Marius's thoughts even when I don't want to do it. And on the night when Marius came to help us, as Marius sat beside you, as he watched you heal from your wounds as you drank from me, Marius thought of many mysteries and secrets, and though I gave you blood, I read Marius's mind."

I was too saddened by this to respond to anything said by either of them. My eyes drifted to the garden outside. I listened for the sound of the fountain. Then I sat back in my chair and looked at the various scrolls of my journal which lay about helter-skelter on my desk for anyone to pillage and read. Oh, but you've written everything in code, I thought. And then again, a clever blood drinker might decipher it. What does it all matter now?

Suddenly I felt a strong impulse to try to reason with Mael.

Once again I saw the weakness of anger. I had to put aside anger and contempt and plead with him to understand.

"This is so," I said. "In Egypt, I did find things. But you must believe me that nothing I found matters. If there is a Queen, a Mother as you call her, and mind you, I don't say she exists, imagine for the moment that she is ancient and unresponsive and can give nothing to her children any longer, that so many centuries have passed since our dim beginnings that no one with any reason understands them, and the matter is left quite literally buried for it matters not one jot."

I had admitted far more than I intended, and I looked from one to the other of them for understanding and acceptance of what I'd said.

Mael wore the astonished expression of an innocent. But the look on the face of Avicus was something else.

He studied me as if he wanted desperately to tell me many things. Indeed his eyes spoke in silence though his mind gave me nothing and then he said,

"Long centuries ago, before I was sent to Britain to take up my time in the oak as the god, I was brought before her. You remember I told you this."

"Yes," I said.

"I saw her!" He paused. It seemed quite painful for him to relive this moment. "I was humiliated before her, made to kneel, made to recite my vows. I remember hating those around me. As for her, I thought she was a statue, but now I understand the strange words that they spoke. And then when the Magic Blood was given me, I surrendered to the miracle. I kissed her feet."

"Why have you never told me this!" begged Mael. He seemed more injured and confounded than angry or outraged.

"I told you part of it," said Avicus. "It's only now that I see it all. My existence was wretched, don't you understand?" He looked to me and then to Mael, and his tone became a little more reasonable and soft. "Mael, don't you see?" he asked. "Marius is trying to tell you. This path in the past is a path of pain!"

"But who is she and what is she?" Mael demanded.

In that fatal instant my mind was decided. Anger did move me and perhaps in the wrong way.

"She is the first of us," I said in quiet fury. "That is the old tale. She and her consort or King, they are the Divine Parents. There's no more to it than that."

"And you saw them," Mael said, as if nothing could make him pause in his relentless questioning.

"They exist; they are safe," I said. "Listen to what Avicus tells you. What was Avicus told?"

Avicus was desperately trying to remember. He was searching so far back that he was discovering his own age. At last he spoke in the same respectful and polite voice as before.

"Both of them contain the seed from which we all spring!" he answered. "They cannot be destroyed on that account for if they were, we would die with them. Ah, don't you see?" He looked at Mael. "I know now the cause of the Terrible Fire. Someone seeking to destroy us burnt them or placed them in the sun."

I was utterly defeated. He had revealed one of the most precious secrets. Would he know the other? I sat in sullen silence.

He rose from the chair and began to walk about the room, incensed by his memories.

"How long did they remain in the fire? Or was it only one day's passage in the desert sand?" He turned to me. "They were white as marble when I saw them. 'This is the Divine Mother,' they said to me. My lips touched her foot. The priest pressed his heel to the back of my neck. When the Terrible Fire came I had been so long in the oak I remembered nothing. I had deliberately slain my memory. I had slain all sense of time. I lived for the monthly blood sacrifice and the yearly Sanhaim. I starved and dreamed as I'd been commanded to do. My life was in rising at Sanhaim to judge the wicked, to look into the hearts of those who were accused and pronounce on their guilt or innocence.

"But now I remember. I remember the sight of them—the Mother and the Father—for I saw both of them before they pressed my lips to her feet. How cold she was. How awful it was. And I was unwilling. I was so filled with anger and fear. *And it was a brave man's fear.*"

I winced at his last words. I knew what he meant. What must a brave general feel when he knows the battle has gone against him and nothing remains but death?

Mael looked up at Avicus with a face full of sorrow and sympathy.

But Avicus was not finished. On he went with his walking, seeing nothing before him but memory, his thick black hair falling forward as he dipped his head under the weight of memories he bore.

His black eyes were lustrous in the light of the many lamps. But his expression was his finest feature.

"Was it the sun, or was it a Terrible Fire?" he asked. "Did someone try to burn them? Did someone believe such a thing could be done? Oh, it's so simple. I should have remembered. But memory is desperate to leave us. Memory knows that we cannot endure its company. Memory would reduce us to fools. Ah, listen to old mortals when they have nothing but memories of childhood. How they go on mistaking those around them for persons long dead, and no one listens. How often I have eavesdropped on them in their misery. How often I have wondered at their long uninterrupted conversations with ghosts in empty rooms."

Still I said nothing.

But he looked at me at last, and asked me:

"You saw them, the King and Queen. You know where they are?"

I waited a long moment before answering. I spoke simply when I answered.

"I saw them, yes. And you must trust me that they are safe. And that you don't want to know where they are." I studied both of them. "If you were to know, then perhaps some night other blood drinkers could take you prisoner and wring the truth from you, and they might strive to claim the King and Queen."

Mael studied me for a long while before he responded. "We fight others who attempt to take Rome from us. You know we've done this. We force them to leave."

"I know you do," I said. "But the Christian vampires continue to come, and they come in numbers, and those numbers grow larger all the time. They are devoted to their Devil, their Serpent, their Satan. They will come again. There will be more and more."

"They mean nothing to us," said Mael disgustedly. "Why would they want this Holy Pair?"

For a moment I said nothing. Then the truth broke from me hatefully, as though I couldn't protect them from it, nor protect myself.

"All right," I said. "Since you know so much, both of you, let me explain the following: many blood drinkers want the Mother and the Father. There are those who come from the Far East who know of them. *They want the Primal Blood. They believe in its strength. It's stronger than any other blood.* But the Mother and Father can move to defend themselves. Yet still thieves will always be in search of them, ready to destroy whoever keeps them in hiding. And such thieves have in the past come to me."

Neither of them spoke. I went on.

"You do not want, either of you," I said, "to know anything further of the Mother and the Father. You do not want rogues to come upon you and try to overpower you for your knowledge. You do not want secrets which can be ripped from your heart."

I glared at Mael as I said these last words. Then I spoke again.

"To know of the Mother and the Father is a curse."

A silence fell, but I could see that Mael would not allow for it to be very long. A light came into his face, and he said to me in a trembling voice:

"Have you drunk this Primal Blood?" Slowly he became incensed. "You have drunk this blood, haven't you?"

"Quiet, Mael," said Avicus. But it was no use.

"You have drunk it," said Mael in fury. "And you know where the Mother and Father are concealed."

He rose from the chair and rushed at me, and suddenly clamped his hands on my shoulders.

Now, I am by nature not given to physical combat, but in a rage I pushed him off me with such force that he was thrown across the floor and back against the wall.

"How dare you?" I asked fiercely. I struggled to keep my voice low so as not to alarm the mortals in the banquet room. "I ought to kill you. What peace of mind it would give me to know you were dead. I could cut you into pieces that no sorcerer could reassemble. Damn you."

I was trembling with this uncharacteristic and humiliating rage.

He gazed at me, his mind unchanged, his will only slightly chastened and then he said with extraordinary fervor:

"You have the Mother and the Father. You have drunk the Mother's blood. I see it in you. You cannot hide it from me. How will you ever hide it from anyone else?"

I rose from my chair.

"Then you must die," I said, "isn't that so? For you know, and you must never tell anyone else." I made to advance on him.

But Avicus who had been staring at all this in shock and horror rose quickly and came between us. As for Mael, he had drawn his dagger. And he seemed quite ready for the brawl.

"No, Marius, please," said Avicus, "we must make peace with each other, we cannot keep up this struggle. Don't fight with Mael. What could be the outcome, but two wounded creatures hating each other even more than now?"

Mael was on his feet. He held his dagger ready. He looked clumsy. I don't think he knew weapons. As for his supernatural powers, I didn't think either of them understood fully what they might do. All this, of course, was defensive calculation. I didn't want this battle any more than Avicus wanted it, yet I looked to Avicus now and said coldly:

"I can kill him. Stay out of the way."

"But that is the point," said Avicus, "I cannot do this, and so you will be fighting the two of us, and such a fight you can't win."

I stared at him for a long moment during which words failed me completely. I looked to Mael with his uplifted dagger. And then in a moment of utter despair I went to my desk and sat down and rested my head on my elbows.

I thought of the night in the far city of Antioch when Pandora and I had slaughtered that bunch of Christian vampires who had come so foolishly into our house talking about Moses in the desert lifting the Serpent, and secrets from Egypt, and all such seemingly marvelous things. I thought of all that blood and the burning afterwards.

And I thought also how these two creatures, though we didn't speak or see each other, had been my only companions all these years in Rome. I thought of everything perhaps that mattered. My mind sought to organize itself round Mael and Avicus, and I looked up from one to the other, and then out to the garden again.

"I'm ready to fight you," said Mael with his characteristic impatience.

"And what will you achieve? You think you can cut out the secret of the Mother and the Father from my heart?"

Avicus came to my desk. He sat down in the nearest chair before me and looked to me as if he were my client or friend.

"Marius, they are close to Rome. I know it. I have known it for a long time. Many a night you have gone out into the hills to visit some strange and lonely place, and with the Mind Gift I have followed you, wondering what could take you to such a distant spot. I believe now that you go to visit the Mother and the Father. I believe you took them out of Egypt. You can trust me with your secret. You can also trust me with your silence if you wish."

"No," said Mael, coming forward immediately. "Speak, or I'll destroy you, Marius, and Avicus and I will go to the very spot and see the Mother and Father for ourselves."

"Never," said Avicus, becoming for the first time angry. He shook his head. "Not without Marius. You're being foolish," he said to Mael.

"They can defend themselves," I said coldly. "I've warned you. I've witnessed it. They may allow you to drink the Divine Blood. They may refuse you. If they refuse, you will be destroyed." I paused for emphasis then went on.

"Once a strong god from the East came into my house in Antioch," I said. "He forced his way into the presence of the Mother and the Father. He sought to drink from the Mother. And when he made to sink his fangs into her neck, she crushed his head, and sent the lamps of the room to burn his flailing body till there was nothing left. I don't lie to you about these things." I gave a great sigh. I was tired of my own anger. "Having told you that, I'll take you there if you wish."

"But you have drunk her blood," said Mael.

"You are so very rash," I answered. "Don't you see what I'm saying? She may destroy you. I cannot say what she will do. And then there is the question of the King. What is his will? I don't know. I'll take you there, as I've said."

I could see that Mael wanted to go. Nothing would stop him from this, and as for Avicus, he was very fearful and very ashamed of his own fear.

"I must go," said Mael. "I was her priest once. I served her god in the oak. I have no choice but to go." His eyes were brilliant with his excitement. "I must see her," he said. "I cannot take your warnings. I must be taken to this place."

I nodded. I gestured for them to wait. I went to the doors of the banquet room and opened them. My guests were happy. So be it. A couple of them cheered my sudden presence, but quickly forgot me. The drowsy slave poured the fragrant wine.

I turned and went back to Avicus and Mael.

We went out into the night, the three of us, and as we made for the shrine, I learnt immediately that neither Mael nor Avicus moved at the speed which their strength allowed. I told them both to walk faster, especially when there were no mortals to watch, and very soon I had them silently exhilarated that they were more in possession of their true gifts.

When we came to the granite door of the shrine, I showed them how it was quite impossible for a team of mortals to open it and then I lighted the torch and took them down the stone steps.

"Now, this is Holy Ground," I remarked before opening the bronze doors. "You do not speak irreverently or idly and you don't speak of them as if they cannot hear."

The two were enthralled.

I opened the door, lighted the torch within, and then let them enter and stand before the dais. I held the torch high.

All was perfect as I had assumed it would be. The Queen sat with her hands on her thighs as she always did. Enkil took the same posture. Their faces, framed so beautifully in their black plaited hair, were beautifully empty of thought or woe.

Who could have known from the sight of them that life pumped inside them?

"Mother and Father," I said distinctly, "I have brought two visitors who have begged to see you. They are Mael and Avicus. They've come in reverence and respect."

Mael went down on his knees. He did it as naturally as a Christian. He held out his arms. He began to pray in the language of the Druid priesthood. He told the Queen she was most beautiful. He told tales of the old gods of the oak. And then he begged her for her blood.

Avicus winced, and I suppose, so did I.

But I was sure something quickened in Akasha. Then again perhaps not.

All of us waited in uneasy stillness.

Mael rose and walked towards the dais.

"My Queen," I said calmly, "Mael asks with all respect and all humility, if he may drink from the primal fount."

He stepped up, bent over the Queen lovingly and daringly and bent to drink from her throat.

It seemed nothing would happen. She would allow it. Her glassy eyes stared forward as if it were of no import. Her hands remained on her thighs.

But all of sudden, with monstrous speed, the heavy boned Enkil turned sideways, as if he were a wooden machine worked by wheels and cogs, and he reached out with his right hand.

I sprang forward, threw my arms around Mael and drew him backwards just under the descending arm and all the way to the wall. I flung him into the corner.

"Stay there!" I whispered.

I stood up. Enkil remained turned, his eyes empty, as if he could not find the object of his rage, his hand still poised in the air. How many times, when I'd dressed them or cleaned them, had I seen them in the same attitude of sluggish inattention?

Swallowing my terror, I mounted the dais. I spoke to Enkil coaxingly.

"My King, please, it's finished," I said. I put my trembling hands on his arm, and I gently returned him to his proper place. His face was hideously blank. Then I put my hands on his shoulders and I turned him until he was staring forward as before. Gently I attended to his heavy golden necklace. I arranged his fingers carefully. I smoothed his heavy kilt.

As for the Queen she remained undisturbed. It was as if none of it had ever taken place, or so I thought, until I saw the droplets of blood on the shoulder of her linen gown. I should have to change it when I could.

But this was evidence that she had allowed the kiss, and he had forbidden it. Well, this was most interesting, for I knew now that when I had last drunk from her, it was Enkil who had thrown me back on the chapel floor.

There was no time to ponder it. I had to get Avicus and Mael away from the shrine.

Only when we were back within the confines of my brightly lighted study did I turn my fury on Mael.

"Two times I've saved your miserable life," I said. "And I will suffer for it, I'm sure of that. For by all rights, I should have let you die the night Avicus sought my help for you, and I should have let the King crush you as he would have done tonight. I despise you, understand it. No end of time will change it. You are rash, willful and crazed with your own desires."

Avicus sat with his head down nodding as if to say he agreed.

As for Mael he stood in the corner, his hand on his dagger, regarding me with begrudging silence.

"Get out of my house," I said finally. "And if you want to end your life, then break the peace of the Mother and the Father. For ancient as they are and silent as they are, they will crush you as you have seen for yourself. You know the location of the shrine."

"You don't even know the measure of your crime," Mael answered. "To keep such a secret. How could you dare!"

"Silence, please," said Avicus.

"No, I won't keep silent," said Mael. "You, Marius, you steal the Queen of Heaven and you keep her as if she were your own? You lock her up in a painted chapel as if she were a Roman goddess made of wood? How dare you do such a thing?"

"Fool," I said, "what would you have me do with her! You spit lies at me. What you wanted is what they all want. You wanted her blood. And what would you do now that you know where she is? Do you mean to set her free and for whom and how and when?"

"Quiet, please," said Avicus again. "Mael, I beg you, let us leave Marius."

"And the snake worshipers who have heard whispers of me and my secret, what would they do?" I demanded, now quite lost in my fury. "What if they were to gain possession of her and take the blood from her, and make themselves an army stronger than us? How then would the human race rise up against our kind with laws and hunts to abolish us? Oh, you cannot begin to conceive of all the ills that would be loosed upon this world were she known to all our kind, you foolish, mad, self-important dreamer!"

Avicus stood before me, imploring me with his upraised hands, his face so sad.

I wouldn't be stopped. I stepped aside and faced the furious Mael.

"Imagine the one who would put them both in the sun again," I declared, "bringing fire on us like the fire which Avicus suffered before! Would you end your life's journey in such agony and by another's hands?"

"Please, Marius," said Avicus. "Let me take him away with me. We will go now. I promise you, no more trouble from us."

I turned my back on them. I could hear Mael leaving, but Avicus lingered. And suddenly I felt his arm enclose me and his lips on my cheek.

"Go," I said softly, "before your impetuous friend tries to stab me in base jealousy."

"It was a very great miracle you revealed," he whispered. "Let him ponder it until he has made its greatness small enough for his mind."

I smiled.

"As for me, I don't wish ever to see it again. It is too sad."

I nodded.

"But allow me to come in the evenings, quietly," he whispered. "Allow me to watch at the garden windows in silence as you paint your walls."

8

THE YEARS PASSED too fast.

The great city of Constantinople in the East was all the talk in Rome. More and more of the honorable Patricians were drained away by its magic. Meanwhile after Constantine the Great there came no end of warring Emperors. And the pressure along the borders of the Empire continued to be intolerable, demanding the complete devotion of anyone elevated to the purple.

A most interesting character proved to be Julian, lately known as the Apostate, who tried to restore paganism and completely failed. Whatever his religious illusions, he proved an able soldier and died on a campaign against the irrepressible Persians many miles from home.

The Empire continued to be invaded by the Goths, the Visigoths, the Germans and the Persians on all sides. Its rich and beautiful cities, with their gymnasiums, theaters, porticoes and temples were overrun by tribes of people who cared nothing for philosophy or manners, poetry, or the old values of the genteel life.

Even Antioch, my old home with Pandora, had been sacked by barbarians—quite an unimaginable spectacle to me, which I could not ignore.

Only the city of Rome itself seemed impervious to such a horror, and indeed, I think the old families, even as houses crumbled around them, believed that the Eternal City could never suffer such a fate.

As for me, I went on with my banquets for the disreputable and despised, and I wrote by the hour in my diaries, and I painted my walls.

When my regular guests inevitably died, I suffered it rather dreadfully. And so I saw to it that the company was always very large.

On I went with the pots of paint no matter who drank or vomited in the garden, and so the house seemed mad with all its lamps and the master filling walls with his illusions, and the guests laughing at him and raising their cups to him, and the music strumming on unto the dawn.

At first I thought it would be a distraction to have Avicus spying upon me, but I grew used to hearing him slip over the wall and come into the garden. I grew used to the nearness of someone who shared these moments as only he could.

I continued to paint my goddesses—Venus, Ariadne, Hera—and gradually I grew resigned that the figment of Pandora would dominate everything I did in that particular, but I worked on the gods as well. Apollo, above all, fascinated me. But then I had time to paint other figures of myth, such as Theseus, Aeneas, and Hercules, and sometimes I turned to reading Ovid or Homer or Lucretius directly for inspiration. Other times, I made up my own themes.

But always the painted gardens were my comfort for I felt I was living in them in my heart.

Over and over again I covered all the rooms of my house, and as it was built as a villa, not an enclosed house with an atrium, Avicus could wander the garden all around it, seeing all that I did, and I couldn't help but wonder if my work was changed by what he saw.

What moved me more than anything perhaps was that he lingered so faithfully. And that he was silent with so much respect. Seldom did a week pass that he did not come and stay almost the entire night. Often he was there for four or five nights in a row. And sometimes even longer than that.

Of course we never spoke to each other. There was an elegance in our silence. And though my slaves once took notice of him and annoyed me with their alarm, I soon put a stop to that.

On the nights when I went out to Those Who Must Be Kept Avicus didn't follow me. And I must confess that I did feel a sort of freedom when I painted alone in the shrine. But melancholy was also coming down upon me, harder than ever in the past.

Finding a spot behind the dais and the Precious Pair, I often sat dejected in the corner, and then slept the day and even the next night without going out. My mind was empty. Consolation was unimaginable. Thoughts of the Empire and what might happen to it were unspeakable.

And then, I would remember Avicus, and I would rise, shaking off my languor and go back into the city and begin painting the walls of my rooms again.

How many years passed in this way, I can't calculate.

It is far more important to note that a band of Satanic blood drinkers again took up their abode in an abandoned catacomb and began to feast upon the innocent which was their custom, being desperately careless so as to scare humans and to cause tales of terror to spread.

I had hoped that Mael and Avicus would destroy this band, as they were all very weak, and blundering, and it wouldn't have been hard at all.

But Avicus came to me with the truth of the matter which I should have seen long before.

"Always these Satan worshipers are young," he said to me, "and never is there one who is more than thirty or forty years from his mortal life. Always from the East they come, speaking of how the Devil is their Ruler and how through serving him, they serve Christ."

"I know the old story," I said. I was going about my painting, as if Avicus was not standing there, not out of rudeness, but out of weariness with the Satan worshipers, who had cost me Pandora so long ago.

"But you see, Marius, someone very old must surely be sending these deadly little emissaries to us, and it is this old one whom we must destroy."

"And how will you do that?" I asked.

"We mean to lure him to Rome," said Avicus, "and we've come to ask you to join us. Come down into the catacombs with us tonight and tell these young ones that you are a friend."

"Ah, no, you are mad to suggest this!" I said. "Don't you realize they know about the Mother and the Father? Don't you remember all I've told you?"

"We mean to destroy them to a one," said Mael who stood behind me. "But to make a fine finish we must lure the old one here before the destruction."

"Come, Marius," said Avicus, "we need you and your eloquence. Convince them that you are sympathetic. That they must bring their leader here, and then and only then will you allow them to remain. Mael and I cannot so impress them as you can. This is no vain flattery, be assured."

For a long time I stood with my paintbrush in hand, staring, thinking, Should I do this, and then finally, I confessed that I could not.

"Don't ask it of me," I said to Avicus. "Lure the being yourselves.

And when he comes here, let me know of it, and then I promise I will come."

The following night, Avicus returned to me.

"They are such children, these Satanic creatures," he said, "they spoke of their leader so willingly, admitting that he resides in a desert place in the North of Egypt. He was burnt in the Terrible Fire, no doubt of it, and has taught them all about the Great Mother. It will be sad to destroy them, but they rampage about the city, seeking the sweetest mortals for their victims, and it cannot be borne."

"I know," I said quietly. I felt ashamed that I had always allowed Mael and Avicus to drive these creatures from Rome on their own. "But have you managed to lure the leader out of his hiding place? How could such a thing be done?"

"We have given them abundant riches," said Avicus, "so that they may bring their leader here. We have promised him our strong blood in return for his coming, and that he sorely needs to make more priests and priestesses of his Satanic cause."

"Ah, your strong blood, of course," I said. "Why did I not think of it? I think of it in regard to the Mother and Father, but I did not think of it in relation to us."

"I cannot claim to have thought of it myself," said Avicus. "It was one of the Satanic children who suggested it for the leader is so weak that he can never rise from his bed, and survives only to receive victims and to make followers. Of course Mael and I immediately promised. For what are we to these children with our hundreds of years?"

I heard nothing further of the matter for the next several months, except I knew through the Mind Gift that Avicus had slain several of the Satan worshipers for their public crimes which he considered to be so dangerous, and on one mild summer night, when I stood in my garden looking down over the city, I heard Mael rather distantly arguing with Avicus as to whether they should slay all the rest.

At last the band was slain, and the catacomb was empty, and drenched in blood, and Mael and Avicus appeared at my house and begged me to come to it for those returning from Egypt were expected within the hour and we must strike fast.

I left my warm happy room, carrying my finest weapons, and went with them as I had promised.

The catacomb was so small and tight, I could scarce stand up in it. And I knew it at once to be the burial place of mortal Christians and a place where they had sometimes gathered in the very first years of the sect.

We traveled through it some eighty or ninety feet before we came into an underground place, and there found the old Egyptian blood drinker on his bier, glaring at us, his youthful attendants horrified to find their abode empty and full of ashes of their dead.

The old creature had suffered much. Bald, and thin, black from the Great Fire, he had given himself up utterly to the making of his Satanic children, and so never healed as another blood drinker might. And now he knew himself to be tricked. Those he had sent on to Rome were gone forever, and we stood before him, looking down upon him in judgment, blood drinkers of unthinkable power who felt no pity for him and his cause.

Avicus was the first to raise his sword, but he was stopped as the old creature cried out,

"Do we not serve God?"

"You'll know sooner than I will," Avicus answered him, and with the blade, cut off his head.

The remaining band refused to run away from us. They fell on their knees and met our heavy blows in silence.

And so too it was with the fire that engulfed them all.

The next night and the night after that we went back, the three of us, to gather the remains and burn them over again, until it was finished and we thought that had put an end to the Satanic worshipers once and for all.

Would that it had been so.

I can't say that this awful chapter of our lives brought me together with Avicus and Mael. It was too dreadful, too against my nature, and too bitter for me.

I went back to my house, and gladly resumed my painting.

I rather enjoyed it that none of my guests ever wondered as to my true age, or why I didn't grow old or die. I think the answer lay in the fact that I had so very much company that no one could pay attention to any one thing for very long.

Whatever it was, after the slaughter of the Satanic children, I wanted more music than before, and I painted more relentlessly and with greater invention and design.

Meantime the state of the Empire was dreadful. It was now quite totally divided between East and West. In the West, which included

Rome, of course, Latin was the language; while in the East the common language was Greek. The Christians too felt this sharp division and continued to quarrel over their beliefs.

Finally the situation of my beloved city became intolerable.

The Visigoth Ruler Alaric had taken the nearby port of Ostia, and was threatening Rome itself. The Senate seemed powerless to do anything about the impending invasion, and there was talk throughout the city that the slaves would side with the invaders, thereby bringing ruin on us all.

At last, at midnight, the Salarian gate of the city was opened. There was heard the horrifying sound of a Gothic trumpet. And in came the rapacious hordes of Goths and Scythians to sack Rome herself.

I rushed out into the streets to see the carnage all around me.

Avicus was immediately at my side.

Hurrying across the roofs, we saw everywhere that slaves had risen against their masters, houses were forced open, jewels and gold were offered up by frantic victims, who were nevertheless murdered, rich statues were heaped upon wagons in those streets large enough to allow such, and bodies soon lay everywhere as the blood ran in the gutters and as the inevitable flames began to consume all that they could.

The young and the healthy were rounded up to be sold into slavery, but the carnage was often random, and I soon realized I could do nothing to help any mortal whom I saw.

Returning to my house, I discovered with horror that it was already in flames. My guests had either been taken prisoner or had fled. My books were burning! All my copies of Virgil, Petronius, Apuleius, Cicero, Lucretius, Homer, Pliny were lying helpless amid the flames. My paintings were blackening and disintegrating. Foul smoke choked my lungs.

I had scarce time to grab a few important scrolls. Desperately I sought for Ovid, whom Pandora had so loved, and for the great tragedians of Greece. Avicus reached out his arms to help me. I took more, seeking to save my own diaries, but in that fatal instant Goth soldiers poured into my garden with loud shouts, their weapons raised.

At once I pulled my sword and began with fierce speed to decapitate them, shouting as they shouted, allowing my preternatural voice to deafen them and confuse them, as I hacked off random limbs.

Avicus proved even more fierce than I was, perhaps being more accustomed to this kind of battle, and soon the band lay dead at our feet.

But by now my house was completely engulfed in flames. The few scrolls we'd sought to save were burning. There was nothing more to be done. I could only pray that my slaves had sought some refuge, for if they hadn't they would soon be taken for loot.

"To the chapel of Those Who Must Be Kept," I said. "Where else is there to go?"

Quickly, we made to the roofs again, darting in and out of the blazes which everywhere lighted up the night sky. Rome was weeping; Rome was crying out for pity; Rome was dying. Rome was no more.

We reached the shrine in safety, though Alaric's troops were pillaging the countryside as well.

Going down into the cool confines of the chapel, I lighted the lamps quickly and then I fell down on my knees before Akasha, uncaring of what Avicus might think of such a gesture, and I poured out for her in whispered words the nature of this tragedy which had struck my mortal home.

"You saw the death of Egypt," I said reverently. "You saw it become a Roman province. Well, now Rome dies in its turn. Rome has lasted for eleven hundred years and now it's no more. How will the world survive? Who will tend the thousands of roads and bridges that everywhere bring men and women together? Who will maintain the fabulous cities in which men and women thrive in safe houses, educating their youth to read and write and worship their gods and goddesses with ceremony? Who will drive back these accursed creatures who cannot farm the land which they have burnt and who live only to destroy!"

Of course there was no response from the Blessed Parents.

But I fell forward and my hand went out to touch Akasha's foot. I breathed a deep sigh.

And finally, forgetting all formality, I crept into the corner and sat rather like an exhausted boy.

Avicus came to sit beside me. He clasped my hand.

"And what of Mael?" I asked softly.

"Mael is clever," said Avicus. "Mael loves to fight. He has destroyed many a blood drinker. Mael will never allow himself to be wounded as he was on that long ago night. And Mael knows how to hide when all is lost."

For six nights we remained in the chapel.

We could hear the shouts, the crying, as the looting and pillaging went on. But then Alaric marched out of Rome to wreak havoc on the countryside to the South.

Finally the need for blood caused both of us to go back to the world above.

Avicus bid me farewell and went in search of Mael, while I found myself in the street near my house, coming upon a soldier who was dying with a spear through his chest. He was no longer conscious. I removed the spear, which caused him to moan in his sleep, and then lifting him I opened my mouth over the gushing wound.

The blood was full of scenes of the battle, and quite soon I had enough. I laid him aside, composing his limbs artfully. And then I discovered I was hungry for more.

This time a dying man would not do. I walked on, stepping over rotted and stinking bodies, and passing the gutted ruins of houses, until I found an isolated soldier with a sack of loot over his back. He made to draw his sword, but quickly I overcame him, and bit into his throat. He died too soon for me. But I was satisfied. I let him fall at my feet.

I then came upon my house utterly destroyed.

What a sight was my garden where the dead soldiers lay swollen and reeking.

Not a single book remained unburnt.

And as I wept I realized with a cruel shock that all the Egyptian scrolls I possessed—all the early tales of the Mother and the Father—had perished in the fire.

These were scrolls I had taken from the old temple in Alexandria on the very night I took the Mother and Father from Egypt. These were scrolls which told the old tale of how an evil spirit had entered into the blood of Akasha and Enkil, and how the race of blood drinkers had come about.

All this was gone now. All this was ashes. All this was lost to me along with my Greek and Roman poets and historians. All this was gone along with all that I had written myself.

It seemed quite impossible that such a thing had happened, and I faulted myself that I had not copied the old Egyptian legends, that I had not saved them in the shrine. After all, in some foreign market-place I could find Cicero and Virgil, Xenophon and Homer.

But the Egyptian legends? I would never recover the loss.

I wondered: Would my beautiful Queen care that the written stories of her had perished? Would she care that I alone carried the tales in my mind and heart?

I walked into the ruin of my rooms, and looked at the little that did still appear visible of the paintings on the blackened plaster walls. I looked up through the black timbers which might at any moment fall on me. I stepped over piles of burnt wood.

At last I left the place where I had lived for so long. And as I went about, I came to see that the city was already rising from its punishment. Not all had been put to the torch. Rome was far too huge, with far too many buildings of stone.

But what was it to me, this piteous sight of Christians rushing to help their brethren, and naked children crying for parents who were no more? So Rome had not been razed to the ground. It did not matter. There would come more invasions. These people who remained in the city, struggling to rebuild it, would endure a humiliation which I could not endure.

I went back out to the chapel again. And going down the stairs, and into the sanctum, I lay in the corner, satiated and exhausted, and I closed my eyes.

It was to become my first long sleep.

Always in my life as an immortal I had risen at night and spent the allotted time which the darkness gave to me, either to hunt, or to enjoy whatever distractions or pleasures that I could.

But now I paid no attention to the setting of the sun. I became like you, in your cave of ice.

I slept. I knew I was safe. I knew Those Who Must Be Kept were safe. And I could hear too much of the misery from Rome. So I resolved that I would sleep.

Perhaps I was inspired with the story of the Gods of the Grove, that they could starve in the oak for a month at a time, and still rise to receive the sacrifice. I'm not sure.

I did pray to Akasha. I prayed, "Grant me sleep. Grant me stillness. Grant me immobility. Grant me silence from the voices that I hear so strongly. Grant me peace."

How long was my slumber? Many months. And I began to feel the hunger terribly and to dream of blood. Yet stubbornly I lay on the floor of the shrine, eyes closed during the night when I might have wandered, deaf to intelligence of the outside world.

I could not bear to see my beloved city again. I could think of nowhere to go.

Then a strange moment came. In a dream, it seemed, Mael and Avicus were there, urging me to rise, offering me their blood for strength.

"You're starved, you're weak," said Avicus. How sad he looked. And how gentle he was. "Rome is still there," he maintained. "So it is over-run with Goths and Visigoths. The old Senators remain as always. They humor the crude barbarians. The Christians gather the poor to them and give them bread. Nothing can really kill your city. Alaric is dead, as if he succumbed to a curse for what he did, and his army long gone."

Was I comforted by this? I don't know. I couldn't allow myself to wake. I could not open my eyes. I wanted only to lie where I was and be alone.

They went away. There was nothing more for them to do. And then it seemed that they came at other times, that I would see them by the light of a lamp and that they would talk to me, but it was dreamlike and did not matter at all.

Surely months passed, and then years. I felt light in all my limbs and only the Mind Gift seemed to have strength.

A vision took hold of me. I saw myself lying in the arms of a woman, a beautiful Egyptian woman with black hair. It was Akasha, this woman, and she comforted me, she told me to sleep, and that nothing could hurt me, not even the thirst, because I had drunk her blood. I was not like other blood drinkers. I could starve and then rise again. I would not become fatally weak.

We were in a splendid chamber with silk hangings. We lay on a bed, draped with silk so fine I could see through it. I could see golden columns with lotus leaves at their crowns. I could feel the soft cushions beneath me. But above all I could feel my comforter who held me firmly and warmly and told me to sleep.

After a very long while I rose and went out into the garden and saw that, yes, it was the garden I had painted, only it had been perfected, and I turned round, trying to see the dancing nymphs only they were too quick for me. They were gone before I could see them, and in the distance the singing was too soft for me to hear.

I dreamed of colors. I wanted the pots of paint before me, the pure colors so that I could make the garden come alive.

Yes, sleep.

At last a divine blackness settled over my mind and no thoughts whatsoever could penetrate. I knew that Akasha still held me because I could feel her arms around me and feel her lips against my cheek. That was all I knew.

And the years passed.

The years passed.

Quite suddenly my eyes opened.

A great sense of alarm came over me, giving me to know that I was a living being with a head and arms and legs. I didn't move, but I stared up into the darkness, and then I heard the sound of sharp footfalls, and a light blinded me for a moment.

A voice spoke. It was Avicus.

"Marius, come with us," he said.

I tried to rise from the stone floor but I couldn't do it. I couldn't lift my arms.

Be still, I told myself and think on this matter. Think on what has happened.

In the lamplight, Avicus stood before me once more holding the small flickering bronze lamp. He was dressed in a rich double tunic with an overshirt, rather like a soldier, and the trousers of the Goths.

Mael stood beside him, finely dressed in similar garments, his blond hair swept back and cleanly combed, and all malice was gone from Mael's face.

"We're leaving, Marius," said Mael, his eyes wide and generous. "Come with us. Stop this sleep of the dead and come."

Avicus came down on one knee and put the light behind me so it wouldn't hurt my eyes any longer.

"Marius, we're going to Constantinople. We have our own ship for this journey, our own galley slaves to row it, our own pilot, and well-paid attendants who will not question our nocturnal disposition. You must come with us. There is no reason to remain."

"We must go," said Mael. "Do you know how long you've lain here?"

"Half a century," I said in a small whisper, "and during that time Rome has been laid waste again."

Avicus shook his head. "Far longer than that, old friend," he said, "I can't tell you how many times we've tried to wake you. Marius, the Western Empire is truly no more."

"Come with us to Constantinople," said Mael. "She is the richest city in the world."

"Take my blood," said Avicus and he moved to bite into his wrist to give me to drink. "We can't leave you behind."

"No," I said. "Let me rise of my own accord." I wondered if they could hear my words, so softly were they spoken. I rose slowly on my elbows, and then I realized I was sitting up, and then I rose to my knees and to my feet.

I was dizzy.

My radiant Akasha, so erect on her throne, stared blindly past me. My King was unchanged. However both were covered with a layer of dust, and it seemed a crime unimaginable that they had been so neglected. The withered flowers were like so much hay in their dried vases. But for this who was to blame?

Hesitantly I made my way to the dais. And then I closed my eyes. I felt Avicus catch me as obviously I'd been about to fall.

"Leave me, please," I said quietly. "Just for a little while. I must say my prayers for the comforts I've received while sleeping. I'll join you soon." And vowing to stand more firmly I closed my eyes again.

At once there came into my mind the vision of myself on the opulent bed within the extraordinary palace and Akasha, my Queen, embracing me.

I saw the silk hangings wavering in the breeze. It was not my vision. That is, it had not come from me. Rather it had been given, and I knew it could only have come from her.

I opened my eyes again and stared at her hard perfect face. Surely a woman less beautiful could never have endured so long. No blood drinker had ever had the courage to really destroy her. No blood drinker ever would.

But my thoughts were confused suddenly. Avicus and Mael were still there.

"I'll come with you," I said to them, "but for now, you must leave me here. You must wait for me above."

At last they obeyed. I heard their steps as they went up the stairs.

And then I mounted the steps of the dais and bent over my seated Queen once more, as reverently as ever, as bravely as ever, and I gave the kiss that might soon mean my death.

Nothing stirred in the sanctuary. The Blessed Pair remained quiet. Enkil did not raise his arm to strike. I felt no motion in Akasha's body.

I sank my teeth quickly. I drank deep draughts of the thick blood as fast as I could, and there came the vision of the sunlit garden again, lovely, full of flowering trees and roses, something made for a palace, where every plant is a part of an imperial design. I saw the bedchamber. I saw the golden columns. It seemed I heard a whisper: Marius.

My soul expanded.

I heard it again as if it were echoing through the silk-hung palace. The light in the garden brightened.

Then, with a violent throb I realized I could take no more. I drew back. I saw the tiny puncture wounds contract and vanish. I pressed my lips to them and held the kiss for a long moment.

On my knees I thanked her with my whole heart. I had not the slightest doubt that she had protected me in my sleep. I knew that she had. I knew also that she had caused me to wake. Avicus and Mael could have never done it without her divine intervention. She belonged to me more surely than when we had left Egypt. She was my Queen.

And then I withdrew, powerful, clear-eyed, and ready for the long journey overseas to Byzantium. After all, I had Mael and Avicus to help me with the Divine Parents who must be secured in stone sarcophagi; and there would be many a long night at sea ahead of us during which I could weep for my beautiful Italy, my Italy which was lost.

9

I N T H E N I G H T S that followed I could not resist visiting Rome, though Avicus and Mael both advised me not to do it. They feared that I did not know how long I had slept, but I knew. Almost a hundred years had passed.

I found the grand buildings of Imperial glory fallen to ruin, overrun with animals, and being used as quarries for those who came to take the stone. Huge statues had been toppled over and lay in the weeds. My old street was unrecognizable.

And the population had dwindled to no more than a few thousand souls.

Yet, the Christians ministered to their own, and their virtue was most inspiring. And because the invaders had been in some cases Christians, many of the churches had gone unharmed. The Bishop of Rome sought to defend them against their overlords, and maintained strong ties with Constantinople, the city that ruled both East and West.

But for the few old families who remained, there was only humiliation as they sought to serve their new barbarian masters, and to tell themselves that somehow the crude Goths and Vandals could acquire some polish and love of literature and some appreciation of Roman law.

Once again I marveled at the pure resistance of Christianity, that it seemed to feed upon disaster as it had fed upon persecution, and as it prospered during interludes of peace.

I also marveled at the resilience of the old Patricians, who as I said, did not withdraw from public life, but strove to inculcate the old values as best they could.

Everywhere one saw barbarians with mustaches, wearing crude trousers, their hair greasy and unkempt. Many were Arian Christians, holding different ceremonies from their "orthodox" Catholic brothers and sisters. What were they? Goths, Visigoths, Alemmani, Huns? Some I couldn't recognize at all. And the ruler of this great state lived not at Rome but at Ravenna in the North.

I was also to discover that a new nest of the Satanic vampires had settled in a forgotten catacomb of the city, where they held ceremonies to their Serpent Devil before going out to prey upon the innocent and the guilty alike.

Avicus and Mael, puzzled as to the origins of these new zealots, and most weary of them, had resolved to leave them alone.

As I walked through ruined streets and through empty houses, these zealot creatures spied upon me. I loathed them. But I hardly considered them a danger. In my starvation I had grown strong. Akasha's blood was in my veins.

But how wrong I was in my judgment upon the Satanic vampires, oh, how very wrong indeed. But I will come to that in time.

Let me return to those nights when I wandered the broken fragments of classical civilization.

I was not as embittered by it as one might think. Indeed Akasha's blood had not only given me great new physical power, it had enhanced the clarity of my mind, my ability to concentrate, to take to myself what I prized, and to dismiss what was no longer good.

Nevertheless the state of Rome was demoralizing, and it was only likely to get worse. I looked to Constantinople to preserve what I called civilization and I was all too ready for the voyage ahead.

Well, it was time to help Avicus and Mael with the last preparations. And they assisted me in carefully wrapping the Divine Pair as mummies, with all reverence, and placing them in granite sarcophagi which no team of men could open, as had been done in the past by me, and would be done in the future every time that the Divine Parents had to be moved.

This was most frightening for Avicus and Mael—to see the pair moved and then so completely covered with the white strips of linen. They knew nothing of the old prayers in Egyptian which I recited, which were charms for the safety of the journey scavenged from my years of reading, and I don't think this comforted them. But the Divine Couple were my concern.

As I moved to wrap the eyes of Akasha, she closed them, and with Enkil there occurred the same thing. What a strange and momentary indication of consciousness. It sent a chill through me. Yet still I went about my duty, as if I were an old Egyptian wrapping a deceased Pharaoh in the Sacred House of the Dead.

At last Mael and Avicus accompanied me down to Ostia, the port from which we would sail, and we boarded the vessel, having the Divine Parents placed below deck.

As for the slaves that Avicus and Mael had purchased I found them most impressive, all handpicked and excellent even to the galley slaves who knew that they worked for future freedom in the East and rich rewards.

A strong band of soldiers were to sail with us, each heavily armed, highly skilled and quite convinced of the same promise, and I was particularly impressed by the captain of this vessel, a Christian Roman by the name of Clement, a man of cleverness and wit, who would maintain the faith of the others in the final rewards as we made the long voyage.

The ship itself was the largest galley I had ever beheld, with an immense and colorful sail, and it contained a massive and impregnable cabin containing three long chests modestly made of bronze and iron in which Mael, Avicus and I would sleep by day. These chests, like the sarcophagi, were impossible for mortals to open without enormous difficulty and also they were far too heavy for even a gang of men to lift.

At last everything was in readiness, and armed to the teeth against pirates, we set out by night, guiding the ship with our supernatural eyes from floundering on any rocks as we moved swiftly along the coast.

This frightened our crew and our soldiery somewhat as can be imagined, for in those times ships almost invariably proceeded only by day. It was too dangerous for them to do otherwise, for they couldn't see the coast or the rocky islands they might encounter, and even though they might have good maps and skilled navigators, there was still the danger of a dreadful accident occurring in the dark.

We reversed this age-old wisdom, and by day, our ship was in port so that those who served us might enjoy what the local town had to offer, and our slaves and soldiers were made all the more happy by this, and all the more devoted, while the captain kept a firm grip by allowing only some to go ashore at certain times, and insisting that some remain and keep watch or sleep.

Always we woke and emerged from our cabin to find our servants in high good humor, musicians playing under the moon for the soldiers, and Clement, the captain, delightfully drunk. There was no suspicion among them that we were other than three extremely bizarre human beings of immense wealth. Indeed, sometimes I eavesdropped on their theories about us—that we were Magi from the Far East like unto the Three Kings who had come to lay gifts before the Christ Child, and I was most amused.

Our only real problem was an absurd one. We had to ask for meals to be brought to us, and then to dispense with the food through the windows of our cabin, directly into the sea.

It sent us into peals of laughter, yet I found it undignified.

We did periodically spend a night on shore so that we might feed. Our years had given us great skill in this matter. And we might even have starved for the entire journey, but this we chose not to do.

As for our camaraderie aboard the ship, it was most interesting to me.

I was living more closely with mortals than ever before. I talked with our captain and our soldiers by the hour. And I found I enjoyed it tremendously, and I was very much relieved that, in spite of my very pale skin, it was so easy to do.

I found myself passionately attracted to our Captain Clement. I enjoyed the tales of his youth spent on merchant ships throughout the Mediterranean, and he amused me with descriptions of the ports he'd visited, some of which I had known hundreds of years before, and some of which were wholly new.

My sadness was lifted as I listened to Clement. I saw the world through his eyes, and knew his hope. I looked forward to a lively household in Constantinople where he could call upon me as his friend.

Another great change had taken place. I was now definitely an intimate companion to both Avicus and Mael.

Many a night we spent alone in the cabin, with the full wine cups before us, talking about all that had occurred in Italy and other things as well.

Avicus was of a keen mind as I had always imagined him to be, eager for learning and reading, and had over the centuries taught himself both Latin and Greek. But there was much he didn't understand about my world and its old piety.

He had with him histories by Tacitus, and Livy, and also the True Tales of Lucian, and the biographies written in Greek by Plutarch; but he was not able to understand this work.

I spent many happy hours reading aloud to him as he followed along with me, explaining to him how the text could be interpreted. And I saw in him a great absorption of information. He wanted to know the world.

Mael did not share this spirit; but he was no longer against it as he had been a very long time ago. He listened to all we discussed, and perhaps he profited somewhat from it. It was plain to me that the two—Avicus and Mael—survived as blood drinkers because of each other. But Mael no longer regarded me with fear.

As for me, I rather enjoyed the role of teacher, and it gave me new pleasure to argue with Plutarch as if he were in the room with me, and to comment on Tacitus as if he were there as well.

Both Avicus and Mael had grown paler and stronger with time. Each had, he confessed, at some moment or other felt the threat of despair.

"It was the sight of you, asleep in the shrine," Mael said without enmity, "that kept me from going down into some cellar and resigning myself to the same slumber. I felt I should never awake from it, and Avicus, my companion Avicus, would not allow me to go."

When Avicus had felt weary of the world and unable to continue, it had been Mael who kept him from the fatal sleep.

Both had suffered extreme anguish over my condition, and during the long decades when I lay unresponsive to their pleas, they had been too afraid of the Noble Parents to lay before them flowers, or to burn incense or to do anything to tend the shrine.

"We feared they would strike out at us," said Avicus. "Even to look at their faces filled us with dread."

I nodded to all this.

"The Divine Parents," I said, "have never showed a need of those things. I am the author of such devotions. Darkness may please them as well as burning lamps. Look how they slumber now in their wrappings and in their coffins, side by side beneath the deck."

I felt emboldened by the visions I had had to say these things, though I never spoke of those visions or bragged that I had drunk the Sacred Blood.

All the while we sailed there was the prospect of one great horror which hung over the three of us—that our ship might be attacked either by day or night, and that the Divine Parents might be sunk into the sea. It was far too awful for us to talk of it, and that, perhaps, is why we did not. And whenever I brooded over this, I realized that we should have taken the safer route over land.

Then in the small hours a terrible truth became known to me—that if we did meet disaster, I might rise from the sea, and Those Who Must Be Kept might not. In the mysterious bottom of the great ocean what would become of these Parents? My agony of mind grew too great.

I put aside my anguish. I continued the pleasant talk with my companions. I went out on deck and looked upon the silvery sea and sent my love to Pandora.

Meantime I did not share the enthusiasm of Mael and Avicus for Byzantium. I had lived in Antioch a long time ago, and Antioch was an Eastern city but with great Western influence, and I had left it to return to Rome, for I was a child of the West.

Now we were heading to what I thought to be a purely Eastern capital, and I was afraid that in its great vitality I would find only what I could not possibly embrace.

One must understand: from the Roman point of view, the East— that is, the lands of Asia Minor and Persia—had always been suspect, for their emphasis on luxury and their general softness. It was believed by me and by many Romans that Persia had softened Alexander the Great thereby softening Greek culture. Then Greek culture with its Persian influence had softened Rome.

Of course immense culture and art had come with this softening. Romans embraced Greek knowledge of all sorts.

Nevertheless, I felt, deep in my soul, this age-old suspicion of the East.

Naturally I said nothing to Avicus and Mael. Their enthusiasm for this mighty seat of the Eastern Emperor was something not to be spoilt.

At last after our long voyage, we came early one evening into the shimmering Sea of Marmara and beheld the high ramparts of Constantinople with their myriad torches, and for the first time, I understood the glory of the peninsula which Constantine had chosen so long ago.

Slowly our ship made its way into the magnificent harbor. And I was chosen to be the one to use his "magic" upon the officials of the dock to arrange our arrival and give us time within the port to find some proper lodgings before removing the sacred cargo which we carried, the sarcophagi of venerable ancestors brought back to be buried in their native land. Of course we had mundane questions as to where we might find an agent to help us with our lodgings, and more than one mortal was called to give us advice.

It was a matter of gold and the Spell Gift, and I had no difficulty. And soon we were onshore and ready to explore this mythic place where God had directed Constantine to create the greatest city in the world.

I cannot say I was disappointed that night.

Our first extraordinary surprise was that the merchants of Constantinople were required to put up torches outside their shops so that the streets were beautifully illuminated. And we at once realized that there was a wilderness of great churches for us to explore.

The city held some million inhabitants, and I sensed at once an immense vigor that had gone out of Rome.

I went immediately—leading my two agreeable companions with me—to the great open square called the Augusteum, and where I could gaze on the facade of Hagia Sophia—the Church of the Holy Wisdom—and upon other immense and regal buildings including the splendid public baths of Zeuxippus, which had been decorated with beautifully executed pagan statues taken from various cities of the world.

I wanted to go in all directions at the same time. For here lay the great Hippodrome in which by day thousands witnessed chariot races which were the passion of the populace, and there the indescribably huge and complex royal palace into which we could easily have crept without being seen.

A great street led westward from this square, and constituted the main thoroughfare of the city, in that there were other squares which opened off it, and also other streets, which fed, of course, innumerable lanes.

Mael and Avicus continued to follow me politely as I led them hither and thither, and into the interior of Hagia Sophia to stand between its magnificent walls and beneath its immense dome.

I was overcome by the beauty of the church with its myriad arches and the high ornate and detailed mosaics of Justinian and

Theodora which were unbelievably splendid and glittering in the light of countless lamps.

In the nights to come, there would be no end of splendid adventures. My comrades might tire of this, but I would not. I would penetrate the Imperial Court very soon, using my swiftness and cleverness to go about the palace. And for better or for worse I was in a city that was thriving where I would know the comfort of the proximity of many many human souls.

In the weeks that followed we purchased for ourselves a splendid house, quite well fortified, its garden entirely enclosed, and made for ourselves a secret and safe crypt beneath the mosaic floor.

As for the Divine Parents, I was adamant that they must be hidden some distance from the city. I had already heard plenty about the riots in Constantinople and I wanted the chapel to be safe.

However I could find no old vaults or tombs in the countryside like the old Etruscan tomb I had used outside of Rome. And finally I had no choice but to have a sanctuary built beneath our house by a gang of slaves.

This unnerved me. In Antioch and in Rome, I had created the chapels. Now I must rely upon others. At last I pursued an intricate plan.

I designed a series of overlapping passages leading deep down to a large chamber which would require anyone going there to turn first right, then left, then right, then left again with exceedingly debilitating affect. Then I set pairs of heavy bronze doors at certain intervals, each pair having a heavy bolt.

The thick stone blocking the entrance to this winding and doubling passage was not only disguised as part of the mosaic flooring of the house, but was, as I so often say when describing such things, far too heavy for even a team of mortals to lift. Even the iron grips were so numerous and intricately designed as to seem part of the ornamentation of the overall floor.

Mael and Avicus thought all this quite extreme, but said nothing.

They approved, however, when I had the walls of the chapel covered with gold mosaic of the very kind I saw in all the splendid churches, and the floor laid with the finest marble tile. A broad and gorgeous throne of hammered gold was prepared for the Royal Couple. And lamps were hung from the ceiling on chains.

How was all this work done, you might ask, without compromising the secret of the underground chamber? Did I murder all those who had participated in the creation of this chapel?

No. It was by use of the Spell Gift to confuse those brought to their labor, and by the use at times of simple blindfolds of which the slaves and even the artists could not complain. Gilded words as to "lovers and brides" smoothed over any mortal objections. And money did the rest.

At last came the night when I must take the Royal Parents to their chapel. Avicus and Mael politely confessed that they thought I would want to do this alone.

I had no objections. Like a powerful Christian Angel of Death, I carried first one sarcophagus and then the other down to the fine chapel and set them side by side.

I took the linen wrappings from Akasha first, holding her in my arms as I knelt on the floor. Her eyes were closed. Then quite suddenly, she opened them, looking past me, her expression meaningless and simple as before.

I think I felt a curious deadening disappointment. But I whispered prayers to her to conceal it, as I cleaned away the linen and lifted her, and carried her, my silent bride, and seated her on the throne. There she rested, her clothes rumpled and incomplete, blind as ever, as I took the wrappings from Enkil.

There came the same strange moment when his eyes opened as well.

I dared say nothing aloud to him. I lifted him, found him more pliant, and even almost light, and placed him on the throne beside his queen.

Several nights passed before I could complete their raiment, but it must look perfect to the memories I still had of fine Egyptian garments, and then I sought to locate for them new and interesting jewels. Constantinople was full of such luxuries, and the craftsmen who dealt in them. All of this I did alone and with no difficulty, praying all the while in the most respectful tone.

Finally the chapel was even more beautiful than the first one which I had made in Antioch, and far more lovely than that which had existed outside of Rome. I put in place the usual braziers in which I would burn incense, and I filled the many hanging lamps with sweet-smelling oil.

Only when all this was done did I go back to the matter of the new city, and how things were to be in it, and whether or not Akasha and Enkil were truly safe.

I was very uneasy. I didn't even know the city yet, I realized. I was preoccupied. I wanted to continue visiting the churches and feasting off the beauty of the city; but I did not know whether or not we were the only vampires here.

It seemed extremely doubtful to me. After all, there were other blood drinkers in existence. Why wouldn't they come to the most beautiful city in the world?

As for the Greek quality of Constantinople, I didn't like it. I am rather ashamed to say it, but it was true.

I didn't like that the populace spoke Greek instead of Latin, though I myself could speak Greek very well, of course. And I didn't like all the Christian monasteries in which there seemed a deep mysticism that was more Oriental than Western.

The art I found everywhere was impressive, yes, but it was losing all ties to the classical art of Greece and Rome.

New statues presented men as stocky and crude with very round heads. Eyes were bulbous, faces without expression. And the Ikons or Holy Pictures which had become so common were highly stylized, with scowling faces.

Even the splendid mosaics of Justinian and Theodora—the figures in their long robes floating against the walls of the church—were rigid and dreamlike rather than classical, or beautiful according to standards that I had not learnt.

This was a magnificent place but it was not my place.

For me, there was something inherently repulsive in the gigantic royal palace with its eunuchs and its slaves. When I crept into it and roamed about, visiting its throne rooms, audience halls, gorgeous chapels, immense dining room, and many bedchambers, I saw the licentiousness of Persia, and though I couldn't blame anyone for it, I felt ill at ease.

And the population, though it was huge and vital, could brawl in the streets over the outcome of the chariot races in the Hippodrome, or riot in the very churches, killing one another, over matters of religion as well. In fact, the endless religious quarrels bordered on sheer madness. And doctrinal differences kept the entire Empire in upheaval most of the time.

As for the problems of the Empire's borders they were as continuous as they had been in the time of the Caesars. The Persians perpetually threatened the East and there was simply no end to the barbarians who poured down into the Empire from the West.

Having long identified my own soul with the salvation of the Empire, I felt no consolation in this city. I felt suspicion and profound distaste.

I did however often roam into Santa Sophia to marvel at the enormous dome which seemed to float above with no means of support. Something ineffable had been captured in that grand church which could humble the most proud spirits.

Avicus and Mael were quite happy in this new city. And both seemed absolutely determined that I be their leader, and as I shopped the marketplace for books in the evening, Avicus was eager to join me, and eager for me to read to him what I found.

Meantime I furnished our house comfortably, and hired artisans to paint the walls. I did not want to become lost in my painted gardens again, and when I thought of my lost Pandora my anguish was worse even than before.

Indeed I searched for Pandora. I told Avicus and Mael a few little stories, harmless and unimportant, of my nights with her, but principally of how I had loved her, so that images of her might exist in their minds in so far as they had the power to keep such images alive.

If Pandora roamed these streets, if she came upon my companions perhaps she could divine from them that I was here and wanted so desperately to be reunited with her.

At once I began to acquire a library, buying whole caskets of scrolls and going through them at my leisure. I set up a fine writing desk and began a rather neutral and impersonal diary of my adventures in the old code I had invented before.

We had been in Constantinople less than six months when it became clear to us that other blood drinkers were coming near to our house.

We heard them in the early morning. They came, apparently to hear of us what they could with the Mind Gift and then they rushed away.

"Why have they taken so long?" I demanded. "They've watched us and they've studied us."

"And perhaps they are the reason," said Avicus, "that we've found no Devil worshipers here."

This was perhaps true, for those who spied on us now were not Devil worshipers. We could tell by the bits and pieces of mental imagery which we were able to glean from their minds.

At last they came at early evening and there was no mistaking their polite invitation to us to come with them to visit their mistress.

I went out of our house to greet them and discovered that there were two of them and that they were pale and beautiful boys.

They couldn't have been more than thirteen when they were made, and they had very clear dark eyes, and had short curly black hair. They were dressed in long Eastern robes of the finest decorated cloth, trimmed in a fringe of red and gold. Their under tunics were of silk, and they wore ornate slippers and many jeweled rings.

Two mortals carried the torches for them, and they appeared to be simple and expensive Persian slaves.

One of the radiant young blood drinker boys placed a small scroll in my hands, which I at once opened to read the beautifully written Greek.

"It is the custom before hunting my city to ask permission of me," it said. "Please come to my palace." It was signed, "Eudoxia."

I did not care for the style of this any more than I had cared for the style of anything else in Constantinople. And I cannot say that it surprised me, but then here was an opportunity to speak with other blood drinkers who were not the fanatical worshipers of the Snake and *that opportunity had never come before.*

Also allow me to note that in all my years as a blood drinker, I had not seen any two others who were as fine and elegant and beautiful as these boys.

No doubt the groups of Satan worshipers contained such blood drinkers, with fine faces and innocent eyes, but for the large part, as I have described, it was Avicus and Mael who slew them or came to terms with them, not me. Besides they had always been corrupted by their zeal.

There was something else here.

These boys seemed infinitely more interesting by virtue of their dignity and their adornments, and the courage with which they looked at me. As for the name Eudoxia, I was ultimately more curious than afraid.

"Let me go with you," I said immediately. But the boys gestured that Avicus and Mael should come as well.

"Why is this?" I asked protectively. But at once my companions let me know that they wanted to go too.

"How many are you?" I asked the boys.

"Eudoxia will answer your questions," said the boy who had given me the scroll. "Please do come with us without further conversation. Eudoxia has been hearing of you for some time."

We were escorted a long way through the streets, until finally we came to a quarter of the city even richer than that in which we lived, and to a house much larger even than our own. It had the usual harsh stone facade, enclosing no doubt an inner garden and rich rooms.

During this time, the boy blood drinkers cloaked their thoughts very well, but I was able to divine, perhaps because they wanted me to do, that their names were Asphar and Rashid.

We were admitted to the house by another pair of mortal slaves who guided us into a large chamber completely decorated with gold.

Torches burned all about us, and in the center of the room, on a gilded couch with purple silk pillows there reclined a gorgeous blood drinker woman, with thick black curls not unlike those of the boys who had come to us, though she wore them long and fretted with pearls, her damask robe and under dress of silk as fine as anything I'd seen in Constantinople so far.

Her face was small, oval, and as close to perfection as anything I've ever beheld, even though she bore no resemblance to Pandora who was for me perfection itself.

Her eyes were round and extremely large. Her lips were perfectly rouged, and there came a perfume from her that was no doubt made by a Persian magician to drive us out of our wits.

There were numerous chairs and couches scattered about on the mosaic floor where rampant Grecian goddesses and gods were as tastefully represented as they might have been some five hundred years before. I saw similar images on the walls surrounding us, though the slightly crude but ornate columns seemed of later design.

As for the vampire woman's skin it was perfectly white, and so totally without a touch of humanity that it sent a chill through me. But her expression, which manifested itself almost entirely by a smile, was cordial and curious in the extreme.

Still leaning on her elbow, her arm covered in bracelets, she looked up at me.

"Marius," she said in cultured and perfect Latin, her voice as lovely as her face, "you read my walls and floor as though they were a book."

"Forgive me," I said. "But when a room is so exquisitely decorated, it seems the polite thing to do."

"And you long for old Rome," she said, "or for Athens, or even for Antioch where you once lived."

This was a formidable blood drinker. She'd plucked this knowledge of me from the deepest of my memories. I closed my mind. But I didn't close my heart.

"My name is Eudoxia," she said. "I wish I could say that I bid you welcome to Constantinople, but it is my city and I am not altogether pleased that you are here."

"Can we not come to some understanding with you?" I asked. "We've made a long and arduous journey. The city is vast."

She made some small gesture, and the mortal slaves withdrew. Only Asphar and Rashid remained, as if waiting for her command.

I tried to tell if there were other blood drinkers in this house, but I couldn't do this without her knowing I was doing it, and so my attempt was rather weak.

"Sit down, all of you, please," she said. And at that invitation, the two beautiful boys, Asphar and Rashid, made to bring the couches in closer so that we might gather in a natural way.

At once I asked if I might have a chair. And Avicus and Mael in an uncertain whisper echoed the same request. It was done. We were seated.

"An old Roman," she said with a sudden luminous smile. "You disdain a couch, and would have a chair."

I laughed a small courteous laugh.

But then something quite invisible yet strong caused me to cast a glance at Avicus and to see that he was staring at this splendid female blood drinker as though Cupid had just sent an arrow right into his heart.

As for Mael, he glared at her as he had glared at me in Rome many centuries before.

"Don't worry about your friends," said Eudoxia suddenly, startling me completely. "They're loyal to you and will follow you in whatever you say. It's you and I who must talk now. Understand that though this city is immense and there is blood enough for many, rogue blood drinkers come here often and must be driven away."

"Are we rogues?" I asked gently.

I couldn't help but study her features, her rounded chin with its single dimple, and her small cheeks. She appeared as young in mortal years as the two boys. As for her eyes they were jet black, with such a fringe of lashes that one might suspect there was Egyptian paint on her face when in fact there was none.

This observation put me suddenly in mind of Akasha, and I felt a panic as I tried to clear my mind. What had I done bringing Those Who Must Be Kept here? I should have stayed in the ruins of Rome. But again, I could not think on this matter now.

I looked directly at Eudoxia, a bit dazzled by the countless jewels of her robe, and the vision of her sparkling fingernails, far brighter than any I'd ever beheld except those of Akasha, and I gathered my strength again and tried to penetrate her mind.

She smiled sweetly at me, and then she said, "Marius, I am far too old in the Blood for what you mean to do, but I will tell you anything you want to know."

"May I call you by the name you've given us?" I asked.

"That was my intent," she replied, "in giving you the name. But let me tell you, I expect honesty from you; otherwise, I will not tolerate you in my realm."

I suddenly felt a wave of anger emanating from Mael. I threw a warning glance to him, and once again I saw that totally entranced expression on the face of Avicus.

I realized suddenly that Avicus had probably never beheld such a blood drinker as this. The young women blood drinkers among the worshipers of Satan were deliberately dirty and disheveled, and here, reclining on her magnificent couch lay a woman who looked like the Empress who reigned over Byzantium.

Indeed, perhaps this was how this creature perceived herself.

She smiled as though all these thoughts were transparent to her, and then with a little movement of her hand she told the two blood drinker boys, Asphar and Rashid, to withdraw.

Then her eyes passed very calmly and slowly over my two companions as though she were drawing from them every single coherent thought which had ever passed through their minds.

I continued my study of her, of the pearls in her hair, and the ropes of pearls about her neck, and the jewels that adorned her naked toes as well as her hands.

At last, she looked to me, and a smile spread itself once more on her features, brightening her entire countenance.

"If I grant you permission to stay—and I am not at all sure that I mean to do it—you must show me loyalty when others come to break the peace that we share. You must never side with them against me. You must keep Constantinople only for us."

"And just what will you do if we don't show you loyalty?" asked Mael with his old anger.

She remained staring at me for a long moment, as though to insult him, and then as though rousing herself from a spell, she looked at Mael.

"What can I do," she asked Mael, "to silence you before you say something foolish again?" Then her eyes returned to me. "Let me make this known to you all. I know that you possess the Mother and the Father. I know that you brought them here for safekeeping and that they are in a chapel deep beneath your house."

I was brutally stunned.

I felt a wave of grief. Once again, I had failed to keep the secret. Even in Antioch long ago, I had failed to keep the secret. Would I not always fail to keep the secret? Was this not my fate? What was to be done?

"Don't be so quick to draw back from me, Marius," said Eudoxia. "I drank from the Mother in Egypt centuries before you took her away."

This statement stunned me all the more. Yet it held some strange promise. It cast a small light into my soul.

I was wondrously excited suddenly.

Here was one who understood everything about the ancient mysteries, just as Pandora had understood. This one, delicate of face and speech, was a world apart from either Avicus or Mael, and how gentle and reasonable she seemed.

"I'll tell you my story if you want it, Marius," she said. "I have always been a worldly blood drinker, never one given to the old religion of the Blood Gods of Egypt. I was three hundred years old in the Blood before you were born. But I'll tell you all you want to know. It is plain that you move through the world by means of questions."

"Yes," I said. "I do move through the world by means of questions, and too often I've asked those questions in utter silence, or long centuries ago of people who gave me answers that were fragments which I had to piece together as though they were bits of old papyri. I hunger for knowledge. I hunger for what you mean to say to me."

She nodded and this seemed to give her extraordinary pleasure.

"Some of us don't require intimate understanding," she said. "Do you require it, Marius? I can read much in your thoughts, but this is a puzzle. Must you be understood?"

I was baffled.

"Must I be understood," I said, thinking it over, as secretly as I might. Did either Avicus or Mael understand me? No, they did not. But once long long ago the Mother had understood me. Or had she? Just possibly when I'd fallen so in love with her, I had understood her.

"I don't have an answer for you," I said softly. "I think I have come to enjoy loneliness. I think when I was mortal I loved it. I was the wanderer. But why do you put this question to me?"

"Because I don't require understanding," she said, and for the first time there came a cold tone into her voice. "But if you wish it, I'll tell you about my life."

"I want so much to hear your story," I answered. I was infatuated. Again, I thought of my beautiful Pandora. Here was an incomparable woman who seemed to have the same gifts. I wanted so to listen to her, and it was more than essential for our safety that I listen to her. But how could we deal with the uneasiness of Mael, and the obvious obsession of Avicus?

She took the thought from me immediately, looking at Avicus gently and then turning her attention for a long sober moment on the infuriated Mael.

"You were a priest in Gaul," she said calmly to him, "yet you have the attitude of a dedicated warrior. You would destroy me. Why is this so?"

"I don't respect your authority here," Mael answered, trying to match her quiet tone. "Who are you to me? You say you never respected the old religion. Well, I respected it. And Avicus respected it. Of this we're proud."

"We all want the same thing," she answered. She smiled, revealing her fang teeth. "We want a hunting ground which is not overcrowded. We want the Satanic blood drinkers to be kept out for they multiply insanely and seek to foment trouble in the mortal world. My authority rests on my past triumphs. It's no more than habit. If we can make a peace . . ." She broke off and in the manner of a man she shrugged her shoulders and opened her hands.

Suddenly Avicus broke in.

"Marius speaks for us," he said. "Marius, make the peace with Eudoxia, please."

"We give you our loyalty," I said, "in so far as we do want the same things, as you've described. But I want very much to speak with you. I want to know how many blood drinkers are here now. As for your history, let me say again that I do want to hear it. One thing we can give to each other is our history. Yes. I want to know yours."

She rose from the couch very gracefully, revealing herself to be a little taller than I had supposed. She had rather broad shoulders for a woman, and she walked very straight, her bare feet not making the slightest sound.

"Come into my library," she said, leading us into a chamber off the main room. "It's better for talking, I believe." Her hair was long down her back, a heavy mass of black curls, and she moved gracefully despite the weight of her beaded and decorated robes.

The library was immense, with shelves for scrolls and codexes, that is, bound volumes such as we have today. There were chairs here and there, and some gathered in the center, and two couches for reclining and tables on which to write. The golden lamps looked Persian to me in their heavy worked designs, but I couldn't be certain of it.

The carpets strewn about were definitely Persian, that much I knew.

Of course the moment I saw the books, I was overcome with pleasure. This always happens with me. I remembered the library in old Egypt in which I had found the Elder who had put the Mother and Father into the sun. I feel foolishly safe with books which can be a mistake.

I thought of all that I had lost in the first siege of Rome. I couldn't help but wonder what Greek and Roman authors were here preserved. For the Christians, though they were kinder to the ancients than people now believe, did not always save the old works.

"Your eyes are hungry," she said, "though your mind is shut. I know you want to read here. You're welcome. Send your scribes to copy what you will. But I go ahead of myself, don't I? We must talk. We must see if we can achieve an agreement. I don't know that we can."

She turned her eyes to Avicus.

"And you, you who are old, you who were given the Blood in Egypt, you are only just learning to love the realm of letters. How strange that it would take you so long."

I could feel his immense excitement and tender confusion.

"I'm learning," he said. "Marius is teaching me." And then the flame rose in his cheeks.

As for Mael, I couldn't help but note his quiet fury, and it struck me that he had for so long been the author of his own unhappiness, but now something was truly happening which might be a legitimate cause of his pain.

Of course it greatly distressed me that neither of them could keep their minds secret. Long ago in Rome when I had sought to find them they had done a better job of it.

"Let's be seated," said Eudoxia, "and let me tell you who I am."

We took the chairs, which brought us closer together, and she began to tell her story in a quiet tone.

10

"**M**Y MORTAL LIFE isn't very important," she said, "but I'll pass over it quickly. I was from a fine Greek family, one of the first wave of settlers to come from Athens to Alexandria to make it the great city that Alexander wanted when he founded it three hundred years before the birth of the Christ.

"I was brought up like any girl in such a Greek household, extremely protected, and never leaving the house. I did however learn to read and write, because my father wanted me to be able to write letters to him after I was married and he thought that I might read poetry to my children later on.

"I loved him for it, though no one else did, and I took to my education with a passion, neglecting all else.

"An early marriage was prepared for me. I wasn't fifteen when I was told of it, and frankly I was rather happy about it because I had seen the man, and I'd found him intriguing and somewhat strange. I wondered if marriage to him wouldn't bring a new existence for me, something more interesting than what I'd had at home. My real mother was dead and I didn't care for my stepmother. I wanted to be out of her house."

She paused for a moment and I was of course calculating. She was older than me by many years, she was making that plain to me, twice over, and that is why she appeared so utterly perfect. Time had done its work on the lines of her face, as it was doing its work on my own.

She watched me and hesitated for a moment, but then she went on:

"A month before the nuptials, I was abducted right out of my bed at night, and taken over the walls of the house to a dark and filthy place where I was flung down in the corner, to cower on the stone floor while several men carried on a crude argument, as to who would be paid how much for having stolen me.

"I expected to be murdered. I also knew that my stepmother was behind my ruin.

"But there came into the place a tall thin man with a head of shaggy black hair, and a face and hands as white as the moon, who murdered all of these men, throwing them about as if they were weightless, and holding the last up to his mouth for a long time, as though he were drinking blood from the corpse, or eating part of it.

"I thought I was on the verge of madness.

"As he dropped the body, the white-faced being realized that I was staring at him. I had nothing but a torn and dirty night dress to cover me. But I rose to my feet to face him bravely.

" 'A woman,' he said. I shall never forget. 'A woman' as if that were remarkable."

"Sometimes, it is," I said.

She smiled at me rather tolerantly. She went on with the story.

"After this remark, he gave a strange little laugh and then he came for me.

"Once again, I expected to be murdered. But he made me a blood drinker. There was no ceremony to it, no words, nothing. He simply did it, right then and there.

"Then ripping off the tunic and sandals from one of the men, he dressed me crudely as a boy and we hunted the streets together for the rest of the night. He handled me roughly as we went along, turning me this way and that, pushing me, instructing me as much with shoves as with crude words.

"Before dawn, he took me back to his curious dwelling. It wasn't in the elite Greek quarter where I had been brought up. But I didn't know that at the time. As a matter of fact, I'd never been out of my father's house. My first experience of the city streets had been frankly enthralling.

"Now here I was being carried up the high wall of a three-story dwelling and then brought down into its barren courtyard.

"The place was an immense and disorderly treasure house. In every room there were riches unimaginable.

" 'See, all this!' the blood drinker said to me proudly.

"There was chaos everywhere. There were silk draperies in heaps and beautiful cushions, and these he brought together to make a kind of nest for us. He put heavy necklaces on me and said, 'These will lure your victims. Then you can quickly take hold of them.'

"I was intoxicated and afraid.

"Then he took out his dagger and, grabbing me by the hair, he cut it off, almost all of it, and that sent me into wailing like nothing that had gone before. I had killed. I had drunk blood. I had run through the streets half mad. That did not make me bellow, but the cutting of my hair was too much.

"He didn't seem at all disturbed by my crying, but quite suddenly he snatched me up, and threw me down into a large casket on a hard bed of jewels and gold chains and he shut the lid on me. Little did I know the sun was rising. Again, I thought I would die.

"But next I opened my eyes, he was there, smiling, and in a gruff voice, with no real wit or talent for a turn of phrase he explained that we must sleep all day away from the sun. It was our nature. And we had to drink plenty of blood. Blood was the only thing that mattered to us.

"Maybe to you, I thought, but I didn't dare argue with him.

"And my hair of course had all grown back as it would every day forever, and he once again hacked it off. Within a few nights, to my relief he did acquire an expensive scissors to make this operation easier, but he, no matter what we had to do, would never tolerate my long locks.

"I was with him several years.

"He was never civil or kind, but never terribly cruel either. I was never out of his sight. When I asked if we might acquire better clothes for me, he agreed, though he obviously didn't care too much about it. As for himself, he wore a long tunic and a cloak, changing only when these became worn, stealing the fresh clothing from one of his victims.

"He often patted me on the head. He had no words for love, and he had no imagination. When I brought back books from the market to read poetry, he laughed at me, if you can call the toneless noise he made a laugh. I read the poetry to him nevertheless, and much of the time after the initial laugh he simply stared at me.

"Once or twice I asked him how he'd been made a blood drinker, and he said it was by a wicked drinker of the blood who had come out of Upper Egypt. 'They're all liars, those old ones,' he said. 'I call them the Temple Blood Drinkers.' And that constituted the entire history he bequeathed to me.

"If I went against him in any particular, he hit me. It wasn't a terribly hard blow, but it was enough to stop me from ever opposing him on any count.

"When I tried to put the household in some sort of order, he stared at me dully, never offering to help but never striking me either. I rolled out some of the Babylonian rugs. I put some of the marble statues along the wall so that they looked respectable. I cleaned up the courtyard.

"Now during this time, I heard other blood drinkers in Alexandria. I even glimpsed them, but never did they come very close.

"When I told him about them, he only shrugged and said that they were no worry of mine. 'I'm too strong for them,' he told me, 'and besides they don't want any trouble. They know that I know too much about them.' He didn't explain further, but he told me I was very blessed in that he'd given me old blood.

"I don't know what kept me so happy during that time. Perhaps it was hunting different parts of Alexandria, or just reading new books, or swimming in the sea. He and I did go out together and swim in the sea.

"I don't know if you can imagine this—what the sea meant to me, that I might bathe in it, that I might walk along the shore. A closeted Greek housewife would never have that privilege. And I was a blood drinker. I was a boy. I hunted the ships in the harbor. I walked with brave and evil men.

"One night my Maker failed to cut off my hair, as was the evening custom, and he took me to a strange place. It was in the Egyptian quarter of the city, and once we opened the door, we had to follow a long descending tunnel, before we came into a great room covered with the old picture writing of Egypt. There were huge square pillars supporting the ceiling. It was rather an awe-inspiring place.

"I think it brought to memory a more refined time to me, when I had known things of mystery and beauty, though I cannot now really say.

"There were several blood drinkers there. They were pale and appeared extremely beautiful, but nothing as white as my Maker and they were clearly afraid of him. I was quite astonished to see all this. But then I remembered his phrase, 'Temple Blood Drinkers,' and I thought, So we are with them.

"He pushed me forward as a little miracle which they had not beheld. There was a quarrel then in their language, which I could just barely understand.

"It seemed they told him that the Mother would make the decision, and then and only then could he be forgiven for his ways. As for him, my Maker, he said that he didn't care whether or not he was forgiven, but he was going off now, and he wanted to be rid of me and if they would take me, that was all he wanted to know.

"I was terrified. I didn't entirely like this gloomy place, grand though it was. And we had spent several years together. And now he was leaving?

"I wanted to ask him, What had I done? I suppose I realized in that moment that I loved him. I would do anything if he would only change his mind.

"The others fell upon me. They took hold of me by both arms and dragged me with unnecessary force into another gigantic room.

"The Mother and the Father were there, resplendent and shining, seated on a huge throne of black diorite, above some six or seven marble steps.

"This was the main room of a temple, and all its columns and walls were decorated beautifully with the Egyptian writing, and the ceiling was covered with plates of gold.

"Naturally I thought, as we all do, that the Mother and the Father were statues, and as I was dragged closer to them, I was mad with resentment that such a thing was taking place.

"I was also curiously ashamed, ashamed that I wore old sandals and a dirty boyish tunic, and that my hair was tumbled down all around me—for on this one night my Maker had failed to hack it off—and I was in no way prepared for what ritual was to take place.

"Akasha and Enkil were of the purest white, and they sat as they have always done, since I have come to know them—as they sit in your underground chapel now."

Mael broke the narrative with an angry question:

"How do you know how the Mother and Father appear in our underground chapel?"

I was deeply disturbed that he had done this.

But Eudoxia remained utterly composed.

"You have no power to see through the minds of other blood drinkers?" she asked. Her eyes were hard, perhaps even a little cruel.

Mael was confused.

And I was keenly aware that he had given away a secret to Eudoxia, the secret being that he didn't have such a power, or that he didn't know that he did, and I wasn't quite sure what I should do.

Understand he knew that he could find other blood drinkers by hearing their thoughts, but he didn't know how to use this power to even greater advantage, seeing what they saw.

Indeed, all three of us were uncertain of our powers. And I realized how foolish this was.

At this moment, when Eudoxia received no answer to her question, I tried vainly to think of some way to distract her.

"Please," I said to Eudoxia, "will you continue? Tell us your story." I didn't dare to apologize for Mael's rudeness because that might have made him furious.

"Very well," said Eudoxia looking straight at me as though she were dismissing my companions as impossible.

"As I was telling you," she said, "My Maker pushed me forward and told me to kneel before the Father and the Mother. And being exceedingly frightened, I did as I was told.

"I looked up at their faces, as blood drinkers have done since time immemorial and I saw no vitality, no subtlety of expression, only the relaxation of dumb animals, no more.

"But then there came a change in the Mother. Her right hand was raised ever so slightly from her lap and it turned and thereby made the simplest beckoning gesture to me.

"I was astonished by this gesture. So these creatures lived and breathed? Or was it trickery, some form of magic? I didn't know.

"My Maker, ever so crude even at this sacred moment, said, 'Ah, go to her, drink her blood. She is the Mother of us all.' And with his bare foot, he kicked me. 'She is the First One,' he said. 'Drink.'

"The other blood drinkers began to quarrel with him fiercely, speaking the old Egyptian tongue again, telling him that the gesture wasn't clear, that the Mother might destroy me, and who was he to give such a command, and how dare he come to this temple with a pitiful female blood drinker who was as soiled and untutored as he was.

"But he overrode them. 'Drink her blood and your strength will be beyond measure,' he said. Then he lifted me to my feet and all but threw me forward so that I landed with my hands on the marble steps before the throne.

"The other blood drinkers were shocked by his behavior. I heard a low laugh from my Maker. But my eyes were on the King and the Queen.

"I saw that the Queen had moved her hand again, opening her fingers, and though her eyes never changed, the beckoning gesture was certain.

" 'From her neck,' said my Maker. 'Don't be afraid. She never destroys those whom she beckons. Do as I say.' And I did.

"I drank as much from her as I was able to drink. And mark my words, Marius, this was over three hundred years before the Elder ever put the Mother and Father in the Great Fire. And I was to drink from her more than once. Heed my words, more than once, long before you ever came to Alexandria, long before you took our King and Queen."

She raised her dark black eyebrows slightly as she looked at me, as though she wanted me to understand her point most keenly. She was very very strong.

"But Eudoxia, when I did come to Alexandria," I answered her. "When I came in search of the Mother and Father, and to discover who had put them in the sun, you weren't there in the temple. You weren't in Alexandria. At least you didn't make yourself known to me."

"No," she said, "I was in the city of Ephesus where I had gone with another blood drinker whom the Fire destroyed. Or I should say, I was making my way home to Alexandria, to find the reason for the Fire, and to drink of the healing fount, when you took the Mother and Father away."

She gave me a delicate but cold smile.

"Can you imagine my anguish when I discovered that the Elder was dead and the temple was empty? When the few survivors of the temple told me that a Roman named Marius had come and stolen our King and Queen?"

I said nothing, but her resentment was plain. Her face displayed its human emotions. A shimmer of blood tears rose in her round dark eyes.

"Time has healed me, Marius," she said, "because I contain a great deal of the Queen's blood, and was from the moment of my making very strong. Indeed, the Great Fire only turned me a dark brown color, with small pain. But if you hadn't taken Akasha away from Alexandria, she would have let me drink her blood again, and I would have been healed quickly. It would not have taken so long."

"And would you drink the Queen's blood now, Eudoxia?" I asked. "Is that what you mean to do? For surely you know why I did what I did. Surely you know it was the Elder who put the Mother and the Father in the sun."

She didn't answer. I couldn't tell whether this information surprised her or not. She was perfectly concealed. Then she said:

"Do I need the blood now, Marius? Look at me. What do you see?"

I hesitated to answer. Then I did:

"No, you don't need it, Eudoxia," I said. "Unless such blood is always a blessing."

She looked at me for a long moment and then she nodded her head slowly, almost drowsily and her dark eyebrows came together in a small frown.

"Always a blessing?" she asked, repeating my words. "I don't know if it is always a blessing."

"Will you tell me more of your story? What happened after you first drank from Akasha? After your Maker went his way?" I put these questions gently. "Did you reside in the temple once your Maker had left?"

This seemed to give her the moment of recollection that she required.

"No, I didn't remain there," she said. "Though the priests coaxed me, telling me wild stories of old worship, and that the Mother was imperishable, save from the sunlight, and should she ever burn, so would we all. There was one among them who made quite a point of this warning, as though the prospect tantalized him—."

"The Elder," I said, "who eventually sought to prove it."

"Yes," she said. "But to me he was no Elder, and I did not heed his words.

"I went out, free of my Maker, and, left with his house and his treasure, I decided upon another way of life. Of course the temple priests often came to me and harried me that I was profane and reckless, but as they did no more than that, I paid them no heed.

"I could easily pass for human then, especially if I covered my skin with certain oils." She sighed. "And I was used to passing for a young man. It was a simple matter for me to make a fine household, to acquire good clothes, that is, to pass from poor to rich in a matter of nights.

"I gave out word in the schools and in the marketplace that I could write letters for people, and that I could copy books, and all this by night when the other copyists had quit and gone home. And arranging a big study in my house, with plenty of light, I set to doing this for human beings, and this was how I came to know them, and came to know what the teachers were teaching by day.

"What an agony it was that I couldn't hear the great philosophers who held forth in the daylight hours, but I did very well with this nocturnal occupation, and I had what I wanted, the warm voices of humans speaking to me. I befriended mortals. And on many an evening my house was filled with banqueting guests.

"I learned of the world from students, poets, soldiers. In the small hours, I slipped into the great library of Alexandria, a place that you should have visited, Marius. It is a wonder that you passed over such a treasure house of books. I did not pass it over."

She paused. Her face was horridly blank, and I knew it was from an excess of emotion. She did not look at any of us.

"Yes, I understand this," I said, "I understand it very very deeply. I feel the same need for mortal voices near me, for mortals smiling on me as though I were their own."

"I know your loneliness," she said in a rather hard voice. And for the first time I had the feeling that the passing expressions on her face were hard as well, that her face was nothing but a beautiful shell for a disturbed soul inside her, of which I knew little from her words.

"I lived well and for a long time in Alexandria," she said. "What greater city was there? And I believed as many blood drinkers do that knowledge alone would sustain me over the decades, that information could somehow stave off despair."

I was quite impressed with these words, but I didn't respond.

"I should have remained in Alexandria," she said, looking off, her voice low and suddenly full of regret. "I began to love a certain mortal, a young man who felt great love for me. One night he made his love known to me, that he would give up all for me—his proposed marriage, his family, all—if only I would go away with him to Ephesus, the place from which his family had come, and where he wanted to return."

She broke off as if she did not mean to go on.

"It was such love," she said, her words coming more slowly, "and all this while he believed that I was a young man."

I said nothing.

"The night he declared his love, I revealed myself. He was quite horrified by the pretense. And I took my revenge." She frowned as though she wasn't quite sure of the word. "Yes," she said, "my revenge."

"You made him a blood drinker," I said softly.

"Yes," she said, still looking off as though she were back in those times. "I did, and by the most brutal and ungraceful force, and once that was done, he saw me with naked and loving eyes."

"Loving eyes?" I repeated.

She looked pointedly at Avicus and then back to me. Then she looked at Avicus again.

I took my measure of him. I had always thought him rather splendid, and assumed from his beauty that the Gods of the Grove were chosen for their beauty as well as their endurance, but I tried to see him as she saw him now. His skin was golden now, rather than brown, and his thick black hair made a dignified frame for his unusually beguiling face.

I looked back to Eudoxia and saw with a little shock that she was looking at me.

"He loved you again?" I asked, locking in immediately upon her story and its meaning. "He loved you even when the Blood flowed in his veins?"

I could not even guess her inner thoughts.

She gave me a grave nod. "Yes, he loved me again," she said. "And he had the new eyes of the Blood, and I was his teacher, and we all know what charm lies in all that." She smiled bitterly.

A sinister feeling came over me, a feeling that something was very wrong with her, that perhaps she was mad. But I had to bury this feeling within me and I did.

"Off we went to Ephesus," she said, going on with her story, "and though it was no match for Alexandria, it was nevertheless a great Greek city, with rich trade from the East, and with pilgrims always coming for the worship of the great goddess Artemis, and there we lived until the Great Fire."

Her voice became small. Mortals might not have heard it.

"The Great Fire destroyed him utterly," she said. "He was just that age when all the human flesh was gone from him, and only the blood drinker remained, but the blood drinker had only just begun to be strong."

She broke off, as though she could not continue, then she went on:

"There were only ashes left to me of him. Ashes and no more."

She fell silent and I dared not encourage her.

Then she said:

"I should have taken him to the Queen before I ever left Alexandria. But you see, I had no time for the temple blood drinkers and when I had gone to them, it was as a rebel, talking my way in proudly with tales of the Queen's gestures to me so that I might lay flowers before her, and what if I had brought my lover, and the Queen had made no such gesture as that which she had made to me? And so, you see, I had not brought him, and there in Ephesus, I stood with the ashes in my hands."

I remained silent out of respect for her. I couldn't help but glance at Avicus again. He was all but weeping. She had possession of him, heart and soul.

"Why did I go back to Alexandria after this terrible loss?" she asked wearily. "Because the temple blood drinkers had told me that the Mother was the Queen of all. Because they had spoken of the sun and of our burning. And I knew that something must have befallen our Mother, something had caused this Great Fire, and that only those in the temple would know what it was. And there was a pain in my flesh, by no means unbearable, but something which I would have healed by the Mother, if I had found her there."

I said nothing.

In all the years since I'd taken Those Who Must Be Kept, I had never come upon such a creature as this woman. And I should say as well that never had such a blood drinker come upon me.

Never had anyone come armed with such eloquence, or history, or old poetry such as this.

"For centuries," I said, my voice low and gentle, "I kept the Mother and Father in Antioch. Other blood drinkers found me—warlike and violent creatures, creatures badly burnt and bound upon stealing the strong blood. But you, you never came."

She shook her head in negation.

"Never did Antioch enter my thoughts," she confessed. "I believed that you had taken the Mother and Father to Rome. Marius, the Roman, that is what they called you. Marius, the Roman, has taken the Mother and the Father. And so you see, I made a severe error in going to the Imperial City, and after that I went to Crete, and I was never to be close to you, never to find you by the Mind Gift, never to hear tell of where you might be.

"But I was not always searching for the Mother and Father," she said. "I had my passions. I made blood drinkers to be my companions. The centuries healed me as you have seen. I am now far stronger than you are, Marius. I am infinitely stronger than your companions. And though touched by your fine Patrician manners and your old-fashioned Latin, and by the devotion of your friend, Avicus, I must lay down for you some hard terms."

"How so, Eudoxia?" I asked calmly.

Mael was in a rage.

She was quiet for a long moment, during which her small delicate features wore nothing but an expression of sweetness and kindness, and then she said with courtesy:

"Give over the Mother and Father to me, Marius, or I shall destroy you and your companions. You will not be allowed either to stay or to go."

I could see the shock in Avicus. As for Mael he was, thank the gods, dumbfounded. And as for me, I was again stunned.

I waited several moments, and then I asked:

"Why do you want the Mother and Father, Eudoxia?"

"Oh, Marius," she shook her head crossly, "don't play the fool. You know the Mother's blood is the strongest. I've already told you that every time I ever appealed to her, she gave me the welcoming gesture, and allowed me to drink. I want her because I want the power in her. And also because I would not have this King and Queen, who can be burnt again or put in the sun, given over to others who might do such rash things."

"Have you thought this through?" I asked coldly. "How would you keep the shrine secret? From what I've seen of your blood drinker companions, they are almost children both in mortal years and in the Blood. Do you know the weight of this burden?"

"I knew it before you ever existed," she said, her face suffused with anger. "You play with me, Marius. And I won't have it. I know what's in your heart. You won't give up the Mother because you won't give up the blood."

"Perhaps so, Eudoxia," I said, straining to remain civil. "I want time to consider what has been said here."

"No, I give you no time," she said, her voice angry, a blush coming to her cheeks. "Answer me now, or I destroy you."

Her rage was so sudden it caught me off guard. Yet quickly, I recovered.

"And how do you mean to do this?" I asked.

Mael jumped to his feet, and moved behind his chair. I gestured for him to be still. Avicus sat in mute despair. The blood tears had begun to flow from him, and they moved down his face. He was far more disappointed than fearful. In fact, he seemed rather solemnly brave.

Eudoxia turned to Avicus, and at once I sensed a threat in her posture. Her limbs stiffened, and it seemed that her eyes became unusually hard. She meant to do something evil to Avicus, and there was no time for me to wait and see what that might be.

I rose, and rushing at her, took hold of her by both wrists, turning her so that inevitably and furiously she looked up at me.

Of course this physical strength could accomplish little here, but what more could I do? What had my powers become over these years? I didn't know. But there was no time to ponder or experiment. I summoned, from the very depths of my being, all the destructive force I might possess.

I felt a pain in my belly and then in my head, and while Eudoxia went limp in my grasp, with her eyes closed, I felt a dreadful heat come full force against my face and chest. But I was not burnt by it. I repelled it and drove it back whence it had come.

In sum, this was a battle, and I had no idea who might win it. I sought again to bring all the force that I could command into action and again I saw her weaken, felt her weaken, and yet there came the heat once more against me but it had no effect.

I threw her down on the marble floor and I stood over her, gathering the force with all my will and directing it towards her, and she writhed on the marble, her eyes closed, and her hands shuddering. My force held her pinioned. My force would not let her rise.

At last she went still. She breathed deeply and then she opened her eyes, and she looked up at me.

Out of the corner of my eye I saw her acolytes Asphar and Rashid coming to assist her. Both brandished huge glittering swords. I looked desperately about for one of the oil lamps in the hope that I could burn one of them with flaming oil, but then my thoughts went before me with all my strength and with utter rage: *Oh, if I could only burn you!* And Rashid stopped, cried out, and then burst into flames.

With utter horror, I beheld this. I knew I had done it. And so did all present. The boy's bones were visible but for an instant and then they collapsed and the flames leapt and danced on the marble floor.

I had no choice but to turn to Asphar. But Eudoxia cried out.

"Enough." She struggled to rise but she couldn't do it. I took both her hands and lifted her to her feet.

With her head bowed she backed away from me. She turned and looked at the remains of Rashid.

"You've destroyed one who was dear to me," she said, her voice quivering. "And you didn't even know you had the power of Fire."

"And you meant to destroy my Avicus," I said, "and you meant to destroy me." I sighed as I looked at her. "What choice did you give me? You have been my teacher in regard to my powers." I trembled with exhaustion and fury. "We might have all lived here in accord."

I looked at Asphar who didn't dare to come any closer. I looked at Eudoxia who sat weak and useless in her chair.

"I mean to leave now," I said, "and take my two companions with me. If you try to harm any of us, I'll turn my full power on you. And as you said, I do not even know what it is myself."

"You threaten from fear," she said wearily. "And you won't leave here without giving me a life for a life. You burnt Rashid. Give me Avicus. Give him to me now of your own free will."

"I will not," I said coldly. I felt my power gathered inside me. I glared at Asphar. The poor child blood drinker quivered in terror.

Eudoxia sat sullenly in her chair, her head still bowed.

"What a loss there has been here, Eudoxia," I said. "We could have given such riches of mind to each other."

"Stop your golden talk, Marius," she said, looking up angrily, her eyes full of blood tears. "You still fear me. Bring me to the Mother and the Father, and let the Mother decide who shall be her keeper, you or I."

I answered quickly,

"I won't have you under my roof, Eudoxia. But I will take the matter before the Mother and the Father. And after they speak to me, I will speak to you."

I turned to Asphar.

"Lead us out of this place now," I said, "or I'll burn you as I did your companion."

He obeyed without hesitation, and once he had led us speedily to the street, we fled.

11

WE FLED.
There is no other way to describe it. We were in terror and we fled. As soon as we reached our house we closed off every window and door with its heaviest shutters.

But what did all this matter against a power such as Eudoxia possessed?

Gathering in the inner court, we took stock of the situation. We must discover our own powers. We must know what had been given us by time and blood.

Within a few hours, we had some answers.

Avicus and I could move objects easily without touching them. We could make them fly through the air. As for the Fire Gift, I alone possessed it and we could find no limit to my gift in terms of the space of our house. That meant I could burn wood no matter how far it was from me. And as for living things, I chose the unfortunate vermin for my victims, and ignited them from a great distance with ease.

As for our physical strength it was far greater than we had ever supposed. Again, I excelled in this as in everything. Avicus was second to me, and Mael was third.

But I had sensed something else when I was with Eudoxia, and I tried to explain it to Avicus and Mael.

"When we fought, she sought to burn me with the Fire Gift. (And we did use those words then in one form or another.) Of this I'm certain. I felt the warmth. But I was confronting her with a different power. I was using a pressure against her. And that is something I must come to understand."

Once again, I chose the unfortunate rats of our dwelling for my exercise, and holding one of these, I exerted the same force I had used when struggling with Eudoxia in my arms. The creature virtually exploded, but there was no fire involved.

I knew then that I possessed a power different from the Fire Gift, which I might call the Killing Gift, which I had used in my defense. Should I use this pressure against a mortal, and I didn't intend to, the mortal's internal organs would be exploded and the poor creature would die.

"Now Avicus," I said, "you being the eldest of us, see if you possess this Killing Gift, for you very well might."

Having caught a rat, I held it as Avicus directed his thoughts with all due concentration, and within seconds the poor creature bled from its ears and mouth and was quite dead.

This had a sobering effect upon Avicus.

I insisted that Mael attempt the same thing. This time the rat squirmed furiously, letting out terrible little squeaks or cries, but did not die. When I put the little creature down on the mosaic floor of the court, it could not run, or even climb to its small feet, and I, out of mercy for it, put it to death.

I looked at Mael. "The power is growing in you," I said. "The powers are increasing in all of us. We have to be more clever, infinitely more clever, as we face our enemies here."

Mael nodded. "It seems that I might cripple a mortal."

"Or even make him fall," I answered. "But let us turn our attention now to the Mind Gift. We've all used it to locate each other, and sometimes to communicate a silent question or thought, but only in the simplest most self-defensive ways."

We went into the library and seated ourselves in a small triangle, and I sought to put into the mind of Avicus images of what I had seen in the great church of Hagia Sophia, specifically the mosaics which I had most loved.

He was at once able to describe them to me, even down to detail.

Then I became a recipient of his thoughts, which were memories of the long ago year when he was brought North out of Egypt, and up to Britain, to take up his long service in the Grove of the Druids. He had been in chains.

I was shaken by these images. Not only did I see them, I felt a deep physical response. I had to clear my eyes as well as my head. There was something overpoweringly intimate about them, yet something indistinct at the same time. I knew that I would never feel quite the same about Avicus again.

Now it was my turn with Mael. I tried to send him vivid pictures of my former house in Antioch, where I had been so happy—or unhappy—with Pandora. And again, he was able to describe in words the images I'd sent.

When it came his turn to send me images, he allowed me to see the first night in his youth that he had ever been allowed to join the Faithful of the Forest in the ceremonies of the God of the Grove. I disliked these scenes, for obvious reasons, and again I felt jarred by them, and that I knew him now a little better than I desired.

After this, we tried to eavesdrop upon each other mentally, a skill we had always known we possessed. We proved far stronger in this than we had anticipated. And as for cloaking our minds, we could all do it quite near to perfection, even Mael.

We resolved then that we would strengthen our powers in so far as we could do this for ourselves. We would use the Mind Gift more often. We would do all that we could to prepare for Eudoxia and what she meant to do.

At last, having completed our lessons, and having heard no more of Eudoxia or her household, I resolved to go down into the shrine of Those Who Must Be Kept.

Avicus and Mael were hesitant to remain upstairs without me, so I allowed them to come down and wait near the doorway, but I insisted that I go into the shrine alone.

I knelt down before the Divine Parents, and in a low voice I told them what had taken place. Naturally there was an absurdity to this, for they probably already knew.

Whatever the case, I spoke frankly to Akasha and Enkil of all that Eudoxia had revealed to me, of our terrible struggle, and I told them that I didn't know what to do.

Here was one who laid claim to them, and I did not trust Eudoxia, because she had no respect for me and those I loved. I told them that if they wished to be given over to Eudoxia, all I needed was a sign, but I begged that I and my companions would be saved.

Nothing broke the silence of the chapel except my whispers. Nothing changed.

"I need the blood, Mother," I said to Akasha. "Never have I needed it more. If I am to defend myself this time, I need the blood."

I rose. I waited. I wished that I would see Akasha's hand rise as it had for Eudoxia. I thought of the words of her Maker, "She never destroys those she beckons."

But there was no warm gesture for me. There was only my courage, as I once more embraced Akasha, and pressed my lips to her neck, and then pierced her skin and felt the delicious indescribable blood.

What did I see in my ecstasy? What did I see in this sublime satisfaction? It was the lush and beautiful palace garden, full of carefully tended fruit trees, and the soft dark grass, and the sun shining through the branches. How could I ever forget that fatal and supremely beautiful sun? Beneath my naked foot, I felt the soft waxy petal of a flower. Against my face, I felt soft branches. I drank and drank, slipping out of time, and the warmth paralyzed me.

Is this your sign, Mother? I was walking in the palace garden, and it seemed I held a paintbrush in my hand, and when I looked up, I was painting the very trees that I saw above me, creating the garden on the wall of my house, the garden in which I walked. I understood this paradox perfectly. This was a garden which I had once painted on the walls of the shrine. And now it was mine to have both on a flat wall, and also surrounding me, as if it really existed. And that was the omen. Keep the Mother and the Father. Do not be afraid.

I drew back. I could take no more. I clung to Akasha like a child. I held to her neck with my left hand, my forehead against her heavy black plaits, and I kissed her, over and over again, I kissed her, as though that and only that were the most eloquent gesture in the world.

Enkil did not stir. Akasha did not stir. I sighed and that was the only sound.

Then I withdrew and knelt down before both of them, and I gave my thanks.

How completely and totally I loved her, my shimmering Egyptian goddess. How I believed that she belonged to me.

Then for a long time I pondered this problem with Eudoxia, and I saw it a little more clearly.

It occurred to me that in the absence of a clear sign to Eudoxia, my battle with her would be to the death. She would never allow me to remain in this city, and she meant to take Those Who Must Be Kept from me, so that I would have to use the Fire Gift against her as best I could. What had happened earlier this night was only the beginning of our little war.

It was dreadfully sad to me, because I admired Eudoxia, but I knew that she had been far too humiliated by our struggle ever to give in.

I looked up at Akasha. "How do I fight this creature to the death?" I asked. "This creature has your blood in her. I have your blood in me. But surely there must be a clearer sign of what you mean for me to do?"

I stayed there for an hour or more, and then finally I went out.

I found Avicus and Mael waiting where I had left them.

"She's given me her blood," I said. "This isn't a boast. I only mean for you to know it. And I believe that that is her sign. But how can I know? I believe that she does not want to be given over to Eudoxia, and she will destroy if provoked."

Avicus looked desperate.

"In all our years in Rome," he said, "we were blessed that no one of great strength ever challenged us."

I agreed with him. "Strong blood drinkers stay away from others like them," I said. "But you must see, surely, that we are challenging her. We could leave as she has asked us to do."

"She has no right to ask this of us," said Avicus. "Why can't she try to love us?"

"Love us?" I asked, repeating his words. "What makes you say such a strange thing? I know that you're enamored of her. Of course. I've seen this. But why should she love us?"

"Precisely because we are strong," he responded. "She has only the weakest blood drinkers around her, creatures no more than half a century in age. We can tell her things, things she may not know."

"Ah, yes, I thought the same things when I first laid eyes on her. But with this one it's not to be."

"Why?" he asked again.

"If she wanted strong ones like us, they would be here," I said. And then I said dejectedly, "We can always go back to Rome."

He had no answer for that. I didn't know whether I meant it myself.

As we went up the steps and through the tunnels to the surface, I took his arm.

"You're mad with thoughts of her," I said. "You must regain your spiritual self. Don't love her. Make it a simple act of will."

He nodded. But he was too troubled to conceal it.

I glanced at Mael, and found him more calm about all this than I had imagined. Then came the inevitable question:

"Would she have destroyed Avicus if you hadn't opposed her?" Mael asked.

"She was going to give it a very good try," I said. "But Avicus is very old, older than you or me. And possibly older than her. And you've seen his strength tonight."

Uneasy, filled with misgivings, and bad thoughts, we went to our unholy rest.

The following night, as soon as I rose, I knew that there were strangers in our house. I was furious, but had some sense even then that anger renders one weak.

Mael and Avicus came to me immediately, and the three of us went to discover Eudoxia and the terrified Asphar with her, and two other young male blood drinkers whom we had not see before.

All were settled within my library as if they were invited guests.

Eudoxia was dressed in splendid and heavy Eastern robes with long bell sleeves, and Persian slippers, and her thick black curls were gathered above her ears with jewels and pearls.

The room was not as fine as the one in which she had received me, as I had not finished with my furnishings and other such things, and therefore she appeared the most sumptuous ornament in view.

I was struck once more by the beauty of her small face, especially I think by her mouth, though her cold dark eyes were as mesmerizing as before.

I felt sorry for the miserable Asphar who was so afraid of me, and as for the other two blood drinkers, both boys in mortal life, and young in immortality, I felt rather sorry for them too.

Need I say that they were beautiful? They had been grown children when they were taken, that is, splendid beings with adult bodies and chubby boyish cheeks and mouths.

"Why have you come without an invitation?" I asked Eudoxia. "You sit in my chair as though you're my guest."

"Forgive me," she said gently. "I came because I felt compelled to come. I've searched your house through and through."

"You boast of this?" I asked.

Her lips were parted as though she meant to answer but then the tears rose in her eyes.

"Where are the books, Marius?" she said softly. She looked at me. "Where are all the old books of Egypt? The books that were in the temple, the books that you stole?"

I didn't answer. I didn't sit down.

"I came because I hoped to find them," she said, staring forward, her tears falling. "I came here because last night I dreamed of the priests in the temple, and how they used to tell me that I ought to read the old tales."

Still I didn't answer.

She looked up, and then with the back of one hand, she wiped at her tears. "I could smell the scents of the temple, the scent of papyrus," she said. "I saw the Elder at his desk."

"He put the Parents in the sun, Eudoxia," I said. "Don't slide into a dream that makes him innocent. The Elder was evil and guilty. The Elder was selfish and bitter. Would you know his ultimate fate?"

"In my dream, the priests told me that you took the books, Marius. They said that, unopposed, you came into the library of the temple and took all the old scrolls away."

I said nothing.

But her grief was heartrending.

"Tell me, Marius. Where are those books? If you will let me read them, if you will let me read the old stories of Egypt, then my soul can find some peace with you. Can you do that much for me?"

How bitterly did I draw in my breath.

"Eudoxia," I said gently. "They're gone, those books, and all that remains of them is here, in my head." I tapped the side of my forehead. "In Rome, when the savages from the North breached the city, my house was burnt and my library destroyed."

She shook her head and put her hands to the side of her face as though she could not bear this.

I went down on my knees beside her and I tried to turn her to me, but she would have none of it. Her tears were shed quietly.

"I'll write it all out, all that I remember, and there is so much that I remember," I said. "Or shall I tell it aloud for our scribes? You decide how you will receive it, and I'll give it to you, lovingly. I understand what you desire."

This was not the time to tell her that much of what she sought came to nothing, that the old tales had been full of superstition and nonsense and even incantations that meant nothing at all.

Even the wicked Elder had said so. But I had read these scrolls during my years in Antioch. I remembered them. They were inside my heart and soul.

She turned to me slowly. And lifting her left hand, she stroked my hair.

"Why did you steal those books!" she whispered desperately, her tears still flowing. "Why did you take them from a sanctum where they had been safe for so long!"

"I wanted to know what they said," I answered candidly. "Why didn't you read them when you had a lifetime to do it?" I asked gently. "Why didn't you copy them when you copied for the Greeks and the Romans? How can you blame me now for what I did?"

"Blame you?" she said earnestly. "I hate you for it."

"The Elder was dead, Eudoxia," I said quietly. "It was the Mother who slew the Elder."

Her eyes suddenly, for all their tears, grew wide.

"You want me to believe this? That you didn't do it?"

"I? Slay a blood drinker who was a thousand years old, when I was just born?" I gave a short laugh. "No. It was the Mother who did it. And it was the Mother who asked me to take her out of Egypt. I did only what she asked me to do."

I stared into her eyes, determined that she must believe me, that she must weigh this final and all-important piece of evidence before she proceeded in her case of hatred against me.

"Look into my mind, Eudoxia," I said. "See the pictures of this for yourself."

I myself relived the grim moments when Akasha had crushed the evil Elder underfoot. I myself remembered the lamp, brought magically from its stand, to pour its flaming oil upon his remains. How the mysterious blood had burnt.

"Yes," Eudoxia whispered. "Fire is our enemy, always our enemy. You are speaking the truth."

"With my heart and soul," I said. "It's true. And having been charged with this duty, and having seen the death of the Elder, how could I leave the books behind? I wanted them as you wanted them. I read them when I was in Antioch. I will tell you all they contained."

She thought on this for a long time and then nodded.

I rose to my feet. I looked down at her. She sat still, her head bowed, and then she drew a fine napkin from inside her robes, and she wiped at her blood tears.

Once again, I pressed my promises.

"I'll write down all I remember," I said. "I'll write down all that the Elder told me when first I came to the temple. I'll spend my nights in this labor until everything is told."

She didn't answer me, and I couldn't see her face unless I knelt down again.

"Eudoxia," I said. "We know much that we can give to each other. In Rome, I grew so weary that I lost the thread of life for a century. I am eager to hear all you know."

Was she weighing this? I couldn't tell.

Then she spoke, without raising her face to me.

"My sleep this last day was feverish," she said. "I dreamed of Rashid crying out to me."

What could I say? I felt desperate.

"No, I don't ask for placating words from you," she said. "I only mean to say, my sleep was miserable. And then I was in the temple and the priests were all around me. And I had an awful sense, the purest sense, of death and time."

I went down on one knee before her. "We can conquer this," I said.

She looked into my eyes as though she were suspicious of me and I were trying to trick her.

"No," she said softly. "We die too. We die when it is right for us to die."

"I don't want to die," I said. "To sleep, yes, and sometimes to sleep almost forever, yes, but not to die."

She smiled.

"What would you write for me?" she asked, "if you could write anything at all? What would you choose to put down on parchment for me to read and know?"

"Not what was in those old Egyptian texts," I said forcefully, "but something finer, more truly universal, something full of hope and vitality that speaks of growth and triumph, that speaks—how shall I put it any other way?—of life."

She nodded gravely, and once again she smiled.

She looked at me for a long and seemingly affectionate moment.

"Take me down into the shrine," she said. She reached out and clasped my hand.

"Very well," I said.

As I rose, so did she, and then she went past me to lead the way. This might have been to show me that she knew it, and, thank the gods, her retinue stayed behind so that I did not have to tell them to do so.

I went down with her, and with the Mind Gift I opened the many doors without touching them.

If this made an impression upon her she didn't acknowledge it. But I didn't know if we were at war with each other any longer. I couldn't gauge her frame of mind.

When she saw the Mother and the Father in their fine linen and exquisite jewelry she let out a gasp.

"Oh, Blessed Parents," she whispered. "I have come such a long way to this."

I was moved by her voice. Her tears were flowing again.

"Would that I had something to offer you," she said, gazing up at the Queen. She was trembling. "Would that I had some sacrifice, some gift."

I didn't know why but something quickened in me when she said those words. I looked at the Mother first and then at the Father, and I detected nothing, yet something had changed within the chapel, something which Eudoxia perhaps felt.

I breathed in the heavy fragrance rising from the censers. I looked at the shivering flowers in their vases. I looked at the glistening eyes of my Queen.

"What gift can I give you?" Eudoxia pressed as she stepped forward. "What would you take from me that I could give with my whole soul?" She walked closer and closer to the steps, her arms out. "I am your slave. I was your slave in Alexandria when first you gave me your blood, and I am your slave now."

"Step back," I said suddenly, though why I didn't know. "Step back and be quiet," I said quickly.

But Eudoxia only moved forward, mounting the first step of the dais.

"Don't you see I mean what I say?" she said to me without turning her head away from the King and Queen. "Let me be your victim, most holy Akasha, let me be your blood sacrifice, most holy Queen."

In a flash Akasha's right arm rose and pulled Eudoxia forward in a brutal and tight embrace.

An awful groan rose from Eudoxia.

Down came the reddened mouth of the Queen, with only the slightest move of her head, and I saw the sharp teeth only for an instant before they penetrated Eudoxia's neck. Eudoxia was helpless, head wrenched to one side, as Akasha drank from her, Eudoxia's arms hanging limp as her legs, Akasha's face as blank as ever, as the grip tightened and the drinking went on.

I stood horrified, not daring to challenge anything that I beheld.

No more than a few seconds passed, perhaps half a minute before Eudoxia gave a raw and terrible scream. She tried desperately to raise her arms.

"Stop, Mother, I beg you!" I cried out and with all my might I took hold of the body of Eudoxia. "Stop, I beg you, don't take her life! Spare her!" I pulled on the body. "Spare her, Mother!" I cried. I felt the body shift in my grasp and quickly I drew it back from the curved arm which remained poised in space.

Eudoxia still breathed, though she was livid, and groaning miserably, and we both fell back off the dais, as the arm of Akasha returned to its age-old position, at her side, fingers laid on her thigh as though nothing had occurred.

Sprawled on the floor I lay with the gasping Eudoxia.

"Did you want to die!" I demanded.

"No," she said desperately. She lay there with her breast heaving, her hands shuddering, seemingly unable to rise to her feet.

I looked up searchingly into the Queen's face.

The sacrifice had given no blush to her cheeks. And on her lips there was no red blood.

I was stupefied. I picked up Eudoxia and rushed to get her out of the shrine, up the steps, through the various tunnels, and finally into the house above ground.

I ordered all the others out of the library, slamming tight the doors with the Mind Gift, and there I laid her down on my couch so that she might at least catch her breath.

"But how?" she asked me, "did you ever have the courage to take me from her?" She clung to my neck. "Hold tight to me, Marius, don't let me go just yet. I cannot. . . . I do not. . . . Hold tight to me. Where did you get the courage to move against our own Queen?"

"She was about to destroy you," I said. "She was about to answer my prayer."

"And what prayer was that?" she asked.

She let me go. I brought up a chair to sit beside her.

Her face was drawn and tragic, her eyes brilliant. She reached out and clung to my sleeve.

"I asked for a sign of her pleasure," I said. "Would she be given over to you or remain with me? She's spoken. And you see how it is."

She shook her head, but it was not a negation to anything that I'd said. She was trying to recover her clarity of mind. She tried to rise from the couch and then fell backwards.

For a long time, she merely lay there, staring at the ceiling and I couldn't know her thoughts. I tried to take her hand, but she withdrew it from me.

Then in a low voice, she said:

"You've drunk her blood. You have the Fire Gift, and you've drunk her blood. And this she has done in answer to your prayer."

"Tell me," I said. "What prompted you to offer yourself to her? Why did you say such words? Had you ever spoken them in Egypt?"

"Never," she said in a heated murmur. "I had forgotten the beauty." She looked confused, weak. "I had forgotten the timelessness," she whispered. "I had forgotten the silence gathered around them—as if it were so many veils."

She turned and looked at me languidly. She looked about her. I sensed her hunger, her weakness.

"Yes," she sighed. "Bring my slaves to me," she said. "Let them go out and obtain for me a sacrifice, for I'm too weak from having been the sacrifice myself."

I went into the courtyard garden and told her little gang of exquisite blood drinkers to go to her. She could give them this disagreeable order on her own.

When they had gone on their dismal errand, I returned to her. She was sitting up, her face still drawn and her white hands trembling.

"Perhaps I should have died," she said to me. "Perhaps it was meant to be."

"What's meant?" I asked scornfully. "What's meant is that we must both live in Constantinople, you in your house with your little companions and I here with mine. And we must have a commingling of households from time to time that is agreeable. I say that is what is meant."

She looked at me thoughtfully as if she were pondering this as much as she could ponder anything after what had befallen her in the shrine.

"Trust in me," I said desperately in a low voice. "Trust in me for some little while. And then if we should part, let it be amicable."

She smiled. "As if we were old Greeks?" she asked.

"Why must we lose our manners?" I said. "Weren't they nourished in brilliance, like the arts which still surround us, the poetry that still comforts us, and the stirring tales of heroism which distract us from the cruel passage of time?"

"Our manners," she repeated thoughtfully. "What a strange creature you are."

Was she my enemy or my friend? I didn't know.

All too quickly, her blood drinker slaves appeared with a miserable and terrified victim, a rich merchant who glared at all of us with bulbous eyes. Frankly he offered us money for his life.

I wanted to stop this abomination. When had I ever taken a victim under my roof? And this was to happen within my house to one who appealed to me for mercy.

But within seconds, the man was forced down upon his knees and Eudoxia then gave herself over to drinking blood from him with no regard for my standing there and watching this spectacle, and I turned on my heel and went out of the library and remained away, until the man was dead, and his richly dressed body was taken away.

At last I came back into my library, exhausted, horrified and confused.

Eudoxia was much better for having feasted on the poor wretch and she was staring at me intently.

I sat down now, for I saw no reason to stand indignantly with regard to something that was finished, and I felt myself plunged into thought.

"Will we share this city?" I asked calmly. I looked at her. "Can that be done in peace?"

"I don't know the answer to your questions," she said. There was something wrong in her voice, wrong in her eyes, wrong in her manner. "I want to leave you now. We will talk again."

She gathered her band of followers and all of them left quietly, by request, through the rear door of the house.

I sat there very still and weary from what had taken place, and wondering if there would be any change in Akasha who had moved to drink Eudoxia's blood.

Of course there would be no change. I thought back to my first years with Akasha, when I'd been so certain that I could bring her back to life. And here, she had moved, yes, she had moved, but how ghastly had been the expression on her smooth innocent face, more blank than the faces of mortals after death.

An awful foreboding came over me, in which the subtle force of Eudoxia seemed both a charm and a curse.

And in the midst of this foreboding I came to know a terrible temptation, a terrible rebellious thought. Why hadn't I given over the

Mother and Father to Eudoxia? I would have been rid of them, rid of this burden which I had carried since the earliest nights of my life among the Undead? Why hadn't I done it?

It would have been so simple. And I would have been free.

And as I recognized this guilty desire inside of me, as I saw it flare up like a fire fed by the bellows, I realized that during those long nights at sea, on the voyage to Constantinople, I had secretly wished that our ship would meet with misadventure, that we would be sunk and Those Who Must Be Kept would have gone down to the bottom of the ocean, never to surface again. I could have survived any shipwreck. But they would have been buried just as the Elder in Egypt had long ago mentioned to me, cursing and carrying on, saying, "Why do I not sink them into the sea?"

Oh, these were terrible thoughts. Did I not love Akasha? Had I not pledged my soul?

I was consumed with self-hatred and dread that the Queen would know my petty secret—that I wished to be rid of her, that I wished to be rid of all of them—Avicus, Mael, Eudoxia most certainly—that I wished—for the very first time—to wander a vagabond like so many others, that I wished to have no name and no place and no destination, but to be alone.

These thoughts were too dreadful. They divided me from all that I valued. I had to banish them from my mind.

But before I could get my wits about me, Mael and Avicus came rushing into the library. There was some sort of disturbance outside the house.

"Can you hear it?" Avicus said frantically.

"Yea gods," I said, "why are all those people shouting in the streets?"

I realized there was a great clamor, and that some of these people were beating on our windows and doors. Rocks were being thrown at our house. The wooden shutters were about to be broken in.

"What is happening? What is the reason for this?" Mael asked desperately.

"Listen!" I said desperately. "They're saying that we seduced a rich merchant into the house, and then murdered him, and threw his corpse out to rot! Oh, damn Eudoxia, don't you see what she's done, it was she who murdered the merchant! She's caused a mob to rise against us. We have only time to retreat to the shrine."

I led them to the entrance, lifted the heavy marble door, and we were soon inside the passage, knowing full well that we were protected, but unable to defend our house.

Then all we could do was listen helplessly as the mob broke in and sacked our entire dwelling, destroying my new library and all I possessed. We did not have to hear their voices to know when they had set the house ablaze.

At last, when it was quiet above, when a few looters picked their way through the smoldering rafters and debris, we came up out of the tunnel, and stared at the ruins in utter disgust.

We scared off the riffraff. Then we made certain that the entrance to the shrine was in fact secure and disguised, which it was, and finally, we went off to a crowded tavern, where, huddled at a table amid mortals, we could talk.

Such a retreat was, for us, quite incredible, but what else could we do?

I told Avicus and Mael what had happened in the shrine, how Eudoxia had been nearly drained of all blood by the Mother and how I had intervened to save Eudoxia's life. I then explained with regard to the mortal merchant, for they had seen him brought in, and seen him removed, but had not understood.

"They dumped his body where it would be found," said Avicus. "They baited the crowd to gather as it did."

"Yes. Our dwelling is gone," I said finally, "and the shrine will be lost to us until such time as I go to bizarre and complex legal measures to purchase under a new name what already belongs to me under an old one, and the family of the merchant will demand justice against the unfortunate individual, whom I was before, if you follow me, so that I might not be able to buy the property at all."

"What does she expect of us?" asked Avicus.

"This is an insult to Those Who Must Be Kept," Mael declared. "She knows the shrine is under the house, yet she incited a riot to destroy it."

I stared at him for a long moment. I was too ready to condemn him for his anger. But quite suddenly I had a confession to make.

"That thought had not occurred to me," I said. "But it seems to me that you are precisely right. It was an insult to Those Who Must Be Kept."

"Oh, yes, she has done an injury to the Mother," said Avicus.

"Surely she has done that. By day, thieves may chip at the very floor that blocks the passage to the shrine below."

A dreadful gloom took hold of me. A pure and youthful anger was part of it. The anger fed my will.

"What is it?" Avicus demanded. "Your entire countenance is changed. Tell us your thoughts, right now, from your soul."

"I'm not so certain I can voice my thoughts," I said, "but I know them, and they don't bode well for Eudoxia or those whom she claims to love. Both of you, seal your minds off from everything so that you give no hint of your whereabouts. Go to the nearest gate of the city, and leave it, and hide yourselves for the coming day in the hills. Tomorrow, come immediately to meet me here at this tavern."

I walked with them part of the distance to the gate, and seeing them safely on their way, I went directly to Eudoxia's house.

It was a simple matter to hear her blood drinker slaves within, and I commanded them brusquely to open the door.

Eudoxia, ever the arrogant one, commanded them to do as I had requested, and once inside, seeing the two young blood drinkers, I began to tremble with anger, but I could not hesitate, and with all my force, I burnt them both at once.

It was appalling to watch, this violent fire, and it set me to gasping and to shaking, but I had no time for observation. Asphar ran from me, and Eudoxia shouted to me fiercely to stop, but I burnt Asphar, wincing as I heard his piteous screams, all the while fighting Eudoxia's enormous powers with all the might I could command.

Indeed so hot was the fire against my chest that I thought I would die, but I hardened all my body, and hurled my own Fire Gift against Eudoxia with full force.

Her mortal slaves were fleeing out every door and window.

She rushed at me, fists clenched, her face a picture of rage.

"Why do you do this to me!" she demanded.

I caught her up in my arms as she fought me, the waves of heat passing over me, and I carried her out of her house and through the dark streets towards the smoking ruins above the shrine.

"So you would send a mob to destroy my house," I said. "So you would do this after I saved you, so you would do this while deceiving me with your thanks."

"I gave you no thanks," she said, twisting, turning, struggling against me, the heat exhausting me as I fought to control her, her hands pushing me with stunning force. "You prayed for my death, you prayed to the Mother to destroy me," she cried. "You told me yourself."

At last I came to the smoking heap of wood and rubble, and finding the mosaic covered door, I lifted it with the Mind Gift, which gave her just time enough to send a scorching blast against my face.

I felt it like a mortal might feel scalding water. But the heavy door was indeed opened, and I protected myself once more against her, as pulling the giant stone down behind me with one arm, I held her with the other, and started to drag her through the complex passages to the shrine.

Again and again, the heat came to burn me, and I could smell my hair scorched by it, and see the smoke in the air around me, as she made some victory no matter how great my strength.

But I fended her off, and I never let go of her. Clutching her with one arm, I opened the doors, one after another, pushing back her power, even as I stumbled. On and on I dragged her towards the shrine. Nothing could stop me, but I could not hurt her with all my force.

No, that privilege was reserved for one far greater than me.

At last we had reached the chapel, and I flung her down on the floor.

Sealing myself off from her with all my strength I turned my eyes to the Mother and Father, only to see the same mute picture which had always greeted my gaze.

And having no further sign than that, and fighting off another crippling wave of heat, I picked up Eudoxia before she could climb to her feet and holding her wrists behind her back, I offered her to the Mother as closely as I dared without disturbing the garments of the Mother, without committing what for me was a sacrilege in the name of what I meant to do.

The right arm of the Mother reached out for Eudoxia, detaching itself, as it were, from the Mother's tranquility, and once again, Akasha's head made that slight, subtle and utterly grotesque movement, her lips parting, fangs bared. Eudoxia screamed as I released her body and stepped back.

A great desperate sigh came out of me. Ah, so be it!

And I watched in quiet horror as Eudoxia became the Mother's victim, Eudoxia's arms flailing hopelessly, her knees pushing against the

Mother, until finally the limp body of Eudoxia was allowed to slip from the Mother's embrace.

Once fallen onto the marble floor, it looked like an exquisite doll of white wax. No audible breath came from it. Its round dark eyes did not move.

But it wasn't dead, no, not by any means. It was a blood drinker's body with a blood drinker's soul. Only fire could kill it. I waited, keeping my own powers in check.

Long ago, in Antioch, when unwelcome vampires had assaulted the Mother, she had used the Mind Gift to lift a lamp to burn their remains with fire and oil. So she had done with the remains of the Elder in Egypt, as I have already described. Would she do this now?

Something simpler happened.

Quite suddenly I saw flames erupt from Eudoxia's breast, and then flames run riot through her veins. Her face remained sweet and unfeeling. Her eyes remained empty. Her limbs twitched.

It was not my Fire Gift that had brought about this execution. It was the power of Akasha. What else could it have been? A new power, lain dormant in her for centuries, now known to her on account of Eudoxia and me?

I dared not guess. I dared not question.

At once the flames rising from the highly combustible blood of the preternatural body ignited the heavy ornate garments and the whole form was ablaze.

Only after a long time did the fire die away, leaving a glittering mass of ash.

The clever learned creature who had been Eudoxia was no more. The brilliant charming creature who had lived so well and so long was no more. The being who had given me such hope when first I saw her and heard her voice was no more.

I took off my outer cloak and, going down on my knees like a poor scrubwoman, I wiped up this pollution of the shrine and then I sat down exhausted in the corner, my head against the wall. And to my own surprise, and who knows?—perhaps to the surprise of the Mother and Father—I gave way to tears.

I wept and wept for Eudoxia, and also for myself that I had brutally burnt those young blood drinkers, those foolish unschooled and undisciplined immortals who had been Born to Darkness as we say now, only to be pawns in a brawl.

I felt a cruelty in myself which I could only abhor.

Finally, being quite satisfied that my underground crypt remained impregnable—for looters were now thick in the ruins above—I laid down for the sleep of the day.

I knew what I meant to do the following night and nothing could change my mind.

1 2

IN THE TAVERN, I met with Avicus and Mael the following night. They were filled with fear and they listened with wide eyes as I told them the tale.

Avicus was crushed by this knowledge, but not Mael.

"To destroy her," said Avicus, "why did it have to be done?"

He felt no false manly need to disguise his grief and sadness and was weeping at once.

"You know why," said Mael. "There would have been no stop to her enmity. Marius knew this. Don't torment him now with questions. It had to be done."

I could say nothing, for I had too many doubts as to what I'd done. It had been so absolute and so sudden. I felt a tightening of my heart and chest when I thought about it, a sort of panic which resides in the body rather than the brain.

I sat back, observing my two companions and thinking hard on what their affection had meant to me. It had been sweet and I did not want to leave them, but that was precisely what I intended to do.

Finally after they had quietly quarreled for some time, I gestured for silence. On the matter of Eudoxia I had only a few things to say.

"It was my anger which required it," I said, "for what other part of me, except my anger, had received the insult of what she had done to us through the destruction of our house? I don't regret that she is gone; no, I cannot. And as I've told you, it was only done by means of an offering to the Mother, and as to why the Mother wanted or took such an offering, I can't say.

"Long ago in Antioch, I offered victims to the Divine Parents. I brought the Evil Doers, drugged and unknowing, into the shrine. But neither the Mother or the Father ever took this blood.

"I don't know why the Mother drank from Eudoxia except that Eudoxia offered herself, and I had prayed for a sign. It's finished, this matter of Eudoxia. She is gone, with all her beauty and her charm.

"But listen hard to what I must tell you now. I'm leaving you. I'm leaving this city, which I detest, and I will take the Mother and the Father with me, of course. I'm leaving you, and I urge you to remain together, as I'm sure you mean to do, for your love for one another is the source of your endurance and your strength."

"But why leave us!" demanded Avicus. His expressive face was charged with emotion. "How can you do such a thing? We've been happy here, the three of us, we've hunted together, we've found Evil Doers aplenty. Why would you go now?"

"I must be alone," I said. "It was so before and it's so now."

"Marius, this is folly," said Mael. "You'll end up in the crypt again with the Divine Parents, slumbering until you're too weak to be awakened on your own."

"Perhaps, but if such a thing happens," I said, "you can be more than certain that Those Who Must Be Kept will be safe."

"I can't understand you," said Avicus. He began to weep again. He wept as much for Eudoxia as for me.

I didn't try to stop him. The tavern was dim and overcrowded and no one took notice of one being, albeit a splendid figure of a male with a white hand covering his face, drunk perhaps over his cup of wine for all anyone knew, weeping into it, and wiping at his tears.

Mael looked dreadfully sad.

"I must go," I tried to explain. "You must realize, both of you, that the secret of the Mother and the Father must be kept. As long as I remain with you, the secret isn't safe. Anyone, even those as weak as Eudoxia's slaves, Asphar and Rashid, can pick it out of your minds."

"But how do you know they did!" Mael protested.

Oh, it was all too sad. But I couldn't be deterred.

"If I am alone," I said, "then I alone possess the secret of where the Divine Parents sit in state, or lie in sleep." I paused, quite miserable and wishing that all of this could have been done simply, and despising myself as much perhaps as I ever have.

I wondered again why I had ever fled Pandora, and it seemed, quite suddenly, that I had put an end to Eudoxia for the same reason—that these two creatures were more surely linked in my mind than I was willing to admit.

But no, that wasn't true. Rather I didn't know it for certain. What I knew was, I was a weak being as well as a strong being and I could have loved Eudoxia, perhaps as much as I'd loved Pandora, if time had given me the chance.

"Stay with us," Avicus said. "I don't blame you for what you did. You mustn't leave because you think I do. I was caught by her spell, yes, I admit it, but I don't despise you for what you did."

"I know that," I said, taking his hand and seeking to reassure him. "But I have to be alone." I couldn't console him. "Now listen to me, both of you," I said. "You know well how to find concealment for yourself. You must do it. I myself will go to Eudoxia's old house to make the plans for my departure, as I have no other house in which I can work. You may come with me if you like and see what crypts there might be beneath the structure but such is a dangerous thing to do."

Neither of them wanted to go near the house of Eudoxia.

"Very well then, you're wise, you always have been. I'll leave you now to your own designs. I promise I won't leave Constantinople for some nights. There are things I want to revisit again, among them the great churches and even the Imperial palace. Come to me at the house of Eudoxia, or I'll find you."

I kissed them both, as men kiss, roughly, with gruff and heated gestures and tight embraces, and then I was off on my own as I so longed to be.

Eudoxia's house was utterly deserted. But some mortal slave had been there, for lamps were lighted in almost every room.

I searched these palatial chambers most carefully and found no trace of any recent occupant. There were no other blood drinkers to be discovered. The sumptuous sitting rooms and spacious library all lay under a thin blanket of silence, the only sound being the several fountains in her lovely inner garden into which the sun might penetrate by day.

There were crypts beneath her house with heavy bronze caskets, and I made a count of these to confirm that I had, indeed, destroyed all her blood drinker slaves.

Then, without difficulty I found the crypt where she had lain during the sunlight hours, with all her treasure and wealth hidden there, and two gorgeous sarcophagi decorated thickly with gold and silver and rubies and emeralds and large, perfect pearls.

Why two? I didn't know, except perhaps that she had had a companion once who was now gone.

As I studied this magnificent chamber, a harrowing pain gripped me, a harrowing pain rather like the grief I felt in Rome when I realized that I had utterly lost Pandora, and that nothing could bring her back. Indeed, it was worse than that, for Pandora might surely exist somewhere, and Eudoxia did not.

I knelt beside one of the sarcophagi and I folded my arms beneath my head and, wearily, I shed tears as I had last night.

For little more than an hour I'd been there, wasting the night away in morbid and miserable guilt, when suddenly I was aware of a footfall on the stairs.

It wasn't a mortal, I knew that immediately, and I knew as well that it was no blood drinker whom I'd seen before.

I didn't bother to move. Whoever it was, it wasn't a strong one, and in fact, the creature was so weak and young as to let me hear its bare feet.

Quietly there appeared in the torchlight a young girl, a girl perhaps no older than Eudoxia when she'd been taken into Darkness, a girl with black hair parted in the middle and streaming down over her shoulders, her clothes as fine as those of Eudoxia had been.

Her face was unblemished, her troubled eyes gleaming, her mouth red. She was blushing with the human tissue which she still possessed. And the painful seriousness of her expression gave a sharpness to all her features and to the strong line of her full lips.

Of course I must have seen someone somewhere who was more beautiful than this child, but I could not think of that one. I was so humbled, indeed, so astonished by this beauty that I felt a pure fool.

Nevertheless I knew in an instant that this girl had been the blood drinker lover of Eudoxia, that this girl had been chosen because she was incomparably beautiful, as well as extremely well educated and clever, and that before Eudoxia's summoning of us, she had closeted this girl away.

The other sarcophagus in this chamber belonged to this young one. This one had been deeply loved.

Yes, all that was logical and evident and I didn't have to speak for the moment. I had only to gaze at this radiant child who stood in the door of the crypt, the torch blazing above her, her tormented eyes on me.

Finally in a hushed whisper she spoke.

"You've killed her, haven't you?" she said. She was fearless, either out of simple youth or remarkable bravery. "You've destroyed her. She's gone."

I rose to my feet as if a queen had ordered me to do it. Her eyes took my measure. And then her face became completely and utterly sad.

It seemed she would fall to the floor. I caught her just before it happened, and then I lifted her, and carried her slowly up the marble stairs.

She let her head fall against my chest. She gave a deep sigh.

I brought her into the ornate bedchamber of the house and laid her down on the huge bed. She wouldn't remain on the pillow however. She wanted to sit there and I sat beside her.

I expected her to question me, to become violent, to turn her hatred on me, though she had hardly any strength. She couldn't have been made ten years ago. And if she'd been fourteen when it happened, I would have been surprised.

"Where were you hiding?" I asked.

"In an old house," she said softly. "A deserted place. She insisted I stay there. She said she would send for me."

"When?" I asked.

"When she had finished with you, when you were destroyed or driven away." She looked up at me.

She was no more than an exquisite baby of a woman! I wanted so to kiss her cheeks. But her sorrow was terrible.

"She said it would be a battle," she said, "that you were one of the strongest who had ever come here. The others had been simple. But with you, she wasn't sure of the outcome, and so she had to hide me away."

I nodded. I didn't dare to touch her. But I felt nothing but a desire to protect her, to enfold her in my arms, to tell her that if she meant to pound her fists on my chest and curse me she should do it, that if she meant to weep she might do that as well.

"Why don't you speak?" she asked me, her eyes full of hurt and wonder. "Why are you so quiet?"

I shook my head. "What can I say?" I asked. "It was a terrible quarrel. I didn't want it. I thought that we could all exist here in peace."

At this she smiled. "She would never have allowed that," she said to me quickly. "If you knew how many she's destroyed . . . but then I don't know myself."

This was a small comfort to my conscience, but I didn't seize upon it. I let it go.

"She said that this city belonged to her, and that it took the power of an empress to protect it. She took me from the palace, where I was a slave. She brought me here by night and I was so frightened. But then I came to love her. She was so certain that I would. She told such stories of her wanderings. And then when others came, she would hide me, and she would go against them until the city was hers again."

I nodded, listening to all this, sad for her and the drowsy sorrowful manner in which she spoke. It was no more than I'd supposed.

"How will you exist if I leave you here?" I asked.

"I can't!" she answered. She looked into my eyes. "You can't leave me. You must take care of me. I beg you. I don't know what it means to exist alone."

I cursed under my breath. She heard it, and I saw the pain in her expression.

I stood up and walked about the room. I looked back at her, this baby woman, with her tender mouth and her long loose black hair.

"What's your name?" I asked her.

"Zenobia," she replied. "Why can't you read it from my mind? She could always read my thoughts."

"I could do it," I said, "if I wanted to do it. But I would rather talk to you. Your beauty confuses me. I would rather hear your voice. Who made you a vampire?"

"One of her slaves," she said. "The one named Asphar. He's gone too, isn't he?" she asked. "They're all gone. I saw the ashes." She gestured vaguely to the other rooms. She murmured a string of names.

"Yes," I said, "they're all dead."

"You would have slain me too if I'd been here," she said, with the same wondering and hurt-filled expression.

"Perhaps," I said. "But it's over now. It was a battle. And when a battle is finished, everything changes. Who else has been hidden away?"

"No one," she answered truthfully, "only me, with one mortal slave, and when I woke tonight, he was gone."

I must have looked very dejected for surely I felt that way.

She turned and with the slowness of a dazed person, reached under the heavy pillows at the head of the bed, and withdrew a dagger.

Then she rose and made her way to me. She held up the dagger with two hands, the tip pointed at my chest. She stared before her, but not into my eyes. Her long wavy black hair fell down around her on both sides of her face.

"I should take vengeance," she said quietly, "but you will only stop me if I try."

"Don't try it," I said in the same calm voice I had used for her all along. I pushed the dagger away gently. And putting my arm around her, I led her back to the bed.

"Why didn't she give you the Blood?" I asked.

"Her blood was too strong for us. She told us so. All her blood drinker slaves were stolen or made one by another under her direction. She said that her blood was not to be shared. It would come with strength and silence. Make a blood drinker and you cannot ever hear his thoughts afterwards. That's what she told us. So Asphar made me and I was deaf to Asphar and Asphar was deaf to me. She must keep us all in obedience and that she could not do if we were made from her powerful blood."

It pained me now that Eudoxia was the teacher, and Eudoxia was dead.

This one was studying me, and then she asked in the simplest voice:

"Why don't you want me? What can I do to make you want me?" She went on speaking tenderly. "You're very beautiful," she said, "with your light yellow hair. You look like a god, really, tall as you are and with your blue eyes. Even she thought you were beautiful. She told me you were. I was never allowed to see you. But she told me that you were like the North men. She described you as you walked about in your red robes—."

"Don't say any more, please," I said. "You don't have to flatter me. It won't matter. I can't take you with me."

"Why?" she asked. "Because I know about the Mother and the Father?"

I was shocked.

I should read her thoughts, all her thoughts, ransack her soul for everything she knew, I thought, but I didn't want to do it. I didn't want that feeling of intimacy with her. Her beauty was too much, there was no denying it.

Unlike my paragon, Pandora, this lovely creature had the promise of a virgin—that one could make of her what one wanted while losing nothing—and I believed that promise to contain a lie.

I answered her in a warm whisper trying not to hurt her.

"That's precisely the reason I can't take you, that, and because I must be alone."

She bowed her head. "What am I to do?" she asked. "Tell me. Men will come here, mortal men," she said, "wanting the taxes on this house or some other triviality and I shall be discovered and called a witch or a heretic and dragged into the streets. Or during the day they will come and find me sleeping like the dead beneath the floor, and lift me, hoping to revive me, into the certain death of the sun's light."

"Stop, I know it all," I said. "Don't you see, I'm trying to reason! Leave me alone for now."

"If I leave you alone," she said, "I'll start weeping or screaming in my grief, and you won't be able to bear it. You'll desert me."

"No, I won't," I said. "Be quiet."

I paced the floor, my heart aching for her, and my soul hurting for myself that this had fallen to me. It seemed a terrible justice for my slaughter of Eudoxia. Indeed this child seemed some phantom risen from Eudoxia's ashes to haunt me as I tried to plan my escape from what I'd done.

Finally, I quietly sent out my call to Avicus and Mael. Using my strongest Mind Gift, I urged them, no, commanded them, to come to me at Eudoxia's house and to let nothing keep them from it. I told them I needed them and I would wait until they arrived.

Then I sat down beside my young captive and I did what I had been wanting to do all along: I moved her heavy black hair back behind her shoulders and I kissed her soft cheeks. These were rapacious kisses and I knew it. But the texture of her baby soft skin and of her thick wavy hair drove me to quiet madness, and I wouldn't stop.

This intimacy startled her but she did nothing to drive me away.

"Did Eudoxia suffer?" she asked me.

"Very little, if at all," I said. I drew back from kissing her. "But tell me why she didn't simply try to destroy me," I said. "Why did she invite me here? Why did she talk with me? Why did she give me some hope that we could come to an understanding of the mind?"

She pondered this before she answered.

"You held a fascination for her," said Zenobia, "which others had not. It wasn't only your beauty though that was a large part of it. Always for her a large part of it. She said to me that she had heard tell of you from a woman blood drinker in Crete long ago."

I dared not interrupt her! I stared with wide eyes.

"Many years ago," she said, "this Roman blood drinker had come to the isle of Crete, wandering, looking for you, and speaking of you—Marius, the Roman, Patrician by birth, scholar by choice. The woman blood drinker loved you. She didn't challenge the claim of Eudoxia to all of the island. She searched only for you, and when she found that you weren't there, she moved on."

I couldn't speak! I was so miserable and so excited that I couldn't answer her. It was Pandora! And this was the first that I had heard of her in three hundred years.

"Don't weep over this," she said gently. "It happened in ages past. Surely time can take away such love. What a curse if it can't."

"It can't." I said. My voice was thick. The tears were in my eyes. "What more did she say? Tell me, please, the tiniest things you might remember." My heart was knocking in my chest. Indeed it seemed as if I'd forgotten that I had a heart and must now find out.

"What more. There is no more. Only that the woman was powerful and no easy enemy. You know Eudoxia always spoke of such things. The woman could not be destroyed, nor would she tell the origin of her great strength. To Eudoxia it was a mystery—until you came to Constantinople, and she saw you, Marius, the Roman, in your brilliant red robes, moving through the square at evening, pale as marble, yet with all the conviction of a mortal man."

She paused. She put her hand up to touch the side of my face.

"Don't cry. Those were her words: 'with all the conviction of a mortal man.'"

"How then did you learn of the Mother and the Father?" I asked, "and what do such words mean to you?"

"She spoke of them in amazement," she said. "She said you were rash if not mad. But you see, she would go one way and then the other, that was always in her nature. She cursed you that the Mother and the Father were in this very city, and yet she wanted to bring you here to her house. On account of this, I had to be hidden. Yet she kept the boys for whom she cared so little. And I was put away."

"And the Mother and the Father?" I asked. "Do you know what they are?"

She shook her head. "Only that you have them, or had them when she spoke of it. Are they the First of us?"

I didn't answer her. But I believed her, that this was all she knew, extreme as it was.

And now I did penetrate her mind, calling on my power to know her past and present, to know her most secret and casual thoughts.

She looked at me with clear unquestioning eyes, as if she felt what I was doing to her, or trying to do, and it seemed that she would not hold anything back.

But what did I learn? Only that she had told me the truth. *I know no more of your beautiful blood drinker.* She was patient with me, and then there came a wave of true grief. *I loved Eudoxia. You destroyed her. And now you cannot leave me alone.*

I stood up and went again to walking about the room. Its sumptuous Byzantine furnishings stifled me. The thick patterned hangings seemed to fill the air with dust. And nowhere could I glimpse the night sky from this chamber, for we were too far from the inner garden court.

But what did I want just now? Only to be free of this creature, no, free of the whole knowledge of her, of the whole awareness of her, free of ever having seen her, and that was quite impossible, was it not?

Suddenly a sound interrupted me and I realized that at last Avicus and Mael had come.

They found their way through the many rooms to the bedchamber, and as both of them entered, they were astonished to see the gorgeous young woman seated on the side of the immense heavily draped bed.

I stood silent while the two of them absorbed the shock. Immediately Avicus was drawn to Zenobia, as drawn to her as he had been to Eudoxia, and this creature had yet to speak a single word.

In Mael I saw suspicion and a bit of concern. He looked to me searchingly. He was not spellbound by the young woman's beauty. His feelings were under his command.

Avicus drew near to Zenobia, and as I watched him, as I watched his eyes fire with a passion for her, I saw my way out. I saw it plainly, and when I did, I felt a terrible regret. I felt my solemn vow to be alone weigh heavily upon me, as if I had taken it in the name of a god, and perhaps I had. I had taken it in the name of Those Who Must Be Kept. But there must be no more thoughts of them now, not in Zenobia's presence.

As for the child woman herself, she was far more drawn to Avicus, perhaps because of his immediate and obvious devotion, than she was to the distant and somewhat suspicious Mael.

"Thank you for coming," I said. "I know it was not your choice to set foot in this house."

"What's happened?" Mael asked. "Who is this creature?"

"The companion of Eudoxia, sent away for her own protection until the battle with us could be finished, and now that it is finished, here is the child."

"Child?" asked Zenobia gently. "I am no child."

Avicus and Mael both smiled indulgently at her, though her look was grave and disapproving.

"I was as old as Eudoxia," she said, "when the Blood was given to her. 'Never make a blood drinker of a greater age,' said Eudoxia. 'For a greater mortal age can only lead to misery later on from habits learned in mortal life.' All of Eudoxia's slaves received the Blood at my age, and were therefore no longer children, but blood drinkers prepared for eternal life within the Blood."

I said nothing to this, but I never forgot it. Mark me. I never forgot it. Indeed, there came a time a thousand years after, when these words meant a great deal to me, and they came to haunt my nights and to torture me. But we will come soon enough to that, for I mean to pass over that thousand years very quickly. But let me return to my tale.

This little speech from Zenobia was spoken tenderly as all her words had been spoken, and when she finished it I could see that Avicus was charmed. This did not mean that he would love her completely or forever, mind you, I knew that. But I could see that there was no barrier between the child and himself.

He drew closer still and seemed at a loss to express his respect for her beauty, and then, surprising me completely, he spoke to her:

"My name is Avicus," he said. "I am a long-time friend of Marius." Then he looked at me, and then back to Zenobia. He asked: "Are you alone?"

"Quite alone," said Zenobia, though she did glance at me first to see if I meant to silence her, "and if you—all of you or perhaps one of you—do not take me with you out of here, or remain with me in this house, I'm lost."

I nodded to both my long-time companions.

Mael gave me a withering look and shook his head in negation. He glanced at Avicus. But Avicus was still looking at our child.

"You won't be left here unprotected," said Avicus, "that's unthinkable. But you must leave us alone now, so that we may talk. No, you remain where you are. There are many rooms in this house. Marius, where can we gather?"

"The library," I said at once. "Come, both of you. Zenobia, don't be afraid, and don't try to listen, for you may hear only parts of what we say, and all is what matters. All is what will contain the true sentiments of the heart."

I led the way, and we quickly seated ourselves in Eudoxia's fine library just as we had only a short time before.

"You must take her," I said. "I can't do it. I'm leaving here and I'm taking the Mother and the Father, just as I've told you. Take her under your wing."

"This is impossible," Mael declared, "she's far too weak. And I don't want her! I tell you that plainly, I don't want her!"

Avicus reached out and covered Mael's hand with his own.

"Marius can't take her," said Avicus. "He's speaking the simple truth. It's not a choice. He cannot have such a little creature with him."

"Little creature," said Mael disgustedly. "Say what's really the truth. She is a frail creature, an unknowing creature, and she will bring us harm."

"I beg you both, take her," I said. "Teach her all that you know. Teach her what she needs to be on her own."

"But she's a woman," said Mael disgustedly. "How could she ever be on her own?"

"Mael, when one is a blood drinker such a thing doesn't matter," I said. "Once she is strong, once she truly knows everything, she can live like Eudoxia once lived if she chooses. She can live any way that she likes."

"No, I don't want her," said Mael. "I will not take her. Not for any price or on any terms."

I was about to speak but when I saw the look on his face, I realized he was telling the truth more completely than he knew himself. He would never be reconciled to Zenobia, and if I did leave her with him, I would be leaving her in danger. For he would abandon her or desert her, or even worse. It would only be a matter of time.

I looked to Avicus only to see that he was miserably at the mercy of Mael's words. As always he was in Mael's power. As always he could not break free of Mael's anger.

Avicus pleaded with him. Surely it would not change their lives so very much. They could teach her to hunt, could they not? Why, surely she knew already how to hunt. She wasn't so very human, this lovely little girl. It wasn't hopeless, and shouldn't they do what I had asked?

"I want her to be with us," said Avicus warmly. "I find her lovely. And I see in her a sweetness that touches my heart."

"Yes, there is that," I said. "It's very true, this sweetness."

"And why is such a thing of use in a blood drinker?" asked Mael. "A blood drinker should be sweet?"

I couldn't speak. I thought of Pandora. The pain in me was simply too intense for me to form words. But I saw Pandora. I saw her, and I knew that she had always combined both passion and sweetness, and that both men and women can have such traits, and this child, Zenobia, might grow in both.

I looked off, unable to speak to either of them as they argued, but I realized suddenly that Avicus had grown angry, and that Mael was boiling to a rage.

When I looked back to them, they fell silent. Then Avicus looked at me as if for some authority which I knew that I did not possess.

"I can't command your future," I said. "I'm leaving you as you know."

"Stay and keep her with us," said Avicus.

"Unthinkable!" I said.

"You're stubborn, Marius," said Avicus softly. "Your own strongest passions frighten you. We could be the four of us in this house."

"I've brought about the death of the owner of this house," I said, "I cannot live in it. It is blasphemy against the old gods that I linger this long. The old gods will bring about vengeance not so much because they exist but because I once honored them. As for this city, I've told you, I must leave it, and I must take Those Who Must Be Kept to where they are truly secret and safe."

"The house is yours by right," said Avicus. "And you know this. You've offered it to us."

"You didn't destroy her," I said. "Now let us return to the question at hand. Will you take this girl?"

"We will not," said Mael.

Avicus could say nothing. He had no choice.

I looked away once more. My thoughts were purely and completely with Pandora on the isle of Crete, something which I could not even envision. Pandora, the wanderer. I said nothing for the longest while.

Then I rose without addressing either one of them, for they had disappointed me, and I went back into the bedchamber where the lovely young creature lay on the bed.

Her eyes were closed. The lamplight was soft. What a lush and passive being she seemed to be, her hair cascading over the pillow, her skin flawless, her mouth half closed.

I sat down beside her.

"Besides your beauty, why did Eudoxia choose you?" I asked. "Did she ever say?"

She opened her eyes as if startled, which could be the case with one so young, and then she reflected before answering, to say finally in a soft voice:

"Because I was quick of wit and knew whole books by memory. She had me recite them to her." Without rising from the pillows, she held her hands as if she had a bound book in them. "I could but glance at a page and remember all of it. And I had no mortals to grieve for. I was but one of a hundred attendants to the Empress. I was a virgin. I was a slave."

"I see. Was there anything more?"

I was aware that Avicus had come to the door, but I said nothing to acknowledge him.

Zenobia thought for a moment, then answered:

"She said my soul was incorruptible, that though I'd seen wickedness in the Imperial palace, I could still hear music in the rain."

I nodded. "Do you still hear it, this music?"

"Yes," she said. "More than ever, I think. Though if you leave me here, it won't sustain me."

"I'm going to give you something before I leave you," I said.

"What is that? What can it be?" She sat up, pushing herself back against the pillows. "What can you give me that will help me?"

"What do you think?" I asked gently. "My blood."

I heard Avicus gasp at the doorway, but I paid no attention to it. Indeed, I paid no attention to anything but her.

"I'm strong, little one," I said, "very strong. And after you've drunk from me, as long as you wish and however much you wish, you'll be a different creature from the one you are now."

She was mystified and drawn by the notion. Timidly she lifted her hands and placed them on my shoulders.

"And this I should do now?"

"Yes," I said. I was seated firmly there, and I let her take hold of me, and as I felt her teeth go into my neck, I gave out a long sigh. "Drink, precious one," I said. "Pull hard to take as much blood from me as you can."

My mind was flooded with a thousand tripping visions of the Imperial palace, of golden rooms, and banquets, of music and magicians, of the daylight city with its wild chariot races crashing through the Hippodrome, of the crowd screaming with applause, of the Emperor rising in his Imperial box to wave to those who worshiped him, of the huge processions passing into Hagia Sophia, of candles and incense, and once again of palatial splendor, this time beneath this roof.

I grew weak. I grew sick. But it didn't matter. What mattered was she must take all that she could.

And at last, she fell back on the pillows, and I looked down at her, and I saw her cheeks stark white with the Blood.

Scrambling to sit up, to look at me, she stared like a newborn blood drinker as if she'd never had the true vision of the Blood before.

She climbed off the bed and walked about the room. She made a huge circle, her right hand clenching the fabric of her tunic, her face shining with its new whiteness, her eyes wide and swimming and bright.

She stared at me as if she'd never seen me before. Then she stopped, obviously hearing distant sounds to which she'd been deaf. She put her hands to her ears. Her face was full of quiet awe and sweetness, yes, sweetness, and then her eyes played over me.

I tried to climb to my feet but I was too weak for it. Avicus came to help me but I waved him away.

"What have you done to her!" he said.

"You see what I've done," I answered. "Both of you, you who wouldn't take her. I've given her my blood. *I've given her a chance.*"

I went to Zenobia and made her look at me.

"Pay attention to me," I said. "Did Eudoxia tell you of her early life?" I asked. "Do you know that you can hunt the streets as a man?"

She stared at me with her new eyes, too dazzled, uncomprehending.

"Do you know that your hair, if cut, will grow back in the space of one day, and be as long and full as before?"

She shook her head, her eyes passing over me and over the myriad bronze lamps of the room, and over the mosaics of the walls and the floor.

"Listen to me, lovely creature, I don't have that much time to teach you," I said. "I mean to leave you armed with knowledge as well as strength."

Assuring her again that her hair would grow back, I cut it off for her, watching as it fell to the floor, and then taking her to the rooms of the male blood drinkers, I dressed her in male clothes.

Then ordering Mael and Avicus sternly to leave us, I took her out with me into the city, and tried to show her the manner in which a man would walk, and how fearless he might be, and what was the life of the taverns, which she'd never even dreamt of, and how to hunt on her own.

All the while I found her enchanting as I had before. She seemed now to be her own older, wiser sister. And as she laughed over the usual wasted cup of wine at the table in the tavern, I found myself half resolving that I would urge her to come with me, but then I knew I could not.

"You don't really look like a man, you know," I said to her, smiling, "hair or no hair."

She laughed. "Of course, I don't. I know it. But to be in such a place as this, a place I'd never see if it weren't for you."

"You can do anything now," I told her. "Merely think on it. You can be male. You can be female. You can be neither. Seek the Evil Doer as I do and you will never choke on death. But always, whatever your joys, whatever your misery, don't put yourself in danger of the judgment of others. Measure your strength and take care."

She nodded, her eyes wide with fascination. Of course the men in the tavern shot glances at her. They thought I had brought my pretty boy out drinking with me. Before things got out of hand, I left with her, but not before she had tested her powers to read the minds of those around her, and to daze the poor slave boy who had brought our wine.

As we walked through the streets, I gave her random instructions in the ways of the world which I thought she might need. I enjoyed doing this far too much.

She described for me all the secrets of the Imperial palace so that I might better penetrate it to satisfy my curiosity, and then we found ourselves in a tavern again.

I warned her,

"You'll come to hate me for what I did to Eudoxia, and for what I did to the other blood drinkers as well."

"No, that's not so," she said plainly. "You must understand that Eudoxia never allowed me one moment of freedom, and as for the others they felt only contempt for me or jealousy, I never knew which."

I nodded, accepting this, but then I asked her,

"Why do you think that Eudoxia told me the story of her life, of how she herself had once wandered in a boy's clothing in Alexandria, when she never told you such things?"

"She had some hope of loving you," Zenobia answered. "She confided this to me, not directly you understand, but through her descriptions of you and her enthusiasm for seeing you. But these emotions were mixed up in her mind with wariness and cunning. And I think that her fear of you won out."

I was quiet, thinking it over, the tavern noises like music.

Zenobia was watching me and then she said,

"From me, she wanted no such knowledge of herself or understanding. She was content to have me as a plaything. And even when I read to her or sang for her, she would not really look at me, or care for me. But you? You, she saw as a being who was worthy of her. When she spoke of you, it was as if no one was listening. She went on and on, making her plan to summon you to her house and speak with you. It was an obsession full of fear. Don't you see?"

"It went so wrong," I said. "But come, there are many things I must teach you. We have only so many hours before dawn."

We went out into the night, holding fast to each other. How I loved teaching her! There was such a spell to it for me.

I showed her how she might climb walls effortlessly, and how easy it was to get past mortals in the shadows, and how she could draw mortal victims to herself.

We crept into Hagia Sophia, a thing she believed to be impossible, and for the first time since she'd been given the Blood she saw the great church she'd known so well when she was alive.

Finally, after we'd both claimed victims in the back streets for the night's thirst, at which time she learnt of her considerable new strength, we returned to the house.

There I found the official documents pertaining to its ownership, and I examined these with her, and suggested how she might maintain the house of Eudoxia for her own.

Avicus and Mael were both there. And as it came near to sunrise they asked if they might remain.

"That question you must put to Zenobia," I said. "This house belongs to her."

Immediately, in her kindness of heart she told them to remain. They could take the hidden places that had belonged to Asphar and Rashid.

I could see that she found the well-built Avicus with his finely molded features quite handsome, and she also seemed to look far too kindly and guilelessly upon Mael.

I said nothing. But I was feeling extraordinary confusion and pain. I didn't want to be separated from her. I wanted to lie down in the darkness of the crypt with her. But it was time for me to take my leave.

Being very weary, no matter how good the hunting had been, and it had been marvelous, I went back to the ashes of my house, and down into the shrine of the Divine Parents and lay down to sleep.

13

I AM NOW at an important point in my story, for I mean to come forward in time towards the present by something slightly near to a thousand years.

I cannot say exactly how much time had passed for I am not sure when I left Constantinople, only that it was well after the reign of the Emperor Justinian and Theodora, and before the Arabs had risen with the new religion of Islam and begun their swift and remarkable conquest from East to West.

But the important matter here is that I cannot tell you all my life, and that I choose now to pass over those centuries which history has seen fit to call the Dark Ages, and during which I did in fact live through many small stories which I might confess or make known at a later date.

For now, let me say only that as I left Zenobia's house that night, I was greatly agitated for the safety of Those Who Must Be Kept.

The attack of the mob on our house had left me almost terror stricken. Those Who Must Be Kept had to be taken to safety well away from any city and any lodging of mine within a city. They had to be unreachable save by me.

Where could I take them, that was the question.

I could not go East due to the warring Persian Empire, which had already taken Asia Minor whole and entire from the Greeks, and had even captured the city of Alexandria.

As for my beloved Italy, I wanted to be near it, but not in it as the turmoil there was unendurable for me to behold.

But I did know of a very good place.

The Italian Alps, or the mountain range to the North of the Italian peninsula, was an area I had known in my mortal years. Several passes had been built through the mountains by the Romans, and I myself when young and fearless had traveled the Via Claudia Augusta, and I knew the character of the land.

Of course the barbarians had frequently swept through the Alpine valleys, both as they went down to attack Italy, and as they withdrew. And there was a great deal of Christianity in those lands now, with churches, monasteries and the like.

But I would not be seeking a fertile and populated valley, and certainly not a mountaintop on which a castle or church or monastery had been built.

I needed only the seclusion of a small, high and completely hidden valley that only I could reach.

And I would perform the arduous task of climbing, digging, clearing and creating a vault, and then bringing the Mother and the Father to this safe place. Only a superhuman creature could do this, but I could do it. I had to do it.

There was truly no other path for me.

All the while, as I thought this over, as I hired slaves and purchased wagons for my journey, as I made my preparations, Zenobia was my companion, though Avicus and Mael would have joined us if I had allowed. I was too angry with them still for their early refusal to protect Zenobia. And it did not assuage my anger that they wanted to remain with Zenobia now.

Zenobia sat with me long hours in this tavern or that one, as I made my plan. Did I care that she might read from my mind my thoughts on where I was going? Not at all, for I had only a dim scheme of it myself. The final location of the shrine of Those Who Must Be Kept would be known to no one but me.

From such a safe place, in the Alpine regions, I could venture out to feed upon the populace of any number of different towns. Indeed there had been a great deal of settlement in the land of the Franks, as they were called, and I could even venture into Italy if I wished, for it was very plain now to me that Those Who Must Be Kept did not require my daily vigilance or attendance by any means.

At last the final night came. The wagons had been loaded with their precious sarcophagi, the slaves had been dazed and mildly threatened and wantonly bribed with luxuries and money, the bodyguards were ready for the journey, and I was ready to set out.

I went to the house of Zenobia and found her crying bitterly.

"Marius, I don't want you to go," she declared.

Avicus and Mael were there, staring at me fearfully, as if they didn't dare say what was in their hearts.

"I don't want to go either," I declared to Zenobia, and then I embraced her as warmly as I had ever done and I kissed her all over as I'd kissed her the first night I found her. I could not get enough of her tender baby woman flesh. "I have to go," I said. "My heart will stand for nothing less."

Finally, we broke off, both exhausted with crying, and no better for it, and I turned to the other two.

"You will take care of her," I said sternly to both of them.

"Yes, we mean to remain together," said Avicus. "And I don't understand why you can't remain with us."

As I looked at Avicus, an awful love welled up in me, and I said softly, "I know I have done you wrong in all this. I have been too harsh, but I can't remain."

Avicus gave way to tears now, with no regard for the disapproving looks of Mael.

"You had only begun to teach me so much," he said.

"You can learn it from the world around you," I answered. "You can learn from the books in this house. You can learn from . . . you can learn from those you might some night transform with the Blood."

He nodded. What more was there to say.

It seemed the moment for me to turn and go, but I could not. I walked into the other room, and I stood there, my head bowed, feeling perhaps the worst pain I had ever known.

I wanted desperately to remain with them! There was no doubt of it. And all my plans gave me no strength just now. I put my hand to my waist and I felt of the pain inside me as if it were fire. I couldn't speak. I couldn't move.

Zenobia came to me. And so did Avicus. They put their arms around me, and then Avicus said,

"I understand that you must go. I do. I understand."

I couldn't answer him. I bit down hard on my tongue to make the blood flow and, turning, I put my lips over his and let the blood pass into his mouth. He shivered with this kiss, and his grip tightened on me.

Then I brought the blood up in my mouth again and I kissed Zenobia in the same manner and she held me fast. I picked up her long light perfumed hair, and buried my face in it, or rather brought it as a veil over my face and I could scarce breathe for the pain I felt.

"I love you both," I whispered. I wondered if they could hear.

Then with no more words, and no more gestures, I bowed my head and found my way, somehow, out of the house.

An hour later, I was outside Constantinople, on the well-traveled route to Italy, seated at the front of the first of the wagons where I might talk with the head of my guard who held the reins.

I was playing the mortal game of conversation and laughter, when my heart was broken, and I played it for many nights to come.

I don't remember how long we traveled, only that there were numerous towns in which we might stop, and the roads were nothing as bad as I had feared. I kept a close eye on my bodyguards and gave out the gold generously to buy loyalty and on we went.

After I reached the Alps it took me some time to find the very secluded spot where I would build the shrine.

But finally one evening when the winter was not so cold and the sky very clear, I did spy above me a steep series of unpopulated slopes, just off the main road, that looked more than perfect for my plan.

Taking my caravan into the nearest town, I came back alone. I climbed over rough terrain which would have defeated any mortal, and found the very spot, a tiny valley above which I could build the shrine.

Going back to the town, I purchased a dwelling for myself, and for Those Who Must Be Kept, and then I sent my bodyguards, with my slaves, back to Constantinople, with great rewards for all they'd done.

There were many warm farewells from my confused but amiable mortal companions, and very cheerfully they set out with one of the wagons which I gave them to make their way back home.

As the town where I was lodged was not safe from invasions, no matter how contented its Lombard inhabitants, I set about my work the following night.

Only a blood drinker could have covered the distance with such speed that separated my town dwelling from the final location of the shrine. Only a blood drinker could have dug through hard-packed earth and rock to create the passages that led eventually to the square room of the vault, and then made the ironbound stone door which would separate the King and the Queen from the light of day.

Only a blood drinker could have painted the walls with the old

Greco-Roman gods and goddesses. Only a blood drinker could have made the throne of granite with such skill and in such time.

Only a blood drinker could have carried the Mother and Father one by one up the mountain and into the finished resting place. Only a blood drinker could have set them side by side on their granite throne.

And when it was finished, who else would have lain down in the coldness to weep again out of some habitual loneliness? Who else could have lain for some two weeks in quietude and exhaustion, refusing to move?

It was no wonder that in those first few months I tried to prompt some vitality from Those Who Must Be Kept by bringing to them sacrifices, like unto Eudoxia, but for these poor wretched mortals—Evil Doers, I quite assure you—Akasha refused to move her all-powerful right arm. And so I must finish with these miserable victims and carry their remains high into the mountains where I flung them on jagged peaks as so many offerings to cruel gods.

In the following centuries, I did hunt the nearby towns most carefully, drinking a little from many so as never to rouse a local population, and sometimes I did travel a great distance to discover how things were in the cities I'd once known.

I visited Pavia, Marseilles, and Lyons. There I visited the taverns as had always been my custom, daring to draw mortals into conversation, plying them with wine to tell me all that went on in the world. Now and then I explored the very battlefields where the Islamic warriors achieved their victories. Or followed the Franks into battle, easily using the darkness as my shield. And during this period—for the first time in my immortal existence—I made close mortal friends.

That is, I would choose a mortal, a soldier for instance, and meet with him often in his local tavern to talk about his view of the world, about his life. Never were these friendships very long or very deep, for I wouldn't allow them to be so, and if ever the temptation came over me to make a blood drinker, I would swiftly move on.

But I came to know many mortals in this way, even monks in their monasteries, for I had no shyness about accosting them on the road, especially when they passed through dangerous territory, and accompanying them for some time while asking them polite questions about how it went with the Pope and the church and even the small communities in which they lived.

There are stories I could tell of these mortals, for sometimes I couldn't guard my heart so very well. But there is no time now for that. Let me only confess that I made the friendships, and when I look back on it, I pray to some god who might be willing to answer me, that I gave as good a consolation from this as I received.

When I was most courageous of heart, I went down into Italy as far as Ravenna to see the marvelous churches which possessed the same magnificent mosaics as I had seen in Constantinople. But never did I dare to go further into my native land. I was too afraid to see the destruction of all that had once been there.

As for the news of the world which I learnt from those I befriended, in the main it broke my heart.

Constantinople had abandoned Italy, and only the Pope of Rome stood firm against its invaders. Islamic Arabs conquered all the world it seemed, including Gaul. Then Constantinople became involved in a terrible crisis over the validity of Holy Pictures, condemning them out of hand, which meant the wholesale destruction of mosaics in churches as well as ikons—a horrid war against art which scorched my soul.

The Pope of Rome would have no part of it, thank Heaven, and turning his back officially on the Eastern Empire, he made alliances with the Franks.

This was the end of the dream of the great Empire that included both East and West. It was the end of my dream that Byzantium would somehow preserve the civilization which Rome had once preserved.

But it did not mean the end of the civilized world. Even I, the bitter Roman Patrician, had to admit to that.

There soon rose among the Franks a great leader, eventually to be called Charlemagne, and his victories were many in maintaining some sort of peace in the West. Meantime there gathered around him a court where some of the old Latin literature was encouraged like a fragile flame.

But in the main it was the church which now kept alive the aspects of culture which had been part of the Roman world to which I'd been born. Ah, such an irony, that Christianity, this rebel religion, born of martyrdom during the Pax Romana, now preserved the old writings, the old language, the old poetry, and the old speech.

As the centuries passed, I grew stronger; every gift I possessed was enhanced. While lying in the vault with the Mother and the Father, I could hear the voices of people in towns far away. I could hear an occasional blood drinker pass close to me. I could hear thoughts or prayers.

At last the Cloud Gift came to me. I needn't climb the slope to the vault any longer. I had only to will myself to rise from the road and I stood before the hidden doors to the passage. It was frightening, yet I loved it for I could travel even greater distances when I had the strength for it, which was less often as time went on.

Meantime castles and monasteries had come to appear in this land which had once been the territory of warring barbarian tribes. With the Cloud Gift I could visit the high peaks upon which these marvelous structures were created and sometimes slip into their very rooms.

I was a drifter through eternity, a spy among other hearts. I was a blood thing who knew nothing about death and finally nothing about time.

Sometimes on the winds I drifted. Always through the lives of others I drifted. And in the mountain vault I did my usual painting for Those Who Must Be Kept, covering their walls this time with old Egyptians come to make sacrifice, and I kept my few books there that comforted my soul.

In the monasteries I often spied upon the monks. I loved to watch them writing in their scriptoriums, and it was a comfort to me to see that they kept the old Greek and Roman poetry safe. In the small hours, I went into the libraries, and there, a hooded figure, hunched over the lectern, I read the old poetry and history from my time.

Never was I discovered. I was far too clever. And often I lingered outside the chapel in the evening, listening to the plainsong of the monks, which created a peace inside of me, rather like walking the cloisters, or listening to the steeple bells.

Meantime the art of Greece and Rome which I had loved so much completely died away. A dour religious art took its place. Proportion and naturalism were no longer important. What mattered was that those images which were rendered be evocative of devotion to God.

Human figures in paintings or in stone were often impossibly gaunt, with bold staring eyes. A dreadful grotesquery reigned. It was not for want of knowledge, or skill, for manuscripts were decorated with tremendous patience, and monasteries and churches were built at great cost. Those who made this art could have made anything. It was a choice. Art was not to be sensual. Art was to be pious. Art was to be grim. And so the classical world was lost.

Of course I found wonders in this new world, I cannot deny it. Using the Cloud Gift, I traveled to the great Gothic cathedrals, whose high arches surpassed anything I'd ever beheld. I was stunned by the beauty of these cathedrals. I marveled at the market towns which were growing up all over Europe. It seemed that commerce and crafts had settled the land which war could not settle alone.

New languages were spoken everywhere. French was the language of the elite. But there was English and German and Italian as well.

I saw it all happening, and yet I saw nothing. And then finally, perhaps in the year 1200—I am uncertain—I lay down in the vault for a long sleep.

I was weary of the world and quite impossibly strong. I confessed my intentions to Those Who Must Be Kept. The lamps would eventually burn down, I told them. And there would only be darkness, but please, would they forgive me. I was tired. I wanted to sleep for a long, long time.

As I slept, I learnt. My preternatural hearing was too strong now for me to lie in silence. I could not escape the voices of those who cried out, be they blood drinkers or humans. I could not escape the drifting history of the world.

And so it was with me in the high Alpine pass where I was hidden. I heard the prayers of Italy. I heard the prayers of Gaul which had now become the country known as France.

I heard the souls suffering the terrible disease of the thirteen hundreds known now most appropriately as the Black Death.

In the darkness I opened my eyes. I listened. Perhaps I even studied. And then finally I roused myself and went down into Italy, afraid for the fate of all the world. I had to see the land I loved with my own eyes. I had to go back.

The city that drew me was one I had not known before in my life. It was a new city, in that it had not existed in the ancient time of the Caesars, and was now a great port. In fact, it was very likely the greatest city of all Europe. Venice was the name of it, and the Black Death had come to it by way of the ships in its harbor, and thousands were desperately sick.

Never had I visited it before. It would have been too painful, and now as I came into Venice, I found it a city of gorgeous palaces built upon dark green canals. But the Black Death had ahold of the populace who were dying in huge numbers daily, and ferries were taking the bodies out to be buried deeply in the soil of the islands in the city's immense lagoon.

Everywhere there was weeping and desolation. People gathered together to die in sickrooms, faces covered in sweat, bodies tormented by incurable swellings. The stench of the dead rose everywhere. Some were trying to flee the city and its infestation. Others remained with their suffering loved ones.

Never had I seen such a plague. And yet it was amid a city of such remarkable splendor, I found myself numb with sorrow and tantalized by the beauty of the palaces, and by the wonder of the Church of San Marco which bore exquisite testament to the city's ties with Byzantium to which it sent its many merchant ships.

I could do nothing but weep in such a place. It was no time for peering by torchlight at paintings or statues that were wholly new to me. I had to depart, out of respect for the dying, no matter what I was.

And so I made my way South to another city which I had not known in my mortal life, the city of Florence in the heart of Tuscany, a beautiful and fertile land.

Understand, I was avoiding Rome at this point. I could not bear to see my home, once more in ruin and misery. I could not see Rome visited by this plague.

So Florence was my choice, as I have said—a city new to me, and prosperous, though not as rich as Venice perhaps, and not as beautiful, though full of huge palaces and paved streets.

And what did I find, but the same dreadful pestilence. Vicious bullies demanded payment to remove the bodies, often beating the dying or those who tried to tend them. Six to eight corpses lay at the doors of various houses. The priests came and went by torchlight, trying to give the Last Rites. And everywhere the same stench as in Venice, the stench that says all is coming to an end.

Weary and miserable, I made my way into a church, somewhere near the center of Florence, though I cannot say what church it was, and I stood against the wall, gazing at the distant tabernacle by candlelight, wondering as so many praying mortals wondered: What would become of this world?

I had seen Christians persecuted; I had seen barbarians sack cities; I had seen East and West quarrel and finally break with each other; I had seen Islamic soldiers waging their holy war against the infidel; and now I had seen this disease which was moving all through the world.

And such a world, for surely it had changed since the year when I had fled Constantinople. The cities of Europe had grown full and rich as flowers. The barbarian hordes had become settled people. Byzantium still held the cities of the East together.

And now this dreadful scourge—this plague.

Why had I remained alive, I wondered? Why must I endure as the witness to all these many tragic and wonderful things? What was I to make of what I beheld?

And yet, even in my sorrow, I found the church beautiful with its myriad lighted candles, and spying a bit of color far ahead of me, in one of the chapels to the right side of the high altar, I made my way towards it, knowing full well that I would find rich paintings there, for I could see something of them already.

None of those ardently praying in the church took any notice of me, a single being in a red velvet hooded cloak, moving silently and swiftly to the open chapel so that I might see what was painted there.

Oh, if only the candles had been brighter. If only I had dared to light a torch. But I had the eyes of a blood drinker, didn't I? Why complain? And in this chapel I saw painted figures unlike any I had seen before. They were religious, yes, and they were severe, yes, and they were pious, yes, but something new had been sparked here, something that one might almost call sublime.

A mixture of elements had been forged. And I felt a great joy even in my sorrow, until I heard a low voice behind me, a mortal voice. It was speaking so softly that I doubt another mortal would even have heard.

"He's dead," said the mortal. "They're all dead, all the painters who did this work."

I was shocked with pain.

"The plague took them," said this man.

He was a hooded figure as I was, only his cloak was of a dark color, and he looked at me with bright feverish eyes.

"Don't fear," he said. "I've suffered it and it hasn't killed me and I can't pass it on, don't you see? But they're all dead, those painters. They're gone. The plague's taken them and all they knew."

"And you?" I asked. "Are you a painter?"

He nodded. "They were my teachers," he said as he gestured towards the walls. "This is our work, unfinished," he said. "I can't do it alone."

"You must do it," I said. I reached into my purse. I took out several gold coins, and I gave them to him.

"You think this will help?" he asked, dejectedly.

"It's all I have to give," I said. "Maybe it can buy you privacy and quiet. And you can begin to paint again."

I turned to go.

"Don't leave me," he said suddenly.

I turned around and looked at him. His gaze was level with mine and very insistent.

"Everyone's dying and you and I are not dying," he said. "Don't go. Come with me, have a drink of wine with me. Stay with me."

"I can't," I said. I was trembling. I was too charmed by him, much too much. I was so close to killing him. "I would stay with you if I could," I said.

And then I left the city of Florence, and I returned to the vault of Those Who Must Be Kept.

I lay down again for a long sleep, feeling the coward that I had not gone to Rome, and thankful that I had not drunk dry the blood of the exquisite soul who had approached me in the church.

But something had been forever changed in me.

In the church in Florence I had glimpsed new paintings. I had glimpsed something which filled me with hope.

Let the plague run its course, I prayed, and I closed my eyes.

And the plague did finally die out.

All the voices of Europe sang.

They sang of the new cities, and great victories, and terrible defeats. Everything in Europe was being transformed. Commerce and prosperity bred art and culture, as the royal courts and cathedrals and monasteries of the recent past had done.

They sang of a man named Gutenberg in the city of Mainz who had invented a printing press which could make cheap books by the hundreds. Common people could own their own copies of Sacred Scripture, books of the Holy Hours, books of comic stories and pretty poems. All over Europe new printing presses were being built.

They sang of the tragic fall of Constantinople to the invincible Turkish army. But the proud cities of the West no longer depended upon the far-away Greek Empire to protect them. The lament for Constantinople went unheeded.

Italy, my Italy, was illuminated by the glory of Venice and Florence and Rome.

It was time now for me to leave this vault.

I roused myself from my excited dreams.

It was time for me to see this world which marked its time as the year after Christ 1482.

Why I chose that year I am uncertain except perhaps that the voices of Venice and Florence called me most eloquently, and I had earlier beheld these cities in their tribulation and grief. I wanted desperately to see them in their splendor.

But I must go home first, all the way South to Rome.

So lighting the oil lamps once more for my beloved Parents, wiping the dust from their ornaments and their fragile robes, praying to them as I always did, I took my leave to enter one of the most exciting times which the Western world had ever seen.

14

I WENT TO ROME. I could settle for nothing less.

What I found there was to sting my heart, but also to astonish me. It was an enormous and busy city, determined to rise from layers upon layers of ruin, full of merchants and craftsmen hard at work on grand palaces for the Pope and his Cardinals and for other rich men.

The old Forum and Colosseum were still standing, indeed there were many many recognizable ruins of Imperial Rome—including the Arch of Constantine—but blocks of ancient stone were constantly being pilfered for new buildings. However scholars were everywhere studying these ruins, and many argued for their maintenance as they were.

Indeed the whole thrust of the age was to preserve the remnants of the ancient times in which I'd been born, and indeed to learn from them, and imitate the art and the poetry, and the vigor of this movement surpassed my wildest dreams.

How can I say it more lucidly? This prosperous era, given over to trade and banking, in which so many thousands wore thick and beautiful clothes of velvet, had fallen in love with the beauty of ancient Rome and Greece!

Never had I thought such a reversal would occur as I had lain in my vault during the weary centuries, and I was at first too exhilarated by all I saw to do much but walk about the muddy streets, accosting mortals with as much graciousness as I could muster, asking them questions about what was going on about them, and what they thought of the times in which they lived.

Of course I spoke the new language, Italian, which had grown up from the old Latin, and I soon became used to it on my ears and on my tongue. It wasn't such a bad language. Indeed it was beautiful, though I quickly learnt that scholars were well versed in their Latin and Greek.

Out of a multitude of answers to my questions I also learnt that Florence and Venice were deemed to be far ahead of Rome in their spiritual rebirth, but if the Pope were to have his way that was soon to change.

The Pope was no longer only a Christian ruler. He had made up his mind that Rome must be a true cultural and artistic capital, and not only was he completing work upon the new St. Peter's Basilica but he was working as well upon the Sistine Chapel, a great enterprise within his palatial walls.

Artists had been brought from Florence for some of this painting, and the city was much intrigued as to the merits of the frescoes which had been done.

I spent as much time as I could in the streets and in the taverns listening to gossip of all this, and then I made for the Papal Palace determined to see the Sistine Chapel for myself.

What a fateful night this was for me.

In all the dark centuries since I had left my beloved Zenobia and Avicus, I had had my heart stolen by various mortals and various works of art, but nothing I had experienced could quite prepare me for what I was to see when I entered the Sistine Chapel.

Understand, I do not speak of Michelangelo, so well known to all the world for his work there, for Michelangelo was but a child at this time. And his works in the Sistine Chapel were yet to come.

No, it was not the work of Michelangelo that I saw on this fateful night. Put Michelangelo out of your thoughts.

It was the work of someone else.

Getting by the palace guards easily enough, I quickly found myself within the great rectangle of this august chapel, which though not open to the public at large was destined to be used for high ceremonials whenever it should be complete.

And what caught my eye immediately among any number of frescoes was an enormous one filled with brilliantly painted figures, all involving, it seemed, the same dignified elder with golden light streaming from his head as he appeared with three different groupings of those who responded to his command.

Nothing had prepared me for the naturalism with which the multitudinous figures were painted, the vivid yet dignified expressions on the faces of the people, and the gracefully draped garments with which the beings were clothed.

There was great turbulence among these three exquisitely rendered groups of persons as the white-haired figure with the gold light streaming from his head instructed them or upbraided them or corrected them, his own face quite seemingly stern and calm.

All existed in a harmony such as I could never have imagined, and though their creation alone seemed enough to guarantee that this painting should be a masterpiece there was beyond the figures a marvelous depiction of an extravagant wilderness and an indifferent world.

Two great ships of the present period were anchored in the faraway harbor, and beyond the ships there loomed layers of mountains beneath a rich blue sky, and to the right there stood the very Arch of Constantine which still stood in Rome to this day, finely detailed in gold as if it had never been ruined, and the columns of another Roman building, once splendid, now a fragment standing high and proud, though a dark castle loomed beyond.

Ah, such complexity, such inexplicable combinations, such strange matter, and yet every human face so compelling, every hand so exquisitely wrought.

I thought I would go mad just looking at the faces. I thought I would go mad just looking at the hands.

I wanted nights to memorize this painting. I wanted at once to listen at the portals of scholars who could tell me what it was about, for I myself couldn't possibly decipher it! I needed knowledge for this. And more than anything, its sheer beauty spoke to my soul.

All my gloomy years were gone as if a million candles had been lighted in this chapel.

"Oh, Pandora, that you could see this!" I whispered aloud. "Oh, Pandora, if only you knew of this!"

There were other paintings in the unfinished Sistine Chapel. I gave them a passing glance until my eyes hit upon two others by this same Master, and these were as magical as the first.

Once again there was a multitude of persons, all with the same divine faces. Garments were rendered with sculptural depth. And though I recognized the Christ with his winged angels appearing in more than one place in this exquisite fresco, I could not interpret these paintings any more than I could the first.

It didn't matter finally what these paintings meant. They filled me utterly. And in one, there were two maidens rendered so sensitively and yet so sensuously that I was amazed.

The old art of the churches and the monasteries would never have allowed such a thing. Indeed it had banished such carnality completely.

Yet here in the Pope's chapel were these damsels, one with her back to us, and the other facing us, a dreamy expression in her eyes.

"Pandora," I whispered. "I have found you here, found you in your youth and in your eternal beauty. Pandora, you are here on the wall."

I turned away from these frescoes. I paced the floor. Then I went back to them, studying them with my uplifted hands, careful not to touch them, just moving my hands over them, as if I had to look through my hands as well as through my eyes.

I had to know who this painter was! I had to see his work. I had fallen in love with him. I had to see everything ever done by him. Was he young? Was he old? Was he alive? Was he dead? I had to know.

I went out of the chapel, not knowing whom to ask about these marvelous achievements, for surely I could not wake the Pope in his bed and ask him, and in a dark street at the very top of a hill, I found an Evil Doer, a striding drunkard with a dagger ready for me, and I drank my fill of blood in a rush of eagerness that I had not felt in years.

Poor sad victim. I wonder if in my taking of him I gave him some glimpse of those paintings.

I remember so well the moment, for I stood as the top of a narrow stairs which went down the hill to the piazza below me, and I thought only of those paintings as the blood warmed me and I wanted to go back to the chapel at once.

Something interrupted me at that moment. I heard the distinct noise of a blood drinker near me, the bumbling step of one who was young. One hundred years? No more than that, that was my calculation. The creature wanted me to know he was there.

I turned around and saw a tall, well-muscled and dark-haired figure, clothed in the black robes of a monk. His face was white and he did nothing to disguise it. Around his neck he wore a glittering golden crucifix upside down.

"Marius!" he whispered.

"Damn you," I said in answer. Yea gods, how could he know my name! "Whoever you are. Leave me. Get away from me. I warn you. Don't remain in my presence if you want to live."

"Marius!" he said again and he came towards me. "I have no fear of you. I come to you because we need you. You know who we are."

"Worshipers of Satan!" I said in disgust. "Look at that fool ornament around your neck. If the Christ exists, do you think He pays any attention to you? So you still have your foolish little gatherings. You have your lies."

"Foolish?" he said calmly. "We have never been foolish. We do the work of God as we serve Satan. Without Satan, how could there have been the Christ?"

I made a dismissive gesture.

"Get away from me," I said. "I want no part of you." In my heart was locked the secret of Those Who Must Be Kept. I thought of the paintings in the Sistine Chapel. Oh, those lovely figures, those colors . . .

"But don't you see?" he replied. "If one so old and powerful as you were to become our leader, we could be a legion in the catacombs of this city! As it is, we are a dreadful few."

His large black eyes were full of the inevitable zeal. And his rich black hair shimmered in the dim light. He was a comely creature, even coated with dust and dirt as he was. I could smell the catacombs on his garments. I could smell death on him as though he had lain down with mortal remains. But he was handsome, fine of build and proportion as Avicus had been, not unlike Avicus at all.

"You want to be a legion?" I asked him. "You talk nonsense! I was alive when no one spoke of Satan and no one spoke of a Christ. You're merely blood drinkers, and you make up stories for yourselves. How could you believe that I would come to you and lead you?"

He drew closer so that I could all the better see his face. He was full of exuberance and honesty. He held his head proudly.

"Come to us in our catacomb," he said, "come and see us and be a part of our ritual. Sing with us tomorrow night before we go out to hunt." He was passionate and he waited in silence for my reply. He was not a stupid creature by any means, and he did not seem callow like the other followers of Satan whom I had glimpsed in centuries past.

I shook my head. But he pressed on.

"My name is Santino," he said. "I have heard of you for a hundred years. I have dreamt of the moment when we would come upon each other. Satan has brought us together. You must lead us. Only to you would I give up my leadership. Come see my lair with its hundreds of skulls." His voice was refined, well modulated. He spoke a beautiful

Italian. "Come see my followers who worship the Beast with all their hearts. It's the wish of the Beast that you should lead us. It's the wish of God."

How disgusted I was, how much I deplored him and his followers. And I could see the intellect in him. I could see the cleverness and the hope of understanding and wit.

Would that Avicus and Mael were here to put an end to him and all his kith and kin.

"Your lair with its hundreds of skulls?" I repeated. "You think I wish to rule there? Tonight I've seen paintings of such beauty I can't describe them to you. Magnificent works rich in color and brilliance. This city surrounds me with its beautiful allurements."

"Where did you see such paintings?" he asked.

"In the Pope's chapel," I declared.

"But how did you dare to go there?"

"It was nothing for me to do such a thing. I can teach you how to use your powers—."

"But we are creatures of the dark," he said in all simplicity. "We must never go into places of light. God has cursed us to the shadows."

"What god?" I asked. "I go wherever I will. I drink the blood of those who are evil. And the world belongs to me. And you ask me to come down into the earth with you? Into a catacomb full of skulls? You ask me to rule blood drinkers in the name of a demon? You're too clever for your creed, my friend. Forsake it."

"No," he said, shaking his head and stepping backwards. "Ours is a Satanic purity!" he said. "You can't tempt me from it, not with all your power and your tricks, and I give my welcome to you."

I had sparked something in him. I could see it in his black eyes. He was drawn to me, drawn to my words, but he couldn't admit it.

"You'll never be a legion," I said. "The world will never allow it. You're nothing. Give up your trappings. Don't make other blood drinkers to join this foolish crusade."

He drew closer again, as if I were a light and he wanted to be in it. He looked into my eyes, trying no doubt to read my thoughts of which he could get nothing except what I had said in words.

"We are so gifted," I said. "There is so much to be observed, to be learnt. Let me take you back with me into the Pope's chapel to see the paintings I have described."

He drew even closer and something changed in his face.

"Those Who Must Be Kept," he said, "what are they?"

It was like a harsh blow—that once again another knew the secret, a secret I had guarded so well for a thousand years.

"You will never know," I responded.

"No, listen to me," he said. "Are they something profane? Or are they holy?"

I clenched my teeth. I reached out for him, but with a swiftness that surprised me, he escaped me.

I went after him, caught him, and spinning him around, I dragged him to the head of the narrow stone stairs that went down the hill.

"Never come near me again, do you hear?" I said to him. He struggled desperately against me. "I can kill you by fire with my mind if I choose it," I said. "And why don't I choose it? Why don't I choose to slaughter you all, you miserable vermin? Why don't I do it? Because I loathe the violence of it and the cruelty, even though you're more evil than the mortal whom I killed for my thirst tonight."

He was frantically trying to get loose from me, but of course he had not the slightest chance.

Why didn't I destroy him? Was my mind too filled with the beautiful paintings? Was my mind too attuned to the mortal world to be dragged back into this abysmal filth?

I don't know.

What I know is that I threw him down the stone stairway so that he tumbled over and over again, clumsily, miserably, until he finally scrambled to his feet below.

He glared at me, his face full of hatred.

"I curse you, Marius!" he said with remarkable courage. "I curse you and your secret of Those Who Must Be Kept."

I was taken aback by his defiance.

"I warn you, stay away from me, Santino!" I said as I looked down at him. "Be wanderers through time," I said. "Be witnesses of all splendid and beautiful things human. Be true immortals. Not worshipers of Satan! Not servants of a god who will put you in a Christian Hell. But whatever you do, stay clear of me for your own sake."

He was planted there, looking up at me in his fury.

And then it occurred to me to give him a small warning, if only I could do it. And I meant to try.

I brought up the Fire Gift inside of me, feeling it grow powerful and I quelled it ever so carefully and I sent it down towards him, and willed it to kindle only the edge of his black monkish robes.

At once the cloth around his feet began to smoke and he stepped back in horror.

I stopped the power.

He turned round and round in panic and tore the scorched robes off himself, standing there in a long white tunic staring at the smoking cloth that lay on the ground.

Once again he looked at me, fearless as before, but enraged in his helplessness.

"Know what I could do to you," I said, "and never come near to me again."

And then I turned my back on him. And off I went.

I shivered even to think of him and his followers. I shivered to think that I should have to use the Fire Gift again after all these years. I shivered remembering the slaughter of Eudoxia's slaves.

It wasn't even midnight.

I wanted the bright new world of Italy. I wanted the clever scholars and artists of these times. I wanted the huge palazzi of the Cardinals and the other powerful inhabitants of the Eternal City which had risen after all the long miserable years.

Putting the creature named Santino out of my mind I went near to one of the new palazzi in which there was a feast in progress, a masquerade with much dancing and tables laden with food.

It was no problem to me to gain entry. I had equipped myself with the fine velvet clothes of this period, and once inside among the guests, I was welcomed as was everyone else.

I had no mask, only my white face which seemed like one, and my customary red velvet hooded cloak which set me apart from the guests and yet made me one of them at the same time.

The music was intoxicating. The walls were ablaze with fine paintings, though none as magical as what I had seen in the Sistine Chapel, and the crowd was huge and sumptuously dressed.

Quickly, I fell into conversation with the young scholars, the ones who were talking hotly of painting as well as poetry and I asked my dumb question: Who had done the magnificent frescoes in the Sistine Chapel which I had just beheld?

"You've seen these paintings?" said one of the crowd to me. "I don't believe it. We haven't been allowed in to see them. Describe to me again what you saw."

I laid out everything, very simply as though I were a schoolboy.

"The figures are supremely delicate," I said, "with sensitive faces, and each being, though rendered with great naturalness, is ever so slightly too long."

The company around me laughed good naturedly.

"Ever so slightly too long," repeated one of the elders.

"Who did the paintings?" I said, imploringly. "I must meet this man."

"You'll have to go to Florence to meet him," said the elder scholar. "You're talking about Botticelli, and he's already gone home."

"Botticelli," I whispered. It was a strange almost ridiculous name. In Italian it translates to "little tub." But to me it meant magnificence.

"You're certain it was Botticelli," I said.

"Oh, yes," said the elder scholar. The others with us were also nodding. "Everyone's marveling at what he can do. That's why the Pope sent for him. He was here two years working on the Sistine Chapel. Everyone knows Botticelli. And now he's no doubt as busy in Florence as he was here."

"I only want to see him with my own eyes," I said.

"Who are you?" asked one of the scholars.

"No one," I whispered. "No one at all."

There was general laughter. It seemed to blend rather bewitchingly with the music around us, and the glare of so many candles.

I felt drunk on the smell of mortals, and with dreams of Botticelli.

"I have to find Botticelli," I whispered. And bidding them all farewell I went out into the night.

But what was I going to do when I found Botticelli, that was the question. What was driving me? What did I want?

To see all of his works, yes, that much was certain, but what more did my soul require?

My loneliness seemed as great as my age and it frightened me.

I returned to the Sistine Chapel.

I spent the remainder of the night perusing the frescoes once more. Before dawn a guard came upon me. I allowed it to happen. With the Spell Gift I gently convinced him that I belonged where I was.

"Who is the figure here in these paintings?" I asked, "the elder with the beard and the gold light streaming from his head?"

"Moses," said the guard, "you know, Moses the prophet. It all has to do with Moses, and the other painting has to do with Christ." He pointed. "Don't you see the inscription?"

I had not seen it but I saw it now. *The Temptation of Moses, Bearer of the Written Law.*

I sighed. "I wish I knew their stories better," I said. "But the paintings are so exquisite that the story doesn't matter."

The guard only shrugged.

"Did you know Botticelli when he painted here?" I asked.

Once again, the man only shrugged.

"But don't you think the paintings are incomparably beautiful?" I asked him.

He looked at me somewhat stupidly.

I realized how lonely I was that I was speaking to this poor creature, trying to elicit from him some understanding of what I felt.

"Beautiful paintings are everywhere now," he said.

"Yes," I said, "yes, I know they are. But they don't look like this."

I gave him a few gold coins, and left the chapel.

I had only time enough to reach the vault of Those Who Must Be Kept before dawn.

As I lay down to sleep I dreamt of Botticelli, but it was the voice of Santino that haunted me. And I wished that I had destroyed him, which, all things considered, was a very unusual wish for me.

15

T HE FOLLOWING NIGHT I went to the city of Florence. It was of course splendid to see it quite recovered from the ravages of the Black Death, and indeed a city of greater prosperity and greater ingenuity and energy than Rome.

I soon learnt what I had suspected—that having grown up around commerce, the city had not suffered the ruin of a classical era, but had rather grown progressively strong over the centuries, as its ruling family, the Medici, maintained power by means of a great international bank.

Everywhere about me there were elements of the place—its growing architectural monuments, its interior paintings, its clever scholars—that drew me fiercely, but nothing really could keep me away from discovering the identity of Botticelli, and seeing for myself not only his works, but the man.

Nevertheless, I tormented myself slightly. I took rooms in a palazzo near the main piazza of the city, hired a bumbling and remarkably gullible servant to lay in lots of costly clothes for me, all made in the color red as I preferred it, and still do to any other, and I went at once to a bookseller's and knocked and knocked until the man opened his doors for me, took my gold, and gave me the latest books which "everyone was reading" on poetry, art, philosophy and the like.

Then retiring to my rooms, I sat down by the light of one lamp and devoured what I could of my century's thinking, and at last I lay flat upon the floor, staring at the ceiling, overwhelmed by the vigor of the return to the classical, by the passionate enthusiasm for the old Greek and Roman poets, and by the faith in sensuality which this age seemed to hold.

Let me note here that some of these books were printed books, thanks to the miraculous invention of the printing press, and I was quite amazed by these though I preferred the beauty of the old hand-written codexes, as did many men of the time. In fact, it is an irony that even after the printing press was very well established, people still boasted of having handwritten libraries, but I digress.

I was talking of the return to the old Greek and Roman poets, of the infatuation of the era with the times of my birth.

The Roman church was overwhelmingly powerful as I have suggested.

But this was an age of fusion, as well as inconceivable expansion—and it was fusion which I had seen in the painting of Botticelli—so full of loveliness and natural beauty though created for the interior of the Pope's own chapel in Rome.

Perhaps near to midnight, I stumbled out of my quarters, finding the city under curfew, with the taverns which defied it and the inevitable ruffians roaming about.

I was dazed as I made my way into a huge tavern full of gleeful young drunkards where a rosy-cheeked boy sang as he played the lute. I sat in the corner thinking to control my overwrought enthusiasms, my crazed passions, yet I had to find the home of Botticelli. I had to. I had to see more of his work.

What stopped me from it? What did I fear? What was going on in my mind? Surely the gods knew I was a creature of iron control. Had I not proven it a thousand times?

For the keeping of a Divine Secret had I not turned my back on Zenobia? And did I not suffer routinely and justly for having abandoned my incomparable Pandora whom I might never find again?

At last I could endure my confused thoughts no longer. I came close to one of the older men in the tavern who was not singing with the younger ones.

"I've come here to find a great painter," I told him.

He shrugged and took a drink of his wine.

"I used to be a great painter," he said, "but no more. All I do is drink."

I laughed. I called for the tavern maid to serve him another cup. He gave a nod of thanks to me.

"The man I'm looking for—he's called Botticelli, or so I'm told."

Now it was his turn to laugh.

"You're seeking the greatest painter in Florence," he said. "You won't have any trouble finding him. He's always busy, no matter how many idlers hang about in his workshop. He may be painting now."

"Where is the workshop?" I asked.

"He lives in the Via Nuova, right before the Via Paolino."

"But tell me—." I hesitated. "What sort of man is he? I mean to you?"

Again, the man shrugged. "Not bad, not good, though he has a sense of humor. Not one to make an imprint on your mind except through his painting. You'll see when you meet him. But don't expect to hire him. He has much work already to do."

I thanked the man, laid down money for more wine if he wanted it, and slipped out of the tavern.

With a few questions I found the way to the Via Nuova. A night watchman gave me the way to the home of Botticelli, pointing to a sizable house, but not a great palazzo, where the painter lived with his brother and his brother's family.

I stood before this simple house as if it were a shrine. I could see where the workshop most certainly was by its large doors to the street which were inevitably open by day, and I could see that all the rooms both on the main floor and above it were dark.

How could I go into this workshop? How could I see what work was being done there now? Only by night could I come to this place. Never had I cursed the night so much.

Gold had to do this for me. Gold and the Spell Gift, though how I would dare to daze Botticelli himself I had no idea.

Suddenly, unable to control myself any longer I pounded on the door of the house.

Naturally enough, no one answered, so I pounded again.

Finally a light brightened in the upstairs window, and I could hear footfall within.

At last a voice demanded: Who was I, and what did I want?

What was I to answer to such a question? Was I to lie to someone whom I worshiped? Ah, but I had to get in.

"Marius de Romanus," I answered, making up the name at that very moment. "I've come with a purse of gold for Botticelli. I've seen his paintings in Rome, and I greatly admire him. I must put this purse into his own hand."

There was a pause. Voices behind the door. Two men conferring with each other as to who I might be, or why such a lie might be told.

One man said not to answer. The other man said it was worth a brief look, and it was he who pulled back the latch and opened the door. The other held the lamp behind him, so I saw only a shadowy face.

"I am Sandro," he said simply, "I'm Botticelli. Why would you bring me a purse of gold?"

For a long moment I was speechless. But in this speechlessness, I had the sense to produce the gold. I handed the purse over to the man, and I watched silently as he opened it and as he took out the gold florins and held them in his hand.

"What do you want?" he asked. His voice was as plain as his manner. He was rather tall. His hair was light brown and already threaded with gray though he was not old. He had large eyes that appeared compassionate, and a well-formed mouth and nose. He stood looking at me without annoyance or suspicion, and obviously ready to return my gold. I didn't think he was forty years old.

I tried to speak and I stammered. For the first time in all my memory I stammered. Finally I managed to make myself plain:

"Let me come into your workshop tonight," I said. "Let me see your paintings. That's all I want."

"You can see them by day." He shrugged. "My workshop's always open. Or you can go to the churches in which I've painted. My work is all over Florence. You don't have to pay me for such a thing." What a sublime voice; what an honest voice. There was something patient and tender in it.

I gazed upon him as I had gazed on his paintings. But he was waiting for an answer. I had to pull myself together.

"I have my reasons," I said. "I have my passions. I want to see your work now, if you'll let me. I offer the gold."

He smiled and he gave a little even laugh. "Well, you come like one of the Magi," he said. "For I can certainly use the payment. Come inside."

That was the second time in my long years that I had been compared to the Magi of Scripture and I loved it.

I entered the house which was by no means luxurious, and as he took the lamp from the other man, I followed him through a side door into his workshop where he put the lamp on a table full of paints and brushes and rags.

I couldn't take my eyes off him. This was the man who had done the great paintings in the Sistine Chapel, this ordinary man.

The light flared up and filled the place. Sandro, as he had called himself, gestured to his left, and as I turned to my right, I thought I was losing my mind.

A giant canvas covered the wall, and though I had expected to see a religious painting, no matter how sensual, there was something else there, altogether different, which rendered me speechless once more.

The painting was enormous as I've indicated, and it was composed of several figures, but whereas the Roman paintings had confused me in the question of their subject matter, I knew very well the subject matter of this.

For these were not saints and angels, or Christs and prophets—no, far from it.

There loomed before me a great painting of the goddess Venus in all her glorious nudity, feet poised upon a seashell, her golden hair torn by faint breezes, her dreamy gaze steady, her faithful attendants the god Zephyr who blew the breezes which guided her landward, and a nymph as beautiful as the goddess herself who welcomed her to the shore.

I drew in my breath and put my hands over my face, and then when I uncovered my eyes I found the painting there again.

A slight impatient sigh came from Sandro Botticelli. What in the name of the gods could I say to him about the brilliance of this work? What could I say to him to reveal the adulation I felt?

Then came his voice, low and resigned. "If you're going to tell me it's shocking and evil, let me tell you, I have heard it a thousand times. I'll give you back your gold if you want. I've heard it a thousand times."

I turned and went down on my knees, and I took his hands and I kissed them with my lips as closely as I dared. Then I rose slowly like an old man on one knee before the other and I stood back to gaze at the panel for a long time.

I looked at the perfect figure of Venus again, covering her most intimate secret with locks of her abundant hair. I looked on the nymph with her outstretched hand and her voluminous garments. I looked on the god Zephyr and the goddess with him, and all of the tiny details of the painting came to reside in my mind.

"How has it come about?" I asked. "After so long a time of Christs and Virgins, that such a thing could be painted at last?"

From the quiet figure of the uncomplaining man there came another little laugh.

"It's up to my patron," he said. "My Latin is not so good. They read the poetry to me. I painted what they said to paint." He paused. He looked troubled. "Do you think it's sinful?"

"Certainly not," I responded. "You ask me what I think? I think it's a miracle. I'm surprised that you would ask." I looked at the painting. "This is a goddess," I said. "How could it be other than sacred? There was a time when millions worshiped her with all their hearts. There was a time when people consecrated themselves to her with all their hearts."

"Well, yes," he answered softly, "but she's a pagan goddess, and not everyone thinks that she is the patron of marriage as some say now. Some say this painting is sinful, that I shouldn't be doing it." He gave a frustrated sigh. He wanted to say more, but I sensed that the arguments were quite beyond him.

"Don't listen to such things," I said. "It has a purity I've almost never seen in painting. Her face, the way you've painted it, she's newborn yet sublime, a woman, yet divine. Don't think of sin when you work on this painting. This painting is too vital, too eloquent. Put the struggles of sin out of your mind."

He was silent but I knew he was thinking. I turned and tried to read his mind. It seemed chaotic, and full of wandering thoughts and guilt.

He was a painter almost entirely at the mercy of those who hired him, but he had made himself supreme by virtue of the particularities that all cherished in his work. Nowhere were his talents more fully expressed than in this particular painting and he knew this though he couldn't put it into words. He thought hard on how to tell me about his craft and his originality, but he simply couldn't do it. And I would not press him. It would be a wicked thing to do.

"I don't have your words," he said simply. "You really believe the painting isn't sinful?"

"Yes, I told you, it's not sinful. If anyone tells you anything else they're lying to you." I couldn't stress it enough. "Behold the innocence in the face of the goddess. Don't think of anything else."

He looked tormented, and there came over me a sense of how fragile he was, in spite of his immense talent and his immense energy to work. The thrusts of his art could be utterly crushed by those who criticized him. Yet he went on somehow every day painting the best pictures that he knew how to paint.

"Don't believe them," I said again, drawing his eyes back to me.

"Come," he said, "you've paid me well to look at my work. Look at this tondo of the Virgin Mary with Angels. Tell me how you like this."

He brought the lamp to the far wall and held it so that I might see the round painting which hung there.

Once again I was too shocked by the loveliness of it to speak. But it was plainly obvious that the Virgin was as purely beautiful as the goddess Venus, and the Angels were sensual and alluring as only very young boys and girls can be.

"I know," he said to me. "You don't have to tell me. My Venus looks like the Virgin and the Virgin looks like the Venus and so they say of me. But my patrons pay me."

"Listen to your patrons," I said. I wanted so to clasp his arms. I wanted to gently shake him so that he would never forget my words. "Do what they tell you. Both paintings are magnificent. Both paintings are finer than anything I've ever seen."

He couldn't know what I meant by such words. I couldn't tell him. I stared at him, and for the first time I saw a little apprehension in him. He had begun to notice my skin, and perhaps my hands.

It was time to leave him before he became even more suspicious, and I wanted him to remember me kindly and not with fear.

I took out another purse which I had brought with me. It was full of gold florins.

He gestured to refuse it. In fact, he gave me a very stubborn refusal. I placed it on the table.

For a moment we merely looked at each other.

"Good-bye, Sandro," I said.

"Marius, was it? I'll remember you."

I made my way out the front door and into the street. I hurried for the space of two blocks and then I stopped, breathing too hurriedly, and it seemed a dream that I had been with him, that I had seen such paintings, that such paintings had been created by man.

I didn't go back to my rooms in the palazzo.

When I reached the vault of Those Who Must Be Kept, I fell down in a new kind of exhaustion, crazed by what I had beheld. I couldn't get the impression of the man out of my mind. I couldn't stop seeing him with his soft dull hair and sincere eyes.

As for the paintings, they haunted me, and I knew that my torment, my obsession, my complete abandonment to the love of Botticelli had only just begun.

16

IN THE MONTHS that followed I became a busy visitor of Florence, slipping into various palaces and churches to see the work that Botticelli had done.

Those who praised him had not lied. He was the most revered painter in Florence, and those who complained of him were those for whom he had no time, for he was only a mortal man.

In the Church of San Paolino, I found an altarpiece which was to drive me mad. The subject of the painting was a common one, I had discovered, usually called *The Lamentation*, being the scene of those weeping over the body of the dead Christ only just taken down from the Cross.

It was a miracle of Botticelli's sensuality, most specifically in the tender representation of Christ himself who had the gorgeous body of a Greek god, and in the utter abandon of the woman who had pressed her face against that of his, for though Christ lay with his head hanging downward, she knelt upright and her eyes were therefore very near to Christ's mouth.

Ah, to see these two faces seamlessly pressed to each other, and to see the delicacy of every face and form surrounding them, it was more than I could endure.

How long would I let this torture me? How long must I go through this wanton enthusiasm, this mad celebration before I retreated to my loneliness and coldness in the vault? I knew how to punish myself, didn't I? Did I have to go out of my way to the city of Florence for this?

There were reasons to be gone.

Two other blood drinkers haunted this city who might want me out of it, but so far they had left me alone. They were very young and hardly very clever, nevertheless I did not want them to come upon me, and spread "the legend of Marius" any further than it had already gone.

And then there was that monster I had encountered in Rome—that evil Santino who might come this far to harry me with his little Satan worshipers whom I so desperately deplored.

But these things didn't really matter.

I had time in Florence and I knew it. There were no Satan worshipers here and that was a good thing. I had time to suffer as much as I chose.

And I was mad for this mortal, Botticelli, this painter, this genius, and I could scarce think of anything else.

Meantime, there came from Botticelli's brilliance yet another immense pagan masterpiece which I beheld in the palazzo to which it was sent upon being finished—a place into which I crept in the early hours of the morning to see the painting while the owners of the building slept.

Once again, Botticelli had used Roman mythology, or perhaps the Greek mythology that lay behind it to create a garden—yes, of all things, a garden—a garden of eternal springtime in which mythical figures made their sublime progress with harmonious gestures and dreamy expressions, their attitudes exquisitely gentle in the extreme.

On one side of the verdant garden danced the youthful and inevitably beautiful Three Graces in transparent and billowing garments while on the other side came the goddess Flora, magnificently clothed and strewing flowers from her dress. The goddess Venus once more appeared in the center, dressed as a rich Florentine woman, her hand up in a gesture of welcome, her head tilted slightly to one side.

The figure of Mercury in the far left corner, and several other mythic beings completed the gathering which entranced me so that I stood before the masterpiece for hours, perusing all the details, sometimes smiling, sometimes weeping, wiping at my face, and even now and then covering my eyes and then uncovering them again to see the vivid colors and the delicate gestures and attitudes of these creatures—the whole so reminiscent of the lost glory of Rome, and yet so utterly new and different from it that I thought, for loving all this, I will lose my mind.

Any and all gardens which I had ever painted or imagined were obliterated by this painting. How would I ever rival, even in my dreams, such a work as this?

How exquisite here to die of happiness after being so long miserable and alone. How exquisite to see this triumph of form and color after having studied with bitter sacrifice so many forms I could not understand.

There is no despair in me anymore. There is only joy, continuous restless joy.

Is that possible?

Only reluctantly did I leave this painting of the springtime garden. Only reluctantly did I leave behind its dark flower-rich grass and overhanging orange trees. Only reluctantly did I move on to find more of Botticelli where I could.

I might have staggered around Florence for nights on end, drunk on what I'd seen in this painting. But there was more, much more, for me to see.

Mark, all this time, as I slipped into churches to see more works by the Master, as I crept into a palazzo to see a famed painting by the Master of the irresistible god Mars sleeping helplessly on the grass beside a patient and watchful Venus, as I went about clasping my hands to my lips so as not to cry out crazily, I did not return to the workshop of the genius. I held myself back.

"You cannot interfere in his life," I told myself. "You cannot come in with gold and draw him from his paintings. His is a mortal destiny. Already the entire city knows of him. Rome knows of him. His paintings will endure. He is not someone you need save from a gutter. He is the talk of Florence. He is the talk of the Pope's Palace in Rome. Leave him alone."

And so I did not go back, though I was starving just to look at him, just to talk to him, just to tell him that the marvelous painting of the Three Graces and the other goddesses in the springtime garden was as glorious as anything that he had done.

I would have paid him just to allow me to sit in his shop in the evening, and to watch him at his work. But this was wrong, all of it.

I went back to the Church of San Paolino, and I stayed for a long time, staring at *The Lamentation*.

It was far more stiff than his "pagan" paintings. Indeed, he had seldom done something quite this severe. And there was much darkness to the painting, in the deeply colored robes of the various figures, and in the shadowy recesses of the open tomb. But even in this severity there was a tenderness, a loveliness. And the two faces—that of Mary and Christ—which were pressed together—drew me and would not let me look away.

Ah, Botticelli. How does one explain his gift? His figures though perfect were always slightly elongated, even the faces were elongated, and the expressions on the faces were sleepy and perhaps even ever so slightly unhappy, it is so difficult to say. All the figures of any one painting seemed lost in a communal dream.

As for the paint he used—the paint used by so many in Florence—it was far superior to anything we had had in the ancient days of Rome, in that it mixed simple egg yolk and ground pigment to achieve the colors and the glazes and the varnishes to make an application of unsurpassed brilliance and endurance. In other words, the works had a gloss that seemed miraculous to my eyes.

So fascinated was I by this paint that I sent my mortal servant to procure all the available pigments for me, and the eggs, and to bring me by night an old apprentice who might mix up the colors for me, exactly to the right thickness, so I might paint a bit of work in my rented rooms.

It was only an idle experiment, but I found myself working furiously and soon covering every bit of prepared wood and canvas which my apprentice and my servant had bought.

They were, of course, shocked by my speed, which gave me pause. I had to be clever, not fantastical. Hadn't I learnt that long years ago when I'd painted my banquet room as my guests cheered me on?

I sent them away with plenty of gold, telling them to come back to me with more materials. As for what I had painted? It was some poor imitation of Botticelli, for even with my immortal blood I could not capture what he had captured. I could not make faces like those he had rendered, no, not by a very long way. There was something brittle and hopeless in what I painted. I could not look at my own work. I loathed it. There was something flat and accusatory in the faces I had created. There was something ominous in the expressions that looked back at me from the walls.

I went out into the night, restless, hearing those other blood drinkers, a young pair, fearful of me and rightly so, yet very attentive to what I did, for what reason I was unsure. I sent a silent message to all the immortal trash that might perturb me: Do not come near me for I am in a grand passion and will not tolerate being interrupted now.

I crept into the Church of San Paolino and knelt down as I looked at *The Lamentation*. I ran my tongue against my sharp teeth. I hungered for blood as the beauty of the figures filled me. I could have taken a victim in the very church.

And then the most evil idea came to me. It was purely evil just as the painting was purely religious. The idea came to me unbidden as if there really were a Satan in the world and that Satan had come crawling along the stone floor towards me and put the idea in my mind.

"You love him, Marius," said this Satan. "Well, bring him over to you. Give Botticelli the Blood."

I shivered quietly in the church. I slipped down, sitting against the stone wall. Again I felt the thirst. I was horrified that I had even thought of it yet I saw myself taking Botticelli in my arms. I saw myself sinking my teeth into Botticelli's throat. The blood of Botticelli. I thought of it. And my blood, my blood given to him.

"Think how you have waited, Marius," said the evil voice of Satan. "All these long centuries you have never given your blood to anyone. But you can give it to Botticelli! You can take Botticelli now."

He would go on painting; he would have the Blood and his painting would be unparalleled. He would live forever with his talent—this humble man of some forty years who was grateful for a mere purse of gold—this humble man who had done the exquisite Christ I stared at, his head thrown back in the hand of Mary, whose eyes were pressed to his mouth.

This was not something that would be done. No, this must never be done. I could not do it. I would not do it.

Yet I rose slowly to my feet and I left the church and began walking through the dark narrow street, towards Botticelli's house.

I could hear my heart inside me. And my mind seemed curiously empty, and my body light and predatory and full of evil, an evil which I freely admitted and totally understood. A high excitement filled me. Take Botticelli in your arms. Forever in your arms.

And though I heard those other blood drinkers, those two young ones who followed me, I did not pay it any mind. They were far too fearful of me to come close to me. On I went for what I would choose to do.

It was no more than a few blocks and I was there at Sandro's door and the lights were burning inside, and I had a purse of gold.

Drifting, dreaming, thirsting, I knocked as I had the first time.

No, this is something you will never do, I thought. You will not take someone so vital out of the world. You will not disturb the destiny of one who has given others so much to love and enjoy.

It was Sandro's brother who came to the door, but this time he was courteous to me and he showed me into the shop where Botticelli was alone and at work.

He turned to greet me as soon as I entered the spacious room.

There loomed behind him a large panel, with a shockingly different aspect to it from any of his other work. I let my eyes drift over it for I thought this was what he wanted me to do, and I don't think I could hide from him my disapproval or fear.

The blood hunger surged in me, but I put it away and stared only at the painting, thinking of nothing, not of Sandro, not of his death and rebirth through me, no, of nothing but the painting as I pretended to be human for him.

It was a grim and chilling painting of the Trinity, with Christ on his Cross, the full figure of God the Father behind him, and a dove representing the Holy Spirit, just above the head of the Christ. On one side stood St. John the Baptist opening the scarlet robe of God the Father, and on the other, the penitent Magdalene, her long hair her only clothing as she stared grieving at the crucified Lord.

It seemed a cruel use of Botticelli's talent! It seemed a ghastly thing. Oh, it was expertly done, yes, but how merciless it seemed.

Only now did I know that in *The Lamentation* I had seen a perfect balance of light and dark forces. For I did not see that balance here. On the contrary, it was astonishing that Botticelli could have done something as wholly dark as this. It was a harsh thing. Had I seen it elsewhere I would not have thought it was his work.

And it seemed a profound judgment on me that I had thought for one moment of giving Botticelli the Dark Blood! Did the Christian God really live? Could he deter me? Could he judge me? Is that why I had come face to face with this painting with Botticelli standing beside it looking into my eyes?

Botticelli was waiting for me to speak to him on account of this painting. He was waiting patiently to be wounded by what I meant to say. And deep inside me there was a love of Botticelli's talent which had nothing to do with God or the Devil or my own evil or power. That love of Botticelli's talent respected Botticelli and nothing mattered just now but that.

I looked up again at the painting.

"Where is the innocence, Sandro?" I asked him, making my tone as kind as I could.

Again I fought the blood hunger. Look how old he is. If you don't do it Sandro Botticelli will die.

"Where is the tenderness in the painting?" I asked. "Where is the sublime sweetness that makes us forget everything? I see it only a little perhaps in the face of God the Father, but the rest—it's dark, Sandro. It's so unlike you, this darkness. I don't understand why you do it when you can do so much else."

The blood hunger was raging but I had control of it. I was pushing it deep inside me. I loved him too much to do it. I could not do it. I could not endure the result if it were to be done.

As for my remarks, he nodded. He was miserable. A man divided wanting to paint his goddesses on the one hand, and the sacred paintings as well.

"Marius," he said. "I don't want to do what's sinful. I don't want to do what's evil, or what will make another person, simply by looking at a painting, commit a sin."

"You're very far from ever doing that, Sandro," I said. "That's my view of it—that your goddesses are glorious as are your gods. In Rome, your frescoes of Christ were filled with light and beauty. Why journey into the darkness as you have done here?"

I took out the purse and put it on the table. I would leave now, and he would never know what true evil had come close to him. He would never dream of what I was and what I had meant, perhaps, perhaps to do.

He came to me and picked up the purse and tried to give it back.

"No, you keep it," I said. "You deserve it. You do what you believe you should do."

"Marius, I have to do what is right," he said simply. "Now look at this, I want to show you." He took me to another part of the workshop away from the large paintings.

Here was a table and on it were several pages of parchment covered with tiny drawings.

"These are illustrations for Dante's *Inferno*," he told me. "Surely you've read it. I want to do an illustrated version of the entire book."

My heart sank when I heard this, but what could I say? I looked down at the drawings of the twisted and suffering bodies! How could one defend such an enterprise on the part of the painter who had rendered Venus and the Virgin with miraculous skill?

Dante's *Inferno*. How I had despised the work while recognizing its brilliance.

"Sandro, how can you want to do this?" I asked. I was shaking. I didn't want him to see my face. "I find glory," I said, "in those paintings that are filled with the light of paradise, whether it is Christian or pagan. I find no delight in the illustrations of those who suffer in Hell."

He was plainly confused and perhaps he always would be. It was his fate. I had only stepped into it, and perhaps fed a fire that was already too weak to survive.

I had to go now. I had to leave him now forever. I knew it. I could not come again to this house. I could not trust myself with him. I had to get out of Florence or my resolve would break.

"I won't be seeing you again, Sandro," I said.

"But why?" he said. "I've been looking forward to seeing you. Oh, it's not because of the purse, believe me."

"I know, but I must leave. Remember. I believe in your gods and goddesses. I always will."

I went out of his house, and only as far as the church. I was so overcome with the desire for him, to bring him over to me, and visit upon him all the dark secrets of the Blood, that I could scarce catch my breath or see the street before me, or even feel the air in my lungs.

I wanted him. I wanted his talent. I dreamt dreams of the two of us—Sandro and me—together in a great palazzo, and from there would come paintings tinged with the magic of the Blood.

It would be a confirmation of the Blood.

After all, I thought, he is ruining his own talent, is he not, by turning to what is dark? How can one account for it that he would turn from his goddesses to a poem called the *Inferno*? Can I not turn him back to his celestial visions with the Blood?

But none of this must happen. I knew it even before I'd seen his cruel crucifixion. I had known it before I went into his house.

I must find a victim now; I must find many. And so I hunted cruelly, until I could take no more blood from the few doomed souls I found in the streets of Florence.

At last an hour or so before dawn, I found myself sitting against a church door in a small piazza, looking like a beggar perhaps if beggars fit themselves out with crimson cloaks.

Those two young vampires whom I had heard following me came with fearful steps towards me.

I was weary and impatient.

"Get away from me," I said. "I'll destroy you both if you don't."

A young male, a young female, each taken in youth and both trembling, they would not retreat. At last the male spoke for them, his courage tremulous but real.

"Don't you harm Botticelli!" he declared. "Don't you hurt him! Take the dregs, yes, you're welcome, but not Botticelli, never Botticelli."

Sadly I laughed. My head fell back and very softly I laughed and laughed.

"I won't do it," I said. "I love him as much as you do. Now get away from me. Or believe me, there will be no more nights for either one of you. Go."

Returning to the vault in the mountains, I wept for Botticelli.

I closed my eyes, and I entered the garden where Flora dropped her tender roses to the carpet of grass and flowers. I reached out to touch the hair of one of the young Graces.

"Pandora," I whispered. "Pandora, it's our garden. They were all beautiful like you."

17

IN THE WEEKS that followed, I filled the shrine in the Alps with many new riches. I bought new golden lamps, and censers. I bought fine carpets from the markets in Venice, and golden silks from China as well. From the seamstresses of Florence I commissioned new garments for my Immortal Parents, and then carefully dressed them, relieving them of rags which should have been burnt long ago.

All the while I spoke to them in a consoling voice of the miracles I had seen in the changing world.

I laid before them fine printed books as I explained the ingenious invention of the printing press. And I hung over the doors to the shrine a new Flemish tapestry, also bought in Florence which I described to them in detail, so they might choose to look with their seemingly blind eyes.

Then I went to the city of Florence and gathering up all the pigment and oil and other materials which my servant had procured for me, I brought it to the mountain shrine, and I proceeded to paint the walls in the new style.

I did not seek now to imitate Botticelli. But I did return to the old motif of the garden which I had so loved centuries ago, and I soon found myself rendering my Venus, my Graces, my Flora, and infusing into the work all the details of life which only a blood drinker can behold.

Where Botticelli had painted the dark grass rich with varied flowers, I revealed the small insectile creatures inevitably concealed there, and then the most flamboyant and beautiful of creatures, the butterflies and the varicolored moths. Indeed my style ran to frightening detail in every respect, and soon an intoxicating and magic forest surrounded the Mother and Father, the egg tempera lending a gleam to the whole which I had never achieved in the past.

When I studied it, I became ever so slightly dizzy, thinking of Botticelli's garden, indeed, thinking even of the garden I had dreamt of in old Rome, of the garden I had painted—and soon I had to shake myself and collect myself because I did not know where I was.

The Royal Parents seemed more solid and remote than ever. All trace of the Great Burning was now gone from them in that their skin was purely white.

It had been so long since they had moved that I began to wonder if I had dreamt those things which had happened—if I had imagined the sacrifice of Eudoxia—but now my mind was very much intent upon escaping the shrine for long periods of time.

My last gift to the Divine Parents—after all my painting was done, and Akasha and Enkil were decked out with all new jewels—was a long bank of one hundred beeswax candles which I lighted for them all at once with the power of my mind.

Of course I saw no change in the eyes of the King and Queen. Nevertheless, it gave me great pleasure to offer this to them; and I spent my last hours with them, letting the candles burn down as I told them in a soft voice of all the wonders of the cities of Florence and Venice which I had come to love.

I vowed that every time I came to them I would light the one hundred candles. It would be a small proof of my undying love.

What caused me to do such a thing? I have no true idea. But after that I kept a great supply of candles always in the shrine; I stored them behind the two figures; and after the offering, I would replenish the bronze holder and take away all melted wax.

When all this had been done, I returned to Florence and to Venice, and to the rich high-walled little city of Siena, to study paintings of all sorts.

Indeed, I wandered through palaces and churches throughout Italy, quite drunken on what I beheld.

As I have described, a great fusion had taken place between Christian themes and ancient pagan style, which was developing everywhere. And though I still perceived Botticelli to be the Master, I was taken aback by the plasticity and wonder of much of what I saw.

The voices in the taverns and in the wine shops told me I ought to go North to see paintings as well.

Now this was news to me, for North had always meant the land of the less civilized, but so great was my hunger for the new styles that I did as I was told.

I found throughout all of northern Europe an intense and complex civilization which I had surely underestimated, most particularly I think in France. There were great cities in existence and Royal Courts which supported painting. There was much for me to study.

But I did not love the art which I saw.

I respected the works of Jan van Eyck, and Rogier van der Weyden, of Hugo van der Goes, and of Hieronymus Bosch and many other nameless masters whom I beheld, but their work did not delight me as did the work of the Italian painters. The Northern world was not as lyrical. It was not as sweet. It still bore the grotesque stamp of the work of purely religious art.

So I soon returned to the cities of Italy where I was richly rewarded for my wanderings with no end in sight.

I soon learnt that Botticelli had studied with a great master, Filippo Lippi, and that this one's son, Filippino Lippi, was working with Botticelli right now. Other painters whom I loved included Gozzoli and Signorelli, and Piero della Francesca and beyond that so many that I do not want to mention their names.

But all during my study of painting, my little travels, my long nights of adoring attention to this or that wall, or this or that altarpiece, I did not let myself dream of bringing Botticelli to me, and I never lingered long near any place where he was.

I knew that he prospered. I knew that he painted. And that was quite enough for me.

But an idea had come to brew in me—an idea as strong as the earlier dream of seducing Botticelli had been.

What if I were to reenter the world again, and to live in it as a painter? Oh, not a working painter who took commissions, that would be nonsense, but an eccentric gentleman who chose to paint for his own pleasure, admitting mortals to his house to dine at his table and drink his wine.

Had I not done so in a bumbling way in the ancient nights before the first sack of Rome? Yes, I had painted my own walls with crude, hasty images, and I had let my good-natured guests laugh at me.

Oh yes, a thousand years had passed since then, more in fact, and I could no longer easily pass for human. I was too pale and too dangerously strong. But was I not more clever now, more wise, more practiced with the Mind Gift, and more willing to mask my skin with whatever emollients were required to dim its preternatural gleam?

I was desperate to do it!

Of course it would not be in Florence. That was far too close to Botticelli. I would attract his notice and were he to set foot under my roof, I would be driven to extremes of pain. I was in love with the man. I could not deny it. But I had another, most marvelous choice.

It was the gorgeous and glittering city of Venice which drew me with its indescribably majestic palaces, their windows open to the constant breezes of the Adriatic, and its dark winding canals.

It seemed I should make a new and spectacular beginning there, purchasing for myself the finest house available, and acquiring a bevy of apprentices to prepare my paints for me, and the walls of my own house which would eventually receive my best efforts after I had done some panels and canvases to once again learn my craft.

As for my identity I would be Marius de Romanus, a man of mystery and incalculable wealth. Simply put, I would bribe those I had to bribe to obtain the right to remain in Venice, and thereafter spend freely among those who came to know me in the smallest capacity, and give generously to my apprentices who would be recipients of the finest education I could obtain for them.

Understand please that in this time the cities of Florence and Venice were not part of one country. Far from it. Each was a country unto itself. And so being in Venice I was quite removed from Botticelli, and would be subject to very important laws which the citizens of Venice were required to obey.

Now as to the matter of my appearance I intended to be careful in the extreme. Imagine the effect upon a mortal heart were I to reveal myself in all my coldness, a blood drinker of some fifteen hundred years in age with purely white skin and flashing blue eyes. So the matter of emollients was no small thing.

Renting rooms in the city, I purchased from the perfume shops the very finest tinted salves I could find. Then to my skin I applied these ointments, carefully inspecting the results in the finest mirrors which could be had. I soon made a blending of salves which was most perfect for not only darkening my cold complexion, but for bringing back to visibility in it the finest little wrinkles or lines.

I myself had not known that these lines of human expression still remained to me, and I was most happy to discover them, and I rather liked the image that I presented to the glass. As for the perfume, it was pleasing, and I realized that once settled in my own house, I could have the proper salves made for me and have them always on hand.

It took some months to complete my entire plan.

And this was largely because I had fallen in love with one particular palazzo, a house of great beauty, its facade covered in glistering marble tiles, its arches in the Moorish style, and its immense rooms more luxurious than anything I had ever beheld in all my nights, and even my long ago days. The lofty ceilings amazed me. We had known nothing like them in old Rome, at least not in a private house. And on top of the immense roof was a carefully arranged roof garden from which one could view the sea.

Once the ink was dry upon the parchment, I set out to purchase for myself the finest furnishings imaginable—coffered beds, desks, chairs, tables, all the usual appointments including gold-threaded draperies for every window—and I set to the task of managing all this a clever and genial old man named Vincenzo, a creature of extremely solid health, whom I had bought almost as if he were a slave from a family who had no more use for him and kept him about in shameful neglect because he had once educated their sons.

I saw in Vincenzo just the sort of governor I would need for all the apprentices I meant to buy from their Masters, boys who would bring some skill already learnt to the tasks they had to do for me. I was also pleased with the fact that the man was already old which meant I did not have to be tormented by the spectacle of youth dying in him. Rather I could pride myself, perhaps foolishly, on visiting upon him a rather splendid old age.

How did I find the creature? I went about reading minds to discover what I wanted.

I was now more powerful than ever. I could find the Evil Doer effortlessly. I could hear the secret thoughts of those who sought to cheat me or those who loved the mere sight of me. And the latter was a dangerous thing.

Why dangerous, you might ask? The answer is that I was now more than ever susceptible to love, and when seen with loving eyes I knew it and I slowed my pace.

What a strange mood would descend upon me while walking in the arcade along San Marco if someone should be looking at me admiringly. I would turn about, taking my time, and double back perhaps, and only reluctantly move away, rather like a bird in some northern clime enjoying the warmth of the sun on its wings.

Meantime, with gold in his hands, Vincenzo was sent to buy fine clothes for himself. I would make a gentleman of him, in so far as the sumptuary laws allowed.

And seated at my new desk in a spacious bedchamber floored in marble with windows open to the winds off the canal, I wrote out lists of those additional luxuries which I desired.

I wanted a lavish old Roman-style bath built for me in this bedchamber, so that I could enjoy the warm water whenever I wished. I wanted shelves for my books, and a finer chair for this desk. Of course there should be another library. What was a house to me if it did not possess a library? I wanted the finest clothing, the fashionable hats and leather shoes.

I drew pictures to guide those who would carry out my designs.

These were heady times. I was a part of life once more and my heart was beating to a human pace.

Hailing a gondola at the quais, I traveled the canals for hours looking up at the spectacular facades which made up the waterways of Venice. I listened to the voices everywhere. I lay back sometimes on my elbow and gazed up at the stars.

At various goldsmith shops and painters' workshops I chose my first gathering of apprentices, taking every opportunity to select the brilliant ones who were for various reasons among the wronged, and neglected, and abused. They would show me profound loyalty and untapped knowledge, and I sent them off to their new home with gold coins in their hands.

Of course I procured clever assistants because those were necessary, but I knew I would be very successful with the poorlings. Force was not required.

Meantime, it was my wish that my boys should be educated for the university—not a customary thing with a painter's apprentice—so I chose tutors for them and arranged for these men to come to my house in the daylight hours to perform instruction as required.

The boys would learn Latin, Greek, philosophy, the newfound and much valued "classics," some mathematics and whatever they needed to proceed in life. If they excelled in painting and they chose it, they could of course forget the university and follow the painter's path.

Finally I had a houseful of healthy and noisy activity. There were cooks in the kitchen, and musicians teaching my boys to sing and play the lute. There were dancing instructors and there were fencing matches over the marble floors of the great salons.

But I did not open my doors to the populace as I had done in long ago Rome.

I was too wary to do such a thing in Venice, too unsure of my ruse, too uncertain of what questions my mad painting might arouse.

No, I need only have my young male assistants, I fancied, both to keep me company and to help me, for there was much to be done preparing the walls for my frescoes and covering my panels and canvases with the proper varnishes for my work.

As it turned out, there was not much for anyone to do for some weeks, for during that period I wandered the local workshops and studied the painters of Venice as I had studied the painters of Florence not long before.

There was no doubt in my mind, after this studious examination, that I could mimic mortal work to some extent, but I could not hope to surpass it. And I feared what I would accomplish. And I resolved to keep my house closed to all but the boys and their instructors as arranged.

Taking to my bedroom study, I began a journal of my thoughts, the first I had ever kept since the nights in old Rome.

I wrote of the comforts I enjoyed. And I chastised myself with more clarity than I did in my mind.

"You have become a fool for the love of mortals," I wrote,

far more than you ever did in the ancient nights. For you know you have chosen these boys so that you might instruct them and mold them, and there will be loving in it and hope in it, and the intention of sending them on to be educated at Padua, as though they were your mortal children.

But what if they should come to discover that you are a beast in heart and soul, and they run from your touch, what then? Will you slaughter them in their innocence? This is not ancient Rome with its nameless millions. This is the strict Republic of Venice where you play your games, and for what?

For the color of the evening sky over the piazza that you see when you are first risen, for the domes of the church beneath the moon? For the color of the canals that only you can behold in the starlight? You are a wicked and greedy creature.

Will art satisfy you? You hunt elsewhere, in the surrounding towns and hamlets, or even in distant cities, for you can move with the speed of a god. But you bring evil to Venice because you are evil, and in your fine palazzo, lies are told, lies are lived, lies may fail.

I put down the quill. I read over my words, forever memorizing them, as if they were a foreign voice speaking to me, and only when I'd finished did I look up to see Vincenzo, so polite and humble, and so dignified in his new clothes, waiting to speak to me.

"What is it?" I asked gently so as not to make him think I disapproved of him for coming in.

"Master, only let me tell you . . ." he said. He looked quite elegant in his new velvet, rather like a prince at court.

"Yes, do tell me," I said.

"It's only that the boys are so happy. They are all in bed now and sleeping. But do you know what it means to them that they have plenty to eat and decent clothes, and are learning their lessons with a purpose? I could tell you many stories, too many I think. There's not a dullard among them. It's such luck."

I smiled.

"That's very good, Vincenzo," I said. "Go have your supper. Enjoy as much wine as you wish."

I sat in the stillness after he had left me.

It seemed quite impossible that I had made this residence for myself, and that nothing had stopped me. I had hours before dawn during which I might rest on my bed, or read among my new books before making the short journey to another place within the city where a sarcophagus had been hidden in a gold-lined chamber in which I would sleep by day.

But I chose instead to go to the great room which I had designated as my studio, and there I found the pigments and other materials ready for me, including several wooden panels which my young apprentices had prepared as directed for me to paint.

It was a small matter to blend the tempera and I did it quickly so that I had a wealth of colors at my command, and then glancing over and over again into a mirror which I had brought into the room with me, I painted my own portrait in quick exact strokes with little or no correction until it was complete.

As soon as I was finished, I stood back from my creation, and I found myself staring into my own eyes. It wasn't the man of long ago who had died in the northern forest, or the frantic blood drinker who had taken the Mother and the Father out of Egypt. Nor was it the starved and dogged wanderer who had slipped soundlessly through time for so many hundreds of years.

It was a bold and proud immortal who looked at me, a blood drinker who demanded that the world at last give him some quarter, an aberrant being of immense power who insisted that he might have a place among the human beings of which he had in former times been one.

As the months passed, I discovered that my plan was working quite well. In fact it was working marvelously!

I became obsessed with my new clothing of the period, velvet tunics and stockings, and marvelous cloaks trimmed in rare fur. Indeed mirrors were an obsession with me now as well. I could not stop looking at my own reflection. I applied the salves with great care.

Each evening, after sunset, I arose fully dressed with the requisite disguise on my skin, and I arrived at my palazzo to a warm greeting from all my children, and then dismissing the many teachers and tutors, I presided over a good banquet with my children where all were delighted to have the rich food of princes, as music played.

Then in a mild manner I questioned all my apprentices as to what they had learnt that day. Our conversations were long, complex, and full of wonderful revelations. I could easily surmise which teacher had been successful, and which had not wrought the effects I desired.

As for the boys themselves, I soon saw which of the boys possessed the greater talent, who should be sent off to the University of Padua, and who should be schooled as a goldsmith or a painter. Of failures we had none.

You understand, this was a transcendent enterprise. To repeat, I had chosen all of these boys by means of the Mind Gift, and what I offered them in these months, which soon stretched to years, was something they would never have had if I had not intervened.

I had become a magician for them, aiding them to realize accomplishments of which they hadn't even dreamt.

And there was no doubt that I found immense satisfaction in this achievement, for I was a teacher of these creatures, just as I had long ago wanted to be the teacher of Avicus and Zenobia, and during all this time I thought of Avicus and Zenobia. I could not help but think of them and wonder what had become of them.

Had they survived?

I could not know.

But I knew this about myself: I had loved both Zenobia and Avicus because they allowed me to be their teacher. And I had fought with Pandora because she would not. She was far too finely educated and clever to be anything but a fierce verbal and philosophical opponent and I had left her, stupidly, on that account.

But no amount of such self-knowledge caused me to not long for my lost Zenobia and for Avicus, and to wonder what paths they'd taken through the world. Zenobia's beauty had struck a deeper note in me than the beauty of Avicus, and I could not relinquish the simple recollection of the softness of Zenobia's hair.

Sometimes, when I was alone in my bedroom in Venice, when I sat at my desk watching the curtains blow out from the windows, I thought of Zenobia's hair. I thought of it lying on the mosaic floor in Constantinople, after she had cut all of it so that she might travel the streets as a boy. I wanted to reach back over a thousand years and gather it up in my hands.

As for my own blond hair, I could wear it long now for this was the style of the period, and I rather enjoyed it, brushing it clean without resentment, and going out to walk in the piazza while the sky was still purple knowing people were looking at me, wondering just what sort of man I was.

As for my painting, I went about it using a few wooden panels with only a handful of apprentices in my studio, locked off from the world. I created several successful religious pictures—all of the Virgin Mary and the Angel Gabriel appearing to her, because this theme—The Annunciation—appealed to me. And I was rather amazed at how well I could imitate the style of the times.

Then I set upon a major undertaking which would be a true test of my immortal skill and wits.

18

L ET ME EXPLAIN what this undertaking was to be:

There was a chapel in Florence that existed within a Medici palazzo, and on the walls of this chapel was a great painting by a painter named Gozzoli of the Procession of the Magi—the three wise men of Scripture—coming to visit the Christ Child with their precious gifts.

Now it was a marvelous painting, full of rampant detail. And it was worldly in the extreme, in that the Magi themselves were clothed as wealthy Florentine citizens and there followed behind them a huge gathering of similarly clothed men and churchmen so that the whole was a tribute to the Christ Child and to the times in which the painting had been done.

This painting covered the walls of this chapel, along with the walls of the recess for the place where its altar stood. And the chapel itself was quite small.

Now I was taken with the painting for many reasons. I had not fallen deeply in love with Gozzoli as I had with Botticelli, but greatly admired him, and the details of this painting were fantastic in the extreme.

Not only was the Procession itself enormous, if not actually never ending, but the landscape behind it was wondrous, filled with towns and mountains, with men hunting and animals running, with beautifully realized castles and delicately shaped trees.

Well, choosing in my palazzo one of the largest rooms, I set out to duplicate this painting in the flat mode on one wall. What this meant was that I had to travel back and forth between Florence and Venice, memorizing parts of this painting, and then render it with all my supernatural skill.

To a very large part I succeeded in my task.

I "stole" the Procession of the Magi—this fabulous depiction of a procession so important to the Christians and especially to the Florentines and I laid it out in vivid and exact color on my wall.

There was nothing original to it. But I had passed a test which I had set for myself, and as no one was to be admitted to this chamber, I did not fancy that I had truly robbed Gozzoli of anything he possessed. Indeed if any mortal had found his way into this chamber which I kept locked, I would have explained that the original of this painting was done by Gozzoli, and indeed when the time came for me to show it to my apprentices, for the lessons it contained, I did so explain.

But let me return for a moment to the subject of this stolen work of art. Why did it appeal to me? What in it made my soul sing? I don't know. Except that it had to do with the three kings giving gifts, and I fancied that I was giving gifts to the children who lived in my house. But I'm not sure if that is why I chose the painting for my first excursion into true work with the brush. I'm not sure at all.

Perhaps it was only that all the details of the work were so fascinating. One could fall in love with the horses in the Procession. Or with the faces of the young men. I shall now leave the subject as puzzled about it as I tell my story, as I was then.

Immediately after confirming my success with the copy, I opened a spacious painting studio in the palazzo and began to work on large panels late at night while the boys slept. I did not really need their help and I did not want them to see the speed or the determination with which I worked.

My first ambitious painting was dramatic and strange. I painted a gathering of my apprentices in full fancy dress listening to an old Roman philosopher who wore only his long tunic and cloak and sandals, and this against a backdrop of the ruins of Rome. It was full of vivid color and my boys were well rendered, I give myself that. But I didn't know if it was any good. And I didn't know if it would horrify.

I left the door open to the studio in the hope that the teachers might wander in there by day.

As it turned out they were far too timid to do it.

I proceeded to create another painting, and this time I chose the Crucifixion—an approved theme for any artist—and I rendered it with tender care—and once again I used the backdrop of the ruins of Rome. Was it sacrilege? I couldn't guess. Once again, I was sure of my colors.

Indeed, this time I was sure of my proportions, and of the sympathetic expression on Christ's face. But was the composition itself somehow something that should not be?

How was I to know? I had all this knowledge, all this seeming power. Yet I didn't know. Was I creating something blasphemous and monstrous?

I returned to the subject of the Magi. I knew the conventions. Three kings, the stable, Mary, Joseph, the Infant, Jesus, and this time I did them freely, imputing to Mary the beauty of Zenobia, and glorying in the colors as before.

Soon my giant workroom was full of paintings. Some were correctly hung. Others were simply propped against the wall.

Then one night, at supper to which I'd invited the boys' more refined instructors, one of them, the Greek teacher, happened to mention that he had seen into my workshop through an open door.

"Oh, please, tell me," I said, "what did you think of my paintings?"

"Most remarkable!" he said frankly. "I've never seen anything like them! Why, all of the figures in the painting of the Magi . . ." He broke off, afraid.

"Please go on," I said instantly. "Tell me. I want to know."

"All of the figures are looking out at us, including Mary, and Joseph, and the three kings. I have never seen it done in that way."

"But is it wrong?" I asked.

"I don't think so," he said quickly. "But who's to say? You paint for yourself, don't you?"

"Yes, I do," I answered. "But your opinion matters to me. I find at moments I'm as fragile as glass."

We laughed. Only the older boys were interested in this exchange, and I saw that the very oldest, Piero, had something to say. He too had seen the paintings. He had gone inside the room.

"Tell me everything, Piero," I said, winking at him, and smiling. "Come on. What do you think?"

"The colors, Master, they were beautiful! When will it be time for us to work with you? I'm more skilled than you might think."

"I remember, Piero," I said, referring to the shop from which he'd come. "I'll call upon you soon enough."

In fact, I called upon them the very next night.

Having severe doubts about subject matter more than anything else, I resolved to follow Botticelli in that regard.

I chose the Lamentation for my subject matter. And I made my Christ as tender and vulnerable as I could conceivably do it, and I surrounded him with countless mourners. Pagan that I was, I didn't know who was supposed to be there! And so I created an immense and varied crowd of weeping mortals—all in Florentine dress—to lament the dead Jesus, and angels in the sky torn with anguish much like the angels of the painter Giotto whose work I had seen in some Italian city the name of which I could not recall.

My apprentices were quite astonished by the work and so were the teachers, whom I invited into the huge workroom for the initial view. Once again the faces I painted elicited special comment but so did the bizarre qualities of the painting—the inordinate amount of color and gold—and small touches I had added, such as insects here and there.

I realized something. I was free. I could paint what I wanted. Nobody was going to be the wiser. But then again, I thought, perhaps that's not true.

It was desperately important for me to remain in the middle of Venice. I did not want to lose my foothold in the warm, loving world.

I drifted out in the following weeks to all the churches once more in search of inspiration for my paintings, and I studied many a grotesque and bizarre picture which amazed me almost as much as my own work.

An artist by the name of Carpaccio had created a work called *Meditation on the Passion* which revealed the body of the dead Christ enthroned against a fantastical landscape, and flanked by two white-haired saints who peered at the viewer as if Christ were not there!

In the work of a painter named Crivelli, I found a truly grotesque picture of the dead Savior, flanked by two angels who looked like monsters. And the same painter had done a Madonna almost as lovely and lifelike as Botticelli's goddesses or nymphs.

I arose night after night hungry not for blood, though I certainly fed when I had to feed, but for my time in the workshop, and soon my paintings, all of them on large wooden panels, were propped all over the enormous house.

Finally, because I could keep track of them no longer, and went on to things new, rather than to perfect the old, I gave in to Vincenzo that he might have these works properly mounted as he wished.

Meanwhile our whole palazzo, though it had become famous in Venice as "a strange place," remained somewhat closed to the world.

Undoubtedly my hired teachers spoke of their days and evenings in the company of Marius de Romanus, and all our servants gossiped, no question of it, and I did not seek to put an end to such talk.

But I did not admit the true citizens of Venice. I did not lay out the banquet table as I had done in the old nights. I did not open the doors. Yet all the while I was longing to do it. I wanted the fashionable world of the city to be received under my roof.

What I did instead of extending invitations was to accept those I received.

Often in the early evening, when I didn't want to dine with my children, and long before I needed to begin painting furiously, I went to other palaces where feasting was in progress, and I entered, whispering my name when asked, but more often being received without question and discovering that the guests were eager to have me among them and had heard of my paintings and of my famous little school where the apprentices hardly did any work at all.

Of course I kept to the shadows, spoke in vague but gentle words, read minds well enough to make the most clever conversation and in general almost lost my wits so great was this love to me, this convivial reception of me which was nothing more than most of the noblemen of Venice took for granted every night of their lives.

I don't know how many months passed in this way. Two of my students went on to Padua. I went out into the city and found four more. Vincenzo showed no signs of ill health. I hired new and better teachers from time to time. I painted fiercely. So on it went.

Let me say a year or two had gone by before I was told of a very lovely and brilliant young woman who maintained a house always open to poets and playwrights and clever philosophers who could make their visits worth her while.

Understand the payment in question was not a manner of money; it was that one had to be interesting to be admitted to this woman's company; poems had to be lyrical and meaningful; there had to be wit in conversation; one could play the virginal or the lute only if one knew how.

I was fiercely curious as to the identity of this creature, and the general sweetness of the reports of her.

And so passing her house, I listened, and I heard her voice threading through the voices of those around her, and I knew her to be a mere child, but one filled with anguish and secrets, all of which she concealed with immense skill behind a graceful manner and a beautiful face.

How beautiful, I had no idea, until I mounted the steps, entered her rooms boldly and saw her for myself.

When I came into the room, she had her back to me, and turned as if my arrival had made some noise which it had not. I saw her in profile and then completely as she rose to greet me, and I could not speak for a moment, so great was the impression on my mind of her form and face.

That Botticelli hadn't painted her was a mere accident. Indeed he might well have done so. She looked so very like his women that all other thoughts left my mind. I saw her oval face, her oval eyes, and her thick wavy blond hair, interwound with long strings of tiny pearls, and the fine shape of her body with exquisitely molded arms and breasts.

"Yes, like Botticelli," she said, smiling as if I'd spoken it.

Again, I could say nothing. I was the one who read minds, and yet this child, this woman of nineteen or twenty years seemed to have read mine. But did she know how much I loved Botticelli? That she could not know.

She went on gaily, reaching out for my hand with both of hers.

"Everyone says it," she said, "and I'm honored. You might say I dress my hair this way on account of Botticelli. You know I was born in Florence, but that's not worth talking about here in Venice, is it? You're Marius de Romanus. I was wondering how long it would be before you came."

"Thank you for receiving me," I said. "I fear I come with nothing." I was still shocked by her beauty, shocked by the sound of her voice. "What have I to offer you?" I asked. "I have no poems, nor clever stories about the state of things. Tomorrow, I shall have my servants bring you the best wine I have in my house. But what is that to you?"

"Wine?" she repeated. "I don't want gifts of wine from you, Marius. Paint my picture. Paint the pearls interwound in my hair, I should love it."

There was soft laughter all around the room. I gazed musingly at the others. The candlelight was dim even for me. How rich it all seemed, these naive poets and students of the classics, this indescribably beautiful woman, and the room itself with all the usual splendid trappings, and time passing slowly as though the moments had some meaning and were not a sentence of penitence and grief.

I was in my glory. I realized it quite suddenly and then something else struck me.

This young woman was in her glory too.

Something sordid and evil lay behind her recent fortunes here, yet she displayed nothing of the desperation she must surely feel.

I tried to read her mind and then I chose not to do it! I didn't want anything but this moment.

I wanted to see this woman as she wanted me to see her—young, infinitely kind, yet utterly well defended—a companion for the night's cheerful gatherings, mysterious mistress of her own house.

Indeed, I saw another great drawing room adjacent to this one, and beyond it a marvelously decorated bedroom with a bed made of golden swans and gold-threaded silk.

Why this display if not to tell everyone that in that bed, this woman slept alone? No one was ever to presume to cross that threshold, but all might see where the maiden retired of her own accord.

"Why do you stare at me?" she asked me. "Why do you look about yourself as if this is a strange place to you when surely it's not?"

"All of Venice is lovely to me," I answered, making my voice soft and confidential so that it would not be for the whole room.

"Yes, isn't it?" she said, smiling exquisitely. "I too love it. I'll never return to Florence. But will you paint a picture of me?"

"Perhaps I will," I answered. "I don't know your name."

"You're not serious," she said, smiling again. I realized suddenly how very worldly she was. "You didn't come here not knowing my name. How could you want me to believe such a thing?"

"Oh, but I don't know it," I said, because I had never asked her name, and had learnt of her through vague images and impressions and fragments of conversation overheard by me as a blood drinker, and I stood at a loss because I wouldn't read her mind.

"Bianca," she said. "And my rooms are always open to you. And if you paint my picture, I'll be in your debt."

There were more guests coming. I knew that she meant to receive them. I backed away from her and took a station, so to speak, in the shadows well away from the candles, and from there I watched her, watched her infallibly graceful movements and heard her clever, ringing voice.

Over the years, I had beheld a thousand mortals who meant nothing to me, and now, gazing at this one creature I felt my heart tripping as it had when I had entered Botticelli's workshop, when I had seen his paintings and seen him, Botticelli, the man. Oh, yes, the man.

I stayed in her rooms only for a short time that night.

But I returned within the week with a portrait of her. I had painted it on a small panel and had it framed with gold and jewels.

I saw her shock when she received it. She had not expected something so exact. But then I feared she might see something wrong.

When she looked at me, I felt her gratitude and her affection and something greater collecting inside her, an emotion she denied in dealing with others.

"Who are you . . . really?" she asked me in a soft, lilting whisper.

"Who are *you* . . . really?" I repeated, and I smiled.

She looked at me gravely. Then she smiled too but she didn't answer, and all her secrets folded inside her—the sordid things, things to do with blood and gold.

For a moment, I thought my powerful self-control would be lost. I would embrace her, whether or not she would have it, and take her rapidly by force from the very middle of her warm and safe rooms to the cold and fatal domain of my soul.

I saw her, positively saw her as if the Christian Satan were giving me visions once more—I saw her transformed by the Dark Blood. I saw her as if she were mine, and all her youth burnt out in sacrifice to immortality, and the only warmth or riches known to her those which came from me.

I left her rooms. I couldn't remain there. For nights, no, months I did not return. In that time a letter came to me from her. I was quite astonished to receive it and I read it over and over and then put it in a pocket inside my tunic next to my heart.

My dear Marius,

Why leave me with only a brilliant painting when I would have your companionship as well? We are always seeking for amusement here, and there is much kind talk of you. Do come back to me. Your painting occupies a position of honor on the wall of my salon so that I might share the pleasure of it with all who come.

How had this happened, this craving to make a mortal my companion? After so many centuries, what had I done to bring it on?

I had thought that, with Botticelli, it had to do with his remarkable talent, and that I, with eyes so sharp and heart so hungry, had wanted to mingle the Blood with his inexplicable gift.

But this child, Bianca, was no such seeming miracle, no matter how precious I found her to be. Oh, yes, she was to my taste as if I'd made her—the daughter of Pandora—it was as if Botticelli had created her, even to the somewhat dreamy expression of her face. And she did have a seemingly impossible mingling of fire and poise.

But I had in my long miserable years seen many beautiful humans, rich and poor, younger and older, and I had not felt this sharp, near uncontrollable desire to bring her to me, to take her to the shrine with me, to spill out to her whatever wisdom I possessed.

What was I to do with this pain? How should I be rid of it? How long would it torment me right here in the city of Venice where I had chosen to seek comfort from mortals and give back to the world in secret payment my blessed and well-educated boys?

On rising, I found myself shaking loose light dreams of Bianca, dreams in which she and I were sitting in my bedroom and talking together as I told her of all the long lonely paths I'd trod, talking together as she told me of how she had drawn from common and filthy pain her immeasurable strength.

Even as I attended the feast with my students I couldn't shake off these dreams. They broke in on me as if I were falling asleep over the wine and meats. The boys vied for my attention. They thought they had failed the Master.

When I went to my rooms to paint, I was equally confused. I painted a large picture of Bianca as the Virgin Mary with a chubby Infant Jesus. I laid down the brushes. I wasn't content. I couldn't be content.

I went out of Venice into the countryside. I searched for the Evil Doer. I drank blood until I was glutted. And then I returned to my rooms, and I lay down on my bed and I dreamt of Bianca again.

At last before dawn I wrote my admonitions down in my diary:

This desire to make an immortal companion is no more justified here than it was in Florence. You have survived all your long life without ever taking this evil step, though you know well how to do it—the Druid priest taught you how to do it—and not doing it, you will continue to survive. You cannot bring over this child to you, no matter how you envision it. Imagine her to be a statue. Imagine your evil to be a force that would shatter that statue. See her then in fragments. Know that that is what you would do.

I went back to her rooms.

It was as if I'd never seen her before, so great was her impression upon me, so soft and compelling her voice, so radiant her face and her worldly eyes. It was an agony and also an immeasurable consolation to be near her.

For months I came to her rooms, pretending to listen to the poems recited, sometimes forced to answer in the gentle discussions regarding the theories of aesthetics or philosophy, but all the while simply wanting to be near her, studying the minutia of her beauty, closing my eyes now and then as I listened to the song of her voice.

Visitors came and went from her famous gatherings. No one dared question her supremacy within her own domain. But as I sat, as I observed, as I let myself dream in the candlelight, there came to my observation something subtle and dreadful as ever I had beheld.

Certain men who came into these rooms were marked for a dark and specific purpose. Certain men, well known to the divinely alluring mistress, received in their wine a poison which would follow them as they left the genial company and soon accomplish their deaths!

At first, when I with my preternatural senses had smelled this subtle but certain poison I thought I had imagined such a thing. But then with the Mind Gift, I saw into the heart of this enchantress, and how she lured those whom she must poison, knowing little or nothing of why they had been condemned to death.

This was the sordid lie I had first perceived in her. A kinsman, a Florentine banker, kept her in terror. Indeed it was he who had brought her here, provided her with her nest of lovely chambers and ever playing music. It was he who demanded of her that the poison be placed in the proper cup to do away with those he chose.

How calmly her blue eyes passed over those who drank the fatal potion. How calmly she watched as the poetry was read to her. How calmly she smiled at me when her eyes happened to fall upon the tall blond-haired man who observed her from the corner. And how deep her despair!

Armed with this new knowledge, no, driven to distraction by it, I went out into the night roaming, for now I had the proof on her of guilt immeasurable! Was this not sufficient to bring her over, to force the Dark Blood upon her, and then say, "No, my darling, I haven't taken your life, I've given you eternity with me!"

Beyond the city I walked the country roads for hours, sometimes pounding my forehead with the heels of my palms.

I want her, I want her, I want her. But I could not bring myself to do it. At last I went home to paint her portrait. And night after night, I painted her portrait again. I painted her as the Virgin of the Annunciation, and the Virgin with Child. I painted her as the Virgin in the Lamentation. I painted her as Venus, as Flora, I painted her on small panels that I brought to her. I painted her until I could endure it no longer. I slumped on the floor of my painting room, and when the apprentices came to me in the dark hours of the dawn, they thought me sick and cried out.

But I couldn't bring harm to her. I couldn't bring my Evil Blood to her. I couldn't take her over to me, and now a most great and grotesque quality attached itself to her in my eyes.

She was evil as I was evil, and when I watched her from the corner of her room, I fancied that I studied a thing which was like unto myself.

For her life, she dispatched her victims. For my life, I drank human blood.

And so this tender girl, in her costly gowns with her long blond locks and soft cheeks, took on a dark majesty for me; and I was fascinated by her more than ever before.

One night, so great was my pain, so dire was my need to separate myself from this young woman, that I went alone in my gondola, telling my oarsman to row back and forth through the smallest canals of the city and not bring me back to the palazzo until I gave the command.

What did I seek? The smell of death and rats in the blackest waters. The occasional merciful flashes of the moon.

I lay down in the boat, my head on my pillow. I listened to the voices of the city so that I would not hear my own.

And quite suddenly, as we came into the wider canals again, as we came into a certain district of Venice, there came a voice quite different from all the others, for it was speaking from a desperate and deranged mind.

In a flash I saw an image behind the cry of this voice, the image of a painted face. Indeed, I saw the paint laid on in marvelous strokes. I knew the painted face. It was the face of Christ!

What did this mean? In a solemn silence, I listened. No other voice mattered to me. I banished a city full of whispers.

It was a woeful crying. It was the voice of a child behind thick walls who on account of the recent cruelties done him could not remember his native language or even his name.

Yet in that forgotten language he prayed to be delivered from those who had cast him down in darkness, those who had tormented him and jabbered at him in a tongue he didn't know.

Once again there came that image, the painted Christ staring forward. The painted Christ in a time-honored and Greek style. Oh, how well I knew this fashion of painting; oh, how well I knew this countenance. Had I not seen it a thousand times in Byzantium, and in all those places East and West to which its power had reached?

What did this mean, this mingled voice and imagery? What did it mean that the child thought again and again of an ikon and did not know that he prayed?

Once again there came the plea from one who thought himself to be utterly silent.

And I knew the language in which he prayed. It was no matter to me to disentangle it, to put the words in order, having as I did such a knowledge of languages the world wide. Yes, I knew his tongue and I knew his prayer. "Dear God, deliver me. Dear God, let me die."

A frail child, a hungry child, a child who was alone.

Sitting up in the gondola, I listened. I delved for the images locked away inside the child's most wordless thoughts.

He had once been a painter, this bruised and young one. The face of Christ had been his work. He had once mixed the egg yolk and the pigment just as I mixed them. He had once painted the face of Christ again and again!

Whence came this voice? I had to discover the source of it. I listened with all my skill.

Somewhere very near, this child was imprisoned. Somewhere very near, he offered up his prayer with his last breath.

He had painted his precious ikons in the far country of snowy Russia. Indeed, this child had been supremely gifted in the painting of ikons. But he could not remember that now. That was the mystery. That was the complexity! He could not even see the images which I was seeing, so broken was his heart.

I could understand what he himself could not understand. And he was pleading silently with Heaven in a Russian dialect to be delivered from those who had made him a slave in Venice and sought to make him serve others in a brothel through acts which to him were sins of the flesh which he could not abide!

I told my oarsman to stop.

I listened until I had found the exact source. I directed the boat to go back only a few doors until I found the precise place.

The torches were burning brightly before the entrance. I could hear the music inside.

The voice of the child was persistent, and yet there came that clear understanding on my part that the child did not know his own prayers, his own history, his own tongue.

I was greeted by the owners of the house with great fanfare. They knew of me. I must come in. I could have whatever I wanted under their roof. Just beyond the door lay paradise. Listen to the laughter, and the singing.

"What do you desire, Master?" a pleasant-voiced man asked of me. "You can tell me. We have no secrets here."

I stood listening. How reticent I must have seemed—this tall, blond-haired man with such a chilly manner, who cocked his head to one side and looked away with his thoughtful blue eyes.

I tried to see the boy, but I could not. The boy was locked away where no one saw him. How would I proceed? Ask to see all of the boys of the house? That would not do it, for this one was in a chamber of punishment, cold and quite alone.

Then suddenly the answer came to me as though angels had spoken it, or was it the Devil? It came swiftly and completely.

"To purchase, you understand," I said, "with gold of course, and now, a boy you want to be rid of. One recently arrived here who will not do as he's told."

In a flash I saw the boy in the man's eyes. Only it could not be true. I could not have such luck. For this boy had beauty as bountiful as Bianca's. I did not count upon it.

"Recently come from Istanbul," I said. "Yes, I think that is correct, for the boy was no doubt brought from Russian climes."

I need say no more words. Everyone was scurrying about. Someone had put a goblet of wine into my hands. I smelled the lovely scent of it, and set it down on the table. It seemed a flood of rose petals descended. Indeed there was everywhere the perfume of flowers. A chair was brought for me. I did not sit on it.

Suddenly the man who had greeted me returned to the room.

"You don't want that one," he said quickly. He was greatly agitated. And once again, I saw a clear image of the boy lying on a stone floor.

And I heard the boy's prayers: "Deliver me." And I saw the Face of Christ in gleaming egg tempera. I saw the jewels set into the halo. I saw the egg and pigment mixing. "Deliver me."

"Can't you understand me?" I asked. "I told you what I wanted. I want that boy, the one who won't do what you try to force him to do."

Then I realized it.

The brothel keeper thought the boy was dying. He was afraid of the law. He stood before me in terror.

"Take me to him," I said. I pressed him with the Mind Gift. "Do it now. I know of him and won't leave here without him. Besides, I'll pay you. I don't care if he's sick and dying. Do you hear me? I'll take him away with me. You'll never have to worry about him again."

It was a cruel small chamber in which they'd locked him, and into that chamber the light of a lamp flooded upon the child.

And there I saw beauty, beauty which has always been my downfall, beauty as in Pandora, as in Avicus, as in Zenobia, as in Bianca, beauty in a new and celestial form.

Heaven had cast down upon this stone floor an abandoned angel, of auburn curls and perfectly formed limbs, of fair and mysterious face.

I reached down to take him by the arms and I lifted him, and I looked into his half-opened eyes. His soft reddish hair was loose and tangled. His flesh was pale and the bones of his face only faintly sharpened by his Slavic blood.

"Amadeo," I said, the name springing to my lips as though the angels willed it, the very angels whom he resembled in his purity and in his seeming innocence, starved as he was.

His eyes grew wide as he stared at me. In majesty and golden light, I saw again in his mind those ikons which he had painted. Desperately he struggled to remember. Ikons. The Christ he had painted. With long hair and burning eyes, I resembled the Christ.

He tried to speak, but the language had left him. He tried to find the name of his Lord.

"I'm not the Christ, my child," I said, speaking to that part of him deep within the mind of which he knew nothing. "But one who comes with his own salvation. Amadeo, come into my arms."

19

ILOVED HIM INSTANTLY and impossibly. He was fifteen years old
at the most when I took him out of the brothel that night and
brought him to live in the palazzo with my boys.

As I held him close to me in the gondola, I knew him certainly to
have been doomed—indeed, snatched at the last moment from an
inconsequential death.

Though the firmness of my arms comforted him, the beat of his
heart was barely sufficient to drive the images which I received from
him as he lay against my chest.

Reaching the palazzo, I refused Vincenzo's assistance, sending him
off for food for the child, and I took my Amadeo into my bedchamber
alone.

I laid him upon my bed, a wan and ragged being, amid the heavy
velvet hangings and pillows, and when the soup at last came, I forced it
through his lips myself.

Wine, soup, a potion of honey and lemon, what more could we give
him? Slowly, cautioned Vincenzo, lest he take too much after the starvation, and his stomach suffer as the result.

At last I sent Vincenzo away from us, and I bolted the doors of my
room.

Was that the fateful moment? Was it the moment in which I knew
my soul most completely, the moment in which I acknowledged that
this would be a child of my power, my immortality, a pupil of all I
knew?

As I looked at the child on the bed, I forgot the language of guilt
and recrimination. I was Marius, the witness of the centuries, Marius,
the chosen one of Those Who Must Be Kept.

Taking Amadeo into the bath, I cleansed him myself and covered him with kisses. I drew from him an easy intimacy which he had denied all those who had tormented him, so dazzled and confused was he by my simple kindnesses, and the words I whispered in his tender ears.

I brought him quickly to know the pleasures which he had never allowed himself before. He was dazed and silent; but his prayers for deliverance were no more.

Yet even here in the safety of this bedroom, in the arms of one he saw as his Savior, nothing of his old memory could move from the recesses of his mind into the sanctum of reason.

Indeed, perhaps my frankly carnal embraces made the wall in his mind, between past and present, all the more strong.

As for me, I had never experienced such pure intimacy with a mortal, except with those I meant to kill. It gave me chills to have my arms around this boy, to press my lips to his cheeks and chin, his forehead, his tender closed eyes.

Yes, the blood thirst rose, but I knew so well how to control it. I filled my nostrils with the smell of his youthful flesh.

I knew that I could do anything I wanted with him. There was no force between Heaven and Hell that could stop me. And I did not need a Satan to tell me that I could bring him over to me and educate him within the Blood.

Drying him gently with towels, I returned him to the bed.

I sat down at my desk, where turning to the side I might look directly at him, and there came the full-blown idea of it, as rich as my desire to seduce Botticelli, as terrible as my passion for the lovely Bianca.

This was a foundling who could be educated for the Blood! This was a child utterly lost to life who could be reclaimed specifically for the Blood.

Would his training be a night, a week, a month, a year? Only I need decide it.

Whatever it was, I would make of him a child of the Blood.

My mind went back swiftly to Eudoxia and how she had spoken of the perfect age for the Blood to be received. I remembered Zenobia and her quick wits and knowing eyes. I remembered my own long ago reflection on the promise of a virgin, that one could make of a virgin what one wished without price.

And this child, this rescued slave, had been a painter! He knew the magic of the egg and the pigments, yes, he knew the magic of the color spread upon the wooden panel. He would remember; he would remember a time when he cared about nothing else.

True it had been in far-away Russia, where those who worked in monasteries limited themselves to the style of the Byzantines which I had long ago rejected as I turned my back on the Greek Empire and came to make my home amid the strife of the West.

But behold what had happened: the West had had its wars, yes, and indeed, the barbarians had conquered all it did seem. Yet Rome had risen again through the great thinkers and painters of the 1400s! I beheld it in the work of Botticelli, and Bellini and Filippo Lippi and in a hundred others.

Homer, Lucretius, Virgil, Ovid, Plutarch—they were all being studied once again. The scholars of "humanism" sang songs of "antiquity."

In sum, the West had risen again with new and fabulous cities, whereas Constantinople, old golden Constantinople, had been lost to the Turks who had made it Istanbul.

But far beyond Istanbul, there lay Russia from which this boy had been taken prisoner, Russia which had taken its Christianity from Constantinople so that this boy knew only the ikons of strict somber style and rigid beauty, an art which was as remote from what I painted as night from day.

Yet in the city of Venice both styles existed: the Byzantine style and the new style of the times.

How had it come about? Through trading. Venice had been a seaport since its beginnings. Its great fleet had gone back and forth between East and West when Rome was a ruin. And many a church in Venice preserved the old Byzantine style which filled this boy's tortured mind.

These Byzantine churches had never much mattered to me before, I had to admit. Not even the Doge's chapel, San Marco, had much mattered to me. But they mattered now, because they helped me to understand again and all the better the art which this boy had loved.

I stared at him as he slept.

All right. I understood something of his nature; I understood his suffering. But who was he really? I posed the same question which Bianca and I had exchanged with each other. The answer I did not have.

Before I could think of moving forward with my plan to prepare him for the Blood I must know.

Would it take a night, or a hundred nights? Whatever the time, it would not be endless.

Amadeo was destined for me.

I turned and wrote in my diary. Never had such a design occurred to me before, to educate a novice for the Blood! I described all the events of the night so that I might never lose them to overwrought memory. I drew sketches of Amadeo's face as he slept.

How can I describe him? His beauty did not depend on his facial expression. It was stamped already on the face. It was all wrought up with his fine bones, serene mouth, and his auburn curls.

I wrote passionately in my diary.

This child has come from a world so different from our own that he can make no sense of what has happened to him. But I know the snowy lands of Russia. I know the dark dreary life of Russian and Greek monasteries, and it was in one of these, I am quite convinced, that he painted the ikons which he cannot speak of now.

As for our tongue, he's had no experience with it except in cruelty. Perhaps when the boys make him one of them, he will remember his past. He will want to take up the paintbrush. His talent will come forth again.

I put the quill aside. I could not confide everything to my diary. No, not everything by any means. Great secrets I sometimes wrote in Greek rather than Latin, but even in Greek I could not say all that I thought.

I looked at the boy. I took up the candelabrum and I approached the bed and I looked down at him as he slept there, easy at last, breathing as though he were safe.

Slowly his eyes opened. He looked up at me. There was no fear in him. Indeed, it seemed that he still dreamed.

I gave myself over to the Mind Gift.

Tell me, child, tell me from your heart.

I saw the riders of the Steppes come down upon him and a band of his people. I saw a bundle drop from the boy's anxious hands. The cloth wrapping fell away from it. It was an ikon, and the boy cried out fearfully, but the evil barbarians wanted only the boy. They were the same inevitable barbarians who had never ceased to raid along the Roman Empire's long-forgotten Northern and Eastern frontiers. Would the world never see an end to their kind?

By those evil men, this child had been brought to some Eastern marketplace. Was it Istanbul? And from there to Venice where he fell into the hands of a brothel keeper who had bought him for high payment on account of face and form.

The cruelty of this, the mystery of it, had been overwhelming. In the hands of another, this boy might never be healed.

Yet in his mute expression now I saw pure trust.

"Master," he said softly in the Russian tongue.

I felt the tiny hairs rise all over my body. I wanted so to touch him once more with my cold fingers but I did not dare. I knelt beside the bed and leant over and I kissed his cheek warmly.

"Amadeo," I said to him so that he might know his new name.

And then using the very Russian tongue he knew, but did not know, I told him that he was mine now, that I was his Master just as he had said. I gave him to know that all things were resolved in me. He must never worry, he would never fear again.

It was almost morning. I had to leave.

Vincenzo came knocking. The eldest among the apprentices were waiting outside. They had heard that a new boy had been brought into the house.

I admitted them to the bedroom. I told them they must take care of Amadeo. They must acquaint him with all our common wonders. They must let him rest for a while, surely, but they could take him out into the city. Perhaps it was the perfect thing to do.

"Riccardo," I charged the eldest. "Take this one under your wing."

What a lie it was! I stood thinking of it. It was a lie to give him over to the daylight, to companionship other than my own.

But the rising sun gave me no more time in the palazzo. What else could I do?

I went to my grave.

I lay down in darkness dreaming of him.

I had found an escape from the love of Botticelli. I had found an escape from the obsession with Bianca and her tantalizing guilt. I had found one whom death and cruelty had already marked. The Blood would be the ransom. Yes, all things were resolved in me.

Oh, but who was he? What was he? I knew the memories, the images, the horrors, the prayers, but not the voice! And something tormented me savagely, even in my avowed certainty. Did I not love this child too much to do what I planned to do?

The following night a splendid surprise awaited me.

There was my Amadeo at supper gorgeously turned out in blue velvet, as splendidly clothed as the other boys!

They had hastened to complete the tailoring of his clothes to make me happy and indeed I was, almost to the point of being stunned.

As he knelt to kiss my ring, I was speechless, and with both my hands I bid him rise, and I embraced him, kissing him quickly on both cheeks.

He was still weak from his ordeals, I could see it, but the other boys as well as Vincenzo had gone a long way to put some color into his face.

As we sat down to supper, Riccardo explained that Amadeo could paint nothing. Indeed, Amadeo was afraid of the brushes and the pots of paint. And that he knew no language but he was picking up with amazing quickness our own tongue.

The beautiful boy with the auburn hair who was Amadeo gazed at me calmly as Riccardo spoke. And once again he said in the soft Russian tongue: Master, which the other boys did not hear.

You are for me. That was my answer for him. The soft words in Russian that I gave to him through the Mind Gift. *Remember. Who were you before you came here? Before they hurt you? Go back. Go back to the ikon. Go back to the Face of Christ if need be.*

A look of fear passed over him. Riccardo, not dreaming of the reason why, quickly took his hand. Riccardo began to name the simple objects of the supper table for him. And Amadeo as if waking from a nightmare smiled at Riccardo and repeated the words.

How sharp and fine his voice. How sure the pronunciation. How quick the look of his brown eyes.

"Teach him everything," I said to Riccardo and to the teachers assembled. "See to it that he studies dancing, fencing, and most of all painting. Show him every picture in the house, and every sculpture. Take him everywhere. See that he learns all there is to know about Venice."

Then I retired to the painting room alone.

Quickly I mixed up the tempera, and I painted a small portrait of

Amadeo as I'd seen him at supper, in his fine tunic of blue velvet with his hair shining and combed.

I was weak from the heat of my own miserable thoughts. The fact was, my conviction had left me.

How could I take from this boy the cup he'd barely tasted? He was a dead creature brought back to life. I had robbed myself of my own Child of the Blood by my own splendid designs.

From that moment afterwards for months to come, Amadeo belonged to daylight. Yes, he must have every chance in the daylight to make of himself whatever he would!

Yet in his mind, unbeknownst to the others in any material way, Amadeo perceived himself, at my behest, as secretly and completely belonging to me.

It was for me a great and terrible contradiction.

I relinquished my claim upon the child. I couldn't condemn him to the Dark Blood, no matter how great my loneliness or how great his former misery had been. He must have his chance now among the apprentices and scholars of my household, and should he prove to be a princeling as I fully expected from his immediate brightness, he should have his chance to move on to the University of Padua or the University of Bologna where my students were now going one after the other as my myriad plans came to fruition beneath my all-encompassing roof.

Yet in the late evenings, when the lessons had ceased and the little boys had been put to bed, and the older boys were finishing tasks in my studio, I couldn't stop myself from taking Amadeo into my bedroom study, and there I visited on him my carnal kisses, my sweet and bloodless kisses, my kisses of need, and he gave himself to me without reserve.

My beauty charmed him. Is it pride to say so? I had no doubt of it. I need not work the Mind Gift to render him spellbound. He adored me. And though my paintings terrified him, something in his deep soul allowed him to worship my seeming talent—the deftness of my composition, my vibrant colors, my graceful speed.

Of course he never spoke of this to the others. And they, the boys, who surely must have known that we spent hours together in the bedroom, never dared think of what happened between us. As for Vincenzo, he knew better than to acknowledge this strange relationship in any respect.

Meanwhile, Amadeo recovered nothing of his memory. He could not paint, he could not touch the brushes. It was as if the colors, when raw, burnt his eyes.

But his wit was as sharp as any among the other boys. He learnt Greek and Latin quickly, he was a wonder at dancing, he loved his lessons with the rapier. He absorbed readily the lectures of the brighter teachers. He was soon writing Latin in a clear and steady hand.

In the evening he read aloud his verses to me. He sang to me, softly accompanying himself on the lute.

I sat at my desk, leaning upon my elbow, listening to his low and measured voice.

His hair was always beautifully combed, his clothes elegant and immaculate, his fingers, like mine, covered in rings.

Didn't everyone know he was the boy I kept? My minion, my lover, my secret treasure? Even in old Rome, amid a wilderness of vices, there would have been whispers, low laughter, some bit of mockery.

Here in Venice for Marius de Romanus, there was none. But Amadeo had his suspicions, not as to kisses that were fast becoming all too chaste for him, but as to the man of seeming marble, who never supped at his own table, nor took a drop of wine from a goblet, or ever appeared beneath his own roof during the light of day.

Along with these suspicions, I saw in Amadeo a growing confusion as memories tried to make themselves known to him and he would deny them, sometimes waking beside me as we dozed together, and tormenting me with kisses when I would rather dream.

One evening, in the early and beautiful months of winter when I came in to greet my eager students, Riccardo told me that he had taken Amadeo with him to visit the lovely and gracious Bianca Solderini, and she had made them welcome, delighted by Amadeo's poetry and the manner in which he could pen tributes for her on the very spot.

I looked into the eyes of my Amadeo. He had been enchanted by her. How well I understood it. And how strange a mood descended upon me as the boys talked of her pleasant company and the fascinating English gentlemen now visiting her house.

Bianca had sent a small note to me.

"Marius, I miss you. Do come soon and bring your boys with you. Amadeo is as clever as Riccardo. I have your portraits everywhere. All are curious about the man who painted them, but I say nothing, for in truth I know nothing. Lovingly, Bianca."

When I looked up from the note, I saw Amadeo watching me, probing me as it were with his silent eyes.

"Do you know her, Master?" he asked me soberly, surprising Riccardo, who said nothing.

"You know I do, Amadeo. She told you I had come to visit her. You saw my portraits on her walls."

I sensed a sudden and violent jealousy in him. But nothing changed in his face. *Don't go to her.* That's what his soul said to me. And I knew he wished that Riccardo would leave now and we could have the shadowy bed, with its concealing velvet curtains, to ourselves.

There was something stubborn in him, something directed entirely towards our love. And how it tempted me, how it drew from me the most complete devotion.

"But I want you to remember," I said to him suddenly in his Russian tongue.

It was a shock to him but he didn't understand it.

"Amadeo," I said in the Venetian dialect, "think back to the time before you came here. Think back, Amadeo. What was your world then?"

A flush came to his cheeks. He was miserable. It was as if I'd beaten him.

Riccardo reached out for him with a consoling hand. "Master," he said, "it's too hard for him."

Amadeo seemed paralyzed. I rose from my chair at the desk and I put my arm around him where he sat and I kissed the top of his head.

"Come, forget everything. We'll go to see Bianca. This is the time of night which she likes the best."

Riccardo was amazed to be permitted out at this hour. As for Amadeo he was still dazed.

We found Bianca thickly surrounded by her chattering guests. There were Florentines among them, and Englishmen as I'd been told.

Bianca brightened as she saw me. She took me away from the others, towards her bedchamber where the elaborate swan bed was exquisitely adorned as if it were something on a stage.

"You've come at last," she said. "I'm so glad to see you. You don't know how I've missed you." How warm were her words. "You are the only painter who exists in my world, Marius." She wanted to kiss me but I couldn't risk it. I bent to press my lips to her cheek quickly and then I held her back.

Ah, such radiant sweetness. Gazing into her oval eyes, I stepped into the paintings of Botticelli. I held in my hands, for reasons I could never know, the dark perfumed tresses of Zenobia, gathered up in memory from the floor of a house on the other side of the world.

"Bianca, my darling," I said to her. "I'm ready to open my house if you will receive for me." What a shock it was to hear these words come from my own lips. I had not known what I meant to say. Yet on I pressed with my dream. "I have neither wife nor daughter. Come, open my house to the world."

The look of triumph in her face confirmed it. I would do it.

"I shall tell everyone," she said immediately. "Yes, I'll receive for you, I shall do it proudly, I shall do it gladly, but surely you'll be there yourself."

"May we open the doors in the evening?" I asked her. "It's my custom to come in the evening. The light of candles suits me better than the light of day. You set the night for it, Bianca, and I shall have my servants make everything ready. The paintings are everywhere now. You do understand I offer nothing to anyone. I paint for my pleasure. And for my guests I'll have food and drink as you say."

How happy she looked. Off to one side I saw Amadeo gazing at her, loving her somewhat and loving the sight of us together though it gave him pain.

Riccardo was being drawn into conversation by men who were older than he and flattered him and loved his handsome face.

"Tell me what to lay out on my tables," I said to Bianca. "Tell me what wines to serve. My servants shall be your servants. I shall do everything as you say."

"It's too lovely," she answered. "All of Venice will be there, I promise you, you'll discover the most wonderful company. People are so curious about you. Oh, how they whisper. You can't imagine what a supreme delight this will be."

It came about as she described.

Within the month I opened the palazzo to the whole city. But how different it was from those drunken nights in old Rome when people laid about on my couches and vomited in my gardens and I painted madly away on the walls.

Oh, yes, when I arrived, how proper were my finely clad Venetian guests. Of course I was asked a thousand questions. I let my eyes mist over. I heard the mortal voices around me as if they were kisses. I thought: You are among them; it is truly as if you were one of them. It is truly as if you are alive.

What did it matter their little criticisms of the paintings? I would strive to make my work the finest, yes, truly, but what counted was the vitality, the momentum!

And here amid my best work stood my lovely fair-haired Bianca, free for the moment from those who put her up to her wrongdoings, recognized by all as the Mistress of my house.

Amadeo watched this with silent grudging eyes. The memories inside him tormented him like a cancer, yet he could not see them and know them for what they were.

Not a month after, at sunset, I found him sick in the grand church on the nearby island of Torcello to which he had wandered, apparently on his own. I picked him up from the cold damp floor and took him home.

Of course I understood the reason. There he had found ikons of the very style he had once painted. There he had found old mosaics from centuries past, similar to those he had seen in Russian churches as a child. He had not remembered. He had merely come upon some old truth in his wanderings—the brittle, stark Byzantine paintings—and now the heat of the place had left him with a fever, and I could taste it on his lips and see it in his eyes.

He was no better at sunrise when, half mad, I left him in the care of Vincenzo, only to rise again at sunset and hurry back to the side of his bed.

It was his mind that stoked the fever. Bundling him like a child I took him into a Venetian church to see the wondrous paintings of robust and natural figures that had been done in these last few years.

But I could see now it was hopeless. His mind would never be opened, never truly changed. I brought him home, and laid him down on the pillows once more.

I sought to better understand what I could.

His had been a punitive world of austere devotion. Painting for him had been joyless. And indeed all of life itself in far-away Russia had been so rigorous that he could not give himself over to the pleasure that awaited him now at every turn.

Beset by the memories, yet not understanding them, he was moving slowly towards death.

I would not have it. I paced the floor, I turned to those who attended him. I walked about, whispering to myself in my anger. I would not have it. I would not let him die.

Sternly, I banished others from the bedchamber.

I bent over him, and biting into my tongue I filled my mouth with blood and then I loosed a thin stream of it into his mouth.

He quickened, and licked his lips after it, and then he breathed more easily and the flush came to his cheeks. I felt of his forehead. It was cooler. He opened his eyes and he looked at me, and he said as he did so often, "Master," and then gently, without memories, without terrible dreams, he slept.

It was enough. I left the bed. I wrote in my thick diary, the quill scratching as I quickly inscribed the words:

"He is irresistible, but what am I to do? I claimed him once, declaring him my very own, and now I treat his misery with the blood I wish that I could give him. Yet in treating his misery, I hope to cure him not for me but for the wide world."

I closed the book, in disgust with myself for the blood I'd given him. But it had healed him. I knew it. And were he ill, I would give him blood again.

Time was moving too swiftly.

Things were happening too fast. My earlier judgments were shaken, and the beauty of Amadeo increased with every passing night.

The teachers took the boys to Florence that they might see the paintings there. And all came home more truly inspired to study than before.

Yes, they had seen the work of Botticelli, and how splendid it was. Was the Master painting? Indeed, so, but his work had become almost entirely religious. It was due to the preaching of Savonarola, a stringent monk who condemned the Florentines for their worldliness. Savonarola had great power over the people of Florence. Botticelli believed in him, and was thought to be one of his followers.

This saddened me greatly. Indeed it damn near maddened me. But then I knew that whatever Botticelli painted it would be magnificent. And in Amadeo's progress I was comforted, or rather pleasantly confused as before.

Amadeo was now the most brilliant of all my little academy. New teachers were required for him in philosophy and law. He was outgrowing his clothes at a marvelous rate, he had become quick and charming in conversation, and he was the beloved of all the younger boys.

Night after night we visited Bianca. I became accustomed to the company of refined strangers, the eternal stream of northern Europeans who came to Italy to discover its ancient and mysterious charms.

Only occasionally did I see Bianca hand the poisoned cup to one of her ill-fated guests. Only occasionally did I feel the beat of her dark heart, and see the shadow of desperate guilt in the very depth of her eyes. How she watched the unfortunate victim; how she saw him out of her company at last with a subtle smile.

As for Amadeo, our private sessions within my bedchamber became ever more intimate. And more than once, as we embraced, I gave the Blood Kiss to him, watching his body shiver, and seeing the power of it in his half-lidded eyes.

What was this madness? Was he for the world or for me?

How I lied to myself about it. I told myself the boy might still prove himself and thereby earn his freedom to leave me, safe and rich, for accomplishments beyond my house.

But I had given him so much of the Secret Blood that he pushed me with questions. What manner of creature was I? Why did I never come by day? Why did I take no food or drink?

He wrapped his warm arms around the mystery. He buried his face in the monster's neck.

I sent him off to the best brothels to learn the pleasures of women, and the pleasures of boys. He hated me for it, and yet he enjoyed it, and he came home to me eager for the Blood Kiss and nothing else.

He taunted me when I painted alone, except for him, in my studio, working furiously, creating some landscape or gathering of ancient heroes. He slept beside me when I collapsed in my bed to sleep the last few hours before dawn.

Meantime, we opened the palazzo again and yet again. Bianca, ever the clever and poised one, had outgrown her early beauty, and preserving her delicate face and manner, had now the polish of a woman rather than the promise of a girl.

Often I found myself staring at her, wondering what would have happened if I had not turned my attention to him. Why after all had I done it? Could I not have wooed her and persuaded her; and then, thinking these thoughts, I realized, foolishly, that I might still choose to do so, and cast him off, with wealth and position, to mortality with all the rest of my boys.

No, she was saved.

Amadeo was the one I wanted. Amadeo was the one I was educating, training. Amadeo was the precious student of the Blood.

The nights passed swiftly, as if in a dream.

Several boys went off to university. One of the teachers died. Vincenzo took to walking with a limp, but I hired an assistant to fetch for him. Bianca rearranged several of the large paintings. The air was warm and the windows were open. On the roof garden we gathered for a great banquet. The boys sang.

Never once in all this time did I fail to apply the salve to my skin to darken it and make me appear human. Never once did I fail to work it into the flesh of both my hands. Never once did I fail to dress with fine jewels, and wear rings that would distract everyone. Never once did I move too close to a grouping of candles, or a torch at a doorway or on the quais.

I went to the shrine of Those Who Must Be Kept and remained there in meditation. I laid the case before Akasha.

I wanted this child—this boy who was now two years older than when I'd found him—and yet I wanted everything else for him, and my soul was torn, just as his heart was torn.

Never before had I wanted such a thing, to make a blood drinker for my own companionship, indeed to educate a mortal youth for this very purpose, and to groom him expertly that he might be the finest choice.

But I wanted it now and it filled my thoughts during every waking hour, and I found no consolation looking at my cold Mother and Father. I heard no answer to my prayer.

I lay down to sleep in the shrine and knew only dark and troubled dreams.

I saw the garden, the very one I had painted on the walls eternally, and I was walking in it as always, and there was fruit on the low-hanging trees. There came Amadeo walking near me, and suddenly there came from his mouth a chilling cruel laughter.

"A sacrifice?" he asked, "for Bianca? How can such a thing be?"

I woke with a start, and sat up, rubbing the backs of my arms, and shaking my head, trying to free myself from the dream.

"I don't know the answer," I whispered, as though he were there near me, as though his spirit had traveled to the place where I sat.

"Except she was already a young woman when I came upon her," I responded, "educated and forced into life, indeed a murderess; yes, indeed, a murderess, a child woman guilty of dreadful crimes. And you, you were a helpless child. I could mold you and change you, all of which I've done.

"It's true, I thought you were a painter," I continued, "that you had the gift for painting, and I know that it's still in you, and that did sway me, too. But when all is said and done, I don't know why you distracted me, only that it was done."

I lay back down to sleep once more, lying on my side rather carelessly, staring up at the glimmering eye of Akasha. At the harsh lines of the face of Enkil.

I thought back over the centuries to Eudoxia. I remembered her terrible death. I remembered her burning body as it lay upon the floor of the shrine in the very place where I lay now.

I thought of Pandora. Where is my Pandora? And then finally I drifted into sleep.

When I returned to the palazzo, coming down from the roof as was always my custom, things were not as I would have them, for all the company was solemn at supper, and Vincenzo told me anxiously that a "strange man" had come to visit me, and that he stood in the anteroom and would not come in.

The boys had been finishing one of my murals in the anteroom, and they had hastily left this "strange man" to himself. Only Amadeo had remained behind, doing some small work with little enthusiasm, his eyes upon this "strange man" in a manner which gave Vincenzo concern.

As if that were not enough, Bianca had been to visit, indeed to give me a gift from Florence, a small painting by Botticelli; and she had had "uneasy" conversation with this "strange man" and had told Vincenzo to keep watch on him. Bianca was gone. The "strange man" remained.

I went into the anteroom immediately, but I had felt the presence of this creature before I saw who it was.

It was Mael.

Not for a single second did I not know him. He was unchanged just as I am unchanged, and he had not paid much attention to the fashion of these times, any more than he had paid attention to the fashion of times in the past.

He looked dreadful in fact in a ragged leather jerkin and leggings with holes in them and his boots were tied with rope.

His hair was dirty and tangled but his face wore an amazingly pleasant expression, and when he saw me he came at once to me and embraced me.

"You're really here," he said in a low voice, as though we had to whisper under my roof. He spoke the old Latin. "I heard of it but I didn't believe it. Oh, I'm so glad to see you. I'm glad you're still . . ."

"Yes, I know what you mean to say," I said. "I'm still the watcher of the years passing; I'm still the witness surviving in the Blood."

"Oh, you put it far better than I could," he answered. "But let me say it again, I'm so happy to see you, happy to hear your voice."

I saw that there was dust all over him. He was looking about the room, at its fancy painted ceiling with its ring of cherubs and its gold leaf. He stared at the unfinished mural. I wondered if he knew it was my work.

"Mael, always the astonished one," I said, moving him gently out of the light of the candles. I laughed softly. "You look like a tramp."

"Would you offer me clothes again?" he asked. "I cannot really, you know, master such things. I am in need, I suppose. And you live so splendidly here as you always did. Is nothing ever a mystery to you, Marius?"

"Everything is a mystery, Mael," I responded. "But fine clothes I always have. If the world comes to an end, I shall be well dressed for it, whether it is by the light of day or in the dark of night."

I took his arm and guided him through the various immense rooms that lay between me and my bedchamber. He was suitably awed by the paintings everywhere and let me lead him along.

"I want you to stay here, away from my mortal company," I said. "You'll only confuse them."

"Ah, but you've worked it all so well," he said. "It was easier for you in old Rome, wasn't it? But what a palace you have here. There are kings who would envy you, Marius."

"Yes, it seems so," I answered offhandedly.

I went to the adjacent closets, which were small rooms actually, and pulled out clothes for him, and leather shoes. He seemed quite incapable of dressing himself but I refused to do it for him, and after I had put out everything, on the velvet bed in the correct order, as if for a child or an idiot, he began to examine various articles as if he might manage alone.

"Who told you I was here, Mael?" I asked him.

He glanced at me, and his face was cold for a moment, the old hawk nose as disagreeable as ever, the deep-set eyes rather more brilliant than I'd remembered and the mouth far better shaped than I'd recalled. Maybe time had softened the set of his lips. I'm not certain that such things can happen. But he did seem an interesting-looking immortal male.

"You told me you had heard that I was here," I said, prompting him. "Who told you?"

"Oh, it was a fool of a blood drinker," he said with a shudder. "A maniacal Satan worshiper. His name was Santino. Will they never die out? It was in Rome. He urged me to join him, can you imagine?"

"Why didn't you destroy him?" I asked dejectedly. How grim was all this, how distant from the boys at their supper, from the teachers speaking of the day's lessons, from the light and music to which I longed to return. "In the old times when you encountered them, you always destroyed them. What stopped you now?"

He shrugged his shoulders. "What do I care what happens in Rome? I didn't stay one night in Rome."

I shook my head. "How did this creature discover I was in Venice? I've never heard a whisper of our kind here."

"I'm here," he answered sharply, "and you didn't hear me, did you? You're not infallible, Marius. You have about you many worldly distractions. Perhaps you don't listen as you should."

"Yes, you're right, but I wonder. How did he know?"

"Mortals come to your house. Mortals speak of you. Possibly those mortals go on to Rome. Don't all roads lead to Rome?" He was mocking me naturally. But he was being rather gentle, almost friendly. "He wants your secret, Marius, that Roman blood drinker. How he begged me to explain the mystery of Those Who Must Be Kept."

"And you didn't reveal it, did you, Mael?" I demanded. I began to hate him again, hotly, as I had in nights past.

"No, I didn't reveal it," he said calmly, "but I did laugh at him, and I didn't deny it. Perhaps I should have, but the older I get the harder it is to lie on any account."

"That I understand rather well," I said.

"Do you? With all these beautiful mortal children around you? You must lie with every breath you take, Marius. And as for your paintings, how dare you display your works amongst mortals who have but brief lifetimes with which to challenge you? It seems a terrible lie, that, if you ask me."

I sighed.

He tore open the front of his jerkin and then took it off.

"Why do I accept your hospitality?" he asked. "I don't know the answer. Perhaps I feel that having helped yourself to so many mortal delights, you owe some help to another blood drinker who is lost in time as always, wandering from country to country, marveling sometimes and at others merely getting dust in his eyes."

"Tell yourself anything you like," I said. "You are welcome to the clothes and to shelter. But tell me at once. What's happened to Avicus and Zenobia? Do they travel with you? Do you know where they are?"

"I have no idea where they are," he said, "and surely you sensed it before you asked. It has been so long since I saw either of them that I cannot reckon the years or the centuries. It was Avicus who put her up to it, and off they went together. They left me in Constantinople, and I can't say that it came to me as a dreadful surprise. There had been terrible coldness between us before the parting. Avicus loved her. She loved him more than me. That was all that was required."

"I'm sad to hear it."

"Why?" he asked. "You left the three of us. And you left her with us, that was the worst of it. We were two for so long, and then you forced Zenobia into our company."

"For the love of Hell, stop blaming me for everything," I said under my breath. "Will you never cease with your accusations? Am I the author of every evil that ever befell you, Mael? What must I do to be absolved so that there might be silence? It was you, Mael, you," I whispered, "who took me from my mortal life by force and brought me, shackled and helpless, into your accursed Druid grove!"

The anger spilled from me as I struggled to keep my voice down.

He seemed quite amazed by it.

"And so you do despise me, Marius," he said, smiling. "I had thought you far too clever for such a simple feeling. Yes, I took you prisoner, and you took the secrets, and I've been cursed one way or the other, ever since."

I had to step back from this. I did not want it. I stood calmly until the anger left me. Let the truth be damned.

For some reason this brought out the kindness in him. As he removed his rags, and kicked them away, he spoke of Avicus and Zenobia.

"The two of them were always slipping into the Emperor's palace where they would hunt the shadows," he said. "Zenobia seldom dressed as a boy as you taught her. She was too fond of sumptuous clothes. You should have seen the gowns she wore. And her hair, I think I loved it more than she did."

"I don't know if that's possible," I said softly. I saw the vision of her in his mind, and confused it with the vision of her in my own.

"Avicus continued to be the student," he said with slight contempt. "He mastered Greek. He read everything he could find. You were always his inspiration. He imitated you. He bought books without knowing what they were. On and on, he read."

"Maybe he did know," I suggested. "Who can say?"

"I can say," Mael answered. "I've known you both, and he was an idiot gathering poetry and history for nothing. He wasn't even looking for something. He embraced words and phrases on account of how they felt."

"And where and how did you spend your hours, Mael?" I asked, my voice far more cold than I had hoped.

"I hunted the dark hills beyond the city," he responded. "I hunted the soldiery. I hunted for the brutal Evil Doer, as you know. I was the vagabond, and they were dressed as though they were part of the Imperial Court."

"Did they ever make another?" I asked.

"No!" he said, scoffing. "Who would do such a thing?"

I didn't answer.

"And you, did you ever make another?" I asked.

"No," he responded. He frowned. "How would I find someone strong enough?" he asked. He seemed puzzled. "How would I know that a human had the endurance for the Blood?"

"And so you move through the world alone."

"I'll find another blood drinker to be a companion," he said. "Didn't I find that cursed Santino in Rome? Maybe I'll lure one from among the Satan worshipers. They can't all like a miserable life in the catacombs, wearing black robes and singing Latin hymns."

I nodded. I could see now that he was ready for the bath. I didn't want to keep him any longer.

When I spoke it was in a genial manner.

"The house is enormous as you see," I said. "There is a locked room on the first floor to the far right side. It has no windows. You may sleep there by day if you like."

He gave a low contemptuous laugh. "The clothes are quite enough, my friend, and perhaps just a few hours during which I might rest."

"I don't mind. Stay here, out of sight of the others. See the bath there. Use it. I'll come for you when all the boys are asleep."

When next I saw him it was all too soon.

He came out of the bedroom and into the large salon in which I stood relinquishing my hold on Riccardo and Amadeo with the strong admonition that they could go to Bianca's for the evening and nowhere else.

Amadeo saw him. Again, for several fatal moments, Amadeo saw him. And I knew that something deep inside Amadeo recognized Mael for the creature that he was. But like so many things in the mind of Amadeo, it wasn't conscious, and the boys left me with quick kisses, off to sing their songs to Bianca, and be flattered by everyone there.

I was impatient with Mael that he had come out of the bedchamber, but I didn't say it.

"So you would make a blood drinker of that one," he said, pointing to the door through which the boys had left us. He smiled.

I was in a silent fury. I glared at him, as always in such situations, quite unable to speak.

He stood there smiling at me in sinister fashion and then he said,

"Marius of the many names and the many houses and the many lifetimes. So you have chosen a lovely child."

I shook it off. How had he read from my mind my desire for Amadeo?

"You've grown careless," he said softly. "Listen to me, Marius. I don't speak to insult you. You walk with a heavy step among mortals. And that boy is very young."

"Don't speak another word to me," I answered, pulling hard on my anger to rein it in.

"Forgive me," he said. "I only spoke my mind."

"I know you did, but I don't want to hear any more."

I looked him over. He was rather handsome in his new attire, though a few little details were absurdly crooked and not tucked properly, but I was not the one to make them right. He struck me as not only barbaric, but comical. But I knew that anyone else would think him an impressive man.

I hated him, but not completely. And as I stood there with him, I almost gave way to tears. Quite suddenly, to stem this emotion, I spoke.

"What have you learnt in all this time?" I asked.

"That's an arrogant question!" he said in a low voice. "What have you learnt?"

I told him my theories, about how the West had risen again, once more drawing upon the old classics which Rome had taken from Greece. I spoke of how the art of the old Empire was re-created now throughout Italy and I spoke of the fine cities of the North of Europe, prosperous as those of the South. And then I explained how it seemed to me that the Eastern Empire had fallen to Islam and was no more. The Greek world had been irrevocably lost.

"We have the West again, don't you see?" I asked.

He looked at me as though I were perfectly mad.

"Well?" I responded.

There came a slight change in his face.

"Witness in the Blood," he said, repeating the words I'd spoken earlier, "watcher of the years."

He put his arms forward as though to embrace me. His eyes were clear and I could sense no malice at all.

"You've given me courage," he said.

"For what, may I ask?" I responded.

"To continue my wandering," he said. He let his arms slowly drop.

I nodded. What more was there for us to say?

"You have all you need?" I asked. "I have plenty of Venetian or Florentine coin. You know that wealth is nothing to me. I'm happy to share what I have."

"It's nothing to me either," he said. "I shall get what I need from my next victim, and his blood and wealth will carry me to one after that."

"So be it," I said, which meant that I wanted him to leave me. But even as he realized it, as he turned to go, I reached out and took him by the arm. "Forgive me that I was cold to you," I said. "We've been companions in time."

It was a strong embrace.

And I walked with him down to the front entrance where the torches shone too brightly on us for my taste, and saw him virtually disappear into the dark.

In a matter of seconds, I could hear no more of him. I gave silent thanks.

I reflected. How I hated Mael. How I feared him. Yet I had loved him once, loved him when we'd been mortals even, and I'd been his prisoner and he had been the Druid priest teaching me the hymns of the Faithful of the Forest, for what purpose, I didn't know.

And I had loved him on that long voyage to Constantinople, surely, and in that city when I'd given over Zenobia to him and Avicus, wishing them all well.

But I did not want him near me now! I wanted my house, my children, Amadeo, Bianca. I wanted my Venice. I wanted my mortal world.

How I would not risk my mortal home even for a few hours longer with him. How I wanted so to keep my secrets from him.

But here I was standing in the torchlight, distracted, and something was amiss.

Vincenzo wasn't very far away, and I turned and called to him.

"I'm going away for a few nights," I told him. "You know what to do. I'll be back soon enough."

"Yes, Master," he said.

And I was able to assure myself that he'd sensed nothing strange in Mael whatsoever. He was as always ready to do my will.

But then he pointed his finger.

"There, Master, Amadeo, he's waiting to talk to you."

I was astonished.

On the far side of the canal, Amadeo stood in a gondola, watching me, waiting, and surely he'd seen me with Mael. Why had I not heard him? Mael was right. I was careless. I was all too softened by human emotions. I was too greedy for love.

Amadeo told his oarsman to bring him alongside the house.

"And why didn't you go with Riccardo?" I demanded. "I expected to find you at Bianca's. You must do as I say."

Quite suddenly Vincenzo was gone, and Amadeo had stepped up onto the quais, and he had his arms around me, pressing my hard unyielding body with all his strength.

"Where are you going?" he demanded in a rushed whisper. "Why do you leave me again?"

"I must leave," I said, "but it's only for a few nights. You know that I must leave. I have solemn obligations elsewhere, and don't I always return?"

"Master, that one, the one who came, the one who just left you—."

"Don't ask me," I said sternly. How I had dreaded this. "I'll come back to you within a few nights."

"Take me with you," Amadeo begged.

The words struck me. I felt something within loosened.

"That I cannot do," I answered. And out of my mouth there came words I thought I'd never speak. "I go to Those Who Must Be Kept," I said as if I couldn't hold the secret within me. "To see if they are at peace. I do as I have always done."

What a look of wonder came over his face.

"Those Who Must Be Kept," he whispered. He said it like a prayer. I shivered.

I felt a great release. And it seemed that in the wake of Mael I had drawn Amadeo closer to me. I had taken another fatal step.

The torchlight tormented me.

"Come inside," I said. And into the shadowy entranceway we stepped together. Vincenzo, never very far off, took his leave.

I bent to kiss Amadeo, and the heat of his body inflamed me.

"Master, give me the Blood," he whispered in my ear. "Master, tell me what you are."

"What I am, child? Sometimes I think I know not. And sometimes I think I know only too well. Study in my absence. Waste nothing. And I'll be back to you before you know the hour. And then we'll speak of Blood Kisses and secrets and meantime tell no one that you belong to me."

"Have I ever told anyone, Master?" he responded. He kissed my cheek. He placed his warm hand on my cheek as if he would know how inhuman I was.

I closed my lips over his. I let a small stream of blood pour into him. I felt him shudder.

I drew back from him. He was limp in my arms.

I called for Vincenzo and I gave Amadeo over to him, and off I went into the night.

I left the splendid city of Venice with her glistering palaces, and I withdrew to the chilly mountain sanctuary, and I knew that the fate of Amadeo was sealed.

2 0

H OW LONG I WAS with Those Who Must Be Kept, I don't know. A week, perhaps more.

I came into the shrine, confessing my astonishment that I had confided the mere phrase "Those Who Must Be Kept" to a mortal boy. I confided again that I wanted him, I wanted him to share my loneliness. I wanted him to share all that I could teach and give.

Oh, the pain of it! All that I could teach and give!

What was this to the Immortal Parents? Nothing. And as I trimmed the wicks of the lamps, as I filled them with oil, as I let the light grow bright around the eternally silent Egyptian figures, I knew the same penance I had always known.

Twice with a gust of the Fire Gift, I lighted the long bank of one hundred tall candles. Twice I let it burn down.

But as I prayed, as I dreamt, one clear conclusion did come to me. I wanted this mortal companion precisely because I had put myself into the mortal world.

Had I never stepped into Botticelli's workshop this mad loneliness would not have come over me. It was mixed up with my love of all the arts, but most particularly painting, and my desire to be close to those mortals who nourished themselves gracefully upon the creations of this period as I fed upon blood.

I also confessed that my education of Amadeo was almost complete.

On waking I listened with the powerful Mind Gift to the movements and thoughts of Amadeo who was no more than a few hundred miles away. He was obedient to my instructions. In the night hours he kept to his books, and did not go to Bianca. Indeed he kept to my bedchamber, for he no longer knew simple camaraderie with the other boys.

What could I give this child that would prompt him to leave me?

What could I give him to more purely train him to be the companion I wanted with all my soul?

Both questions tormented me.

At last a plan came to me—one last trial must be passed by him, and should he fail it, I would commit him with irresistible wealth and position to the mortal world. How that might be done, I did not know, but it did not strike me as a difficult thing.

I meant to reveal to him the manner in which I fed.

Of course this was a lie, this question of a trial; for once he had beheld me in the act of feeding, in the act of murder, how then could he pass unscathed into a productive mortality, no matter how great his education, his refinements and his wealth?

No sooner had I put that question to myself than I remembered my exquisite Bianca, who remained quite steadily at the helm of her ship in spite of the poisonous cups she had passed.

All this, evil and cunning, made up the substance of my prayers. Was I asking permission of Akasha and Enkil to make this child a blood drinker? Was I asking permission to admit Amadeo to the secrets of this ancient and unchangeable shrine?

If I did ask, there came no answer.

Akasha gave me only her effortless serenity, and Enkil his majesty. The only sound came from my movements as I rose from my knees, as I laid my kisses at the feet of Akasha, as I withdrew and closed behind me the immense door, and bolted it shut.

There was wind and snow in the mountains on that evening. It was bitter and white and pure.

I was glad to be home in Venice within minutes, though my beloved city was also cold.

No sooner did I reach my bedchamber than Amadeo came into my arms.

I covered his head with kisses and then his warm mouth, taking the breath from him, and then with the smallest bite, giving him the Blood.

"Would you be what I am, Amadeo?" I asked. "Would you be changeless forever? Would you live a secret for eternity?"

"Yes, Master," he said with a feverish abandon. He laid both his warm hands on the sides of my face. "Give it to me, Master. Do you think I've not brooded upon it? I know that you fathom our minds. Master, I want it. Master, how is it done? Master, I'm yours."

"Find the heaviest cloak to protect you against the winter," I said, "And then come up to me on the roof."

It seemed scarcely a moment before he joined me. I looked out towards the sea. The wind was strong. I wondered if it hurt him and I did fathom his mind, and I measured his passion.

And looking into his brown eyes I knew that he had left the mortal world behind him more effortlessly perhaps than any other mortal I might have plucked from my garden, for those memories still festered within him, though he was disposed completely to believe in me.

I wrapped him in my arms and, covering his face, I carried him with me down into a wretched district of Venice, in which thieves and beggars slept where they could. The canals reeked of refuse and dead fish.

There I found a mortal victim within minutes, and to Amadeo's amazement caught the miserable fellow with preternatural speed as he sought to stab me, and brought him up to my lips.

I let Amadeo see the cunning teeth with which I pierced the throat of the wretch, and then my eyes closed and I became Marius, the blood drinker, Marius, the slayer of the Evil Doer, and the blood flowed into me, and it did not matter to me that Amadeo was witness, that Amadeo was there.

When it was finished, I dropped the body silently into the filthy water of the canal.

I turned, feeling the blood in my face and in my chest and then slowly moving into my hands. My vision was dim, and I knew that I was smiling—not a vicious smile, you understand, but something secretive and beyond anything the child had ever beheld.

When at last I looked at him, I saw only amazement.

"Have you no tears for the man, Amadeo?" I asked. "Have you no questions as to the disposition of his soul? Without Sacred Rites, he died. He died only for me."

"No, Master," he answered, and then a smile played on his lips as though it were a flame which had sprung from mine. "It's marvelous what I saw, Master. What do I care for his body or his soul?"

I was too angry to respond. There had been no lesson in it! He was too young, the night too dark, the man too wretched, and all that I had foreseen had come to nought.

Once again, I wrapped him in my cloak, covering his face so that he could see nothing as I traveled through the air silently, moving over the rooftops and then breaking deftly and silently through an upper window that had been shuttered against the night air.

Through the rear chambers of the house, I moved from this breach till we stood together in the shadowy and sumptuous bedroom of Bianca, and through the salons before us, I saw her turn from her guests. I saw her coming to us.

"Why are we here, Master?" asked Amadeo. He looked towards the front rooms fearfully.

"You would see it again to understand it," I said angrily. "You would see it among those whom we claim to love."

"But how, Master?" Amadeo demanded. "What are you saying? What do you mean to do?"

"I hunt the Evil Doer, child," I said to him. "And you shall see that there is evil here as rich as there was in that poorling whom I committed to the dark water, unconfessed and unmourned."

Bianca stood before us, asking us as gently as she could, How had we come to be in her private rooms? Her pale eyes looked at me searchingly.

Quickly I accused her.

"Tell him, my beloved beauty," I said, my voice muted so that the company should take no notice, "tell him what awful deeds lie behind your gentle composure. Tell him what poison guests have drunk beneath your roof."

How calm she was as she answered me.

"You anger me, Marius. You come improperly. You accuse me without authority. Leave me and come again in the gentle manner in which you have come so many times before."

Amadeo was trembling. "Please, Master, let us leave here. We have nothing but love for Bianca."

"Oh, but I would have more of her, rather than love of her," I said to him. "I would have her blood."

"No, Master," Amadeo whispered. "Master, I beg you."

"Yes, for it's evil blood," I said, "and it's all the more savory to me. I would drink the stuff of murderers. Tell him, Bianca, of wine laced with potions, and lives forfeit for those who have made you the instrument of their most wicked plans."

"Leave me now," she said again without the slightest fear of me. Her eyes blazed. "Marius de Romanus, you cannot judge me. Not you with your magician's powers, not you with your boys. I will say nothing except that you must leave my house."

I moved to take her in my arms. I did not know when I would stop but only that I would reveal the horror of it to him, that he must see it, he must see the suffering, he must see the pain.

"Master," he whispered, struggling to come between us, "I will give up my petitions to you forever, if only you do not harm her. Do you understand? Master, I will beg nothing further. Let her go."

I held her, looking down at her, smelling the sweetest perfume of her youth, her hair, her blood.

"Take her and I die with her, Master," said Amadeo.

It was enough. It was more than enough.

I moved away from her. I felt a strange confusion. The music in the rooms became a noise. I think I sat upon her bed. The blood thirst in me was terrible. I might have slain them all, I thought, looking toward the crowd beyond, and then I believe I said:

"We are murderers together, you and I, Bianca."

I saw that Amadeo was weeping. He stood with his back to the company. His face was glistening with tears.

And she, she the fragrant beauty with her braided blond hair came to sit beside me, so boldly, and to take my hand, my very hand.

"We are murderers together, my lord," she said, "yes, I can speak for myself as you demanded. But understand that I am given the commissions by those who would as easily send me to Hell in the same way. It is they who mix the potions for the fatal wine. It is they who mark those who would receive it. And I know not the reasons. I know only that if I do not obey, I shall die."

"Then tell me who they are, my exquisite darling," I said. "I am hungry for them. So hungry you can't dream."

"They are my kinsmen, sir," she said. "Such has been my heritage. Such has been my family. Such have been my guardians here."

She had begun to weep but she clung to me, as though my strength were the only truth for her suddenly and indeed I realized it was.

My threats of moments ago had only bound her to me all the more firmly, and Amadeo drew close, urging me to kill all those who kept her under their power, all those who made her wretched, whatever the ties of blood.

I held her as she bowed her head. From her mind, so often confusing to me, I read the names as though they were written in plain script.

I knew the men, all Florentines who had come often to call on her. Tonight they held a feast in a neighboring house. They were moneylenders, some might have called them bankers, but those they murdered were those from whom they had borrowed and did not wish to repay.

"You shall be rid of them, my beauty," I said to her. I touched her lightly with my lips.

She turned to me, and gave me countless and violent small kisses.

"And what shall I owe for this?" she asked, even as she kissed me, even as her hands reached to stroke my hair.

"Only that you say nothing of what you saw in me tonight."

She gazed at me with her tranquil oval eyes, and her mind closed up, as though she would never reveal to me her thoughts again.

"You have my pledge, my lord," she whispered. "And so my soul grows ever more heavy."

"No, I shall take the weight from it," I said, as we made to go.

How sad seemed her sudden tears. I kissed her, tasting them, wishing they were blood and forever forswearing the blood within her.

"Don't weep for those who have used you," I whispered. "Go back to the gaiety and the music. Leave the dark commissions to me."

We found the Florentines drunk at their banquet, paying us no heed as we entered without introduction or explanation and took our places at the overladen table. A noisy band of musicians played. The floor was slippery with spilt wine.

Amadeo was eager for it, filled with excitement, attentive to my slow and methodical seduction of each one of them, as I drank the blood lustily, and let the bodies tip forward upon the groaning board. The musicians fled.

Within an hour I had slain them all, these kinsmen of Bianca, and only for the very last of them, he who had talked the longest with me, quite unawares of what was happening all about him—only for him did Amadeo beg and weep. Was I to show this one mercy when his heart was as guilty as all the rest?

We sat alone in the ruined supper room, the dead bodies around us, the food cold upon its silver and gold plates and platters, the wine running from overturned goblets, and for the first time, as Amadeo cried and cried, I saw dread in his eyes.

I looked at my hands. I had drunk so much blood that they looked human and I knew that were I to look into a mirror, I would see a florid human face.

The heat in me was delicious and unendurable, and I wanted nothing more than to take Amadeo, bring him over to me now, and yet there he sat before me, the tears streaming down his face.

"They are all gone," I said, "those who tormented Bianca. You come with me. Let's leave this gory scene. I would walk with you, before the sun rises, near the sea."

He followed me as a child might, the tears staining his face as they ran still from his eyes.

"Wipe your tears," I said firmly. "We're going out into the piazza. It's almost dawn."

He slipped his hand into mine as we went down the stone stairs.

I put my arm around him, sheltering him from the sharp wind.

"Master," he pleaded, "they were evil men, weren't they? You were certain of it. You knew it."

"All of them," I answered. "But sometimes men and women are both good and evil," I continued, "and who am I to choose for my vicious appetite, yet I do. Is Bianca not both good and evil?"

"Master," he asked, "if I drink the blood of those who are evil, will I become like you?"

We stood before the closed doors of San Marco. The wind came mercilessly off the sea. I drew my cloak about him all the more tightly, and he rested his head against my chest.

"No, child," I said, "there's infinitely more magic in it than that."

"You must give me your blood, isn't that so, Master?" he asked as he looked up at me, the tears clear and glistening in the cold air, his hair mussed.

I didn't answer.

"Master," he said, as I held him close to me, "long years ago, or so they seem to me, in some far-away place, where I lived before I came to you, I was what they called a Fool for God. I don't remember it clearly and never will as both of us well know.

"But a Fool for God was a man who gave himself over to God completely and did not care what happened, whether it was mockery, or starvation, or endless laughter, or dreadful cold. That much I remember, that I was a Fool for God in those times."

"But you painted pictures, Amadeo, you painted beautiful ikons—."

"But listen to me, Master," he said firmly, forcing me to silence, "whatever I did, I was a Fool for God, and now I would be a Fool for you." He paused, snuggling close to me as the wind grew stronger. The mists moved in over the stones. There came noises from the ships.

I started to speak but he reached to stop me. How obdurate and strong he seemed, how seductive, how completely mine.

"Master," he went on. "Do it when you will. You have my secrecy. You have my patience. Do it when and how you will."

I thought on what he'd said.

"Go home, Amadeo," I answered him. "You know the sun is coming, and I must leave you with the arrival of the sun."

He nodded, puzzling over it, as though for the very first time it mattered to him, though how he couldn't have thought of it before I didn't know.

"Go home, and study with the others, talk with them, and shepherd the little ones at their play. If you can do that—go from the bloody banquet room to the laughter of children—then when I come tonight, I shall do it. I shall bring you over to myself."

I watched him walk away from me in the mist. He went towards the canal where he would find the gondola to take him back to our door.

"A Fool for God," I whispered aloud so that my mind might hear it, "yes, a Fool for God, and in some miserable monastery you painted the sacred pictures, convinced your life would mean nothing unless it was a life of sacrifice and pain. And now, in my magic you see some similar burning purity. And you turn away from all the riches of life in Venice for that burning purity; you turn away from all that a human may have."

But was it so? Did he know enough to make such a decision? Could he forsake the sun forever?

I had no answer. It was not his decision that mattered now. For I had made mine.

As for my radiant Bianca, her thoughts were forever after closed to me, as though she knew the knack of it like a wily witch. As for her devotion, her love, her friendship, that was something else.

2 1

NOW, WHERE I SLEPT in the daylight hours in Venice, was in a beautiful granite sarcophagus in a hidden chamber just above the level of the water in an uninhabited palazzo which belonged to me.

The room itself was lined with gold, a quite marvelous little cell, replete with torches, and a stairway led up from this chamber to a door which only I could force back.

On coming out of the palazzo one had to walk down a flight of steps to the canal—that is, if one were walking at all, which I, of course, was not.

Some long months ago I had arranged for the creation of another sarcophagus of the same beauty and weight, so that two blood drinkers could have lain down together in this chamber, and it was from this gilded resting place that I arose the following night.

I knew at once that my true house was in an uproar. I could hear the distant wailing of the little boys, and the frantic prayers of Bianca. Some carnage had taken place beneath my roof.

Of course I thought it had to do with the Florentines I had slaughtered, and as I rushed to my palazzo, I cursed myself that I had not taken greater care with this spectacular deed.

But nothing could have been further from the truth.

No one had to tell me, as I rushed down the stairs from the roof, that a drunken violent English lord had come rampaging into my house in search of Amadeo for whom he harbored a forbidden passion, which had been somewhat fed by Amadeo's dalliance on random nights when I had been away.

And with the same knowledge, I quickly imbibed the horror that

Lord Harlech, this Englishman, had cruelly, wantonly slain children no older than seven before he met in combat Amadeo himself.

Of course Amadeo knew how to use both sword and dagger and had swiftly fought this evil man with both in hand. Indeed, he had slain Lord Harlech but not before Lord Harlech had slashed his face and arms with a poisoned blade.

I came into the bedchamber to find Amadeo in a fatal fever, his senses having left him, the priests in attendance, and Bianca bathing him with a cool cloth.

Everywhere there were candles. Amadeo lay in his clothes of last night with the sleeve cut away where Lord Harlech had wounded his arm.

Riccardo was weeping. The teachers were weeping. The priests had given Amadeo the Last Rites. There was nothing more to be done.

At once Bianca turned to greet me. Her lovely dress was stained with blood. She came to me, her face pale, her hands gripping my sleeves.

"For hours, he's struggled," she told me. "He's spoken of visions. He has crossed a great sea and seen a wondrous celestial city. He has seen that all things are made of love. All things! Do you understand?"

"I do," I said.

"He has seen a city of glass as he described it," she said, "made of love as are all growing things. He has seen priests from his homeland, and these priests have told him that it is not his time to reach the city. They have sent him back."

She appealed to me.

"They are right, are they not," she asked, "these priests he's seen? It is not his time to die."

I didn't answer her.

She went to his side again and I stood behind her. I watched as she bathed his forehead again.

"Amadeo," she said, her voice calm and strong, "breathe for me, breathe for your Master. Amadeo, breathe for me."

I could see that he tried to obey her command.

His eyes were closed and then opened, but they saw nothing. His skin was the color of old ivory. His hair was swept back from his face. How cruel was the cut in his face made by Lord Harlech's blade.

"Leave me with him now," I said gently to the entire company.

No one protested. I heard the doors close.

I bent down and, cutting my tongue as I had so often done, I let the blood drip on the evil cut on his face. I marveled silently as the flesh healed.

Once again his eyes opened. He saw me and then he spoke.

"It's Marius," he said softly. He had never once in all our time together called me by name. "Marius has come," he said. "Why didn't the priests tell me? They told me only that it wasn't my time to die."

I lifted his right hand. There too the blade of Lord Harlech had made a cut and now I kissed it with the healing blood and watched the miracle once again.

Amadeo shuddered. It was painful for him and his lips drew back for a moment and then he settled as if into deeper sleep. The poison was eating inside him. I could see the cruel evidence of it.

He was dying, no matter what his visions had told him, and no slight tender kiss of blood could save him now.

"Did you believe what they said?" I asked him. "That it was not your time to die?"

Reluctantly, painfully, his eyes opened.

"Master, they returned me to you," he answered. "Oh, if only I could remember all they told me, but they warned me that I would forget. Why was I ever brought here, Master?" He struggled, but he would not be quieted. He went on talking.

"Why was I taken out of some distant land and brought to you? I remember riding through the grasslands. I remember my father. And in my arms, as I rode, I held an ikon that I had painted, and my father was a great horseman and a great fighter, and there came down on us the evil ones, the Tatars, and they took me, and Master—the ikon, it fell into the tall grass. Master I know now. I think they killed my father when they took me away."

"Did you see him, child?" I asked, "when you dreamt these things?"

"No, Master. But then again, I don't remember." He began to cough suddenly and then the coughing stopped and he breathed deeply as if it were the only thing he had the strength to do.

"I know I painted the ikon, and we were sent out in the grasslands to place the ikon in a tree. It was a sacred thing to do. The grasslands were dangerous, Master, but my father always hunted there. Nothing frightened my father, and I could ride as well as he. Master, I know now the story of all my life, I know it yet I can't quite tell you—."

His voice dried up suddenly, and his whole body shuddered once more.

"This is death, Master," he whispered, "and yet they said it was not my time."

I knew his life was being measured now in moments. Had I ever loved anyone more than I loved him? Had I ever revealed more of my soul to anyone than I had revealed to him? If my tears spilled now, he would see them. If I trembled now, he would know.

Long ago, I'd been taken prisoner, just as he had! Was that not why I had chosen him?—that thieves had taken him from his life as I'd been taken from mine?

And so I'd thought that I would give him this great gift which was eternity! Was he not worthy in all things? Yes, he was young, but how would it harm him to be forever beautiful with the countenance of a young man?

He was not Botticelli. He was not a man of immense talent and fame.

He was a boy dying here whom few would remember except for me.

"How could they have said it?" he whispered, "that it was not my time?"

"They sent you back to me!" I gasped. I couldn't bear this. "Amadeo, did you believe these priests whom you saw? Did you believe in the glass city, tell me."

He smiled. And it was never innocent, no matter how beautiful, his smile.

"Don't weep for me, Master," he answered. He struggled to rise a little from the pillow, his eyes very wide. "When the ikon fell, my fate was made, Master."

"No, Amadeo, I don't believe it," I said.

But there was no more time.

"Go to them, child, call to them!" I said. "Tell them to take you now."

"No, Master. They may be insubstantial things," he said. "They may be dreams of the feverish mind. They may be phantoms wrapped in the garments of memory. *But I know what you are, Master.* I want the Blood. I've tasted it, Master. I want to stay with you. And if you refuse me, then let me die with Bianca! Send back my mortal nurse to me, Master, for she comforts me far better than you in your coldness. I would die with her alone."

He fell back exhausted on the pillow.

Desperately, I cut my tongue and filled my mouth with blood. I gave it to him. But the poison was moving too fast.

He smiled as the blood warmed him and a film of tears covered his eyes.

"Beautiful Marius," he said, as if he were far older than I would ever be. "Beautiful Marius who gave me Venice. Beautiful Marius, give me the Blood."

We had no more time. I was weeping miserably.

"Would you truly have the Blood, Amadeo?" I asked. "Say it to me, that you forsake the light of the sun forever, and forever you will thrive on the blood of the Evil Doer as I thrive."

"I vow it, I will it," he answered.

"You'll live forever, unchanging?" I asked, "feeding upon mortals who can be your brothers and sisters no more?"

"Yes, forever unchanging," he answered, "among them, though they are my brothers and sisters no more."

Once again, I gave him the Blood Kiss. And then I lifted him and carried him to the bath.

I stripped off his thick and soiled velvet clothes. And into the warm water I placed him, and there with the blood from my mouth I sealed all the cuts in the flesh made by Lord Harlech. I shaved off for all time any beard that he might have.

Now he was ready for the magic as one who had been prepared for sacrifice. And his heart beat slowly and his eyes were too heavy to open anymore.

And in a simple long silk shirt I clothed him and carried him out of the room.

The others were waiting anxiously. What lies I told them I do not know. How mad I was in these moments. To Bianca I gave some solemn charge that she must comfort and thank the others, and that Amadeo's life was safe in my hands.

"Leave us now, my beauty," I said to her. Even as I held him, I kissed her. "Trust in me, and I shall see that you never come to harm."

I could see that she believed in me. All fear was gone from her.

Within moments Amadeo and I were alone.

Then into my grandest painted salon I took him. It was the room into which I'd copied Gozzoli's magnificent painting *The Procession of the Magi*, stolen from the original in Florence as a test of my memory and skill.

Into this intense color and variation, I plunged him, setting him down on his feet on the cold marble, and then giving him through the Blood Kiss, the greatest draught of blood which I had given so far.

With the Fire Gift I lighted the candelabra up one side of the chamber and down the other. The painting was bathed in light.

"You can stand now, my blessed pupil," I told him. "My blood runs through you after the poison. We have begun."

He trembled, fearing to let go of me, his head hanging heavily, his luxuriant hair soft against my hands.

"Amadeo," I said, kissing him once again as the blood flowed over my lips and into his mouth, "what was your name in that lost land?" Again I filled my mouth with blood and I gave it to him. "Reach back for the past, child, and make it part of the future."

His eyes opened wide.

I stepped away from him. I left him standing. I let loose my red velvet cloak and pushed it away from me.

"Come to me," I said. I held out my arms.

He took the first steps, unsure of himself, so full of my blood that surely the light itself must have amazed him, but his eyes were moving over the multitude of figures painted on the wall. Then he looked directly at me.

How knowing, how clever was his expression! How full of triumph he seemed suddenly in his silence and patience. How utterly damned.

"Come, Amadeo, come and take it from me," I said, my eyes full of tears. "You are the victor. Take what I have to give."

He was in my arms instantly, and I held him warmly, whispering close to his ear.

"Don't be afraid, child, not even for a moment. You'll die now to live forever, as I take your blood and give it back to you. I won't let you slip away."

I sank my teeth into his throat and tasted the poison in his blood as soon as it flowed into me, my body destroying the poison, my body consuming his blood effortlessly, as it might have consumed a dozen such young ones, and into my mind there came the visions of his childhood—of the Russian monastery where he had painted his flawless ikons, of the cold chambers in which he'd lived.

I saw monks half walled up alive as they fasted, eating only what would sustain them. I smelled the earth. I smelled decay. Oh, how ghastly was this passage to salvation. And he had been part of it, half in love with the sacrificial cells and their starving inhabitants, save for his gift: that he could paint.

Then for one instant I saw nothing but his paintings, one image tumbling upon another, rapt faces of Christ, the Virgin—I saw the halos studded with costly jewels. Ah, such riches in the dark, cheerless monastery. And then came the rich bawdy laughter of his father, wanting him to leave the monastery, to ride out with him into the grasslands where the Tatars rode.

Prince Michael, their ruler, wanted to send Amadeo's father into the grasslands. It was a foolish mission. The monks railed against it, that Amadeo's father would take him into such danger. The monks wrapped the ikon and gave it to Amadeo. Out of the darkness and bitter earth of the monastery, Amadeo came into the light.

I stopped; I drew back from the blood and the visions. I *knew* him. I knew the relentless and hopeless darkness inside of him. I knew the life that had been forecast in hunger and bitter discipline.

I cut the flesh of my throat and I held his head near me. "Drink," I said. I pushed his head forward. "Put your mouth to the wound. Drink."

At last, he obeyed me, and suddenly with all his force he drew on the blood. Had he not tasted it enough to crave it? And now it came without measure, and he was passionate for it, and I closed my eyes, and felt an exquisite sweetness that I had not known since the long ago night when I had given my blood to my blessed Zenobia to make her all the more strong.

"Be my child, Amadeo," I whispered in this sweetness. "Be my child forever," I said. "Have I ever loved anyone more than you?"

I drew him back away from the wound, and as he cried out I sank my teeth into his throat again. This time it was my blood mingled with his that flowed into me. The poison was no more.

Again, I saw the ikons. I saw the dim corridors of the monastery, and then in the falling snow, I saw the two on their horses, Amadeo and his father. Amadeo held the ikon, and the priest ran beside him, telling him that he must place the ikon in a tree, that the Tatars would find it and count it as a miracle, and Amadeo, how innocent he looked to be such a bold rider, to be chosen to ride with his father for Prince Michael's mission, as the snow came down heavily, as his hair was whipped by the wind.

And so it was your undoing. Turn your back on it now. You have seen it for what it was. Look to the fabulous painting on the wall, Amadeo. Look to the riches which I have given you. Look to the glory and virtue which lie in beauty as varied and magnificent as what you see here.

I let loose of him. He gazed at the painting. I pressed his lips to my throat again.

"Drink," I said. But he needed no counsel. He held fast to me. He knew the blood, as I knew him.

How many times did we do it, the passing of blood from one to the other? I know not. I know only that never having done it completely since that long ago night in the Druid grove, I trusted to nothing, and made of him the strongest fledgling that I could.

And as he drank from me, I gave him my lessons, my secrets. I told him of the gifts that might one night come to him. I told him of my long ago love for Pandora. I told him of Zenobia, of Avicus, of Mael. I told him all but the final secret. That I kept from him.

Oh, thank the gods that I kept it. I kept it close in my heart!

Well before morning it was finished. His skin was wondrously pale, and his dark eyes fiercely bright. I ran my fingers through his auburn hair. Once again, he smiled at me so knowingly, with such a quiet air of triumph.

"It's complete now, Master," he said, as if he were speaking to a child.

And together we walked back to the bedchamber where he put on his handsome velvets, and we went out to hunt.

I taught him how to find his victims, to use the Mind Gift to make certain that they were Evil Doers, and I also remained with him through the few hours of his mortal Death.

His powers were very simply enormous. It would not be long before he could use the Cloud Gift; and I could not find a test to outdo his strength. He could not only read the minds of mortals, he could make spells as well.

His mind, quite naturally, was closed to me, though this was still something I did not completely accept. Of course it had happened with Pandora, yet I hoped that it would not happen with Amadeo and only reluctantly explained it to him.

Now I must read his facial expressions, his gestures, the depth of his secretive and faintly cruel brown eyes.

Never had he been more beautiful, of course.

And having done all this, I took him with me to my very grave, as one says, to the gilded room of the two stone sarcophagi which awaited us, and I showed him how he must sleep by day.

It didn't frighten him. Indeed, nothing frightened him.

"What of your dreams now, Amadeo?" I asked him as I held him in my arms. "What of your priests and the distant glass city?"

"Master, I've reached paradise," he answered. "What has Venice in all her beauty been to me but a prelude for the Blood?"

As I had done a thousand times, I gave him the Blood Kiss and he received it and then drew back smiling.

"How different it is now," he said.

"Sweet or bitter?" I asked.

"Oh, sweet, very sweet, for you've fulfilled my heart's desires. You don't pull me heartlessly after you by a bloody thread."

I crushed him in my warm embrace.

"Amadeo, my love," I whispered, and it seemed the long centuries I had endured had been but preparation for this. Old images came to me, bits and pieces of dreams. Nothing was substantial but Amadeo. And Amadeo was here.

And so we went to our separate sleep, and as I closed my eyes I feared only one thing in the whole world—that this bliss should not last.

22

THE NEXT FEW MONTHS passed in freedom and pleasure such as I could have never imagined.

Amadeo was truly my companion and also my pupil, and I forced him with gentle discipline to learn all that I thought he should know. This included his lessons in law and government, in history and philosophy, and also his lessons with me in being a blood drinker, to which he gave himself with a cheerful willingness that surpassed my dreams.

I had thought that, being young, he might want to feed on the innocent, but when I instructed him as to how guilt would soon destroy his soul if he did this, I found that he listened; and he took my instructions in how to feed upon evil without allowing it to darken his own soul.

He was also my eager pupil in the lessons on how to be in mortal company, and he soon felt strong enough to have some conversation with the mortal boys. Indeed, he was soon expert in deceiving them, just as I was, and though they sensed that something had changed with Amadeo they did not know what, and they could not know, and they dared not risk the peace of our wondrous house with even their slightest doubts.

Even Riccardo, the eldest of my apprentices, suspected nothing really, except that his Master was somehow a powerful magician and the magic had saved Amadeo's life.

But now we had to deal with our beloved Bianca, whom we had not seen since the night of the terrible illness, and I knew that this would be Amadeo's most arduous trial.

What was she to make of Amadeo's swift recovery from his terrible battle with Lord Harlech, and what did she think when she laid eyes upon Amadeo with his luminous skin and shimmering hair? What was he to think when he looked into her eyes?

It was no secret to me that he adored her, indeed, that he had loved her as I had loved her. And so we must go to her. Indeed, we had put it off for too long.

Abruptly one evening, we went to visit her, having fed well on this night so that we might feel and appear quite warm.

As soon as we came into her room, I saw immediately the strain in Amadeo, that he could not tell her of what had happened to him, and only in that moment did I realize how difficult this secrecy was for him, and how in spite of all his strength, he was still quite young and even weak.

Indeed, Amadeo's frame of mind was far greater cause for alarm than that of Bianca, who seemed only happy to see Amadeo restored.

They were like a brother and sister together, and I thought of course of the vow I had extracted from him when I made him, and I wished I could take him aside and remind him of it now. But we were in her drawing room and there were many other visitors, with all the usual music and talk going on.

"Come into my bedroom," she said to both of us. Her lovely oval face was beaming. "I am so very glad to see you. Why didn't you come before now? Of course everyone in Venice knew that Amadeo was recovered, and that Lord Harlech had gone back to England, but you should have written to me if you couldn't come."

I showered her with my apologies. It was my thoughtlessness. And indeed I should have written a letter. What had blinded me on such a score was my love for Amadeo. I had cared for nothing else.

"Oh, I forgive you, Marius," she declared. "I would forgive you anything, and look at Amadeo. It's as if he were never sick at all."

Gratefully I accepted her embrace, but I could see how Amadeo suffered when she kissed him, when she clasped his hand. He could not endure the gulf which separated them, but he must endure it, and so I did not move to leave.

"How goes it with you, my beautiful nurse," I said to her, "you who kept Amadeo by a thread until I could come to him. You and your kinsmen? Are you a happy lot?"

She gave a soft gentle laugh. "Oh, yes, my kinsmen, some of them have met with the most unfortunate end. Indeed, it is my understanding that the Grand Council of Venice believes they were murdered by those from whom they exacted heavy payments. My kinsmen should have never come to Venice with their evil designs. But I am blameless as everyone knows. Members of the Grand Council of Venice have told me as much. And you would not think it but I am now richer on account of all this."

Of course I saw it in a moment. Those who had owed money to her miserable kinsmen had, after their murders, given her costly gifts. She was richer than she had ever been.

"I am a happier woman," she said softly, looking at me. "Indeed, I am someone altogether different, for I know a freedom now that was inconceivable before."

Hungrily her eyes moved over me and over Amadeo. I felt a desire emanating from her. I felt it as she looked at both of us, that she wanted a new familiarity, and then she came to me, and putting her arms around me, she kissed me.

Quickly, I held her back and away from me, but this only impelled her to embrace Amadeo, and she kissed him on his cheeks and on his mouth.

She gestured towards the bed.

"All of Venice wonders about my magician and his apprentice," she said warmly. "And they come to me, only to me."

With my eyes, I let her know my love for her, that I would trespass now if she didn't strictly forbid it, and moving past her, I seated myself on her bed.

Never had I taken such a liberty with her, but I knew her thoughts. We dazzled her. She idolized us.

And how lovely she was in her luminous silk and jewels.

She came and took her place beside me, nestled close, and unafraid of whatever she saw when she looked into my eyes.

Amadeo was astonished and soon sat beside her on her right. Though he'd fed well, I could sense his blood hunger, and that he fought bravely to keep it down.

"Let me kiss you, my exquisite one," I said. And I did so, counting upon the dim light and my sweet words to bedazzle her, and then of course she saw what she wanted to see—not some dreadful thing quite beyond her comprehension, but a mysterious man who had rendered her an invaluable service and left her wealthy and free.

"You will be safe always, Bianca," I said to her. "As long as I am here." Twice and once more I kissed her. "Help me open my house again, Bianca, with even more splendid food and entertainments. Help me prepare a greater feast perhaps than Venice has ever seen. We'll have wondrous theatricals and dancing. Help me fill my many rooms."

"Yes, Marius, I shall do it," she answered drowsily, her head leaning against me. "I shall be so happy."

"I shall give you all the money you require for it. And Vincenzo will carry out your instructions. Only tell me when you would have this take place."

I looked into her eyes as I spoke and then I kissed her, and though I did not dare to give her the smallest taste of my blood, I breathed my cold breath into her, and I pierced her mind with my desire.

Meantime, with my right hand I reached beneath her skirts and found her sweet naked secrets and easily moved them with my fingers, which inflamed her with immediate and undisguised desire.

Amadeo was confused.

"Kiss her," I whispered. "Kiss her again."

He obeyed me, and soon had her ravished with his kisses.

And as my fingers tightened and caressed her, as his kisses grew more fervent, she grew bloodred with her cresting passion and fell softly against Amadeo's arm.

I withdrew, kissing her forehead as though she were chaste again.

"Rest now," I said, "and remember you are safe from those evil kinsmen, and that I am in your debt forever because you kept Amadeo alive until I could come."

"Did I, Marius?" she asked me. "Wasn't it his strange dreams?" She turned to Amadeo. "Again and again you spoke of wondrous places, of those who told you that you must return to us."

"Those were but memories caught in a web with fear," said Amadeo softly. "For long before I was born again in Venice, I knew a harsh and pitiless life. It was you who brought me back from some thick margin of consciousness which lies just this side of death."

She gazed at him, wondering.

How he was suffering that he could not tell her what he was.

But having accepted these words from him, she allowed us to, in the manner of common attendants, help her with her disheveled dress and hair.

"We'll leave you now," I said, "and of the feast we'll make our plans at once. Allow me to send Vincenzo to you."

"Yes, and on that night I promise you," she said, "your house will be more splendid than even the Doge's palace, you will see."

"My princess," I said as I kissed her.

Back to her guests she went, and off we hurried down the stairs.

In the gondola, Amadeo began his entreaties.

"Marius, I can't bear it, this separation from her, that we can't tell her."

"Amadeo, say nothing more to me of this!" I cautioned.

When we reached the bedchamber and locked the door, he gave way to terrible tears.

"Master, I could tell her nothing of what had happened to me! And to Bianca I would always tell all. Oh, not the secrets of you and me or the Blood Kisses, no, but of other things. How often I sat with her, and talked with her. Master, I went to her so often by day and you didn't know it. She was my friend. Master, this is unendurable. Master, she was my sister." He sobbed like a small boy.

"I cautioned you on this, did I not?" I said furiously. "And now you weep like a child?"

In a rage, I slapped him.

And in shock he fell back away from me, but his tears flowed all the more.

"Master, why can we not make her one of us! Why can we not share the Blood with her?"

I took him roughly by the shoulders. He didn't fear my hands. He didn't care.

"Amadeo, listen to me. We cannot give way to this desire. I have lived a thousand years and more without making a blood drinker, and now you, within months of your own transformation, would make the first mortal for whom you feel inordinate love?"

He was crying bitterly. He tried to free himself from me, but I would not allow it.

"I wanted so to tell her of the things I see with these new eyes!" he whispered. The blood tears spilled down his boyish cheeks. "I wanted so to tell her how all the world is changed."

"Amadeo, know the value of what you possess and the price of what you give. Two years I prepared you for the Blood, and even so the giving of it was too rapid, spurred on by Lord Harlech's poisoned blade. Now you would visit this power upon Bianca? Why? Because you would have her know what has befallen you?"

I released him. I let him fall on his knees beside the bed, spilling his tears as he cried.

I sat at the desk.

"How long do you think I've wandered this Earth?" I asked. "Do you know how many times it had crossed my mind in carelessness and wanton temper to make another blood drinker? But I did not do it, Amadeo. Not until my eyes fell upon you. I tell you, Bianca is not to be what we are."

"She'll grow old and die!" he whispered. His shoulders moved with his sobs. "Are we to see it? Are we to watch this happen? And what will she think of us as the years pass?"

"Amadeo, stop with this. You cannot make all of them what we are. You cannot make one after another without conscience or imagination. You cannot! For everyone there must be preparation, learning, discipline. For everyone there must be care."

Finally he dried his tears. He stood up and he turned to face me. There seemed an awful calm in him, an unhappy and grim calm.

And then there came a solemn question from his lips.

"Why did you choose me, Master?" he asked.

I was frightened at this question, and I think he saw it before I could hide it. And I marveled that I had been so unprepared to answer such a thing.

I felt no tenderness for him suddenly, for he seemed so strong as he stood there, so very certain of himself and of the question which he had just put to me.

"Did you not ask me for the Blood, Amadeo?" I responded, my voice cool. I was trembling. How deeply I loved him, and how I didn't want him to know.

"Oh, yes, sir," he responded in a small, calm voice, "indeed I did ask you but that was after many a taste of your power, was it not?" He paused, then continued. "Why did you choose me for those kisses? Why did you choose me for the final gift?"

"I loved you," I said without further ado.

He shook his head.

"I think there's more to it," he answered.

"Then be my teacher," I answered.

He came closer to me, and looked down at me as I remained seated at my desk.

"There's a bitter cold in me," he said, "a cold which comes from a distant land. And nothing ever really makes it warm. Even the Blood did not make it warm. You knew of this cold. You tried a thousand times to melt it, and transform it to something more brilliant, but you never succeeded. And then on the night that I came near to death—no, was, in fact, dying—you counted upon that cold to give me the stamina for the Blood."

I nodded. I looked away, but he put his hand on my shoulder.

"Look at me, please, sir," he said. "Isn't it so?" His face was serene.

"Yes," I said, "it's so."

"Why do you shrink from me as I ask this question?" he pressed.

"Amadeo," I said, speaking firmly, "is this a curse, this Blood?"

"No," he answered quickly.

"Think on it before you answer. Is it a curse!" I declared.

"No," he said again.

"Then cease your questions. Don't seek to anger me or embitter me. Let me teach you what I have to teach."

He had lost this little battle and he walked away from me, looking once more like the child, though his full seventeen years as a mortal had rendered him more than that.

He climbed upon the bed, and curled his legs beneath him, sitting there motionless in the alcove of red taffeta and red light.

"Take me back to my home, Master," he said. "Take me back to Russia where I was born. You can take me there, I know you can. You have that power. You can find the place."

"Why, Amadeo?"

"I must see it to forget it. I must know for certain that it was . . . what it was."

I thought on this for a long time before I answered.

"Very well. You will tell me all you remember and I will take you where you want to go. And into the hands of your human family you can place whatever wealth you wish."

He said nothing to this.

"But our secrets will be kept from them, as our secrets are kept from everyone."

He nodded.

"And then we shall return."

Again he nodded.

"All this will happen after the great feast that Bianca will start preparing. On that night, here, we will dance with our invited guests.

Over and over again, you will dance with Bianca. We will use our greatest skill to pass among our guests as human. And I shall count upon you as much as I count upon Bianca or Vincenzo. And the feast will leave all of Venice in awe."

A faint smile came over his face. Again he nodded.

"Now you know what I want of you," I declared. "I want that you befriend the boys all the more lovingly. And I want that you go to Bianca all the more often, after you've fed of course, and your skin is ruddy, and that you tell her nothing, nothing of the magic by which you were saved."

He nodded.

"I thought . . ." he whispered.

"You thought?" I asked.

"I thought if I had the Blood I would have all things," he said. "And now I know that it's not so."

23

No MATTER how long we exist, we have our memories—points in time which time itself cannot erase. Suffering may distort my backward glances, but even to suffering, some memories will yield nothing of their beauty or their splendor. Rather they remain as hard as gems.

So it is with me and the night of Bianca's most supreme feast, and indeed I call it that because it was Bianca who created it, merely using the wealth and rooms of my palazzo for her finest achievement in which all the apprentices participated and in which even humble Vincenzo was given a dramatic role.

All of Venice did come to partake of our never ending banquet, and to delight in the singing and the dancing, whilst the boys performed in numerous and grandly staged tableaux.

It seemed that every room had its own singers or divine pageants. The music of the lute, the virginal, and a dozen other instruments blended to make the lovely songs that lulled and enchanted everyone, as the younger boys, royally costumed, went about filling cups from golden pitchers of wine.

And Amadeo and I did dance ceaselessly, stepping carefully and gracefully as was the fashion then—one walked to music, really—clasping hands with many a Venetian beauty as well as our beloved genius of the whole affair.

Many a time, I snatched her away from the illumination of the candles and told her how dear to me she was that she could bring about such magic. And I begged from her a promise that she might do it again and again.

But what could compare to this night of dancing and wandering amid mortal guests who commented gently and drunkenly on my paintings, sometimes asking me why I had painted this or that? As in the past, no critical word struck my heart deeply. I felt only the loving heat of mortal eyes.

As for Amadeo, I watched over him constantly, and saw only that he was divinely happy, seeing all this splendor as a blood drinker, divinely thrilled by the theatricals in which the boys played wonderfully designed roles.

He had taken my advice and continued in his love of them, and now amid the blazing candelabra and the sweet music, he was radiant with happiness and whispered in my ear when he could that he could ask for nothing finer than this night.

Having fed early, and far away, we were warm with blood and keen of vision. And so the night belonged to us in our strength and in our happiness, and the magnificent Bianca was ours and ours only as all men seemed to know.

Only as sunrise approached did the guests begin to take their leave, with the gondolas lined up before the front doors, and we had to break from the duty of accepting farewells to find our own way to the safety of our gold-lined grave.

Amadeo embraced me before we parted to lie in our coffins.

"Do you still want to make the journey to your homeland?" I asked him.

"Yes, I want to go there," he said quickly. He looked at me sadly. "I wish I could say no. On this night of all nights, I wish I could say no." He was downcast, and I would not have it.

"I'll take you."

"But I don't know the name of the place. I can't—."

"You needn't torture yourself on that account," I said. "I know it from all you've told me. It's the city of Kiev, and I shall take you there very soon."

There came a look of bright recognition to his face. "Kiev," he said and then he said it in Russian. He knew now it was his old home.

The following night I told him the story of his native city.

Kiev had once been magnificent, its cathedral built to rival Hagia Sophia in Constantinople from which its Christianity had come. Greek Christianity had shaped its beliefs and its art. And both had flourished beautifully there in a wondrous place. But centuries ago, the Mongols had sacked this grand city, massacred its population, destroying forever its power, leaving behind some accidental survivals, among them monks who kept to themselves.

What remained of Kiev? A miserable place along the banks of the Dnieper River where the cathedral still stood, and the monks still existed in the famous Monastery of the Caves.

Quietly, Amadeo listened to this intelligence and I could see the pure misery in his face.

"All through my long life," I said, "I have seen such ruin. Magnificent cities are created by men and women with dreams. Then there come the riders of the North or the East and they trample and destroy the magnificence; all that men and women have created is no more. Fear and misery follow this destruction. And nowhere is it more visible than in the ruins of your home—Kiev Rus."

I could see that he was listening to me. I could sense that he wanted me to continue to explain.

"There exists now in our beautiful Italy a land that will not be sacked by those warriors, for they no longer menace the northern or eastern borders of Europe. Rather they long ago settled into the continent and became the very population of France and Britain and Germany today. Those who would still pillage and rape have been pushed back forever. Now throughout Europe what men and women can do in cities is being discovered again.

"But in your land? There is still sorrow, and bitter poverty. The fertile grasslands are useless—thousands of miles of them are useless!— save for the occasional hunter as mad as your father must have been. That is the legacy of Genghis Khan—a monster." I paused. I was becoming too heated. "The Golden Horde is what they call that land, and it is a wasteland of beautiful grass."

He nodded. He saw the sweep of it. I knew this from his solemn eyes.

"Would you still go?" I pressed him. "Would you still revisit the place where you suffered so much?"

"Yes," he whispered. "Though I do not remember her, I had a mother. And without my father, there might be nothing for her. Surely he died that day when we rode out together. Surely he died in the hail of arrows. I remember the arrows. I must go to her." He broke off as though struggling to remember. He groaned suddenly as though some sharp physical pain had humbled him. "How colorless and grim is their world."

"Yes," I said.

"Let me take them only a small amount—."

"Make them rich if that's your wish."

For a long moment, he was silent and then he made a small confession, murmuring it as though he were communing with himself:

"I must see the monastery where I painted the ikons. I must see the place where at times I prayed I would have the strength to be walled up alive. You know it was the way of the place, don't you?"

"Very well, I know it," I answered. "I saw it when I gave you the Blood. I saw you moving down the corridors, giving sustenance to those who still lived in their cells, half immured and waiting for the will of God to take them as they starved themselves. They asked you when you would have the courage for it, yet you could paint ikons that were magnificent."

"Yes," he said.

"And your father hated them that they did not let you paint, that they made you a monk above all things."

He looked at me as if he had not truly understood this until now, and perhaps he had not. And then came from his lips a stronger statement.

"So it is with any monastery, and you know it, Master," he retorted. "The will of God comes first."

I was faintly shocked by the expression on his face. Was he speaking to his father or to me?

It took us four nights to reach Kiev.

I could have made the journey much more quickly had I been on my own, but I carried Amadeo close to me, his head bowed, his eyes closed, my fur-lined cloak wrapped around him to shelter him from the wind as best I could.

At last on the sunset of the fifth night, we reached the ruins of the city which had once been Kiev Rus. Our clothes were covered in dirt and our fur cloaks dark and nondescript, which would help to render us unremarkable to mortal eyes.

A thick snow lay over the high abandoned battlements, and covered the roofs of the Prince's wooden palace, and beneath the battlements simple wooden houses that ran down to the Dnieper River—the town of Podil. Never have I seen a place more forlorn.

As soon as Amadeo had penetrated the wooden dwelling of the European ruler, and glimpsed to his satisfaction this Lithuanian who paid tribute to the Khan for his power, he wanted to move on to the monastery at once.

And into it he slipped using his immense blood drinker's skill to play the shadows and confuse those who might have seen him as he cleaved to the mud walls.

I was near to him always but it was not my place to interfere or instruct. Indeed, I was gripped with horror, for the place seemed infinitely worse than I had ever guessed from the probing of his fevered mind.

With quiet misery, he saw the room in which he'd made ikons with its tables and pots of paints. He saw the long mud corridors through which he'd walked once as a young monk, giving food and drink to those half buried alive.

At last he came out of it, shivering, and he clung to me.

"I would have perished in a mud cell," he whispered, looking at me, begging me to understand the import of it. His face was twisted with pain.

Then turning away swiftly, he went down towards the half-frozen river, searching for the house in which he'd been born.

With no difficulty he found it, and he entered it—the splendid Venetian, dazzling and confusing the family gathered there.

Once again I kept my distance, settling for the silence and the wind, and the voices I could hear with preternatural ears. Within moments he had left them with a fortune in gold coin and come out again into the falling snow.

I reached out to take his arm and comfort him. But he turned away. He wouldn't look at me. Something obsessed him.

"My mother was there," he whispered, as he looked down once more towards the river. "She didn't know me. So be it. I gave them what I had to give."

Again I tried to embrace him, but he shook me off.

"What's wrong then?" I asked. "Why do you stare? Why do you look that way towards the river? What would you do?"

How I wished I could read his mind! His mind, and his alone, was shut to me! And how angry and determined he looked.

"My father wasn't killed in the grasslands," he said, his voice quavering, the wind whipping his auburn hair. "My father is alive. He's in the tavern down there."

"You want to see him?"

"I have to see him. I have to tell him that I didn't die! Didn't you listen to them talking in my house to me?"

"No," I said. "I gave you your time with them. Was I wrong?"

"They said he'd become the drunkard because he had failed to save his son." He glared at me as if I had done him some dreadful wrong. "My father, Ivan, the brave one, the hunter. Ivan, the warrior, the singer of songs whom everyone loved—Ivan is the drunkard now because he failed to save his son!"

"Be calm. We'll go to the tavern. You can tell him in your own way—."

He waved me off as though I were annoying him, and he set off down the street with a mortal tread.

Together we entered the tavern. It was dark and full of the scent of burning oil. Fishermen, traders, killers, drank here together. Everyone took notice of us for a moment and then ignored us, but Amadeo at once spied a man lying on a bench to the back of the rectangular room which made up the place.

Again, I wanted to leave him to what he meant to do, but I feared for him and I listened as he sat down now close to this sleeping man.

It was the man of memory and the man of visions, that I knew, as soon as I studied him. I recognized him by his red hair and red mustache and beard. Amadeo's father, the hunter who had taken him out of the monastery that day for a dangerous mission, to ride out in search of a fort which the Mongols had already destroyed.

I shrank back into the shadows. I watched as the luminous child removed his left glove and laid his chill supernatural hand upon the forehead of the sleeping father. I saw the bearded man wake. I heard them speak.

In rambling drunken confession, the father gave forth his guilt in abundance as though it belonged to anyone who roused him.

He had shot arrow after arrow. He had gone after the fierce Tatars with his sword. Every other man in the party had died. And his son, my Amadeo, stolen, and he was now Ivan the Drunkard, yes, he confessed it. He could scarcely hunt enough to buy his drink. He was a warrior no more.

Patiently, slowly, Amadeo spoke to him, pulling him out of his ramblings, revealing the truth with carefully chosen words.

"I am your son, sir. I did not die that day. Yes, they took me. But I am alive."

Never had I seen Amadeo so obsessed with either love or misery, with either happiness or grief. But the man was stubborn, the man was drunk, and the man wanted one thing from this strange person prodding him and that was more wine.

From the proprietor I bought a bottle of sack for this man who wouldn't listen, who wouldn't look at this exquisite young one who sought to claim his attention now.

I gave the bottle of sack to Amadeo.

Then I moved along the wall so that I might better see Amadeo's face, and all I saw there was obsession. He must make this man understand.

Patiently, he spoke until his words had penetrated the drunken haze from which the man stared at him.

"Father, I've come to tell you. They took me to a far-away place, to the city of Venice, and I fell into the hands of one who made me rich, Father, rich, and gave me learning. I'm alive, sir. I'm as you see me now."

Oh, how strange was this speech coming from one infused with the Blood. Alive? How so, alive, Amadeo?

But my thoughts were my own in the darkness. I had no role in this reunion.

At last, the man, sitting up to face his son, began to understand.

Amadeo was trembling, his eyes fixed on those of his father.

"Forget me now, please, Father," he begged. "But remember this, for the love of God. I shall never be buried in the muddy caves of the monastery. No. Other things may happen to me, but that, I won't suffer. Because of you, that you wouldn't have it, that you came that day and demanded I ride out with you, that I be your son!"

What on earth was Amadeo saying? What did these words mean?

He was on the verge of crying the terrible blood tears which we can never really hide. But as he rose from the bench where his father sat, the elder caught him tightly by his hand.

He knew his son! Andrei, he called him. He had recognized him for who he was.

"Father, I must go," said Amadeo, "but you must never forget that you saw me. You must never forget what I said, that you saved me from those dark and muddy caves. Father, you gave me life, not death. Don't be the drunkard anymore, Father. Be the hunter again. Bring the Prince meat for his table. Be the singer of songs. Remember that I came to tell you this myself."

"I want you, my son, stay with me," said the man. His drunken languor had left him, and he held tight to Amadeo's hand. "Who will ever believe that I saw you?"

Amadeo's tears had risen. Could the man see the blood?

At last Amadeo pulled back, and removing his glove, he pulled off his rings, and he placed these in his father's hands.

"Remember me by these," he said, "and tell my mother that I was the man who came to see her tonight. She didn't know me. Tell her the gold is good gold."

"Stay with me, Andrei," said the father. "This is your home. Who is it that takes you away now?"

It was more than Amadeo could bear.

"I live in the city of Venice, Father," he said. "It's what I know now. I have to go."

He was out of the tavern so quickly his father could not see it, and I, once seeing what he meant to do, had preceded him, and we stood in the snow-covered muddy street together.

"It's time for us to leave this place, Master," he said to me. His gloves were gone, and the cold was fierce. "Oh, but that I had never come here and never seen him and never known that he suffered that I had been lost."

"But look," I said, "your mother comes. I'm sure of it. She knew you and there, she comes," I pointed at the small figure approaching who held a bundle in her arms.

"Andrei," she said as she drew closer. "It's the last one you ever painted. Andrei, I knew it was you. Who else would have come? Andrei, this is the ikon your father brought back on the day you were lost."

Why didn't he take it from her hands?

"You must keep it, Mother," he said of this ikon which he had once linked to his destiny. He was weeping. "Keep it for the little ones. I won't take it, no."

Patiently, she accepted this.

And then another small present she entrusted to him, a painted egg—one of those treasures of Kiev which mean so much to the people who decorate them with intricate designs.

Quickly, gently, he took it from her, and then he embraced her, and in a fervent whisper assured her that he had done nothing wicked to acquire his wealth and that he might some night be able to come again. Oh, what lovely lies.

But I could see that this woman, though he loved her, did not matter to him. Yes, he would give her gold, for that meant nothing. But it was the man who had mattered. The man mattered as the monks had mattered. It was the man who had wrung the strong emotions from him. The man had brought from him bold words.

I was stunned by all. But wasn't Amadeo stunned by it himself? He had thought the man dead, and so had I.

But finding him alive, Amadeo had revealed the obsession—the man had fought the monks for Amadeo's very soul.

And as we made our journey back to Venice, I knew that Amadeo's love for his father was far greater than any love he had ever felt for me.

We did not speak of it, you understand, but I knew that it was the figure of his father who reigned in Amadeo's heart. It was the figure of that powerful bearded man who had so vigorously fought for life rather than death within the monastery who held supremacy over all conflicts that Amadeo was ever to know.

I had seen it with my own eyes, this obsession. I had seen it in a matter of moments in a riverfront tavern, but I had known it for what it was.

Always before this journey to Russia I had thought the split in Amadeo's mind was between the rich and varied art of Venice and the strict and stylized art of old Russia.

But now I knew that was not so.

The split in him was between the monastery with its ikons and its penance on the one hand, and his father, the robust hunter who had dragged him away from the monastery on that fateful day.

Never again did Amadeo speak of his father and mother. Never again did he speak of Kiev. The beautiful painted egg he placed within his sarcophagus without ever explaining its significance to me.

And on certain nights when I painted in my studio, working fiercely on this or that canvas, he would come to keep me company, and it seemed he perused my work with new eyes.

When would he finally pick up the brushes and paint? I didn't know, but such a question didn't matter anymore. He was mine and mine forever. He could do what he pleased.

Yet silently in my secret soul, I suspected that Amadeo held me in contempt. All I taught of art, of history, of beauty, of civilization—all this was meaningless to him.

When the Tatars captured him, when the ikon fell from his arms into the grass, it was not his fate that was sealed; it was his mind.

Yes, I could dress him in finery and teach him different languages, and he could love Bianca, and dance with her exquisitely to slow and rhythmic music, and he could learn to talk philosophy, and write poetry as well.

But his soul held nothing sacred but that old art and that man who lay drinking out his nights and days by the Dnieper in Kiev. And I, with all my power, and all my blandishments, could not replace Amadeo's father in Amadeo's mind.

Why was I so jealous? Why did this knowledge sting me so much?

I loved Amadeo as I had loved Pandora. I loved him as I had loved Botticelli. Amadeo was among these, the great loves of my long life.

I tried to forget my jealousy or ignore it. After all, what was to be done about it? Should I remind him of this journey and torment him with questions? I could not do such a thing.

But I sensed that these concerns were dangerous to me as an immortal, and that never before had anything of this nature so tortured me or made me weak. I had expected Amadeo, the blood drinker, to look upon his family with detachment and no such thing had taken place!

I had to admit that my love for Amadeo was all caught up with my involvement with mortals, that I had plunged myself into their company, and he himself was still so very hopelessly close to them that it would take him centuries to gain the distance from mortals which I had experienced on the very night when I was first given the Blood.

There had been no Druid grove for Amadeo. There had been no treacherous journey to Egypt; there had been no rescue of the King and Queen.

Indeed, as I mulled this over quickly I resolved I would not entrust him with the mystery of Those Who Must Be Kept even though the words had once or twice passed my lips.

Perhaps before the making of him, I had thought idly that I would take him to the shrine at once. I would beg Akasha to receive him, as she had once received Pandora.

But now I thought otherwise. Let him be more advanced; let him be more nearly perfected. Let him become more wise.

And was he not company and consolation for me now more than I ever dreamt? Even if a bad mood overtook him he remained with me. Even if his eyes were dull as though the dazzling colors of my paintings did not matter to him, was he not near at hand?

Yes, he was quiet for a time after the journey to Russia. But I knew his frame of mind would pass. And indeed it did.

Within a few short months, he was no longer aloof and moody but had come back to be my companion, and was once again visiting the various feasts and balls of the great citizens which I attended regularly, and writing short poems for Bianca, and arguing with her about various paintings which I had done.

Ah, Bianca, how we loved her. And how often did I search her mind to make certain that she had no inkling even now that we were not human beings.

Bianca was the only mortal I admitted to my studio, but naturally I could not work with my full speed and force when she was there. I had to lift a mortal arm to hold the paintbrush but it was more than worth it to hear her pleasant commentary with Amadeo who also perceived in my works some grand design which was not there.

All was going well when, one night as I came down upon the roof of the palazzo, quite alone, for I had left Amadeo in the company of Bianca, I sensed that a very young mortal was watching me from the roof of the palazzo across the canal.

Now I had come down so swiftly that not even Amadeo could have seen it had he been watching, yet this distant mortal marked my presence and when I realized it, I realized quite a deal more as well.

Here was a mortal spy who suspected me to be other than human. Here was a mortal spy who had been observing me for some time.

Never in all my years had I known any such a threat to my secrecy. And naturally I was tempted to immediately conclude that my life in Venice had failed. Just when I thought I had fooled an entire city, I was to be caught for what I was.

But this young mortal had nothing to do with the grand society in which I moved. I knew it the moment I penetrated his mind. He was no great Venetian, no painter, no cleric, no poet, no alchemist, and certainly no member of the Grand Council of Venice. On the contrary, he was a most strange sort of being, a scholar of the supernatural, a spy upon creatures such as me.

What could this mean? What could this be?

At this point, meaning to confront him and terrify him, I came to the very edge of the roof garden and peered across the canal at him, and there I made out his stealthy shape, and how he meant to cloak himself, and how fearful yet fascinated he was.

Yes, he knew me to be a blood drinker. Indeed, he had some name for me: *vampire*. And he had been watching me for several years! He had in fact glimpsed me in grand salons and ballrooms, so I might indeed write this off to my carelessness. And on the night that I had first opened my house to the citizens of Venice, he had come.

All this his mind gave me rather easily without the young man realizing it, obviously, and then using the Mind Gift I sent a very direct message to him.

This is folly. Interfere with me and you will surely die. I won't give you a second warning. Move away from my household. Leave Venice. Is it worth your life to know what you want to know of me?

I saw him visibly startled by the message. And then to my pure shock I received a distinct mind message from him:

We mean you no harm. We are scholars. We offer understanding. We offer shelter. We watch and we are always here.

Then he gave way to utter fear and fled the roof.

With little difficulty I heard him make his way down the staircases through the palazzo and then I saw him come out into the canal and hail a gondola which took him away. I had caught a good look at him as he stepped into the boat. He was a tall man, lean and fair of skin, an Englishman, and he was dressed in severe clothes of black. He was very frightened. He did not even look up as the boat took him away.

I stood on the roof for a long time, feeling the blessed wind, and wondering in its silence, what I should do about this strange discovery. I thought over his distinct message and the power of mind with which he'd sent it to me.

Scholars? What sort of scholars? And the other words. How very remarkable indeed.

I cannot exaggerate how odd this was.

It struck me with full force that there had been moments in my long life when I would have found his message irresistible, so great had been my loneliness, so great had been my longing to be understood.

But now, with all of Venice receiving me into its finest company, I did not feel such a thing. I had Bianca when I wanted to ramble on about the work of Bellini or my beloved Botticelli. I had Amadeo with whom to share my golden tomb.

Indeed, I was enjoying a Perfect Time. I wondered if for every immortal there was a Perfect Time. I wondered if it corresponded to the prime of life in mortals—those years when you are strongest and can see with the greatest clarity, those years when you can give your trust most truly to others, and seek to bring about a perfect happiness for yourself.

Botticelli, Bianca, Amadeo—these were the loves of my Perfect Time.

Nevertheless, it was a stunning promise, that which the young Englishman had made. "We offer understanding. We offer shelter. We watch and we are always here."

I resolved to ignore this, to see what came of it, not to allow it to impede me in the slightest as I enjoyed my life.

Yet in the weeks that followed I listened for this strange creature, this English scholar, and indeed, I kept a sharp lookout for him as we made our way through the usual lavish and dizzying social events.

I also went so far as to question Bianca about such a person, and to warn Vincenzo that such a man might attempt to engage him in conversation and that he must be very wise on that account.

Vincenzo shocked me.

The very fellow—a tall lean Englishman, young, but with pale gray hair—had already come calling. He had questioned Vincenzo, Would his Master wish to purchase certain unusual books?

"They were books of magic," said Vincenzo, frightened that I would be angry. "I told him that he must bring the books if he meant to offer them to you, and leave them here for you to see."

"Think back on it. What more was said between you?"

"I told him you had many, many books already, that you visited the booksellers. He . . . he saw the paintings in the portego. He asked if these had been done by you."

I tried to make my voice comforting.

"And you told him that the paintings had been done by me, didn't you?"

"Yes, sir, I'm sorry, so very sorry if this was more than I should have said. He wanted to purchase a painting. I told him that no purchase could be made."

"It doesn't matter. Only be careful on account of this man. Tell him nothing further. And when you see him, report it at once to me."

I had turned to go when a question came to me and I turned to see my beloved Vincenzo in tears. Of course I reassured him at once that he had served me perfectly, and told him he must worry about nothing. But then I asked him:

"Give me your impression of this man. Was he good or bad?"

"Good, I think," he said, "though what sort of magic he meant to sell, I don't know. Yes, good, I would say so, very good, though why I say it I can't tell. He had a kindness to him. And he liked the paintings. He praised them. He was most polite and rather serious for one so young. Rather studious."

"It's quite enough," I said. And indeed it was.

I did not find the man though I searched the city. And I had no fear.

Then two months later, I met, in the most auspicious circumstances, with the man himself.

It was at a luxurious banquet and I was seated at the table, among a great number of drunken Venetians watching the young people before us in their measured and leisurely dance.

The music was poignant, and the lamps were just brilliant enough to give the vast room the most enchanting glow.

There had been several fine spectacles before with acrobats and singers, and I think I was faintly dazed.

I know I was thinking again that this was my Perfect Time. I meant to write it in my diary when I returned home.

As I sat at the table, I leant on my right elbow, my left hand playing idly with the rim of a cup from which I now and then pretended to drink.

And then and there appeared this Englishman, this scholar, at my left side.

"Marius," he said softly, and in full command of classical Latin: "Count me a friend and not a meddler, I beg you. I have watched you for a long time from afar."

I felt a deep shiver. I was startled in the purest sense of the word. I turned to look at him, and saw his sharp clear eyes fixed fearlessly on me.

Again there came that message, mentally, without words, from his mind quite confidently to my own:

We offer shelter. We offer understanding. We are scholars. We watch and we are always here.

Once again a deep shiver stole over me. All the company round was blind to me, but this one saw. This one knew.

Now he passed to me a round gold coin. On it was stamped one word:

Talamasca

I looked it over, concealing my complex shock, and then I asked politely in the same classical Latin:

"What does it mean?"

"We are an Order," he said, his Latin effortless and charming. "That is our name. We are the Talamasca. We are so old we don't know our origins and why we are so called." He spoke calmly. "But our purpose in every generation is clear. We have our rules and our traditions. We watch those whom others despise and persecute. We know secrets that even the most superstitious of men refuse to believe."

His voice and his manners were very elegant, but the power of the mind behind his words was quite strong. His self-possession was stunning. He could not have been more than twenty.

"How did you find me?" I demanded.

"We watch at all times," he said gently, "and we saw you when you lifted your red cloak, as it were, and stepped into the light of torches and the light of rooms such as this."

"Ah, so, it began for you then in Venice," I said. "I have blundered."

"Yes, here in Venice," he said. "One of us saw you and wrote a letter to our Motherhouse in England, and I was dispatched to make certain of who and what you were. Once I glimpsed you in your own house I knew it to be true."

I sat back and took his measure. He had put on handsome velvet of a fawn color, and wore a cloak lined with miniver, and there were simple silver rings on his hands. His pale ashen hair was long and combed plainly. His eyes were as gray as his hair. His forehead was high and bare of lines. He seemed to be shining clean.

"And what truth is this that you speak of?" I asked as gently as I could. "What is it that you know to be true of me?"

"You are a vampire, a blood drinker," he said without flinching, his voice as polite as ever, his manner composed. "You've lived for centuries. I can't know your age. I don't presume to know. I wish that you would tell me. You have not blundered. It is I who have come to greet you."

It was charming to be speaking in the old Latin. And his eyes, reflecting the light of the lamps, were full of an honest excitement tempered only by his dignity.

"I have come into your house when it was open," he said. "I have accepted your hospitality. Oh, what I would give to know how long you've lived, and what you have seen."

"And what would you do with that intelligence?" I asked him, "if I did tell you such things?"

"Commit it to our libraries. Increase the knowledge. Let it be known that what some say is legend is in fact truth." He paused and then he said: "Magnificent truth."

"Ah, but you have something to record even now, don't you?" I asked. "You can record that you have seen me here."

Quite deliberately I looked away from him and towards the dancers before us. Then I looked back at him to see that he had followed, obediently, the direction of my gaze.

He watched Bianca as she made her circle in the carefully modulated dance, her hand clasped by that of Amadeo who smiled at her, the light glimmering on his cheek. She seemed the girl again when the music played so very sweetly, and when Amadeo gazed on her with such approving eyes.

"And what else do you see here?" I asked, "my fine scholar of the Talamasca?"

"Another," he answered, his eyes returning to me without fear. "A beautiful boyish one, who was human when I first laid eyes on him, and now he dances with a young woman who may soon be transformed as well."

My heart beat furiously as I heard this. My heart beat in my throat and in my ears.

But he laid no judgment down upon me. On the contrary, he was without all judgment and for a moment I could do nothing but search his young mind to make certain this was true.

He shook his head gently.

"Forgive me," he said. "I have never been close to one such as you." He was flushed suddenly. "I have never spoken to one such as you. I pray I shall have time to commit to parchment what I've seen tonight, though I swear to you on my honor and on the honor of the Order that if you let me go from here alive I will write nothing until I reach England, and the words will never do you harm."

I shut the soft seductive music out of my hearing. I thought only of his mind, and I searched it and found there nothing but what he had just said to me, and behind it, an Order of scholars as he had described it, a seeming wonder of men and women who wanted only to know, and not to destroy.

Indeed a dozen marvels presented themselves of shelter given to those who could genuinely read minds, and others who from the cards could somehow with uncanny accuracy predict fortunes, and some who might have been burnt as witches, and behind it libraries in which time-honored books of magic were stored.

It seemed quite impossible that in this Christian era, such a secular force could exist.

I reached down and picked up the gold coin with the engraved word, Talamasca. I put it in one of my pockets, and then I took his hand.

He was fiercely afraid now.

"Do you think I mean to kill you?" I asked gently.

"No, I don't think you will do it," he said. "But you see, I have studied you so long and with such love, I can't know."

"Love, is it?" I asked. "How long has your Order known of creatures like us?" I asked. I held his hand firmly.

His high clear forehead was suddenly creased by a small expressive frown.

"Always, and I told you we are very old."

I thought on it for a long moment, holding on to his hand. I searched his mind again, and found no lie in it. I looked out at the young dancers moving decorously, and I let the music fill me once more as though this strange disturbance had never come about.

Then I released his hand slowly.

"Go then," I said, "leave Venice. I give you a day and a night to do it. For I would not have you here with me."

"I understand," he said gratefully.

"You have watched me too long," I said reprovingly. But the reproof was really for myself. "I know that you have already written letters to your Motherhouse describing me. I know because I would have done so if I were you."

"Yes," he said again. "I have studied you. But I have done it only for those who would know more of the world and all its creatures. We persecute no one. And our secrets are well kept from those who would use them for harm."

"Write what you will," I said, "but go, and never suffer your members to come to this city again."

He was about to rise from the table when I asked him his name. As so often happened with me, I had not been able to take it from his mind.

"Raymond Gallant," he responded softly. "Should you ever want to reach me—."

"Never," I said sharply under my breath.

He nodded, but then refusing to go with that admonition he stood his ground and said: "Write to the castle, the name of which is engraved on the other side of the coin."

I watched him leave the ballroom. He wasn't a figure to attract attention, and indeed one could picture him working with quiet dedication in some library where everything was splattered with ink.

But he did have a marvelously appealing face.

I sat brooding at the table, only talking now and then to others when I had to, wondering on it, that this mortal had come so close to me.

Was I too careless now? Too absolutely in love with Amadeo and Bianca to be paying attention to the simplest things that should have sounded an alarm? Had the splendid paintings of Botticelli separated me too much from my immortality?

I didn't know, but in truth what Raymond Gallant had done could be explained fairly well.

I was in a room full of mortals and he was but one of them, and perhaps he had a way of disciplining his mind so that his thoughts did not go out before him. And there was no menace to him in gesture or face.

Yes, it was all simple, and when I was home in my bedchamber I felt much more at ease about it, even enough to write several pages about it in my diary as Amadeo slept like a Fallen Angel on my red taffeta bed.

Should I fear this young man who knew where I dwelt? I thought not. I sensed no danger whatsoever. I believed the things that he said.

Quite suddenly, a couple of hours before dawn a tragic thought crossed my mind.

I must see Raymond Gallant once more! I must speak to him! What a fool I had been.

I went out into the night, leaving the sleeping Amadeo behind.

And throughout Venice I searched for this English scholar sweeping this and that palazzo with the power of my mind.

At last I came upon him in modest lodgings very far from the huge palaces of the Grand Canal. I came down the stairway from the roof, and tapped on his door.

"Open to me, Raymond Gallant," I said, "It's Marius, and I don't mean you any harm."

No answer. But I knew that I had given him a terrible start.

"Raymond Gallant, I can break the door but I have no right to do such a thing. I beg you to answer. Open your door to me."

Finally he did unfasten the door, and I came inside, finding it to be a little chamber with remarkably damp walls in which he had a mean writing table, and a packing case and a heap of clothes. There stood against the wall a small painting which I had done many months ago and which I had, admittedly, cast aside.

The place was overcrowded with candles, however, which meant that he had a rather good look at me.

He drew back from me like a frightened boy.

"Raymond Gallant, you must tell me something," I said at once, both to satisfy myself and to put him at his ease.

"I will do my best to do this, Marius," he answered, his voice tremulous. "What can you possibly want to know of me?"

"Oh, surely it's not so hard to imagine," I responded. I looked about. There was no place to sit. So be it. "You told me you have always known of our kind."

"Yes," he answered. He was shaking violently. "I was . . . I was preparing to leave Venice," he volunteered quickly. "As you advised."

"I see that, and I thank you. But this is my question." I spoke very slowly to him as I went on.

"In all of your study, did you ever hear tell of a woman blood drinker, a woman vampire as you call it—a woman with long rippling brown hair . . . rather tall and beautifully formed, a woman made in the full bloom of life rather than in the budding flower of youth . . . a woman with quick eyes, a woman who walks the night streets alone."

All this quite impressed him and for a moment he looked away from me, registering the words, and then he looked back.

"Pandora," he said.

I winced. I couldn't prevent it. I couldn't play the dignified man with him. I felt it like a blow to the chest.

I was so overcome that I walked a few paces away from him, and turned my back on him so that he could not see the expression on my face.

He knew her very name!

Finally I turned around. "What do you know of her?" I said. I searched his mind as he spoke for the truth of every word.

"In ancient Antioch, carved in stone," he said, "the words, 'Pandora and Marius, drinkers of the blood, once dwelt together in happiness in this house.' "

I could not answer him. But this was only the past, the bitter sad past in which I'd deserted her. And she, full of hurt, must have inscribed the words in the stone.

That he and his scholars had found such a remnant left me humbled and respecting of what they were.

"But now," I declared, "do you know of her now? When did you learn of her? You must tell me all."

"In the North of Europe now," he said, "there are those who say they have seen her." His voice was growing stronger, but he was still quite afraid. "And once a young vampire, a young blood drinker, came to us, one of those who cannot bear the transformation. . . ."

"Yes, go on," I said. "I know. You say nothing that is offensive to me. Continue, please."

"The young one came, hoping we held some magic by which he might reverse the Blood and give him back his mortal life and his immortal soul. . . ."

"Yes, and he spoke of her? That's what you mean to say?"

"Precisely. He knew all about her. He told us her name. He counted her a goddess among vampires. It was not she who made him. Rather coming upon him, she had pity on him, and often listened to his ravings. But he described her as you did. And he told us of the ruins in Antioch where we would find the words she'd written in the stone.

"It was she who spoke to him of Marius. And so the name came to be known to us. Marius, the tall one with the blue eyes, Marius whose mother came from Gaul and whose father was a Roman."

He stopped, plainly afraid of me.

"Oh, go on, please, I beg you," I said.

"This young vampire is gone now, destroyed by his own will without our compliance. He went out into the morning sun."

"Where did he come upon her?" I asked. "Where did she listen to his ravings? When did this take place?"

"Within my lifetime," he said. "Though I myself did not see this blood drinker. Please, do not press me too hard. I am trying to tell you all I know. The young vampire said that she was ever on the move, through the northern countries as I told you, but in the disguise of a rich woman, and with an Asian companion, a blood drinker of very great beauty and abrupt cruelty who seemed to oppress her nightly and force her into what she did not want to do."

"I can't bear it!" I declared. "Go on, tell me—what northern countries? I can't read from your mind any faster than I can hear your words. Tell me all that the young one said."

"I don't know the countries in which she traveled," he answered. My passion was unnerving him.

"This young one, he loved her. He imagined that she would repel the Asian. But she would not. It drove him mad, this failure. And so, feeding upon the populace of a small German town, the young one soon blundered into our arms."

He paused, to gather his courage and to make his voice steady as he went on.

"Within our Motherhouse he talked incessantly of her, but it was all the same theme—her sweetness, her kindness and the cruelty of the Asian from whom she would not break away."

"Tell me the names under which they traveled," I said. "There must have been names, names they used as mortals, for how else could they have lived as rich mortals? Give me the names."

"I don't know them," he said. He gathered all his reserve now. "Give me time and perhaps I can obtain them. But I do not in truth think the Order will give me such information to give to you."

Again I turned away from him. I put my right hand up to shield my eyes. What gestures does a mortal man make at such a moment? I made of my right hand a fist, and held my right arm firmly with my left hand.

She lived. Was I not content with that? She lived! The centuries had not destroyed her. Was that not enough?

I turned around. I saw him standing there, so very bravely, though his hands trembled at his sides.

"Why are you not terrified of me?" I whispered, "terrified that I may come to your Motherhouse and find this information for myself?"

"Perhaps no such action is necessary," he responded quickly. "Perhaps I can obtain it for you, if you must have it, for it breaks no vows we've taken. It was not Pandora herself who sought shelter with us."

"Ah, yes, you make a lawyer's point on this score," I answered. "What more can you tell me? What more did Pandora tell this young one of me?"

"No more," he answered.

"Of Marius, this young one spoke, having heard the name from Pandora—." I repeated.

"Yes, and then here we discovered you in Venice. I have told you all!"

I drew back once more. He was exhausted with me and so frightened of me that his mentality was almost to the point where it might break.

"I have told you all," he said again gravely.

"I know you have," I said. "I see that you are capable of secrecy but quite incapable of a lie."

He said nothing.

I took the gold coin from my pocket, the one which he had given me. I read the word:

Talamasca

I turned it over.

There imprinted on it was the picture of a high and well-fortified castle, and beneath it the name: Lorwich, East Anglia.

I looked up.

"Raymond Gallant," I said. "I thank you."

He nodded.

"Marius," he said suddenly, as though screwing up his courage, "can you not send out some message to her over the miles?"

I shook my head.

"I made her a blood drinker, and her mind has been closed to me from the beginning. So it is with the beautiful child you saw dancing this very night. Maker and offspring cannot read each other's thoughts."

He mulled this over as though we were speaking of human things, just that calmly, and then he said:

"But surely you can send the message with your powerful mind to others who may see her and tell her that you search for her, and where you are."

A strange moment passed between us.

How could I confess to him that I could not beg her to come to me? How could I confess to myself that I had to come upon her and take her in my arms and force her to look at me, that some old anger separated me from her? I could not confess these things to myself.

I looked at him. He stood watching me, growing ever more calm, but certainly enrapt.

"Leave Venice, please," I said, "as I have asked you to do." I untied my purse and I put a good many gold florins on his desk, just as I had done twice with Botticelli. "Take this from me," I said, "for all your trouble. Leave here, and write to me when you can."

Again he nodded, his pale eyes very clear and determined, his young face rather willfully calm.

"It will be an ordinary letter," I said, "come to Venice by ordinary means, but it will contain the most marvelous information, for I may find in it intelligence of a creature whom I have not embraced in over a thousand years."

This shocked him, though why I did not understand. Surely he knew the age of the stones in Antioch. But I saw the shock penetrate him and course through his limbs.

"What have I done?" I said aloud, though I wasn't speaking to him. "I shall leave Venice soon, on account of you and on account of many things. Because I do not change and therefore cannot play the mortal for very long. I will leave soon on account of the young woman you saw dancing tonight with my young apprentice, for I have vowed that she shall not be transformed. But oh, I have played my role most splendidly here. Write it in your histories. Describe my house as you saw it, full of paintings and lamps, full of music and laughter, full of gaiety and warmth."

His expression changed. He grew sad, agitated, without moving so much as a muscle and the tears came up in his eyes. How wise he seemed for his years. How strangely compassionate.

"What is it, Raymond Gallant?" I asked. "How can you weep for me? Explain it to me."

"Marius," he said. "I was taught in the Talamasca that you would be beautiful and you would speak with the tongue of an angel and a demon."

"Where is the demon, Raymond Gallant?"

"Ah, you have me. I have not heard the demon. I have struggled to believe in it. But I have not heard it. You are right."

"Did you see the demon in my paintings, Raymond Gallant?"

"No, I did not, Marius."

"Tell me what you saw."

"Fearful skill and marvelous color," he answered, not even hesitating a moment, as though he had thought it through. "Wondrous figures and great invention, which gave everyone utter delight."

"Ah, but am I better than the Florentine Botticelli?" I asked him.

His face darkened. There came a small frown to him.

"Let me answer for you," I said, "I am not."

He nodded.

"Think on it," I said. "I am an immortal, and Botticelli is a mere man. Yet what are the wonders which Botticelli has done?"

It was too painful for me to be here any longer.

I reached out with both hands and gently took hold of his head before he could stop me. His hands rose and they gripped mine but they could do nothing of course to soften my own grip.

I came close to him, and I spoke in a whisper.

"Let me give you a gift, Raymond. Now pay attention to me. I will not kill you. I will not harm you. I want only to show you the teeth and the Blood, and if you will allow—and mark, I ask for your permission—I shall give you a drop of the Blood on your tongue."

I opened my mouth so that the fang teeth were visible to him and I felt his body stiffen. He uttered a desperate prayer in Latin.

Then I cut my tongue with my teeth as I had done a hundred times with Amadeo.

"Do you want this blood?" I asked.

He closed his eyes.

"I will not make this decision for you, scholar. Will you take this lesson?"

"Yes!" he whispered when in fact his mind said No.

I clamped his mouth in an ardent kiss. The blood passed into him, and violently, he convulsed.

As I let him go, he could scarcely stand. But he was no coward, this man. And he bowed his head for only an instant and then he looked at me with clouded eyes.

He was enchanted for these small moments, and patiently, I let them pass.

"My thanks to you, Raymond," I said. I prepared to take my leave through the window. "Write to me with all you know of Pandora, and if you cannot I will understand."

"Don't ever see an enemy in us, Marius," he said quickly.

"Don't fear it," I said. "I never really forget anything that happens. I will always remember that you spoke to me of her."

And then I was gone.

I came back to my bedroom study, where Amadeo still slept as though wine had drugged him when it had only been mortal blood.

For a little while I wrote in my diary. I tried to describe sensibly the conversation which had just taken place. I tried to describe the Tala-masca from all that Raymond Gallant had revealed to me.

But at last I gave in to writing the name Pandora over and over, foolishly, Pandora, and then I put my head down on my folded arms and dreamt of her, and whispered to her in my dreams.

Pandora in the northern countries, what countries, what could this mean?

Oh, if I were to find her Asian companion, how I would deal with him, how quickly and brutally would I free her from such oppression. Pandora! How could you let such a thing happen? And no sooner had I asked such a question than I realized I was quarreling with her as I had done so often of old.

When it came time to leave the house that night to find our resting place, I discovered Bianca asleep in my studio on a long silken couch.

"Oh, but you're too lovely," I said to her, kissing her hair tenderly and squeezing her beautifully curved arm.

"I adore you," she whispered, then went on with her dreaming—my fine and wonderful girl.

On we went to the golden room in which our coffins awaited us. I helped Amadeo lift the lid of his coffin before I lifted my own.

Amadeo was tired. The dancing had wearied him. But he whispered something sleepily to me.

"What is it?" I said.

"When the time comes, you will do it, you will give Bianca the Blood."

"No," I said, "stop speaking of that, you're infuriating me."

He laughed his cold uncompassionate little laugh. "I know you will. You love her too much to see her begin to wither."

I told him No.

And then I went to my rest, never dreaming that it was the last night of our life together, the last night of my supreme power, the last night of Marius de Romanus, citizen of Venice, painter and magician, the last night of my Perfect Time.

24

O N THE FOLLOWING NIGHT I rose as was my custom and
waited the hour or so for Amadeo to open his eyes.

Being young he did not follow the sunset so quickly as I
did, and the time of rising differs among blood drinkers even when age
is not a question at all.

I sat in the gold-lined chamber, deep in my thoughts about the
scholar named Raymond Gallant, and wondered if he had left Venice
as I had advised him to do. What danger could he bring to me, I
thought, even if he meant to do it, for whom would he incite against
me and on what charge?

I was far too strong to be overcome or imprisoned. Such a thing was
preposterous. The very worst that could happen was that if this man
marked me as some sort of dangerous alchemist, or even a demon, I
should have to take Amadeo and go.

But I did not like these thoughts, and so I chose during these quiet
moments to believe in Raymond Gallant, to be fond of him and to
trust in him, and to let my mind search the city around me to see if I
might find a trace of his presence, which would displease me in the
extreme.

I had only started this search when something utterly ghastly blot-
ted out my reason.

I heard screams coming from my own house. And I heard the cry
of blood drinkers! I heard the cry of Satan worshipers—the chant of
condemnations—and in my mind's eye I saw my rooms filled with
spreading fire.

I beheld Bianca's face in the minds of others. I heard the cries of my
boys.

Quickly I threw off the cover of Amadeo's coffin.

"Come, Amadeo, I need you," I cried in this frantic, foolish moment. "They're burning the house. Bianca is in danger. Come."

"Who is it, Master," he said, flying up the steps beside me. "Is it Those Who Must Be Kept?"

"No, Amadeo," I said, taking him under my arm and flying to the roof of the palazzo, "It's a band of demon-worshiping blood drinkers. They're weak. They will burn by their own torches! We must save Bianca. We must save the boys."

As soon as I reached the house, I realized that they were attacking it in unimaginable numbers. Santino had realized his crazed dreams. In every room there was a zealous assailant putting to the torch whatever he could.

The entire house was filled with fire.

As I rushed to the top of the main stairs I saw Bianca far below me, surrounded by the black-cloaked demons, who tormented her with torches as she screamed. Vincenzo lay dead before the open front doors.

I could hear the shouts of the gondoliers pleading with those inside to come out.

I dropped to the bottom of the stairway, and with the Fire Gift burnt Bianca's young and blundering attackers, who all but tripped on their black robes as they went up in flames. Some I could only force away with physical blows because I had no time to direct my powerful gifts.

Quickly I carried Bianca through the thick smoke and out onto the quais. I heaved her into the arms of a boatman who at once moved to take her away.

As soon as I turned back to save the screaming boys, a host of black-clad monsters surrounded me and again I burnt them with the Fire Gift, battering at their torches clumsily as I did.

The house was everywhere in chaos. Statues fell over the railings. Tapestries were set ablaze and paintings smoldered, but the boys, what could I do to protect the boys?

As soon as I burnt one ring of monsters there came another, and from all sides the condemnations:

"Heretic, blasphemer, Marius, the idolater, Marius, the pagan. Santino condemns you to burn."

Again and again I knocked the torches aside. Again and again I burnt the intruders. Again and again I heard their dying cries.

The smoke blinded me as it might have a mortal. The boys were roaring in panic as they were carried out of the house and over the rooftops.

"Amadeo!" I called out.

From above, I heard him desperately call to me.

I ascended, yet at every landing they accosted me and I found myself whipping around and playing the same game of force and Fire Gift as rapidly as I could.

"Amadeo, use your strength," I called out to him. I could not see him. "Use the gifts I've given you." I could only hear his cries.

I set ablaze those who crowded close to me. I could see nothing but the creatures burning, and then more torches thrust towards me as I hurled them back.

"Do you want to burn!" I declared, seeking to threaten them but no lesson of power stopped them.

In their fervor they came on.

"Santino sends you his holy fire. Santino sends you his justice. Santino claims your pupils. Santino claims your fledglings. Now it is time for you to burn."

All of a sudden and indeed, it was all of sudden—there did come the fatal circle of some seven or eight of them swift enough to plunge the fire at me so that it caught all of my garments and my hair.

Against my body itself this fire burnt, swallowing my head and all of my limbs.

For one slight moment I thought I shall survive this, this is nothing, I am Marius, the Immortal One, and then there came to me in a fury the horrid memory of the blood of the Elder in Egypt set afire by a lamp, burning with lurid smoke on the floor of my room.

There came a memory of the blood of Euxodia in Constantinople, bursting into flame on the floor of the shrine.

There came the memory of the Druid god in the grove with his black burnt skin.

And I knew in the next instant, without memory or thought, that my blood had been fatally ignited—that no matter how strong my skin or my bone, or my will, I was now burning, burning with such pain and such speed that nothing could keep me from being destroyed.

"Marius," Amadeo cried out in terror. "Marius." I heard his voice like a bell.

I cannot say reason drove me in any direction.

I did know I had reached the rooftop, and the cries of Amadeo and the boys were moving far off.

"Marius," cried Amadeo one more time.

I was blind to all who still tormented me. I was blind to the sky. In my ears, I heard the old God of the Grove on the night of my making telling me that I was immortal, that I could only be destroyed by the sun or by fire.

For life, I reached with all my remaining power. And in this state, I willed myself to reach the proper railing of the roof garden and to plummet down into the canal.

"Yes, down, down, into the water, under the water," I said aloud, forcing myself to hear the words, and then through the fetid waters I swam as fast as I could, clinging to the bottom, cooled and soothed and saved by the filthy water, leaving behind the burning palazzo from which my children had been stolen, in which my paintings had been destroyed.

An hour, perhaps longer, I remained in the canal.

The fire in my veins had been quenched almost immediately, but the raw pain was almost unendurable, and when at last I rose it was to seek that gold-lined chamber where my coffin lay.

I was unable to walk to this room.

Fearfully, on hands and knees, I sought the back entrance of the house, and managed by means of both the Mind Gift and my fingers to unlatch the door.

Then moving slowly through the many chambers I came at last to the heavy barrier which I had made to my tomb. For how long I struggled with it I do not know, only that it was the Mind Gift which finally unfastened it, not the strength of my burnt hands.

At last I crept down the stairs to the dark quiet of the golden room.

It seemed a miracle when at last I lay beside my coffin. I was too exhausted to move further, and with every breath I felt pain.

The sight of my burnt arms and legs was stultifying. And when I reached to feel my hair, I realized that most of it was gone. I felt my ribs beneath the thickened black flesh of my chest. I needed no mirror to tell me that I had become a horror, that my face was gone.

But what grieved me far worse was that when I leant against my coffin and listened, I could hear the boys wailing, wailing as a ship took them to some distant port, and I could hear Amadeo pleading with his captors for some kind of reason. But no reason came. Only the chants of the Satan worshipers were sung to my poor children. And I knew these Satan worshipers were taking my children South to Rome, South to Santino, whom I had foolishly condemned and dismissed.

Amadeo was once more a prisoner, once more a captive of those who would use him for their evil ends. Amadeo had once more been stolen from a way of life to be taken to another inexplicable place.

Oh, how I hated myself that I had not destroyed Santino! Why had I ever suffered him to live!

And even now, as I tell you this story, I despise him! Oh, how heartily and eternally I despise him because he destroyed, in the name of Satan, all that I held precious, because he took my Amadeo away from me, because he took those whom I protected, because he burnt the palazzo which contained the fruits of my dreams.

Yes, I repeat myself, don't I? You must forgive me. Surely you must understand the pure arrogance and utter cruelty of what Santino did to me. Surely you must understand the pure destructive force with which he changed the course of Amadeo's journey. . . .

And I knew that this journey would be changed.

I knew it as I lay against the side of my coffin. I knew it because I was too weak to recover my pupil, too weak to save the wretched mortal boys who would suffer some unspeakable cruelties, too weak even to hunt for myself.

And if I could not hunt, how would I gain the blood to heal?

I lay back on the floor of the room and I tried to quell the pain in my burnt flesh. I tried only to think and to breathe.

I could hear Bianca. Bianca had survived. Bianca was alive.

Indeed, Bianca had brought others to save our house, but it was far beyond saving. And once again, as in war and pillage, I had lost the beautiful things I cherished; I had lost my books; I had lost my writings, such as they were.

How many hours I lay there I don't know, but when I rose to take the lid from my coffin I found that I still could not stand. Indeed, I could not remove the lid with my burnt arms. Only with the Mind Gift could I push it and then not very far.

I settled back down on the floor.

I was too full of pain to move again for a long time.

Could I hope to travel over the miles to reach the Divine Parents? I didn't know. And I couldn't risk leaving this chamber to find out.

Nevertheless I pictured Those Who Must Be Kept. I prayed to them. Deeply, vividly I envisioned Akasha.

"Help me, my Queen," I whispered aloud. "Help me. Guide me. Remember when you spoke to me in Egypt. Remember. Speak to me now. I have never suffered before as I am suffering now."

And then an old taunt came back to me, a taunt as old as prayers themselves.

"Who will tend your shrine if I am not restored?" I demanded. I trembled in my misery. "Beloved Akasha," I whispered. "Who will worship you if I am destroyed? Help me, guide me, for some night in these passing centuries you may have need of me! Who has cared for you for so long!"

But what good is it ever to taunt the gods and the goddesses?

I sent out the Mind Gift with all its strength to the snowy Alps in which I had built and concealed the chapel.

"My Queen, tell me how I may come to you? Could something as dreadful as this draw you from your solitude, or do I ask too much? I dream of miracles but I cannot imagine them. I pray for mercy, yet I cannot envision how it would come about."

I knew it was vain, if not blasphemy, to beg her to rise from her throne for me. But was she so powerful that she could give some miraculous strength over the miles?

"How will I return to you?" I prayed. "How will I ever fulfill again my duties if I am not healed?"

The silence of the golden room answered. It was as cold as the shrine in the mountains. I imagined I could feel the snow of the Alps on my burnt flesh.

But slowly the horror sunk in.

I think I gave a soft, sad little laugh.

"I can't reach you," I said, "not without assistance, and how can I obtain that assistance unless I forsake the secret of what I am? Unless I forsake the secret of the Chapel of Those Who Must Be Kept?"

At last I climbed to my knees and struggled up the stone stairs very slowly; and painfully, I managed to stand, and with the Mind Gift, fasten the bronze door.

Safety, that was important, very important. I must survive this, I thought. I must not despair.

Then collapsing again and crawling down the stairs to the golden chamber, in the manner of something loathsome and lurid, I pushed doggedly against the lid of my coffin until it was open sufficiently for me to go to my rest.

Never had I known such injury, never had I known such pain.

A monstrous humiliation was mingled with the torture. Oh, there was so much I had not known about existence, so much I had not understood about life.

Soon the cries of the boys were gone from my ears, no matter how keenly I listened. The boat had carried them over the waters.

But I could still hear Bianca.

Bianca wept.

In misery and pain, my mind searched Venice.

"Raymond Gallant, member of the Talamasca," I whispered, "I need you now. Raymond Gallant, pray you haven't left Venice. Raymond Gallant of the Talamasca, please hear my prayers."

I could find no trace of him, but who knew what had happened to my powers? Perhaps all had dwindled. I could not even remember clearly his room or where it had been.

But why did I hope to find him? Had I not told him to leave the Veneto? Had I not impressed upon him that he must leave? Of course he had done as I had told him to do. No doubt he was miles beyond the point where he might hear my call.

Nevertheless I continued to say his name over and over as if it were a prayer.

"Raymond Gallant of the Talamasca, I need you. I need you now."

Finally, the approaching dawn brought a frigid relief to me. The roaring pain subsided slowly and my dreams began as they will do if I sleep before the rise of the sun.

In my dreams, I saw Bianca. She had her servants about her, and they comforted her, and she said:

"They are dead, both of them, I know it. They have died in the fire."

"No, my sweet one," I said. With all the power of the Mind Gift I called to her:

Bianca, Amadeo is gone, but I live. Do not fear me when you set eyes upon me, for I am badly burnt. But I live.

In the eyes of the others, I saw a mirror of her as she stopped and turned away from them. I saw her rise from her chair and move towards the window. I saw her open it and peer out into the dampness at the approaching light.

Tonight, when the sun sets, I will call to you. Bianca. I am a monster now in my own eyes and will be a monster in yours. But I will endure this suffering. I will call to you. Don't be afraid.

"Marius," she said. The mortals who gathered around her heard her speak my name.

But the sleep of the morning had come over me. I couldn't resist it. The pain was at last gone.

25

WHEN I AWOKE the pain was excruciating. I lay for an hour or more without moving. I listened to the voices of Venice. I listened to the movement of the waters beneath my house and all around it, and through the canals and into the sea.

I listened for Santino's miscreants, in quiet dignified terror that they might yet be abroad in search of me. But they were gone completely, at least for now.

I tried to lift the marble lid of the sarcophagus and I couldn't do it. Once again, with the Mind Gift I pushed against it, and then, with the aid of my feeble hands I was able to push it aside.

Most strange and wondrous, I thought, that the power of the mind was greater than the power of the hands.

Slowly, I managed to rise from this cold and handsome grave which I had fashioned for myself, and I did at last, after great effort, sit on the cold marble floor, seeing the glint of the golden walls through a bit of light that seeped into the chamber around the edges of the upper door.

I felt a terrible agony and weariness. A sense of shame overcame me. I had imagined myself invulnerable, and oh, how I had been humbled, how I had been dashed against the stones of my own pride.

The taunts of the Satan worshipers came back to me. I remembered Amadeo's cries.

Where was he now, my beauteous pupil? I listened but I heard nothing.

I called to Raymond Gallant once more, though I knew it was in vain. I pictured him traveling overland to England. I called his name aloud so that it resounded off the walls of the golden chamber, but I could not find him. I knew that I would not find him. I did it only to be certain that he was far beyond my reach.

And then I thought of my precious and fair Bianca. I sought to see her as I had last night, through the minds of those around her. I sent the Mind Gift wandering to her fashionable rooms.

Into my ears there came the sound of playful music; and at once I saw her many regular guests. They drank and talked as though my house had not been destroyed, or rather as if they knew nothing of it, and I had never been one of them; on they went as the living do, after a mortal is taken away.

But where was Bianca?

"Show me her face," I whispered, directing the mysterious Mind Gift by the sheer simplicity of my voice.

No picture came to me.

I shut my own eyes, which gave me exquisite pain, and I listened, hearing the hum of the entire city, and then begging, begging of the Mind Gift that it give me her voice, her thoughts.

Nothing, and then at last I hit upon it. Wherever she was, she was alone. She was waiting for me, and there were none around her to look upon her, or talk to her, and so I must find her in her silence or solitude, and at last I sent out my call to her.

Bianca, I am living. I am monstrously burnt as I've told you. As you once nursed Amadeo, can you extend your great kindness to me?

Scarcely a moment passed before I heard her distinct whisper.

"Marius, I can hear you. Only direct me. Nothing will frighten me. I will bind up your burnt skin. I will bind up your wounds."

Oh, this was wondrous comfort, but what was I planning here? What did I mean to do?

Yes, she would come, and would bring to me fresh garments with which I could conceal my miserable flesh, and perhaps even a hooded cloak that my head should be concealed, and even a Carnival mask for my face.

Yes, all that was most true, she would do it, but what then when I found I could not hunt in this miserable state? And what if, hunting somehow, I discovered that the blood of one or two mortals meant nothing to me, that my injuries had been too great?

How then should I depend upon this tender darling to assist me? How deep into the horrors of my debility should I allow her to come?

Again I heard her voice.

"Marius," she pleaded with me. "Tell me where you are. I'm in your house, Marius. It is much destroyed but not entirely. I wait for you in your old bedchamber. There is clothing here that I have gathered for you. Can you come?"

For a long while I did not answer her, not even to comfort her. I thought upon it in so far as one can think when one is feeling such pain. My mind was not my mind. Of that, I was certain.

And it did seem to me that in this great distress I could betray Bianca. I could betray her utterly were she to allow. Or I might only take from her some mercy, and leave her finally with a mystery which she would never understand.

The betrayal would be the more simple thing, obviously. The alternative, to take her mercy and leave her with a mystery, that would demand immense self-control.

I did not know whether or not I had such self-control. I did not know anything about myself in my misery. I remembered my long ago vow to her, that she would always be safe as long as I was in Venice, and I shuddered in agony envisioning the strong creature I had been on that night. Yes, I had vowed forever to protect her for the care she had given Amadeo, that she had saved him from death until I could come at sunset and take him out of her arms.

What did it all mean now? Was I to break that vow as though it were nothing?

And on and on there came her calls like prayers. She called to me as I had called to Akasha.

"Marius, where are you? Surely you can hear me. Marius, I have soft clothing for you that will not harm you. I have linen for your bandages. I have soft boots for your feet." She wept as she spoke. "Marius, I have a soft tunic of velvet for you. I have one of your many red cloaks. Let me bring these things and come to you, and I shall bandage you and assist you. You are no horror to me."

I lay there listening to her weeping, and then finally, I made up my mind.

You must come to me, precious one. I cannot move from where I am. Bring the clothing which you described, but bring also a mask, and you will find plenty of these in my closets. Bring one that is made of dark leather and decorated with gold.

"Marius, I have these things," she answered. "Tell me where I must come."

I then sent her another strong message, quite infallibly identifying the house in which I lay, and told her how she must come inside, find the door made of plated bronze, and then knock.

I was exhausted from the exchange. And once again, I listened in quiet panic for the sound of Santino's monsters, wondering if and when they would return.

Yet in the eyes of Bianca's boatman I soon caught an image of her coming out of the burnt ruin of my house. The gondola was on its way to me.

At last, there came the inevitable knock on the bronze door.

With all my strength I began my slow progress up the stone stairs.

I placed my hands upon the door.

"Bianca," I said. "Can you hear me?"

"Marius!" she cried out. She began to sob. "Marius, I knew it was you. It was no trick of my mind. You're truly alive, Marius. You're here."

I was aroused by the scent of her blood.

"Listen to me, precious darling," I said. "I was burnt as you cannot imagine. When I open this door a very small space, you must give over to me the clothing and the mask. Do not seek to look at me no matter how curious you may be."

"No, Marius," she answered, her tone resolute. "I love you, Marius. I'll do what you say."

How plaintive were her sobs as they suddenly broke through. And how strong the smell of blood inside her. How hungry I was.

With all my strength, my blackened fingers managed to loosen the latch, and then I opened the door a small space.

The scent of her blood was as painful as all else that I suffered. I thought for a moment I cannot go on.

But the badly needed clothes were thrust at me, and I knew I must take them. I must somehow move to my restoration. I could not sink back in agony for that would breed but more agony. I must go on. Here was the mask of black leather, decorated in gold. Garments for a ball in Venice, not for one so miserable and ghastly as I.

Leaving the door with its small opening, I managed to dress myself fairly well.

She had brought a long tunic rather than a short one, and this was wise, for the stockings I might never have managed to put on. As for the boots, I was able to slip my feet inside them, much as this pained me, and the mask I tied to my face.

The cloak was of generous proportions and with a hood, which I cherished. I was soon covered from head to toe.

But what must I do now? What should I tell this angel of a young woman who stood in the chilled and dark corridor outside?

"Who has come with you?" I asked her.

"Only the boatman," she said. "Did you not say come alone?"

"Perhaps I said it," I answered. "My mind is clouded by pain."

I heard her crying.

I struggled to think. I realized a harsh and terrible truth.

I could not hunt on my own because I wasn't strong enough to venture forth from this place with any of my old gifts of speed or ascent and descent.

I could not rely upon her strength to help me in the hunt because she was entirely too weak for it, and to use her boatman was foolish if not downright impossible. The man would witness what I did, and he knew that I resided in this house!

Oh, how mad it all was. How weak I was. How very possible it was that Santino's monsters might return. How important it was for me to leave Venice and seek the shrine of Those Who Must Be Kept. But how could this be done?

"Marius, please let me in," she said softly. "I'm not afraid to see you. Please, Marius. Let me come in."

"Very well," I said. "Trust in me that I won't harm you. Come down the stairs. Make your way carefully. Trust in me that whatever I tell you is the truth."

With agonizing effort, I pushed the door open sufficiently so that she might come inside. A faint light filled the stairway and the chamber below. It was enough for my eyes. But not for hers.

With her delicate pale hand she groped her way after me, and she could not see how I crawled with my hands resting heavily again and again against the wall.

At last we had come to the bottom of the steps, and there she struggled to see, but she could not.

"Marius, speak to me," she said.

"I'm here, Bianca," I said.

I knelt down, then seated myself on my heels, and gazing up at the torches that hung on the walls, I tried to light one of them with the Fire Gift.

I directed the power with all my strength.

I heard a faint crackling and then the torch kindled and the light exploded, hurting my eyes. The fire made me shiver, but we could not endure without it. The darkness had been worse.

She raised her tender hands to shelter her eyes from the brightness. Then she looked at me.

What did she see?

She covered her mouth and gave a muffled scream.

"What have they done to you?" she asked. "Oh, my beautiful Marius. Tell me how to remedy this and I will."

I saw myself in her gaze, a hooded being of burnt black sticks for neck and wrists with gloves for hands and a floating leather mask for a face.

"And how do you think that can be done, my beautiful Bianca?" I asked. "What magic potion can bring me back from what I am now?"

Her mind was in confusion. I caught a tangle of images and memories, of misery and hope.

She looked about herself at the glittering golden walls. She stared at the shining marble sarcophagi. Then her eyes returned to me. She was aghast but unafraid.

"Marius," she said, "I can be your acolyte as surely as Amadeo was. Only tell me how."

At the mention of Amadeo's name my eyes filled with tears. Oh, to think this burnt body had within it the blood of tears.

She dropped to her knees so that she might look directly into my eyes. Her cloak fell open and I saw the rich pearls around her throat and her pale breasts. She had worn one very fine gown for this enterprise, not caring how its hem would catch the dirt or the damp.

"Oh, my lovely jewel," I said to her, "how I have loved you both in innocence and guilt. You don't know how much I have lusted after you, both as monster and man. You don't know how I've turned my hunger from you when it was something I could scarce control."

"Oh, but I do know," she said. "Do you not remember the night you came to me, accusing me for the crimes I'd committed? Do you not remember how you confessed your thirst for my blood? Surely I have not become since then the pure and simple damsel of a children's tale."

"Perhaps you have, my pretty one," I said. "Perhaps you have. Oh, it's gone, isn't it? My whole world. It's gone. I think of the feasts, the masquerades, the dancing, it's gone, all my paintings burnt."

She began to cry.

"No, don't cry. Let me cry for it. It was all my doing. Because I didn't slay one who despised me. And they have taken Amadeo prisoner. Me, they burnt because I was too strong for their designs, but Amadeo they took!"

"Stop it, Marius, you rave," she said fearfully. She put out her hand and touched my gloved fingers.

"Oh, but I must rave just for a moment. They took him and I could hear him begging them for explanations, and all the boys, they took the boys too. Why did they do this?"

I stared at her through the mask, unable to imagine what she saw or read from this strange artificial countenance in her heated mind. The scent of her blood was almost overpowering and her sweetness seemed part of another world.

"Why did they let you live, Bianca, for surely I had not come in time?"

"Your pupils, those were the ones they wanted," she answered, "they captured them in nets. I saw the nets. I screamed and screamed and screamed out of the front doorway. They did not care about me except to draw you on, and what could I do when I saw you but cry out for your help against them? Did I do wrong? Is it wrong that I'm alive?"

"No, don't think such. No." I reached out as carefully as I could and squeezed her hand with my gloved fingers. "You must tell me if this grip is too strong."

"Never too strong, Marius," she said. "Oh, trust in me as you ask that I trust in you."

I shook my head. The pain was so terrible I couldn't speak for a moment. My mind and body both were pain. I could not endure what had befallen me. I could not endure the hopeless climb which stood before me and my future self.

"We remain here together, you and I," she said, "when surely there is much to be done to heal you. Let me serve your magic. I have already told you that I will."

"But what do you truly know of it, Bianca? Have you truly understood?"

"Is it not blood, my lord?" she asked. "Do you think I cannot remember when you took Amadeo, dying, into your own arms? Nothing could have saved him such as that transformation which I saw forever after in him. You know that I saw it. I knew. You know that I did."

I closed my eyes. I took my breaths slowly. The pain was terrible. Her words were lulling me and making me believe that I was not miserable, but where would this path lead?

I tried to read her mind but in my exhaustion I could not.

I wanted so to touch her face, and then believing in the softness of the glove, I did it, stroking her cheek. The tears welled in her eyes.

"Where is Amadeo gone?" she said desperately.

"South by sea," I confessed, "and to Rome, that is my belief on it, but don't question me now as to why. Let me say only that it was an enemy of mine who made this siege upon my house and those I love, and in Rome is where he dwells, and those he sent to harm me and Amadeo come from Rome.

"I should have destroyed him. I should have foreseen this. But in vanity I displayed my powers to him, and brushed him aside. And so he sent his followers in great numbers so that I couldn't overcome them. Oh, how foolish I was not to divine what he would do. But what is the use of saying it now? I'm weak, Bianca. I have no means to reclaim Amadeo. I must somehow regain my own strength."

"Yes, Marius," she said. "I understand you."

"I pray with all my heart that Amadeo uses the powers I gave him," I confessed, "for they were great and he's very strong."

"Yes, Marius," she said. "I understand what you say."

"It's to Marius that I look now," I said again guiltily and sadly. "It's to Marius that I look, for I must."

A silence fell between us. There was no sound except the crackling of the torch in its sconce high on the wall.

Again I tried to read her mind, but I could not. It was not only my weakness. It was a resolute quality in her just now. For though she loved me, there were thoughts conflicting in her, and a wall had been thrown up to keep me from knowing what they were.

"Bianca," I said in a low voice, "you saw the transformation in Amadeo, but did you really understand?"

"I did, my lord," she said.

"You can guess the source of his strength forever after that night?"

"I know it, my lord," she answered.

"I don't believe you," I said gently. "You dream when you say you know."

"Oh, but I do know, Marius. As I have only just reminded you, I recall only too well how you came into my very bedchamber thirsting for my blood."

She reached out to touch the sides of my face in consolation.

I put up my gloved hand to stop her.

"I knew then," she said, "that you fed upon the dead somehow. That you took their souls, or perhaps only their blood. I knew then it was one or the other, and the musicians who fled that banquet at which you'd slain my kinsmen—they spoke of your giving my unfortunate cousins a kiss of death."

I gave a low soft laugh.

"How very careless I was, and believed myself to be so masterly. What a strange thing. And no wonder is it that I have fallen so far."

I took again a deep breath, feeling the pain all through me, and the thirst unbearably. Had I ever been that powerful creature who so dazzled many that he could slaughter a gathering of mortals and no one would dare accuse save in whispers? Had I ever. . . ? But there was too much to remember, and for how long would I remember before even the smallest part of my power was restored?

But she was staring at me with brilliant inquisitive eyes.

Then came from my lips the truth which I could no longer hide.

"It was the blood of the living, beautiful girl, always the blood of the living," I said desperately. "It is the blood of the living and only the blood of the living and must be the blood of the living, do you understand? It's how I exist and always have existed since I was taken out of mortal life by malicious and disciplined hands."

She made a small frown as she stared at me, but she did not look away. Then she nodded as if to tell me that I might go on.

"Come close to me, Bianca," I whispered. "Believe me when I tell you that I existed when Venice was nothing. When Florence had not risen, I was alive. And I cannot linger long here suffering. I must find blood to restore me. I must have it. I must have it as soon as I can."

Again she nodded. She stared at me as firmly as before. She was shivering, and she brought up out of her clothes a linen handkerchief and wiped at her tears.

What could these words mean to her? They must have sounded like old poetry. How could I expect her to grasp what I had said?

Her eyes never wavered.

"The Evil Doer," she confessed suddenly. "My lord, Amadeo told me," she whispered. "I cannot play the game any longer that I don't know. You feed upon the Evil Doer. Don't be angry. Amadeo confided his secret a long time ago."

I was angry. Instantly and completely, I was angry, but what did it matter? Hadn't this dreadful catastrophe swept everything in its path? So Amadeo had confided the secret to our beauteous Bianca after all his tears and promises to me! So I had been the fool for confiding in a mere child. So I had been the fool to let Santino live! What did it matter now?

She had grown still and was staring at me yet, her eyes full of the fire of the torch, her lower lip trembling, and a sigh coming out of her as though she was about to cry again.

"I can bring the Evil Doer here to this chamber," she said, her face quickening. "I can bring the Evil Doer down these very steps."

"And suppose such a being should overpower you before you have reached this place," I said in a low voice, "how then should I establish any justice or revenge? No, you cannot take such a risk."

"But I will do it. Rely upon me." Her eyes grew brighter and it seemed she looked about, as though absorbing the beauty of the walls. "How long have I kept your secret? I don't know, only that nothing could pry it from me. And no matter what others suspected never did I betray you with one word."

"My precious, my darling," I whispered. "You will not take such risks for me. Let me think now, let me use whatever powers of mind still remain to me. Let us sit here in quiet."

She seemed perturbed and then her face hardened.

"Give me the Blood, my lord," she said suddenly, her voice low and quick. "Give it to me. Make me what you made Amadeo. Make me a blood drinker, and then I will have the strength to bring the Evil Doer to you. You know it is the way."

I was completely caught off guard.

I cannot say that in my burnt soul I had not thought of this very action—I had thought of it immediately when I had heard her weeping—but to hear it come from her own lips, and with such spirit, that was more than I had ever expected, and I knew as I had known from the beginning that it was the perfect plan.

But I must think on this! Not only for her sake, but for my own. Once the magic had worked in her—assuming that I had the strength to give it—how then would we, two weak blood drinkers, hunt the city of Venice for the blood we needed and then make the long journey North?

As a mortal she might have brought me to the Alpine pass of Those

Who Must Be Kept by means of a wagon and armed guards, whom I might have left in the small hours to visit the chapel alone.

As a blood drinker, she would have to sleep by day with me, and therefore we would both be at the mercy of those who transported the sarcophagi.

In my pain, I could not imagine it.

I could not take all the steps necessary. Indeed, it seemed suddenly that I could think of nothing, and shaking my head, I tried to prevent her from embracing me, from frightening herself all the more by embracing me and feeling the stiff dried creature that I had become.

"Give me the Blood," she said again with urgency. "You have the strength to do it, don't you, my lord? And then I shall bring here all the victims you require! I saw the change in Amadeo afterwards. He didn't have to show me. I will be that strong, will I not? Answer me, Marius. Or tell me, tell me how else I may cure you, or heal you, or bring you comfort in this suffering that I see."

I could say nothing. I was trembling with desire for her, with anger at her youth—at the conspiracy of her and Amadeo against me that he had told her—and consumed with desire for her here and now.

Never had she seemed more alive, more purely human, more utterly natural in her rosy beauty—a thing not to be despoiled.

She settled back as if she knew that she had pushed me a little too hard. Her voice came softer, yet still insistent.

"Tell me again the story of your years," she said, her eyes blazing. "Tell me again of how it was that Venice did not exist or Florence either when you were already Marius, tell me this story once more."

I went for her.

She couldn't have escaped.

In fact I think that she tried to escape. Surely she screamed.

No one outside heard her. I had her too quickly for that, and we were too deep in the golden room.

Pushing the mask aside and covering her eyes with my left hand, I sank my teeth into her throat, and her blood came into me in a rush. Her heart pounded faster and faster. And just before it made to stop I drew back from her, shaking her violently and crying out against her ear:

"Bianca, wake!"

At once I slashed my tight dried wrist until I saw the seam of blood and this I forced across her open mouth against her tongue.

I heard her hiss and then she clamped her mouth, only to moan hungrily. I drew back the burnt unyielding flesh and cut it open once again for her.

Oh, it was not enough for her—I was too burnt, too weak—and all the while her blood went on a rampage through me, forcing its way into the collapsed and burnt cells that had once been alive.

Again and again I cut my twisted bony wrist and forced it against her mouth, but it was useless.

She was dying! And all the blood she'd given me had been devoured.

Oh, this was monstrous. I couldn't endure it—no, not to see the life of my Bianca snuffed out like one small candle. I should go screaming mad.

At once I stumbled up the stone steps, not caring what my pain or weakness, forging my mind and heart together, and rising up, I opened the bronze door.

Once at the head of the steps above the quais I called to her boatman: "Hurry," and then went back inside that he should follow me, which he did.

Not one second after he entered the house did I fall upon the poor unfortunate innocent and drink all the blood from him, and then, scarce able to breathe for the comfort and soothing pleasure it gave me, I made my way back to the golden room, to find her where I had left her, dying still, at the foot of the stairs.

"Here now, Bianca, drink, for I have more blood to give," I said against her ear, my cut wrist on her tongue once more. This time the blood flowed from it, scarce a deluge but what she must have and her mouth closed over the fount and she began to pull against my heart.

"Yes, drink, my Bianca, my sweet Bianca," I said, and she in her sighs answered me.

The Blood had imprisoned her tender heart.

The night's dark journey had only begun. I could not send her in search of victims! The magic in her was scarce complete.

Bent over like a hunchback in my weakness, I carried her out and into the gondola, each step achingly painful, my movements slow and unsure.

And, once I had her seated against the cushions, half awake and answering me, her face never more beautiful, never more pale, I took up the solitary oar.

Into the darker regions of Venice I traveled, the mist hanging thick over the canals, to those dimly lighted places where ruffians abound.

"Wake, princess," I said to her, "we are on the silent battlefield, and very soon will see our enemy, and the little war we love so much will begin."

In my pain I could scarcely stand upright, but as always happens in such situations, those we sought came out to do harm to us.

Sensing in my posture and her beauty the very shape of weakness, they forfeited their strength at once.

Into her arms, I easily enticed a proud and youthful victim, "who would pleasure the lady if that's what we wished" and from this one she easily consumed a fatal draught, his dagger falling into the bottom of the boat.

The next victim, a swaggering drunkard who hailed us down with promises of a nearby banquet to which we'd all be admitted, stepped fatally into my grasp.

I had barely the strength for it, and once again the blood ran riot within me, healing me with such violent magic that it bordered upon an increasing pain.

The third who came into our arms was a vagabond, whom I enticed with a coin I did not possess. Bianca took him, her words slurred, disappointed that he had been so frail.

And all of this, beneath the veil of the ink-black night, and far away from the lights of the houses such as our own.

On and on we went. The Mind Gift in me grew stronger with each kill. My pain was eased with each kill. My flesh was more fully restored with each kill.

But it would take a wilderness of kills to restore me, an inconceivable wilderness of victims to bring back to me the vigor which I had possessed before.

I knew that beneath my clothes, I appeared as one made of ropes dipped in pitch, and I could not imagine the dreadful terror that my face had become.

Meantime, Bianca waked from her daze and suffered the pains of her mortal death, and now longed to return to her rooms for fresh clothing so that she might return with me to the golden lined room, in garments fit for her to be my bride.

She had had all too much of the blood of the victims and needed more of mine, but she did not know this, and I did not tell her as much.

Only reluctantly did I concede to her request, taking her back to her palazzo, and waiting uneasily in the gondola until she came, marvelously dressed, to join me, her skin like her purest white pearls.

Forsaking forever her many rooms, she brought with her many bundles, indeed all the clothes she wished to take with her, and all her jewels, and many candles, that we might be together in our hiding place without the roar of the torch.

At last we were in the golden chamber by ourselves, and she was brimming with happiness as she gazed at me, her secretive and silent masked bridegroom.

And only a single candle gave its slender light for us both.

She had spread out a cloak of green velvet that we might sit on it, and so we did.

My legs were crossed, and she leant back on her ankles. My pain was quiet in me yet terrible. Quiet in that it did not lurch with each breath I took but remained steady and allowed me to breathe as I would.

Out of her many bundles she produced for me a polished mirror with a bone handle.

"Here, take the mask off, if you wish," she said, her oval eyes very brave and hard. "You will not frighten me!"

I looked at her for a long moment, cherishing her beauty, studying all the subtle changes which the Blood had worked in her—how it had made her so extravagantly and richly the replica of her former self.

"You find me pleasing, do you not?" she asked.

"Always," I said. "There was a time when I wanted so to give you the Blood that I couldn't look at you. There was a time when I would not go to your rooms for fear that I should lure you to the Blood with all my charms, such as they ever were."

She was amazed. "I never dreamt it," she said.

I looked into the mirror. I saw the mask. I thought of the name of the Order: Talamasca. I thought of Raymond Gallant.

"You can read nothing of my mind now, can you?" I asked her.

"No," she said, "nothing." She was most puzzled.

"It's the way," I said. "Because I made you. You can read the minds of others, yes. . . ."

". . . yes," she answered. "The minds of our victims, yes, and when the blood flows, I see things. . . ."

". . . yes. And always you will see things, but never with that tool fall for the allure of the innocent, or the blood you drink will suddenly appear on your hands."

"I understand it," she answered too quickly. "So Amadeo told me all that you'd taught him. Only the Evil Doer. Never the innocent, I know."

Again, I felt a terrible anger, that these two, these blessed children, had shut me out. I wondered when and how Amadeo had told her these secrets.

But I knew that I should put such jealousy aside.

The awful, awful sadness was that Amadeo was gone from me. Gone. And I could not possibly bring him back. Amadeo was in the hands of those who meant to do unspeakable things. I could not think of it. I could not. I would go mad.

"Look into the mirror," she said again.

I shook my head.

I removed my left glove and stared at my bony fingers. She gave an awful little cry and then she was ashamed.

"Would you still see my face?" I asked.

"No, not for both our sakes," she said. "Not till you've hunted more and I have traveled with you more and am stronger, the better to be your pupil as I promised, as I will be."

She nodded as she spoke, her voice quite determined.

"Lovely Bianca," I said softly, "meant for such harsh and strong things."

"Yes, and I shall do them. I will always be with you. You will come in time to love me as you loved him."

I didn't answer. The agony of losing him was monstrous. How could I deny it with a single syllable?

"And what is happening to him?" I asked, "or have they merely destroyed him in some hideous fashion, for you know of course that we can die by the light of the sun, or by the heat of a terrible fire."

"No, not die, only suffer," she said quickly, looking at me questioningly. "Are you not the living proof?"

"No, die," I said. "With me it's what I told you, that I have lived for over a thousand years. But with Amadeo? It could be death very easily. Pray that they do not design cruelties but only horrors, that whatever they do, they do it quickly or not at all."

She was filled with fear, and her eyes were watching me as if there were an actual expression on the leather face mask that I wore.

"Come now, you must learn to open this coffin," I said to her. "And before that, I must give you more of my blood. I've taken so many victims, I have more now to give and you must have it or you won't be strong as Amadeo, not at all."

"But . . . I've changed my clothes," she said. "I don't want to get them bloody."

I laughed. I laughed and laughed. The whole golden chamber echoed with my laughter.

She stared at me blankly.

"Bianca," I said gently. "I promise you, I won't spill a drop."

26

WHEN I AWOKE, I lay quiet for an hour, weak and keenly in pain. So bad was the pain, in fact, that sleep seem preferable to wakefulness, and I dreamt of things long ago, times when Pandora and I had been together and when it had not seemed possible that we would ever part.

What finally jarred me from my uneasy slumber was the sound of Bianca screaming.

Over and over in terror she screamed.

I rose, somewhat stronger than the night before, and then once I was certain that I had my gloves and mask in place, I crouched beside her coffin and called out to her.

At first she couldn't hear me, so loud were her frantic screams. But at last, she grew quiet in her desperation.

"You have the strength to open the coffin," I said. "I revealed this to you last night. Put your hands against the lid and move it."

"Let me out of it, Marius," she pleaded, sobbing.

"No, you must do it for yourself."

Softer sobs came from her, but she followed my instructions. There came a grinding noise from the marble and the lid moved to one side, and then she rose, pushing the lid out of her way, and she freed herself from the box altogether.

"Come here to me," I said.

She obeyed me, shivering with sobs, and with my gloved hands I stroked her mussed hair.

"You knew you had the strength," I said. "I showed you that even with your mind you could move it."

"Please light the candle," she begged. "I need the light."

I did as she asked me to do. "You must try to quiet your soul," I said. I took a long deep breath. "You're strong now, and after we hunt tonight you'll be even stronger. And as I grow ever more strong, I will give you more of my blood."

"Forgive me for my fear," she whispered.

I had little strength myself to comfort her, but I knew that she needed what little strength I had. It was hitting me again like so many violent blows that my world was dashed, that my house was ruined, that Amadeo was stolen from me.

And then in a half swoon I saw Pandora of long ago, smiling at me, not recriminating me or tormenting me, but only speaking with me, as though we were in the garden together, at the stone table, and talking as we used to do of so many things.

But that was gone. All was gone. Amadeo was gone. My paintings were gone.

And there came again the desperation, the bitterness, the humiliation. I had not thought that such things could be done to me. I had not thought that I could be so miserable. I had believed myself so powerful, so very clever, so very beyond this abject grief.

"Come now, Bianca," I said. "We must go out, we must seek the blood. Come." I consoled her as I consoled myself. "Here, where is your mirror? Where is your comb? Let me comb your pretty hair for you. Look at yourself in the mirror. Did Botticelli ever paint a woman more beautiful?"

She wiped at her red tears.

"Are you happy again?" I asked. "Reach into the depths of your soul. Tell yourself that you are immortal. Tell yourself that death has no power over you. A glorious thing has befallen you here in the darkness, Bianca. You have become forever young, forever beautiful."

I wanted so to kiss her, but I couldn't do this, and so I labored to make my words so many kisses.

She nodded, and as she looked at me a lovely smile broke over her face, and for one moment she fell into a dreaminess which brought back all my memories of Botticelli's genius, and even of the man himself so safely away from all these horrors, living out his life in Florence beyond what I might ever do.

I took the comb from her bundle. I ran it through her hair. I watched her stare at the mask that was my face.

"What is it?" I asked of her gently.

"I want to see how badly—"

"No you don't," I said.

She began to cry again. "But how will you ever be healed? How many nights will it take?"

All her happiness of last night was shattered.

"Come," I said. "We go to hunt. Now put on your cape, and follow me up the steps. We do as we've done before. And don't for a moment doubt your strength, and do always as I tell you."

She would not do as I asked her. She hovered near the coffin, her elbow on the lid, her face stricken.

At last I settled near to her, and I began to speak words I never thought I would hear myself utter.

"You must be the strong one, Bianca," I said, "you must lead us. I haven't the strength for two just now and that is what you are demanding of me. I am ruined inside. I am ruined. No, wait, don't interrupt what I mean to say. And don't shed tears. Listen to me. You must give to me your small reserve of strength for I require it. I have powers quite beyond your imagining. But those powers I cannot reach just now. And until I can reach them, you must lead us forward. Lead us with your thirst and lead us with your wonder, for surely in this state you do see things as never before and you are filled with that wonder."

She nodded her head. Her eyes grew colder and more beautifully calm.

"Don't you see?" I asked. "If you can only come with me through these few nights, you do indeed have immortality?"

She closed her eyes and moaned. "Oh, I love the very sound of your voice," she said, "but I am afraid. In the coffin in the dark when I awoke, it all seemed a poisoned dream, and I fear what they may do to us if they discover what we are, if we fall into their hands, and if . . . if . . ."

"Yes, if?"

"If you cannot protect me."

"Ah, yes, if I cannot protect you."

I fell into a silence, sitting there.

Again, it did not seem possible that this had happened to me. My soul was burnt. My spirit was burnt. My will was scarred and my happiness ruined.

I remembered the very first ball, the ball which Bianca had given at our house, and I remembered the dancing and the tables with their golden platters of fruit and spiced meats, the smell of the wine, and the sound of the music, and the many rooms so filled with contented souls, and the paintings looming over all, and it did not seem possible that anyone could bring me down from that when I was so firmly placed in the realm of unsuspecting mortals.

Oh, Santino, I thought, how I do hate you. How I do despise you.

I pictured him again as he had come to me in Rome. I pictured him in his black robes smelling of the earth, his black hair rather vainly clean and long, and his face so very expressive with its large dark eyes, and I hated him.

Would I ever, I thought, have the chance to destroy him? Oh, surely there would come a time when he was not surrounded by so many numbers, when I might have him firmly in my hands and with the Fire Gift make him pay for what he'd done to me.

And Amadeo, where was my Amadeo, and where were my boys who had been so brutally yet carefully taken? I saw again my poor Vincenzo murdered on the floor.

"Marius, my Marius," Bianca said suddenly. "Please, don't sit in such quiet with me." She reached out, her hand pale and fluttering, not daring to touch me. "I am sorry for being so weak. Believe me, I am. What is it that makes you so silent?"

"Nothing, my darling, only the thoughts of my enemy, the one who brought those brandishing the fire, those who destroyed me."

"But you're not destroyed," she said, "and I will somehow get the strength."

"No, stay here for now," I said. "You have done enough. And your poor gondolier, he gave his life for me last night. You stay here now until I return."

She shuddered and reached out as if to take hold of me.

I forced her to remain at a distance.

"You cannot embrace what I am just yet. But I will go out and I will hunt until I am strong enough to take you from this place and to one that is safe and one where I will be healed completely."

I closed my eyes, though of course she could not see it on account of the mask, and I thought of Those Who Must Be Kept.

My Queen, I pray to you, and I am coming and when I do you will give me the Blood, I thought, but could you not have given me one small vision of warning?

Oh, I had not even thought of this before and now it exploded in my mind. Yes, from her distant throne she could have done it, she could have warned me, could she not?

But how could I ask such a thing from one who for a thousand years had not moved or spoken? Would I never learn?

But what of Bianca who was trembling and begging me to pay attention to her now? I waked from my sleep.

"No, we'll do it as you wanted, I'll go with you," she said piteously. "I'm sorry I was weak. I promised you I would be as strong as Amadeo. I want to be. I'm ready now to go with you."

"No, you aren't," I responded. "You're only more afraid of being left here alone than you are of going. You're afraid that if you stay behind I'll never come back to you."

She nodded her head as if I had forced her to admit it when I had not.

"I'm thirsting," she said softly. She said it with an elegance. And then in wonder. "I'm thirsting for blood. I must go with you."

"Very well then," I answered. "My lovely sweet companion. Strength will come to you. Strength will take up its abode in your heart. Don't fear. I have so much to teach, and as these nights pass, when you and I are comforted, I'll tell you of the others I've known, of their strength and of their beauty."

She nodded again, her eyes widening.

"Do you love me the most," she asked, "that is all I want to know for now and you may lie to me." She smiled, even as the tears stained her cheeks.

"Of course I do," I said. "I love you more than anyone. You're here, are you not? And finding me crushed, you gave your strength to save me."

It was a cold answer, lacking in flattery or kindness, yet it seemed quite enough for her, and it struck me how very different she was from those I had loved before, from Pandora in her wisdom, or Amadeo in his cunning. She seemed endowed with sweetness and intellect in equal measure.

I brought her up the steps with me. We left the small candle behind as if it would be a beacon for our return.

Before I opened the door I listened carefully for the sound of any of Santino's brood. I heard nothing.

We made our way silently through the narrowest canals of the most dangerous portions of the city. And there we found our victims again, struggling little, drinking much. Into the dirty water we released them afterwards.

Long after she was fragrant and warm from her many kills, a sharp observer of the dark and shining walls, I was still parched and burning. Oh, how dreadful was the pain. How soothing the blood as it flooded my arms and legs.

Near dawn we returned. We had encountered no danger. I was much healed but my limbs were still like sticks, and when I reached beneath my mask, I felt a face which seemed irreparably scarred.

How long would this take? I could not tell Bianca. I could not tell myself.

I knew that in Venice we could not reckon upon too many such nights. We would become known. Thieves and killers would begin to watch for us—the white-faced beauty, the man with the black leather mask.

I had to test the Cloud Gift. Could I carry Bianca with me towards the shrine? Could I make the full journey in one night or would I blunder and leave us scrambling desperately before dawn for some hiding place?

She went to her sleep quietly, with no fear of the coffin. It seemed she would show me her strength to comfort me, and though she could not kiss my face, she put a kiss on her slender fingers and gave it to me with her breath.

I had an hour then until the sunrise, and slipping out of the golden room, I went up and out over the rooftop and lifted my arms. Within moments I was high above the city, moving effortlessly, as though the Cloud Gift had never been harmed in me, and then I was beyond Venice, far beyond it, looking back at it with its many golden lights, and at the satin glimmer of the sea.

My return was swift and accurate, and I came down silently to the golden room with ample time to go to my rest.

The wind had hurt my burnt skin. But it was no matter. I was overjoyed with this discovery, that I could take to the air as well as I had ever done. I knew now that I could soon attempt the journey to Those Who Must Be Kept.

On the next night, my beauty did not wake screaming as she had before.

She was far more clever and ready for the hunt and full of questions.

As we made our way through the canals, I told her the old story of the Druid grove and how I'd been taken there. And how the magic had been given me in the oak. I told her of Mael and how I despised him still and how he had come once to visit me in Venice, and how very strange it had all seemed.

"But I saw this one," she said in a hushed voice, her whisper nevertheless echoing up the walls. "I remember the night that he came to you here. It was the night that I came back from Florence."

I could not think clearly of these things. And it was soothing to me to hear her talk of them.

"I had brought you a painting by Botticelli," she said. "It was small and very pretty and you later thanked me for it. This tall blond one was waiting upon you when I came, and he was ragged and dirty."

These things came clear to me as she spoke. The memories enlivened me.

And then came the hunt, the gush of blood, the death, the body dropped into the canal, and once more the pain rising sharp above the sweetness of the cure, and I fell back into the gondola, weak from the pleasure of it.

"Once more, I have to do it," I told her. She was satisfied, but on we went. And out of another house I drew yet another victim into my arms, breaking his neck in my clumsiness. I took another victim and another, and finally it was only exhaustion which stopped me, for the hurt in me would have no end of blood.

At last when the gondola was tethered, I took her in my arms and wrapping her close to my chest as I had so often done with Amadeo, I rose above the city with her, and flew out and high until I could not even see Venice at all.

I heard her small desperate cries against me, but I told her in a low whisper to be still and trust in me, and then bringing her back, I set her down on the stone stairs above the quais.

"We were with the clouds, my little princess," I said to her. "We were with the winds, and the purest things of the skies."

She was shivering from the cold.

I brought her down with me into the golden room.

The wind had made a wild tangle of her hair. Her cheeks were flushed and her lips bloodred.

"But what did you do?" she asked. "Did you spread wings like a bird to carry me?"

"I had no need of them," I said, as I lighted the candles one by one until we had many and the room seemed warm.

I reached up beneath my mask. And then I took it off and turned to look at her.

She was shocked, but only for a moment, and then she came to me, peering into my eyes, and she kissed my lips.

"Marius, I see you again," she said. "You are there."

I smiled. I went past her and lifted the mirror.

I couldn't see myself in this monstrosity. But my lips did cover my teeth at last, and my nose had taken some shape, and my eyes once again had lids. My hair was thick and white and full as it had been before and it hung to my shoulders. It made my face all the more black. I put aside the looking glass.

"Where will we go when we leave here?" she asked me. How steady she seemed, how unafraid.

"To a magical place, a place you would not believe if I told you of it," I answered. "Princess of the skies."

"Can I do this?" she asked. "Go up into the heavens?"

"No, darling one," I said, "not for centuries. It takes time and blood to make such strength. Some night however it will come to you, and you'll feel the strangeness, the loneliness of it."

"Let me put my arms around you," she said.

I shook my head.

"Talk to me, tell me stories," she said. "Tell me of Mael."

We made a place to sit against the wall, and we were warm together.

I began to talk, slowly I think, pouring out old tales.

I told her of the Druid grove again, and how I had been the god there and fled those who would have entrapped me, and I saw her eyes grow wide. I told her of Avicus and Zenobia, of our hunting in the city of Constantinople. I told her of how I cut Zenobia's beautiful black hair.

And telling these tales, I felt calmer and less sad and broken and able to do what I must do.

Never in all my time with Amadeo had I told such stories. Never with Pandora had it been so simple. But with this creature it seemed only natural to talk and to find consolation in it.

And I remembered that when first I had set eyes upon Bianca I had dreamt of this very thing, that she would be with me in the Blood and that we should speak together so easily.

"But let me tell you prettier stories," I said, and I talked of when I had lived in old Rome, and I had painted on the walls, and my guests had laughed and drunk their wine, and rolled about on the grass of my garden.

I made her laugh and then it seemed my pain was gone for a moment, gone in the sound of her voice.

"There was one I loved very much," I said.

"Tell me of him," she said.

"No, it was a woman," I replied. I amazed myself to speak of such a thing. Yet I went on speaking. "I knew her when we were mortals together. I was a young man and she was a child. In those times, as now, marriages were made when women were but children but her father refused me. I never forgot her.

"And then later, after the Blood was in me, we came together she and I. . . ."

"Go on, you must tell me. Where did you come together?"

"And the Blood went into her," I said, "and the two of us were together. We were together for two hundred years."

"Oh, such a long time," she said.

"Yes, it was a long time, though it did not seem so then. Every night was new and I loved her and she loved me, of course, and we quarreled so often. . . ."

"But was it a good quarreling?" she asked.

"Yes, it was, how very right of you to ask that question," I said. "It was a good quarreling until the last."

"What was the last?" she asked gently.

"I did a cruel and mistaken thing to her. I did a wrong thing. I left her without warning and without recourse, and now I can't find her."

"You mean you search for her even now?"

"I don't search because I don't know where to search," I said, lying just a little, "but I look always. . . ."

"Why did you do it?" she asked. "Why did you leave her as you described?"

"Out of love and anger," I said. "And it was the first time that the Satan worshipers had come, you see. Those of the very same ilk that burnt my house and took Amadeo. Only it was centuries ago, can you understand? They came. Oh, not with my enemy, Santino. Santino didn't exist then. Santino is no ancient one. But it was the same tribe, the same ones who believe they are put here on Earth as blood drinkers to serve the Christian God."

I could feel her shock, though for a moment she said nothing, and then she spoke.

"So this was why they cried out about blasphemy," she said.

"Yes, and long long ago, they said similar things as they came to us. They threatened us, and they wanted, they wanted what we knew."

"But how did this divide you and the woman?"

"We destroyed them. We had to. And she knew that we had to do it, and afterwards, when I fell sullen and listless and would say nothing, she was angry with me, and I grew angry with her."

"I see," she answered.

"It didn't have to be, this quarrel. I left her. I left her because she was resolute and strong and had known that the Satan worshipers had to be destroyed. And I had not known and even now, all these many centuries later, I have fallen into the same error.

"In Rome, I knew they existed, these creatures; in Rome, this Santino came to me. In Rome, I should have destroyed him and his followers. But I would have no part of it, you see, and so he came after me, and burnt my house and all I loved."

She was shocked and for a long time said nothing.

"You love her still, this woman," she said.

"Yes, but you see, I never stop loving anyone. I will never stop loving you."

"Are you certain of it?"

"Completely," I answered. "I loved you when first I saw you. Haven't I told you?"

"In all these years, you've never stopped thinking of her?"

"No, never stopped loving her. Impossible to stop thinking of her or loving her. Even the details of her remain with me. Loneliness and solitude have imprinted her most strongly on my mind. I see her. I hear her voice. She had a lovely clear voice." I mused. I went on.

"She was tall; she had brown eyes, with thick brown eyelashes. Her hair was long and rippling and dark brown. She wore it loose when she wandered. Of course I remember her in the softly draped clothes of those ancient times, and I cannot envision her as she might be in these years. And so she seems some goddess to me or saint, I'm not certain which. . . ."

She said nothing. Then finally she spoke.

"Would you leave me for her if you could?"

"No, if I found her, we would all of us be together."

"Oh, that's too lovely," she said.

"I know it can be that way, I know it can and it will be, all of us together, you and she and I. She lives, she thrives, she wanders, and there will come a time when you and I will be with her."

"How do you know that she lives? What if . . . but I don't want my words to hurt you."

"I have hope that she lives," I said.

"Mael, the fair one, he told you."

"No. Mael knows nothing of her. Nothing. I don't believe I ever spoke one sacred word of her to Mael. I have no love for Mael. I have not called out to him in these terrible nights of suffering to aid us. I would not have him see me as I am now."

"Don't be angry," she said soothingly. "Don't feel the pain of it. I understand. You were speaking softly of the woman. . . ."

"Yes," I said. "Perhaps I know that she lives because I know that she would never destroy herself without first finding me and making certain that she had taken her leave of me, and not having found me, and having no proof that I am lost, she can't do it. Do you understand me?"

"Yes, I do," she said. She crept closer to me, but she understood when with my gloved hand I touched her gently and moved her away.

"What was the woman's name?" she asked.

"Pandora," I said.

"I shall never be jealous of her," she said softly.

"No, you must never but how can you say such a thing so quickly? How do you know?"

She answered calmly, sweetly.

"You speak too reverently of her for me to be jealous," she said, "and I know that you can love both of us, because you loved Amadeo and me. I saw this with my own eyes."

"Oh, yes, you are so right," I said. I was almost weeping. I thought in my secret heart of Botticelli, the man himself standing in his studio staring at me, wondering helplessly what sort of strange patron I was, and never dreaming that my hunger and adoration were commingled, never dreaming of a danger which had come so close.

"It's almost dawn," she said. "I feel cold now. And nothing matters. Do you feel the same way?"

"Soon we will leave here," I said in answer, "and we will have golden lamps around us. And a hundred fine candles. Yes, one hundred white candles. And we'll be warm where there is snow."

"Ah, my love," she said softly. "I believe in you with my soul."

The next night we hunted once more and this time as if it were to be our last in Venice. There seemed no end to the blood I could imbibe.

And without confiding it to Bianca, I was eternally listening for Santino's brigands, quite certain that at any moment they might return.

Long after I had brought her back for safekeeping in the golden room, and seen her nestled there amid her bundles of clothes and soft burning candles, I went out to hunt again, moving swiftly over the rooftops, and catching the worst and strongest of the killers of the city.

I wondered that my hunger did not bring some reign of peace to Venice, so savage was I in cleaning out those bent upon evil. And when I was done with blood I went to the secret places in my burnt-out palazzo and gathered the gold which others hadn't been able to find.

Finally, I went to the very highest roof that I could discover and I looked out over Venice, and I said my farewell to it. My heart was broken and I did not know what would restore it.

My Perfect Time had ended for me in agony. It had ended for Amadeo in disaster. And perhaps it had ended for my fair Bianca as well.

At last I knew from my gaunt and blackened limbs—so little healed by so many kills—that I must press on to Those Who Must Be Kept, and I must share the secret with Bianca, for young as she was, I had no real choice.

It faintly excited me in my crushing misery that I could share the secret at last. Oh, what a terrible thing it was to put such a weight upon such tender shoulders, but I was weary of the pain and the loneliness. I had been conquered. And I only wanted to reach the shrine with Bianca in my arms.

2 7

A T LAST it was time for the journey. It was far too dangerous
for us to remain in Venice, and I knew that I could carry us to
the shrine.

Taking one bundle of clothing with us, and as much of my gold as I
could carry, I wrapped Bianca tightly against me and in less than half of
one night, crossed the mountains, in bitter winds and snow.

By now Bianca was accustomed to certain wonders, and to be set
down in a snow-filled mountain pass did not alarm her.

But within moments we were both painfully aware that I had made
a desperate error in judgment. I was not strong enough in my present
state to open the door of the shrine.

It was I, of course, who had created this ironbound stone door to
block any human assault, and after several pathetic attempts to open it,
I had to confess that it was not within my power, and we must find
some other shelter before dawn.

Bianca began to weep, and I became angry with her. I made another
assault upon the door just to spite her, and then stood back and bid the
door open with all the power of my mind.

There was no result, and the wind and the snow beat down hard
against us, and Bianca's weeping infuriated me to where I spoke words
that weren't true.

"I made this door and I shall open it," I declared. "Only give me
time to determine what I must do."

She turned away from me, visibly hurt by my anger, and then in a
miserable yet humble voice she asked me,

"What is inside this place? I can hear a dreadful sound from beyond
the door, all too like the sound of a heartbeat. Why have we come
here? Where shall we go if we cannot find shelter here?"

All of these questions angered me, but when I looked at Bianca, when I saw her sitting on the rock where I had placed her, the snow falling on her head and shoulders, her head bowed, her tears glistening and red as always, I felt ashamed that I had so used her in my weakness and that I needed so to be angry with her now.

"Be still and I shall open it," I said to her. "You have no knowledge of what lies within. But you will in time."

I gave a great sigh and stood back from the door, my burnt hand still tightened on the iron handle and with all my strength I pulled, but I could not make the door budge.

The absolute folly of it gripped me. I could gain no admittance! I was too weak, and for how long I would be too weak I didn't know. And yet I made one attempt after another, only so that Bianca would believe that I could protect her, that I could gain entry to this strange place.

Finally I turned my back on the Holy of Holies, and I went to her, and gathered her to me, and covered her head and tried to warm her as best I could.

"Very soon, I shall tell you all," I said, "and I shall find us shelter this night. Don't doubt. For now, let me say only that this is a place which I built and which is known to me only and which I'm too weak now to enter as you can see."

"Forgive me that I cried," she said gently. "You won't see tears from me again. But what is the sound I hear? Can't humans hear it?"

"No, they cannot," I answered. "Please be still for now, my brave darling."

But at that moment, that very single moment, another new and altogether different sound caught my ear, a sound which could have been heard by anyone.

It was the sound of the stone door opening behind me. I knew the sound infallibly and I turned around, unbelieving and as fearful as I was amazed.

Quickly I gathered Bianca to me, and we stood before the door as it opened wide.

My heart was racing. I could hardly fill my lungs with air.

I knew that only Akasha could have done this, and as the door fell all the way back, I perceived another miracle of equal kindness and beauty of which I'd never dreamt.

A rich and abundant light poured forth from the door of the stone passage.

For a moment I was too stunned to move. Then pure happiness

descended upon me as I gazed upon this flood of beautiful light. And it seemed I could not possibly fear it or doubt its meaning.

"Come now, Bianca," I said to her, as I guided her forward at my side.

She clutched her bundle to her chest as though she would die if she let go of it, and I held her as though without her to witness with me I would fall.

We stepped into the stone passage and made our way slowly into the bright and flickering light of the chapel. All its many bronze lamps were aglow. Its one hundred candles blazed exquisitely. And no sooner had I taken note of these things, amid a subdued glory that filled me with joy, than the stone door was closed behind us with a crushing sound as rock sounded against rock.

I found myself staring over the row of one hundred candles up into the faces of the Divine Mother and Father, seeing them as perhaps Bianca would see them, and certainly with refreshed and grateful eyes.

I knelt down, and Bianca knelt at my side. I was trembling. Indeed my shock was so great that I could not for a moment fill my lungs with air. There was no way that I could explain to Bianca the full import of what had taken place. I would only frighten her if I tried to do so. And careless words spoken before my Queen would be unforgivable.

"Don't speak," I finally said in a whisper. "They are our Parents. They have opened the door, when I could not. They have lighted the lamps for us. They have lighted the candles. You cannot imagine the worth of this blessing. They have welcomed us inside. We can answer them only with prayers."

Bianca nodded. Her face was full of piety and wonder. Did it matter to Akasha that I had brought to her feet an exquisite blood drinker?

In a low reverent voice I recounted the story of the Divine Parents but only in the simplest and grandest terms. I told Bianca how they had come to be the very first blood drinkers thousands of years ago in Egypt, and that now they no longer hungered for blood or even so much as spoke or moved. I was their keeper and their guardian and had been so for all of my life as a blood drinker and so it would always be.

I said these things so that nothing would alarm Bianca and she would feel no dread of the two still figures who stared forward in horrifying silence, and did not seem even to blink. And so it was that tender Bianca was initiated into these powerful mysteries with great care and thought them beautiful and nothing more.

"It was to this chapel," I explained, "that I would come when I left Venice, and I would light the lamps for the King and the Queen, and bring fresh flowers. You see, there are none now. But I will bring them when I can."

Once again, I realized that in spite of my enthusiasm and gratitude, I couldn't really make her know what a miracle it was that Akasha had opened the door for us, or lighted the lamps. Indeed, I didn't dare to do it, and now that I had finished this respectful recital, I closed my eyes, and in silence I thanked both Akasha and Enkil that they had admitted me to the sanctuary, and that they had greeted us with the gift of light.

Over and over I offered my prayers, perhaps unable myself to grasp the fact that they had so welcomed me, and not too certain of what it really meant. Was I loved? Was I needed? It seemed I must accept without presumption. It seemed I must be grateful without imagining things that weren't so.

I knelt in quietude for a long time and Bianca must surely have observed me for she too was quiet, and then I could bear the thirst no longer. I stared at Akasha. I desired the Blood. I could think of nothing but the Blood. All my injuries were as so many open wounds in me. And my wounds bled for the Blood. I had to attempt to take the all-powerful Blood from the Queen.

"My beauty," I said, placing my gloved hand on Bianca's tender arm. "I want you to go to the corner there and to sit quiet, and to say nothing of what you see."

"But what will happen?" she whispered. For the first time she sounded afraid. She looked about herself at the shivering flames of the lamps, at the glowing candles, at the painted walls.

"Do as I tell you," I said. I had to say it, and she had to do it, for how was I ever to know whether the Queen would let me drink?

As soon as Bianca was in the corner with her heavy cloak wrapped around her and as far away as possible, for whatever good it would do, I prayed in silence for the Blood.

"You see me and what I am," I said silently, "you know that I have been burnt. This is why you opened the door for me and admitted me, because I could not do it, and surely you see what a monster I have become. Have mercy on me and let me drink from you as you have done in the past. I need the Blood. I need it more than I have ever needed it. And so I come to you with respect."

I removed my leather mask and laid it aside. I was as hideous now as those old burnt gods whom Akasha had once crushed when they came to her. Would she refuse me in the same manner? Or had she known all along what had befallen me? Had she understood completely all things before the door was ever opened?

I rose slowly until I knelt at her feet and I could put my hand upon her throat, all the while tensed for the threat of Enkil's arm, but it did not come.

I kissed her throat, feeling her plaited hair against me and looking at her white skin before me, and hearing only Bianca's soft tears.

"Don't cry, Bianca," I whispered.

Then I sank my teeth suddenly, viciously, as I had so often done, and the thick blood flooded into me, brilliant and hot as the lamplight and the light of the candles, pouring into me as if her heart were pumping it willingly into me, racing the beat of my own heart. My head grew light. My body grew light.

Far away Bianca wept. Why was she afraid?

I saw the garden. I saw the garden I had painted after I had fallen in love with Botticelli, and it was filled with his orange trees and with his flowers and yet it was my garden, the garden of my father's house outside Rome long long ago. How could I ever forget my own garden? How could I ever forget the garden where I had first played as a child?

In memory I went back to those days in Rome when I had been mortal, and there was my garden, the garden of the villa of my father, and I was walking in the soft grass and listening to the sound of the fountain, and then it seemed that all through time, the garden changed but never changed, and it was always there for me.

I lay down on the grass, and the branches of the trees moved above me. I heard a voice speaking to me, rapidly and sweetly, but I didn't know what it was saying, and then I knew that Amadeo was hurt, that he was in the hands of those who would bring pain and evil to him, and that I could not go to him now, I would only stumble into their snares if I did, and that I must stay here.

I was the Keeper of the King and the Queen as I had told Bianca, yes, the Keeper of the King and the Queen, and I must let Amadeo go in Time, and perhaps were I to do as I should, perhaps Pandora would be returned to me, Pandora who traveled the northern cities of Europe now, Pandora who had been seen.

The garden was verdant and fragrant and I saw Pandora clearly. I saw her in her soft white dress, her hair loose as I had described it to

Bianca. Pandora smiled. She walked towards me. She spoke to me. *The Queen wants us to be together,* she said. Her eyes were large and wondering and I knew she was very close to me, very close, so close that I could almost touch her hand.

I can't be imagining this, no, I cannot, I thought. And there came back to me again vividly the sound of Pandora's voice, as she quarreled with me on our first night as bride and groom: *Even as this new blood races through me still, eats at me and transforms me, I cling to neither reason nor superstition for my safety. I can walk through a myth and out of it! You fear me, because you don't know what I am. I look like a woman, I sound like a man, and your reason tells you the sum total is impossible.*

I was looking into Pandora's eyes. She sat on the garden bench, pulling the flower petals out of her brown hair, a girl again in the Blood, a woman-girl forever, as Bianca would be a young woman forever.

I reached out on either side of me and felt the grass beneath my hands.

Suddenly I fell backwards, out of the dream garden, out of the illusion and found myself lying quite still on the floor of the chapel, between the high bank of perfect candles, and the steps of the dais where the enthroned couple kept their ancient place.

Nothing seemed changed about me. Even Bianca's crying came as before.

"Be quiet now, darling," I said to her. But my eyes were fastened to the face of Akasha above me, and to her breasts beneath the golden silk of her Egyptian dress.

It seemed that Pandora had been with me, that she had been in the very chapel. And the beauty of Pandora seemed bound up with the beauty and presence of Akasha in some intimate way which I could not understand.

"What are these portents?" I whispered. I sat up and then rose to my knees. "Tell me, my beloved Queen. What are these portents? Did you once bring Pandora to me because you wanted us to be together? Do you remember when Pandora spoke those words to me?"

I fell silent. But my mind spoke to Akasha. My mind pleaded with her. Where is Pandora? Will you bring Pandora to me again?

A long interval passed and then I rose to my feet.

I went round the bank of candles and found my precious companion quite distraught over the simple wonder she had beheld of me drinking from the immobile Queen.

"And then you fell back, as though you were lifeless," she recounted. "And I didn't dare to go to you, as you'd said that I mustn't move."

I comforted her.

"And then finally you waked, and you spoke of Pandora, and I saw that you were so . . . so much healed."

This was true. I was more robust all over, my arms and legs thicker, heavier, and my face had more of its natural contour. Indeed, I was still badly burnt, but a man of some stature and seeming strength now, and indeed I could feel more of the old strength in my limbs.

But it was now only two hours from dawn, and being quite unable to open the door, and not in any mood to pray that Akasha work common miracles for anyone, I knew I had to give my blood to Bianca, and so this is what I did.

Would it offend the Queen, that I, having just drunk from her would offer this powerful blood to a child? There was nothing to do but find out.

I didn't frighten Bianca with any warnings or doubts on the matter. I beckoned to her that she should come to me and lie in my arms.

I cut my wrist for her and told her to drink. I heard her gasp with the shock of the powerful blood and her delicate fingers stiffened to make her two hands into claws.

At last of her own volition she drew back and sat up slowly beside me, her eyes vague and full of reflected light.

I kissed her forehead.

"What did you see in the Blood, my beauty?" I asked.

She shook her head as though she had no words for it, and then she laid her head on my chest.

There was only serenity and peace in the chapel, and as we lay down to sleep together, the lamps slowly burnt out.

At last the candles were down to a few, and I could feel the dawn coming, and the chapel was warm as I had promised, and glittering with its riches, but above all with its solemn King and Queen.

Bianca had lost consciousness. I had perhaps three quarters of an hour before the day's slumber would come for me as well.

I looked up at Akasha, delighting in the last shimmer of the dying candles in her eyes.

"You know what a liar I am, don't you?" I asked her. "You know how wicked I have been. And you play my game with me, don't you, my Sovereign?"

Did I hear laughter?

Maybe I was going mad. There had been enough pain for it and enough magic; there had been enough hunger, and enough blood.

I looked down at Bianca who rested so trustingly on my arm.

"I have planted in her mind the image of Pandora, haven't I?" I whispered, "so that wherever she goes with me she will search. And from her angel mind, Pandora cannot fail to pluck my image. And so we may find each other, Pandora and I, through her. She doesn't dream of what I've done. She thinks only to comfort me with her listening, and I, though loving her, take her North with me, into the lands where Raymond Gallant has told me that Pandora was last seen.

"Oh, very wicked, but what does it take to sustain life when life is bruised and burnt as badly as my life has been? For me it is this extravagant and slender ambition, and for it I abandon Amadeo whom I should rescue as soon as my strength is restored."

There was a sound in the chapel. What was it? The sound of the wax of the last candle?

It seemed a voice was speaking to me soundlessly.

You cannot rescue Amadeo. You are the keeper of the Mother and the Father.

"Yes, I grow sleepy," I whispered. I closed my eyes. "I know such things, I have always known them."

You go on, you seek Raymond Gallant, you must remember. Look at his face again.

"Yes, the Talamasca," I said. "And the castle called Lorwich in East Anglia. The place he called the Motherhouse. Yes. I remember both sides of the golden coin."

I thought dreamily of that supper when he had come upon me so stealthily and stared at me with such innocent and inquisitive eyes.

I thought of the music and the way Amadeo smiled at Bianca as they danced together. I thought of everything.

And then in my hand I saw the golden coin and the engraved image of the castle, and I thought, Am I not dreaming? But it seemed that Raymond Gallant was talking to me, talking very distinctly:

"Listen to me, Marius, remember me, Marius. We know of her, Marius. We watch and we are always here."

"Yes, go North," I whispered.

And it seemed that the Queen of Silence said without a word that she was content.

28

As I LOOK BACK NOW, I have no doubt that Akasha turned me away from the rescue of Amadeo, and as I consider all that I have revealed here I have no doubt of her intervention in my life at other periods.

Had I attempted to go South to Rome, I would have fallen into Santino's hands and met with destruction. And what better lure was there than the promise that I might soon meet with Pandora?

Of course my encounter with Raymond Gallant was quite real, and the details of this were vivid within my mind, and Akasha no doubt subtracted these details by virtue of her immense power.

The description of Pandora which I had confided to Bianca was also quite real, and this too might have been known to the Queen had she opened her ears to listen to my distant prayers from Venice.

Whatever the case, from the night we arrived at the shrine I was set upon a course of recovery and of a search for Pandora.

If anyone had told me that both would take some two hundred years, I might have met with despair, but I did not know this. I knew only that I was safe within the shrine, and I had Akasha to protect me, and Bianca to content me.

For well over a year I drank from the fount of the Mother. And for six months of this time, I fed my powerful blood to Bianca.

During those nights, when I could not open the stone door, I saw myself grow more robust in appearance with each divine feast, and I spent the long hours talking in respectful whispers with Bianca.

We took to conserving the oil for the lamps, and the fine candles which I had stored behind the Divine Parents, for we had no inkling of how long it would be before I could open the door and take us to hunting in the distant Alpine towns or cities.

At last there came a night when it occurred to me most strongly to venture out, and I was clever enough to know that this thought had not come to me at random. It had been suggested to me by a series of images. I could open the door now. I could go out. And I could take Bianca with me.

As for my appearance to the mortal world, my skin was coal black, and heavily scarred in places as though from the stroking of a hot poker. But the face I saw in Bianca's mirror was fully formed, with the serene expression that has always been so familiar to me. And my body was strong once more, and my hands of which I am so vain were a scholar's hands with long deft fingers.

For another year, I could not dare to send to Raymond Gallant a letter.

Carrying Bianca with me to far-flung towns, I searched hastily and clumsily for the Evil Doer. As such creatures often run in packs, we would enjoy a gluttonous feast; and then I would take such clothes and gold as needed from the dead; and off we would go to the shrine well before daylight.

I think when I look back on it that ten years at least went by in this fashion. But time is so strange with us, how can I be certain?

What I remember was that a powerful bond existed between me and Bianca that seemed absolutely unshakable. As the years passed, she was as much my companion in silence as she had ever been in conversation.

We moved as one, without argument or consultation.

She was a proud and merciless hunter, dedicated to the majesty of Those Who Must Be Kept, and always drank from more than one human victim whenever possible. Indeed, there seemed no limit to the blood she could imbibe. She wanted strength, both from me and the Evil Doer whom she took with righteous coldness.

Riding the winds in my arms, she turned her eyes to the stars fearlessly. And often she spoke to me softly and easily of her mortal life in Florence, telling me the stories of her youth, and of how she had loved her brothers who had so admired Lorenzo the Magnificent. Yes, she had seen my beloved Botticelli many a time and told me in detail of paintings which I had not seen. She sang songs to me now and then which she composed herself. She spoke in sadness of the death of her brothers and how she had fallen into the power of her evil kinsmen.

I loved listening to her as much as I loved talking to her. Indeed, it was so fluid between us that I still wonder at it.

And though on many a morn, she combed out her lovely hair and replaited it with her ropes of tiny pearls, she never complained of our lot, and wore the cast-off tunics and cloaks of the men we slew as I did.

Now and then, slipping discreetly behind the King and Queen, she took from her precious bundle a gorgeous gown of silk and clothed herself with care in it, this to sleep in my arms, after I had covered her with warm compliments and kisses.

Never had I known such peace with Pandora. Never had I known such warm simplicity.

Yet it was Pandora who filled my mind—Pandora traveling the cities of the North, Pandora with her Asian companion.

At last there came an evening when, after a furious hunt, in exhaustion and satiation, Bianca asked to be returned early to the shrine, and I found myself in possession of a priceless three hours before dawn.

I also found myself in possession of a new measure of strength which I had perhaps unwittingly concealed from her.

To a distant Alpine monastery I went, one which had suffered much due to the recent rise of what scholars call the Protestant Reformation. Here I knew I would find frightened monks who would take my gold and assist me in sending a letter to England.

Entering the empty chapel first, I gathered up every good beeswax candle in the place, these to replenish those of the shrine, and I put all of the candles into a sack which I had brought with me.

I then went to the scriptorium where I found an old monk who was writing very fast by his single candle.

He looked up as soon as he found me standing in his presence.

"Yes," I said at once, speaking his German dialect. "I am a strange man come to you in a strange way, but believe me when I say that I am not evil."

He was gray-haired, tonsured, and wore brown robes, and he was a bit cold in the empty scriptorium. He was utterly fearless as he gazed at me.

But I told myself that I had never looked more human. My skin was as black as that of a Moor and I wore the rather drab gray garments which I had taken from some doomed miscreant.

Now as he continued to stare, quite obviously not in any mood to sound a general alarm, I did my old trick of placing before him a purse of gold coins for the good of the monastery which needed it badly.

"I must write a letter," I said, "and see that it reaches a place in England."

"A Catholic place?" he asked as he looked at me, his gray eyebrows thick and arched as he raised them.

"I should think so," I said with a shrug. Of course I couldn't describe to him the secular nature of the Talamasca.

"Then think again," he said. "For England is no longer Catholic."

"What on earth do you mean?" I asked. "Surely the Reformation has not reached such a place as England."

He laughed. "No, not the Reformation precisely," he said. "Rather the vanity of a King who would divorce his Spanish Catholic wife, and who has denied the power of the Pope to rule against him."

I was so dejected that I sat down on a nearby bench though I'd been given no invitation to do it.

"What are you?" asked the old monk. He laid down his quill pen. He stared at me in the most thoughtful manner.

"It's no matter," I said wearily. "Do you think there's no chance that a letter from here could reach a castle called Lorwich in East Anglia?"

"I don't know," said the monk. "It might well happen. For there are some who oppose King Henry VIII and others who do not. But in general he has destroyed the monasteries of England. And so any letter you write from me cannot go to one of them, only directly to the castle. And how is that to happen? We have to think on it. I can always attempt it."

"Yes, please, let us attempt it."

"But first, tell me what you are," he asked again. "I won't write the letter for you unless you do so. Also I want to know why you stole all the good candles in the chapel and left the bad ones."

"You know I did this?" I asked. I was becoming extremely agitated. I thought I had been silent as a mouse.

"I'm not an ordinary man," he said. "I hear things and see things that people don't. I know you're not human. What are you?"

"I can't tell you," I said. "Tell me what you think I am. Tell me if you can find any true evil in my heart. Tell me what you see in me."

He gazed at me for a long time. His eyes were deeply gray, and as I looked at his elderly face I could easily reconstruct the young man he had been, rather resolute, though his personal strength of character was far greater now even though he suffered human infirmity.

At last he turned away and looked at his candle as though he had completed his examination of me.

"I am a reader of strange books," he said in a hushed but clear voice. "I have studied some of those texts which have come out of Italy pertaining to magic and astrology and things which are often called forbidden."

My pulse quickened. This seemed extraordinary good fortune. I did not interrupt.

"I have a belief that there are angels cast out of Heaven," he said, "and that they do not know what they are any longer. They wander in a state of confusion. You seem one of those creatures, though if I am right, you will not be able to confirm it."

I was so struck by the curiosity of this concept that I could say nothing. At last I had to answer.

"No, I'm not such. I know it for certain. But I wish that I were. Let me confide in you one terrible secret."

"Very well," he said. "You may go to Confession to me if you like, for I am an ordained priest, not simply a monk, but I doubt I shall be able to give you Absolution."

"This is my secret. I have existed since the time when Christ walked the Earth though I never knew of him."

He considered this calmly for a long time, looking into my eyes and then away to his candle, as if this were a little ritual with him. Then he spoke:

"I don't really believe you," he said. "But you are a mystifying being, with your black skin and blue eyes, with your blond hair, and with your gold which you so generously put before me. I'll take it, of course. We need it."

I smiled. I loved him. Of course I wouldn't tell him such a thing. What would it mean to him?

"All right," he said, "I'll write your letter for you."

"I can write it myself," I said, "if only you give me the parchment and the pen. I need for you to send it, and establish this place for the receipt of an answer to it. It's the answer which is so important."

He obeyed me at once, and I turned to the task, gladly accepting the quill from him. I knew he was watching me as I wrote but it didn't matter.

Raymond Gallant,

I have suffered a dreadful catastrophe, following upon the very night which I met with you and talked to you. My palazzo in Venice was destroyed by fire, and I myself injured beyond my own imagining. Please be assured that this was not the work of mortal hands, and some night should we meet I shall most willingly explain to you what happened. In fact, it would give me great satisfaction to describe to you in detail the identity of the one who sent his emissaries to destroy me. As for now, I am far too weakened to attempt vengeance either in words or actions.

I am also too weakened to journey to Lorwich in East Anglia, and thanks to forces which I cannot describe I do have shelter similar to that which you offered me.

But I beg you to tell me if you have had any recent intelligence of my Pandora. I beg you to tell me if she has made herself known to you. I beg you to tell me if you can help me to reach her by letter.

Marius.

Having finished the letter, I gave it over to the priest who promptly added the proper address of the monastery, folded the parchment and sealed it.

We sat in silence for a long moment.

"How shall I find you," he asked, "when an answer reaches here?"

"I'll know," I said, "as you knew when I took the candles. Forgive me for taking them. I should have gone into a city and bought them from a proper merchant. But I have become such a traveler of the sleepy night. I do things far too much at random."

"So I can see," he answered, "for though you began with me in German, you are now speaking Latin in which you wrote your letter. Oh, don't be angry. I didn't read a single word, but I knew it was Latin. Perfect Latin. A Latin such as no one speaks today."

"Is my gold recompense enough?" I asked. I rose from the bench. It was now time for me to be off.

"Oh, yes, and I look forward to your return. I'll see the letter is sent tomorrow. If the Lord of Lorwich in East Anglia has sworn his allegiance to Henry VIII, you'll no doubt have your answer."

I was off so swiftly that to my new friend, it no doubt seemed that I had disappeared.

And as I returned to the shrine, I observed for the first time the beginnings of a human settlement all too close to us.

Of course we were concealed in a tiny valley high upon an ominous cliff. Nevertheless, a small group of huts had caught my eye far below at the foot of the cliff, and I knew what was going to happen.

When I entered the shrine I found Bianca sleeping. No question came from her as to where I had been, and I realized the lengths I had gone to avoid her knowledge of my letter.

I wondered if I might reach England were I to travel the skies alone. But what would I say to her? I had never left her alone and it seemed wrong ever to do so.

Little less than a year went by during which time I passed nightly within hearing distance of the priest to whom I had entrusted my letter.

By this time, Bianca and I had frequently hunted the streets of small Alpine cities in one guise, while buying from their merchants in another.

Now and then we rented rooms for ourselves so that we might enjoy common things, but we were far too fearful to remain anywhere but in the shrine at morning.

All the while, I continued to approach the Queen at intervals. How I chose my moments, I do not know. Perhaps she spoke to me. All I can avow is that I knew when I might drink from her and I did it, and always there came the rapid healing afterwards, the renewal of vigor, and the desire to share my replenished gifts with Bianca.

At last there came a night, when having left a weary Bianca in the shrine once more, I came near to the Alpine monastery and saw my monk standing in the garden with his arms out to the sky in a gesture of such romance and piety that I almost wept to see it.

Softly, without a sound, I entered the cloister behind him.

At once he turned to face me, as if his powers were as great as mine. The wind swept his full brown robes as he came towards me.

"Marius," he said in a whisper. He gestured to me to be quiet, and led me into the scriptorium.

When I saw the thickness of the letter he drew from his desk I was astonished. That it was open, that the seal was broken, gave me pause.

I looked at him.

"Yes, I read it," he said. "Did you think I would give it to you without doing so?"

I couldn't waste any more time. I had to read what was inside the letter. I sat down and unfolded the pages immediately.

Marius,

Let these words not move you to anger or to hasty decision. What I know of Pandora is as follows. She has been seen by those of us who are knowledgeable in such things in the cities of Nuremberg, Vienna, Prague and Gutenberg. She travels in Poland. She travels in Bavaria.

She and her companion are most clever, seldom disturbing the human population through which they move, but from time to time they set foot in the royal courts of certain kingdoms. It is believed by those who have seen them that they take some delight in danger.

Our archives are filled with accounts of a black carriage that travels by day, comporting within two huge enameled chests in which these creatures are presumed to sleep, protected by a small garrison of pale-skinned human guards who are secretive, ruthless and devoted.

Even the most benign or clever approach to these human guards is followed by certain death as some of our members have learnt for themselves when seeking to penetrate the mystery of these dark travelers.

It is the judgment of some among us here that the guards have received a small portion of the power so generously enjoyed by their master and mistress, thus binding them irrevocably to Pandora and her companion.

Our last sighting of the pair was in Poland. However these beings travel very fast and remain in no one place for any given length of time, and indeed seem more than content to move back and forth across the length and breadth of Europe ceaselessly.

They have been known to go back and forth in Spain and to travel throughout France, but never to linger in Paris. As regards this last city, I wonder if you know why they do not stay there long, or if I must be the one to enlighten you.

I shall tell you what I know. In Paris, now, there exists a great dedicated group of the species which we both understand, indeed, so large a group that one must doubt that even Paris can content them. And having received into our arms one desperate infidel from this group we have learnt much of how these unusual Parisian creatures characterize themselves.

I cannot commit to parchment what I know of them. Let me only say that they are possessed of a surprising zeal, believing themselves to serve God Himself with their strenuous appetite. And should others of the same ilk venture into their domain they do not hesitate to destroy them, declaring them to be blasphemers.

This infidel of which I speak has averred more than once that his brothers and sisters were among those who participated in your great loss and injury. Only you can confirm this for me, as I do not know what is madness here or boasting, or perhaps a blending of the two, and you can well imagine how confounded we are to have one so loquacious and hostile beneath our roof, so eager to answer questions and so frightened to be left unguarded.

Let me also add that piece of intelligence which may matter to you as much now as any which I have pertaining to your lost Pandora.

He who guides this voracious and mysterious band of Paris creatures is none other than your young companion from Venice.

Won over by discipline, fasting, penance and the loss of his former Master—so says this young infidel—your old companion has proved to be a leader of immeasurable strength and well capable of driving out any of his kind who seek to gain a foothold in Paris.

Would that I could tell you more of these creatures. Allow me to repeat what I have suggested above. They believe themselves to be in the service of Almighty God. And from this principle, a considerable number of rules follow.

Marius, I cannot imagine how this information will affect you. I write here only that of which I am most certain.

Now, allow me to play an unusual role, given our respective ages.

Whatever your response to my revelations here, under no circumstances travel overland North to see me. Under no circumstances travel overland North to find Pandora. Under no circumstances travel overland North to find your young companion.

I caution you on all these accounts for two reasons. There are at this time, as you must surely know, wars all over Europe. Martin Luther has fomented much unrest. And in England, our sovereign Henry VIII has declared himself independent of Rome, in spite of much resistance.

Of course we at Lorwich are loyal to our King and his decisions earn only our respect and honor.

But it is no time to be traveling in Europe.

And allow me to warn you on another account which may surprise you. Throughout Europe now there are those who are willing to persecute others for witchcraft on slender reasons; that is, a superstition regarding witches reigns in villages and towns, which even one hundred years ago would have been dismissed as ridiculous.

You cannot allow yourself to travel overland through such places. Writings as to wizards, Sabbats and Devil worship cloud human philosophy.

And yes, I do fear for Pandora that she and her companion take no seeming notice of these dangers, but it has been communicated to us many times that though she travels overland, she travels very swiftly. Her servants have been known to purchase fresh horses twice or three times within a day, demanding only that the animals be of the finest quality.

Marius, I send you my deepest good wishes. Please write to me again as soon as possible. There are so many questions I wish to ask you. I dare not do so in this letter. I do not know if I dare at all. Let me only express the wish and hope for your invitation.

I must confess to you that I am the envy of my brothers and sisters that I have received your communication. I shall not let my head be turned by this. I am in awe of you and with justification.

Yours in the Talamasca,
Raymond Gallant.

At last I sat back on the bench, the many sheaves of parchment trembling in my left hand, and I shook my head, hardly knowing what I might say to myself, for my thoughts were all a brew.

Indeed, since the night of the disaster in Venice, I had frequently been at a loss for private words, and never did I know it as keenly as now.

I looked down at the pages. My right fingers touched various words, and then I drew back, shaking my head again.

Pandora, circling Europe, within my grasp but perhaps eternally beyond it.

And Amadeo, won over to the creed of Santino and sent to establish it in Paris! Oh, yes, I could envision it.

There came back to me once more the vivid image of Santino that night in Rome, in his black robes, his hair so vainly clean as he approached me and pressed me to come with him to his wretched catacomb.

And here lay the proof now that he had not destroyed my beautiful child, rather he had made of him a victim. He had won him over; he had taken Amadeo to himself! He had more utterly defeated me than ever I had dreamt.

And Amadeo, my blessed and beautiful pupil, had gone from my uncertain tutelage to that perpetual gloom. And yes, oh, yes, I could imagine it. Ashes. I tasted ashes.

A cold shudder ran through me.

I crushed the pages to myself.

Then quite suddenly I became aware that, beside me sat the gray-haired priest, looking at me, very calm as he leaned on his left elbow.

Again I shook my head. I folded the pages of the letter to make of them a packet that I might carry with me.

I looked into his gray eyes.

"Why don't you run from me?" I asked. I was bitter and wanted to weep but this was no place for it.

"You're in my debt," he said softly. "Tell me what you are, if only so that I may know if I've lost my soul by serving you."

"You haven't lost your soul," I said quickly, my wretchedness too plain in my voice. "Your soul has nothing to do with me." I took a deep breath. "What did you make of what you read in my letter?"

"You're suffering," he said, "rather like a mortal man, but you aren't mortal. And this one in England, he is mortal, but he isn't afraid of you."

"This is true," I said. "I suffer, and I suffer for one has done me wrong and I have no vengeance nor justice. But let's not speak of such things. I would be alone now."

A silence fell between us. It was time for me to go but I had not the strength quite yet to do it.

Had I given him the usual purse? I must do it now. I reached inside my tunic and brought it out. I laid it down, and spilled the golden coins so that I might see them in the light of the candle.

Some vague and heated thoughts formed in my mind to do with

Amadeo and the brilliance of this gold and of how angry I was, and of how I seethed for vengeance against Santino. I saw ikons with their halos of gold; I saw the coin of the Talamasca made of gold. I saw the golden florins of Florence.

I saw the golden bracelets once worn by Pandora on her beautiful naked arms. I saw the golden bracelets which I had put upon the arms of Akasha.

Gold and gold and gold.

And Amadeo had chosen ashes!

Well, I shall find Pandora once more, I thought. I shall find her! And only if she swears against me will I let her go, will I let her remain with this mysterious companion. Oh, I trembled as I thought of it, as I vowed, as I whispered these wordless thoughts.

Pandora, yes! And some night, for Amadeo, there would be the reckoning with Santino!

A long silence ensued.

The priest beside me was not frightened. I wondered if he could possibly guess how grateful I was that he allowed me to remain there in such precious stillness.

At last, I ran my left fingers over the golden coins.

"Is there enough there for flowers?" I asked, "flowers and trees and beautiful plants in your garden?"

"There is enough there to endow our gardens forever," he answered.

"Ah forever!" I said. "I have such a love of that word, forever."

"Yes, it is a timeless word," he said, raising his mossy eyebrows as he looked at me. "Time is ours, but forever belongs to God, don't you think?"

"Yes, I do," I said. I turned to face him. I smiled at him, and I saw the warm impression of this on him just as if I'd spoken kind words to him. He couldn't conceal it.

"You've been good to me," I said.

"Will you write to your friend again?" he asked.

"Not from here," I answered. "It's too dangerous for me. From some other place. And I beg you, forget these things."

He laughed in the most honest and simple way. "Forget!" he said.

I rose to go.

"You shouldn't have read the letter," I said. "It can only cause you worry."

"I had to do it," he answered. "Before I gave it to you."

"I cannot imagine why," I answered. I walked quietly towards the door of the scriptorium.

He came beside me.

"And so you go then, Marius?" he asked.

I turned around. I lifted my hand in farewell.

"Yes, neither angel nor devil, I go," I said, "neither good nor bad. And I thank you."

As I had before, I went from him so swiftly he couldn't see it, and very soon I was alone with the stars, and staring down on that valley all too near to the chapel where a city was forming at the foot of my high cliff which had been neglected by all mankind for over a millennium.

29

I WAITED A LONG TIME before showing the letter to Bianca.
I never really concealed it from her, for I thought such a thing
was dishonest. But as she did not ask me the meaning of the pages
which I kept with my few personal belongings, I did not explain them
to her.

It was too painful for me to share my sorrow with regard to
Amadeo. And as for the existence of the Talamasca, it was too bizarre a
tale, and too fully interwoven with my love for Pandora.

But I did leave Bianca alone in the shrine more and more often.
Never of course did I abandon her there in the early part of the
evening when she depended upon me totally to reach those places
where we might hunt. On the contrary, I always took her with me.

It was later in the night—after we had fed—that I would return her
to safety and go off alone, testing the limits of my powers.

All the while a strange thing was happening to me. As I drank from
the Mother my vigor increased. But I also learned what all injured
blood drinkers learn—that in healing I was becoming stronger than I
had been before my injury.

Of course I gave Bianca my own blood, but as I grew ever stronger
the gap between us became very great and I saw it widening.

There were times, of course, when I put the question in my prayers
as to whether Akasha would receive Bianca. But it seemed that the
answer was no, and so in fear I didn't dare to test it.

I remembered only too well the death of Eudoxia, and I also
remembered the moment when Enkil had lifted his arm against Mael. I
could not subject Bianca to possible injury.

Within a short time, I was easily able to take Bianca with me through the night to the nearby cities of Prague and Geneva, and there we indulged ourselves with some vision of the civilization we had once known in Venice.

As for that beautiful capital, I would not return to it, no matter how much Bianca implored me. Of course she possessed nothing of the Cloud Gift herself, and was dependent upon me in a manner which neither Amadeo nor Pandora had ever been.

"It is too painful to me," I declared. "I will not go there. You've lived here so long as my beautiful nun. What is it you want?"

"I want Italy," she said in a soft crestfallen voice. And I knew only too well what she meant, but I didn't answer her.

"If I cannot have Italy, Marius," she said at last, "I must have somewhere."

She was in the front corner of the shrine when she spoke these all too significant words, and they were in a hushed voice, as if she sensed a danger.

We were always reverent in the shrine. But we did not whisper behind the Divine Parents. We considered it ill-mannered if not downright disrespectful.

It's a strange thing when I think of it. But we could not presume that Akasha and Enkil did not hear us. And therefore we often spoke in the front corner, especially the one to the left, which Bianca favored, often sitting there with her warmest cloak about her.

When she said these words to me, she looked up at the Queen as though acknowledging the interpretation.

"Let it be her wish," she said, "that we not pollute her shrine with our idleness."

I nodded. What else could I do? Yet so many years had passed in this fashion that I had grown accustomed to this place over any other. And Bianca's quiet loyalty to me was something I took for granted.

I sat down beside her now.

I took her hand in mine, and noticed perhaps for the first time in some while that my skin was now darkly bronzed rather than black, and most of the wrinkles had faded.

"Let me make a confession to you," I said. "We cannot live in some simple house as we did in Venice."

She listened to me with quiet eyes.

I went on.

"I fear those creatures, Santino and his demon spawn. Decades have passed since the fire, but they still threaten from their hiding places."

"How do you know this?" she said. It seemed she had a great deal more to say to me. But I asked for her patience.

I went to my belongings and took from them the letter from Raymond Gallant.

"Read this," I said. "It will tell you, among other things, that they have spread their abominable ways as far as the city of Paris."

For a long time I remained silent as she read, and then her immediate sobs startled me. How many times had I seen Bianca cry? Why was I so unprepared for it? She whispered Amadeo's name. She couldn't quite bring herself to speak of it.

"What does this mean?" she said. "How do they live? Explain these words. What did they do to him?"

I sat beside her, begging her to be calm, and then I told her how they lived, these Satan worshiping fiends, as monks or hermits, tasting the earth and death, and how they imagined that the Christian God had made some place for them in his Kingdom.

"They starved our Amadeo," I said, "they tortured him. This is plain here. And when he had given up all hope, believing me to be dead, and believing their piety to be just, he became one of them."

She looked at me solemnly, the tears standing in her eyes.

"Oh, how often I've seen you cry," I said. "But not of late, and not so bitterly as you cry for him. Be assured I have not forgotten him either."

She shook her head as if her thoughts were not in accord with mine but she was not able to reveal them.

"We must be clever, my precious one," I said. "Whatever abode we choose for ourselves, we must be safe from them, always."

Almost dismissively she spoke now.

"We can find a safe place," she said. "You know we can. We must. We cannot remain as we are forever. It is not our nature. If I have learnt nothing from your stories I have learnt that much, that you have wandered the Earth in search of beauty as well as in your search for blood."

I did not like her seriousness.

"We are only two," she went on, "and should these devils come again with their fiery brands, it will be a simple thing for you to remove me to some lofty height where they can't harm me."

"If I am there, my love, if I am there," I said, "and what if I am not? All these years, since we have left our lovely Venice behind, you have lived within these walls where they can't harm you. Now, should we go to some other place, and lodge there, I shall have to be on guard always. Is that natural?"

This felt dreadful to me, this talk. I had never known anything so difficult with her. I didn't like the inscrutable expression on her face, nor the way her hand trembled.

"Perhaps it is too soon," she said. "But I must tell you a most important thing, and I cannot keep it from you."

I hesitated before I answered.

"What is it, Bianca?" I asked. I was fast becoming miserable. Utterly miserable.

"I think you have made a grievous error," she said.

I was quietly stunned. She said nothing more. I waited. Still there came this silence commingled with her sitting back against the wall, her eyes fixed upwards on the Divine Parents.

"Will you tell me what this error is?" I asked. "By all means, you must tell me! I love you. I must hear this."

She said nothing. She looked at the King and Queen. She did not appear to be praying.

I picked up the parchment pages of the letter. I moved through them and then looked at her again.

Her tears had dried, and her mouth was soft, but her eyes were filled with some strange look that I could not explain to myself.

"Is it the Talamasca that causes you fear?" I asked. "I shall explain all this to you. But see here that I wrote to them from a distant monastery. I left few footprints there, my beauty. I traveled the winds while you were sleeping here."

There followed nothing but her silence. It seemed not dark or cold but merely reserved and thoughtful. But when she moved her eyes to me, the change in her face was slow and ominous.

With quiet words I hastened to explain to her my strange meeting with Raymond Gallant on my last night of true happiness in Venice. I explained in the simplest manner how he had sought knowledge of us, and how I had learnt from him that Pandora had been seen in northern Europe.

I talked of all the things contained in the letter. I talked of Amadeo once more. I spoke of my hatred of Santino, that he had robbed me of all I loved save her, and how on that account she was, of all things, most precious to me.

At last I was willing to say no more. I was growing angry. I felt wronged and I couldn't understand her. Her silence hurt me more and more, and I knew that she could see this in my face.

Finally, I saw some change in her. She sharpened her gaze and then she spoke:

"Don't you see the grievous error you've made?" she asked. "Don't you hear it in the lessons you've made known to me? Centuries ago, the young Satan worshipers came to you for what you could give when you lived with Pandora. You denied them your precious knowledge. You should have revealed to them the mystery of the Mother and the Father!"

"Good Lord, how could you believe such a thing?"

"And when Santino asked you in Rome, you should have brought him to this very shrine! You should have shown to him the mysteries you revealed to me. Had you done it, Marius, he would never have been your enemy."

I was enraged as I stared at her. Was this my brilliant Bianca?

"Don't you see!" she went on. "Over and over, these unstoppable fools have made a cult of nothing! You could have shown them something!" She gestured towards me dismissively as though I disgusted her. "How many decades have we been here? How strong am I? Oh, you needn't answer. I know my own endurance. I know my own temper.

"But don't you see, all my understanding of our powers is reinforced by their beauty and their majesty! I know whence we come! I have seen you drink from the Queen. I have seen you wake from your swoon. I have seen your skin healing.

"But what did Amadeo ever see? What did Santino ever see? And you marvel at the extent of their heresy."

"Don't call it heresy!" I declared suddenly, the words bursting from my lips. "Don't speak as if this were a worship! I have told you that yes, there are secret things, and things which no one can explain! But we are not worshipers!"

"It is a truth you revealed to me," she said, "in their paradox, in their presence!" Her voice rose, ill-tempered and utterly alien to her. "You might have smashed Santino's ill-founded crusade with a mere glimpse of the Divine Parents."

I glared at her. A madness took hold of me.

I rose to my feet. I looked about the shrine furiously.

"Gather up all you possess," I said suddenly. "I'm casting you out of here!"

She sat still as she had been before, gazing up at me in cold defiance.

"You heard what I said. Gather your precious clothes, your looking glass, your pearls, your jewels, your books, whatever you want. I'm taking you out of here."

For a long moment she looked at me, glowering, I should say, as if she didn't believe me.

Then all at once she moved, obeying me in a series of quick gestures. And within the space of a few moments, she stood before me, her cloak about her, her bundle clasped to her chest, looking as she had some countless years before when first I had brought her here.

I don't know whether she looked back at the face of the Mother and the Father. I did not. I did not for one moment believe that either would prevent this dreadful expulsion.

Within moments, I was on the wind, and I didn't know where I would take her.

I traveled higher and faster than I had dared to do before, and found it well within my power. Indeed, my own speed amazed me. The land before me had been burnt in recent wars and I knew it to be spotted here and there with ruined castles.

It was to one of these that I took her, making certain that the town all around had been pillaged and deserted, and then I set her down in a stone room within the broken fortress, and went in search of a place where she might sleep by day in the ruined graveyard.

It did not take me long to be confident that she could survive here. In the burnt-out chapel there were crypts beneath the floor. There were hiding places everywhere.

I went back to her. She was standing as I had left her, her face as solemn as before, her brilliant oval eyes fixed on me.

"I want no more of you," I said. I was shuddering. "I want no more of you that you could say such a thing, that you could blame me that Santino took from me my child! I can have no more of you. You have no grasp of the burden I have carried throughout time or how many times I have lamented it! What do you think your precious Santino would do had he the Mother and the Father in his possession? How many demons could he bring to drink from them? And who knows what the Mother and Father might permit in their silence? Who knows what they have ever wanted?"

"You are an evil and negligent brother to me," she said coldly, glancing about herself. "Why not leave me to the wolves in the forest? But go. I want no more of you either. Tell your scholars in the Talamasca where you have deposited me and perhaps they will offer me their kind shelter. But be gone. Whatever, be gone! I don't want you here!"

Though up to that second I had been hanging upon her every word, I abandoned her.

Hours passed. I traveled the skies, not knowing where I went, marveling at the blurred landscape beneath me.

My power was far greater than it had ever been! Would I to try it, I could easily reach England.

I saw the mountains and then the sea, and then suddenly my soul ached so completely that I could do nothing but will myself to go back to her.

Bianca, what have I done?

Bianca, pray that you have waited for me!

Out of the deep dark heavens I somehow returned to her. I found her in the stone room, sitting in the corner, collected and still, just as if she had been in the shrine, and as I knelt before her, she reached up and threw her arms about me.

I sobbed as I embraced her.

"My beautiful Bianca, my beautiful one, I am so sorry, so sorry, my love," I said.

"Marius, I love you with my whole heart eternally." She cried as freely and completely as I did. "My precious Marius," she said. "I have never loved anyone as I love you. Forgive me."

We could do nothing but weep for the longest time and then I took her home to the shrine, and comforted her, combing her hair as I so loved to do and trimming it with her slender ropes of pearls until she was my perfect lovely one.

"What did I mean to say?" she implored. "I don't know. Of course you could not have trusted any of them. And had you shown them the Queen and the King some horrid anarchy might well have come from it!"

"Yes, you have said the perfect word," I answered, "some awful anarchy." I glanced quickly at the still impassive faces. I went on. "You must understand, oh, please, if you love me at all, understand what power exists within them." I stopped suddenly. "Oh, don't you see, as much as I lament their silence, perhaps it is for them a form of peace which they have chosen for the good of everyone."

This was the very essence of it and I think we both knew it.

I feared what might happen if Akasha were ever to stand up from her throne, if she were ever to speak or move. I feared it with all my reason.

Yet still, that night and every night I believed that if and when Akasha were ever waked, a divine sweetness would pour forth from her.

Once Bianca had fallen asleep, I knelt before the Queen in the abject manner which was so common to me now, and which I would never have revealed to Pandora.

"Mother, I hunger for you," I whispered. I opened my hands. "Let me touch you with love," I said. "Tell me if I have been in error. Should I have brought the Satan worshipers to your shrine? Should I have revealed you in all your loveliness to Santino?"

I closed my eyes. I opened them.

"Unchangeable Ones," I said in a soft voice, "speak to me."

I approached her and laid my lips on her throat. I pierced the crisp white skin with my teeth, and the thick blood came into me slowly.

The garden surrounded me. Oh, yes, this I love above all. And it was the garden of the monastery in spring, how wondrous, and my priest was there. I was walking with him in the clean swept cloister. This was the supreme dream, for its colors were rich and I could see all the mountains around us. *I am immortal*, I said.

The garden dissolved. I could see colors washed from a wall.

Then I stood in a midnight forest. In the light of the moon, I beheld a black carriage coming down the road, drawn by many dark horses. It passed me, its huge wheels stirring up the dust. There came behind it a team of guards all clothed in black livery.

Pandora.

When I woke, I was lying against Akasha's breast, my forehead against her throat, my left hand clasping her right shoulder. It was so sweet that I didn't want to move, and all the light of the shrine had become one golden shimmer in my eyes, rather the way that light would become in those long Venetian banquet rooms.

At last I kissed her tenderly and withdrew and then lay down and placed my arms around Bianca.

My thoughts were troubled and strange. I knew it was time to find some habitat other than the shrine itself, and I knew as well that strangers were coming into our mountains.

The small city at the foot of our cliff was now thriving.

But the most dreadful revelation of this night was that Bianca and I could quarrel, that the solid peace between us could be violently and painfully ruptured. And that I, at the first hard words from my jewel, could crumple into mental ruin.

Why had I been so surprised? Could I not remember my painful quarrels with Pandora? I must know that in anger, Marius is not Marius. I must know and never forget it.

30

THE FOLLOWING NIGHT we hunted down a pair of brigands who were traveling the lower passes of our mountains. The blood was good, and from this small feast we went on to a little German town where we could find a tavern.

Here we sat, a man and his wife, one might presume, and over our mulled wine we talked for hours.

I told Bianca all I had ever known of Those Who Must Be Kept. I told her the legends of Egypt—of how the Mother and Father had centuries ago been bound and ill used by those who would steal their Precious Blood. I told her of how Akasha herself had come to me in a vision begging me to take her out of Egypt.

I told her of the few times Akasha had ever spoken to me in the Blood. And I told her finally, finally, of what a pure miracle it had been that the Divine Parents had opened the door of the Alpine shrine when I had come to them too weak to budge it.

"Do they need me?" I asked. I looked into Bianca's eyes. "I can't know. That's the horror. Do they want to be seen by others? I am in ignorance.

"But let me make my final confession. I became so angry last night because centuries ago when Pandora first drank the Mother's blood, she was full of dreams of bringing back to the Divine Parents the old worship. By that I mean, a worship that included the Druidic Gods of the Grove, a religion that went back to the temples of Egypt.

"I was furious that Pandora could believe in such a thing, and on the very night of Pandora's making I broke her dreams with my forceful logic. And I went beyond that. I pounded with my fist upon the Mother's very breast and demanded that she speak to us."

Bianca was amazed.

"Can you guess what happened?" I asked.

"Nothing. The Mother gave no answer."

I nodded. "And there came no rebuke or punishment either. Perhaps the Mother had brought Pandora to me. We could never know. But please understand how I fear the very notion that the Divine Parents might ever be worshiped.

"Bianca, we are immortals, yes, and we possess our King and Queen, but we must never for a moment believe that we understand them."

To all this she nodded. She weighed it all for a long time and then she spoke:

"I was very simply wrong in what I said to you," she told me.

"Not in all of it," I answered. "Perhaps if Amadeo had seen the King and Queen, he would have escaped the Roman blood drinkers and come back to us. Yet there is another way of looking at it."

"Tell me."

"If he had known the secret of the Mother and the Father, he might have been forced to reveal it to Santino, and the demons would have returned to Venice, searching for me. They might have found both of us."

"Ah, yes, all this is true," she said. "I begin to see all of it."

We were easy now with each other in the tavern. The mortals around us took no notice. I talked on in a soft voice, telling her the story of how Mael had once tried, with my permission, to drink Akasha's blood and Enkil had moved to stop him.

I told her the dreadful tale of Eudoxia. I told her of how I had left Constantinople.

"I don't know what it is with you, my love," I said, "but somehow I can tell you everything. It was never so with Pandora. It was never so with Amadeo."

She reached out and put her left hand on my cheek.

"Marius," she said. "Speak freely always of Pandora. Don't ever think that I shall fail to understand your love for Pandora."

I thought this over for many long moments. I took her right hand in mine and I kissed her fingers.

"Listen to me, my love," I said. "With every prayer, I ask the Queen if you might drink. But I gain no clear answer. And after what I witnessed with Eudoxia and Mael, I cannot take you to her. And so I shall continue to give you my blood in so far as it will make you strong, but—."

"I understand you," she said.

I leant across the table and kissed her.

"Last night in my anger I learnt many things. That I cannot live without you was one. But I learnt another. I can now cover great distances with ease. And I suspect my other powers have also increased beyond recent measure. I must test these powers. I must know how easily I can defeat those demons if ever they come near to me. And tonight I want to test my power of flight more than any other."

"And so you are telling me that you want to take me back to the shrine now, and go off to England."

I nodded. "The moon is full tonight, Bianca. I must see the isle of Britain in the light of the moon. I must discover this Order of the Talamasca with my own eyes. It's scarcely possible to believe in such purity."

"Why don't you take me with you?"

"I must be swift," I answered. "And if there's danger I must be swifter still to escape it. These are mortals after all. And Raymond Gallant is only one of them."

"You will be careful then, my love," she said. "You know now more than ever that I very simply adore you."

It seemed then we would never quarrel again, that such a thing was impossible. And it seemed imperative that I never lose her.

As we went out into the darkness, as I wrapped her in my cloak, I pressed my lips to her forehead as I took her into the clouds and homeward.

When I left her, it was two hours before midnight, and I meant to see Raymond Gallant before morning.

Now, it had been many years since my meeting with him in Venice. He had been a young man then, and perhaps middle-aged at the time that I wrote my letter to him.

So it did occur to me as I set out on my journey that he might no longer be living.

Indeed, it was a terrible thought.

But I believed in all he had told me about the Talamasca and so I was determined to approach them.

As I moved towards the stars, the pleasure of the Cloud Gift was so divine that I almost lost myself in the rapture of the skies, dreaming above the isle of Britain, plunging to where I could see the land perfectly against the sea, not wanting to touch the solid Earth so soon or roam it so clumsily.

But I had consulted many a map in recent years to find the location of East Anglia, and I soon saw below me an immense castle with ten rounded towers which I believed to be the very one engraved upon the gold coin which Raymond Gallant had long ago given me.

The sheer size of the castle gave me doubts, however, but I willed myself to set foot on the steep hillside quite close to it. Some deep preternatural instinct told me that I had reached the right place.

The air was cold as I began to walk, indeed as cold as it had been in the mountains which I had left behind me. Some of the woods had come back, which had no doubt been cut down once upon a time for the safety of the castle, and I rather liked the terrain and I enjoyed walking in it.

I wore a full fur-lined cloak which I had taken from one of my victims. I had my customary weapons, a thick short broadsword, and a dagger. I wore a longer velvet tunic than was favored at the time, but this did not matter to me. My shoes were new and I had bought them from a cobbler in Geneva.

As for the style of the castle, I figured it to be some five hundred years old, built in the time of William the Conqueror. I surmised that it had once had a moat and drawbridge. But these elements had long been abandoned, and I could see a great door before me, flanked by torches.

At last I reached this door, and pulled the bell, hearing a loud clang deep within the courtyard.

It did not take long for someone to come, and only then did I realize the curious propriety of what I'd done. In my reverence for this Order of Scholars I had not "listened" outside to discover who they were. I had not hovered near their lighted tower windows.

And now I found myself, a curious figure no doubt with my blue eyes and dark skin, standing before the porter.

This young man couldn't have been more than seventeen, and he seemed both sleepy and indifferent as though my clarion had awakened him.

"I've come in search of Lorwich," I said, "in East Anglia. Have I reached the right place?"

"You have," said the boy, wiping at his eyes and leaning upon the door. "Can I say for what reason?"

"I seek the Talamasca," I replied.

The young man nodded. He opened the door widely, and I soon found myself in a great courtyard. There were wagons and coaches parked within. I could hear the faint sound of the horses in the stables.

"I seek Raymond Gallant," I said to the boy.

"Ah," he replied, as if these were the magic words that he needed from me. And then he led me further inside and shut the giant wood door behind us. "I'll take you where you might wait," he said. "I think that Raymond Gallant is sleeping."

But he's alive, I thought. That's what matters. I caught the scent of many mortals in this place. I caught the scent of food that had recently been cooked. I caught the scent of oak fires and as I looked up I saw the faint smoke of chimneys against the sky which I had not perceived earlier.

With no further questioning, I was soon led by torchlight up a winding stone stairway in one of the many towers. Over and over again I looked out of small windows at the bleak land. I saw the dim outline of a nearby town. I could see the patches of the farmers' fields. All looked so very peaceful.

At last the boy anchored his torch, and, lighting a candle from it, opened two heavily carved doors to reveal a huge room with sparse but beautiful furnishings.

It had been a long time since I had seen heavily carved tables and chairs, and fine tapestries. It had been a long time since I had seen rich golden candlesticks and handsome chests with velvet draperies.

It all seemed a feast for the eyes, and I was about to sit down when there came rushing into the room a spry elderly man with streaming gray hair in a long heavy white nightshirt who gazed at me with brilliant gray eyes, crying out:

"Marius!"

It was Raymond Gallant, it was Raymond in his final years, and I felt a terrible shock of pleasure and pain as I looked at him.

"Raymond," I said, and I opened my arms, and gently enfolded him. How frail he felt. I kissed him on both cheeks. I held him back tenderly that I might look at him.

His hair was still thick and his forehead smooth as it had been so long ago. And when he smiled, his mouth seemed that of the young man I remembered.

"Marius, what a wonder it is to see you," he cried. "Why did you never write to me again?"

"Raymond, I've come. I can't account for time and what it means to us. I've come, and I'm here, and I'm glad to be with you."

He stopped, turning from right to left suddenly and then he cocked his head. He seemed as agile and quick as he had ever been. He was listening.

"They're all aware that you're here," he said, "but don't worry. They won't dare to come into this room. They're far too disciplined for that. They know I will not permit it."

I listened for a moment, and I confirmed what he had said. Mortals throughout the immense sprawling castle had sensed my presence. There were mind readers among these mortals. Others seemed to possess some keen hearing.

But I distinguished no supernatural presence here. I caught no inkling of the "infidel" he had described in his letter.

And I caught no menace from anyone either. Nevertheless, I marked the nearby window, and noting that it was heavily barred though otherwise open to the night, wondered if I could easily break through it. I thought that I could. I felt no fear. In fact, I felt no fear of this Talamasca because it seemed to feel no fear of me and had admitted me so guilelessly.

"Come, sit down with me, Marius," Raymond said. He drew me near to an immense fireplace. I tried not to gaze with concern at his thin palsied hands, or his thin shoulders. I thanked the gods that I had come tonight, and that he was still here to greet me.

He called out to the sleepy boy who remained still at the door.

"Edgar, build the fire and light it, please. Marius, you will forgive me," he said. "I'm very cold. Do you mind it? I understand what happened to you."

"No, not at all, Raymond," I said. "I can't fear fire forever on that account. Not only am I healed now, I'm stronger than ever I was before. It's quite a mystery. And you, how old are you? Tell me, Raymond. I can't guess it."

"Eighty years, Marius," he said. He smiled. "You don't know how I've dreamed of your coming. I had so much more to tell you. I didn't dare to write it in a letter."

"And rightly so," I said, "for the letter was read, and who knows what might have happened? As it was, the priest who received it for me could not make much of it. I understand everything, however."

He motioned to the door. Two young men at once entered the

room, and I made them out to be the simple sort rather like the busy Edgar who was piling up the oak in the fireplace. There were richly carved stone gargoyles above the fire. I rather liked them.

"Two chairs," said Raymond to the boys. "We'll talk together. I'll tell you all I can."

"Why are you so generous to me, Raymond?" I asked. I wanted so to comfort him, to stop his agitation. But as he smiled at me, as if to reassure me, as he put his hand gently on my arm, and urged me towards the two wooden chairs which the boys had brought to the hearth, I saw that he did not need my comfort.

"I'm only very excited, my old friend," he said. "You mustn't be concerned for me. Here, sit down. Is this comfortable enough for you?"

The chairs were as heavily carved as every bit of ornament in the room, and the arms were the paws of lions. I found them beautiful as well as comfortable. I looked about myself at the many bookshelves, and mused as I have often done on how all libraries subdue me and seduce me. I thought of books burnt and books lost.

May this be a safe place for books, I thought, this Talamasca.

"I have been decades in a stone room," I said in a muted voice. "I am quite comfortable. Will you send the boys away now?"

"Yes, yes, of course, only let them bring me some warm wine," he replied. "I need it."

"Please, how could I be so inconsiderate?" I replied.

We were now facing each other, and the fire had begun with a riot of deep good fragrance coming from the burning oak, and a warmth that I even enjoyed, I had to admit it.

One of the boys had brought Raymond a red velvet dressing gown, and once he was clothed in this, and settled in his chair, he did not seem so fragile. His face was radiant after all, his cheeks actually rosy, and I could easily see the young man in him that I had once known.

"My friend, should anything come between us," he said, "let me give you to know that *she* still travels in her old way, rapidly through many European cities. Never to England, for I don't think they want to cross the water, though no doubt they can, contrary to folklore."

I laughed. "Is that the folklore? That we can't cross water? It's nonsense," I said. I would have said more, but I wondered if it were wise.

He apparently took no note of my hesitation. He plunged on:

"She has for the last few decades traveled under the name of the Marquisa De Malvrier, and her companion the Marquis of the same name, though it is she who goes to Court more often than he does. They're seen in Russia, in Bavaria, in Saxony—in countries in which old ceremony is honored, seeming from time to time to need the courtly balls and the immense Roman church ceremonies. But understand, I have gleaned my account of this from many different reports. I'm sure of nothing."

The warm wine was being set upon a small stand beside him. He took the cup in his hands. His hands were shaking. He drank from the wine.

"But how do such reports come to you?" I asked. I was fascinated. There was no doubt he was telling me the truth. As for the rest of the house, I could hear its many inhabitants all around us, waiting in silence it seemed for some kind of summons.

"Forget them," he said. "What can they learn from this audience?" he asked. "They are all faithful members. To answer your questions, we go out sometimes in the guise of priests seeking information about those whom we call vampires. We inquire as to mysterious deaths. And so we gather information which is meaningful to us when it may not be meaningful to others."

"Ah, of course. And you take note of the name when it is mentioned in Russia or Saxony or Bavaria."

"Exactly. I tell you it is De Malvrier. They have a liking for it. And I shall tell you something else."

"Please, you must."

"Several times we have found upon the wall of a church inscribed the name, Pandora."

"Ah, she's done this," I said, desperately trying to conceal my emotion. "She wants to be discovered by me." I paused. "This is painful for me," I said. "I wonder if the one who travels with her even knows her by that name. Ah, this is painful, but why do you assist me?"

"By my very life, I don't know," he said, "except somehow I believe in you."

"What do you mean believe, believe that I'm a wonder? That I'm a demon? Believe what, Raymond, tell me? Oh, never mind, it doesn't matter, does it? We do things because our hearts impel us."

"Marius, my friend," he said, leaning forward and touching my knee with his right hand, "long ago in Venice when I spied upon you, you know that I spoke to you with the purity of my mind. I read your thoughts also. I knew that you slew only those who were the degraded killers of their own sisters or brothers."

"That's true, Raymond, and it was that way with Pandora. But is it now?"

"Yes, I think so," he said, "for every ghastly crime imputed to the vampires whom these creatures may in fact be is connected to one who was known to be guilty of many murders. So you see it's not difficult for me to help you."

"Ah, so she is true to our vow," I whispered. "I didn't think so, not when I heard of her harsh companion."

I looked intently at Raymond, seeing with every passing moment more of the young man I had once known so briefly. It was saddening to me. It was dreadful. And the more I felt it, the more I tried to conceal it.

What was my suffering to this, the slow triumph of old age? Nothing.

"Where was she seen last?" I asked.

"On that point," he said, "allow me to give you my interpretation of her behavior. She and her companion follow a pattern in their roamings. They go in rude circles, returning over and over again to one city. Once they have been some time in that city they begin their circles once more until they have gone as far afield as Russia. The central city of which I speak is Dresden."

"Dresden!" I said. "I don't know the place. I've never been there."

"Oh, it cannot rival your gorgeous Italian cities. It cannot equal Paris or London. But it is the capital of Saxony and it lies on the Elbe River. It has been much adorned by the various Dukes who have ruled there. And invariably, I say invariably, these creatures—Pandora and her companion—return to Dresden. It may not be for twenty years, but they come back to Dresden."

I fell silent in my excitement. Was this some pattern meant for me to interpret? Was this pattern meant for me to discover? Was it like a great round spiderweb meant sooner or later to ensnare me?

Why else would Pandora and her companion follow such a life? I couldn't imagine it. But how did I dare to think Pandora even remembered me. She had written her name in the stone of the church wall, not mine.

At last I heaved a great sigh.

"How can I tell you what all this means to me?" I asked. "You have given me marvelous news. I'll find her."

"Now," he said in the most confident manner, "shall we take up the other matter which I mentioned to you in my letter?"

"Amadeo," I whispered. "What happened to the infidel? I sense no blood drinker in this place. Am I deceived? The creature's either very far afield or he's left you."

"The monster left us soon after I wrote to you. When he realized he could hunt for his victims throughout the countryside, he was gone. We could do nothing to control him. Our appeals to him that he feed only on evil men meant nothing to him. I don't even know if he still exists."

"You must guard yourselves against this individual," I said. I looked about myself at the spacious stone room. "This seems a castle of remarkable size and strength. Nevertheless, we speak of a blood drinker."

He nodded.

"We are well protected here, Marius. We do not admit everyone as we admitted you, take my word for it. But would you hear now what he told us?"

I bowed my head. I knew what Raymond would tell me.

"The Satan worshipers," I said, using the more specific words, "the very ones who burnt my house in Venice, they prey upon humans in Paris. And my brilliant auburn-haired apprentice, Amadeo, is still their leader?"

"As far as we know," he said. "They are very clever. They hunt the poor, the diseased, the outcast. The renegade who told us so much explained that they fear 'places of light,' as they call them. They have taken to believing that it is not God's will for them to be richly clothed, or to enter churches. And your Amadeo now goes by the name of Armand. The renegade told us that Armand has the zeal of the converted."

I was too miserable to say anything.

I shut my eyes, and when I opened them I was looking at the fire which was burning very well in the deep fireplace.

Then slowly my gaze shifted to Raymond Gallant who was staring at me intently.

"I have told you everything, really," he said.

I gave him a faint, sad smile and I nodded.

"You've been generous indeed. And many a time in the past when one was generous to me, I took from my tunic a purse of gold. But is such needed here?"

"No," he said agreeably, shaking his head. "We need no gold, Marius. Gold we have always had in great abundance. What is life without gold? But we have it."

"What can I do for you, then?" I asked. "I'm in your debt. I've been in your debt since the night we spoke in Venice."

"Talk to several of our members," he replied. "Let them come into the room. Let them see you. Let them ask you questions. That is what you can do for me. Tell them only what you will. But create a truth for them which can be recorded for study by others."

"Of course. I'll do this willingly, but not in this library, Raymond, beautiful as it is. We must be in an open place. I have an instinctive fear of mortals who know what I am." I paused. "In fact, I'm not sure I've ever been surrounded by such."

He thought on this for a moment. Then he spoke:

"Our courtyard is too noisy, too close to the stables. Let it be on one of the towers. It will be cold, but I shall tell them all that they must dress warmly."

"Shall we elect the South Tower for our purpose?" I asked. "Bring no torches with you. The night is clear and the moon is full and all of you will be able to see me."

I slipped out of the room then, hurrying down the stairs, and easily passing through one of the narrow stone windows. With preternatural speed I went to the battlements of the South Tower, and there waited in the mild wind for all of them to gather around me.

Of course it seemed I had traveled by magic, but that I had not was one of the things which I meant to tell them.

Within a quarter of an hour they were all assembled, some twenty well-dressed men, both young and old, and two handsome women, and I found myself in the midst of a circle.

No torches, no. I was not in any conceivable danger.

For a long moment I allowed them to look at me, and form whatever conception they desired, and then I spoke:

"You must tell me what you want to know. For my part, I tell you plainly that I am a blood drinker. I have lived for hundreds of years, and I can remember clearly when I was a mortal man. It was in Imperial Rome. You may record this. I have never separated my soul from that mortal time. I refuse to do it."

For a moment only silence followed, but then Raymond began with the questions.

Yes, we had a "beginning," I explained but I could say nothing of it. Yes, we became much much stronger with time. Yes, we tended to be lone creatures or to choose our companions very carefully. Yes, we could make others. No, we were not instinctively vicious, and we felt a deep love for mortals which was often our spiritual undoing.

There were countless other little questions. And I answered them all to the best of my ability. I would say nothing of our vulnerability to the sun or fire. As for the "coven of vampires" in Paris and Rome, I knew little.

At last I said:

"It's time for me to leave now. I will travel hundreds of miles before dawn. I lodge in another country."

"But how do you travel?" one of them asked.

"On the wind," I said. "It's a gift that has come to me with the passing centuries."

I went to Raymond and I took him in my arms again, and then turning to several of the others I bade them come and touch me so that they could see I was a real being.

I stood back, took my knife and cut my hand with it, and held out my hand so that they could see the flesh heal.

There were gasps from them.

"I must be gone now. Raymond, my thanks and my love," I said.

"But wait," said one of the most elderly of the men. He had been standing back all the while, leaning on a cane, listening to me as intently as all the others. "I have one last question for you, Marius."

"Ask me," I said immediately.

"Do you know anything of our origins?"

For a moment I was puzzled. I couldn't quite imagine what he meant in this question. Then Raymond spoke:

"Do you know anything about how the Talamasca came to be? That is what we are asking you."

"No," I said in quiet astonishment.

A silence fell over them all, and I realized quickly that they themselves were confused about how the Talamasca had come about. And it did come back to me that Raymond had told me something of this when first I met him.

"I hope you find your answers," I said.

Then off I went into the darkness.

But I didn't stay away. I did what I had failed to do on my arrival. I hovered quite close but just beyond their hearing and their vision. And with my powerful gifts, I listened to them as they roamed their many towers and their many libraries.

How mysterious they were, how dedicated, how studious.

Some night in the far future perhaps I would come to them again, only to learn more of them. But just now, I had to return to the shrine and to Bianca.

She was still awake when I came into the blessed place. And I saw that she had lighted the hundred candles.

This was a ceremony that I sometimes failed to do, and I was pleased to see it.

"And are you happy with your visit to the Talamasca?" she asked in her frank voice. She had that beguiling look of simplicity on her face which always prompted me to tell her everything.

"I was most pleased. I found them the honest scholars they professed to be. I gave them what knowledge I could, but by no means what I might, for that would have been too foolish. But all they seek is knowledge and I left them more than happy."

She narrowed her eyes as if she could not quite imagine what the Talamasca was and I understood her.

I sat down beside her, folded her close and wrapped the fur cloak around us both.

"You smell of the cold, good wind," she said. "Perhaps we are meant to be creatures of the shrine only, creatures of the cold sky and the inhospitable mountains."

I said nothing, but in my mind I thought of only one thing: the far-off city of Dresden. Pandora sooner or later always returned to Dresden.

31

A HUNDRED YEARS would pass before I found Pandora.
During that time my powers increased enormously.
That night after my return from the Talamasca in England,
I tested all of them and made certain that, never again would I be at the
mercy of Santino's miscreants. For many nights I left Bianca to herself
as I made certain of my advantages.

And once I was utterly sure of my swiftness, of the Fire Gift, and of
an immeasurable power to destroy with invisible force, I went to Paris
with no other thought but to spy upon Amadeo's coven.

Before I left for this little venture, I confessed my goals to Bianca
and she had at once beseeched me not to court such danger.

"No, let me go," I responded. "I could hear his voice now over the
miles perhaps if I chose to do it. But I must be certain of what I hear
and what I see. And I shall tell you something else. I have no desire to
reclaim him."

She was saddened by this, but she seemed to understand it. She kept
her usual place in the corner of the shrine, merely nodding to me and
exacting the promise from me that I would be most careful.

As soon as I reached Paris, I fed from one of several murderers, lur-
ing him by the powerful Spell Gift from his place in a comfortable inn,
and then I sought refuge in a high bell tower of Notre Dame de Paris
itself to listen to the miscreants.

Indeed, it was a huge nest of the most despicable and hateful
beings, and they had sought out a catacomb for their existence in Paris
just as they had in ancient Rome centuries ago.

This catacomb was under the cemetery called Les Innocents, and
those words seemed tragically apt when I caught their addle-brained

vows and chants before they poured out into the night to bring cruelty as well as death to the people of Paris.

"All for Satan, all for the Beast, all to serve God, and then return to our penitential existence."

It was not difficult for me to find, through many different minds, the location of my Amadeo, and within an hour or so of my arrival in Paris, I had him fixed as he walked through a narrow medieval street, never dreaming that I watched him from above in bitter silence.

He was dressed in rags, his hair caked with filth, and when he found his first victim, he visited upon her a painful death which appalled me.

For an hour or more my eyes followed him as he proceeded on, feeding on another hapless creature, and then circling back to walk his way to the enormous cemetery.

Leaning against the cold stone of the tower room, I heard him deep in his underground cell drawing together his "coven" as he himself now called it and demanding of each how he or she had harried, for the love of God, the local population.

"Children of Darkness, it is almost dawn. Each of you shall now open his or her soul to me."

How firm, how clear was his voice. How certain he was of what he said. How quick he was to correct any Child of Satan who had not slain mortals ruthlessly. It was a man's voice I heard coming from the lips of the boy I once knew. It was chilling to me.

"Why were you given the Dark Gift?" he demanded of a laggard. "Tomorrow night you must strike twice. And if all of you do not give me greater devotion, I shall punish you for your sins, and see that others are brought into the coven."

At last I couldn't listen anymore. I was repelled.

I dreamt of going down into his underground world, of pulling him out of it as I burnt his followers, and forcing him into the light, of taking him with me to the shrine of Those Who Must Be Kept, and pleading with him to renounce his vocation.

But I didn't do it. I couldn't do it.

For years and years, he had been one of them. His mind, his soul, his body belonged to those he ruled; and nothing that I had taught him had given him the strength to fight them.

He was not my Amadeo anymore. That is what I had come to Paris to learn and now I knew the truth of it.

I felt sadness. I felt despair. But maybe it was anger and revulsion which caused me to leave Paris that night, saying to myself in essence that he must free himself from the dark mentality of the coven on his own. I could not do it for him.

I had labored long and hard in Venice to erase his memory of the Monastery of the Caves. And now he had found another place of rigid ritual and denial. And his years with me had not protected him from it. Indeed, a circle had long ago closed for him. He was the priest once more. He was the Fool for Satan, as he had once been the Fool for God in far-away Russia. And his brief time with me in Venice had been nothing.

When I told these things to Bianca, when I explained them as best I could, she was sad but she didn't press me.

It was easy between us as always, with her listening to me, and then offering her own response without anger.

"Perhaps in time, you'll change your mind," she said. "You are the one with the power to go there, to fight those who would restrain him if you tried to take him. And that is what it would require, I think, that you would have to take him by force, insist that he come here to be with you, and see the Divine Parents. I don't possess the power to do these things. I ask only that you think on it, that you make no bitter iron resolve against it."

"I give you my word," I said, "I have not done that. But I do not think the sight of the Divine Parents would change the heart of Amadeo." I paused.

I thought on all this for a long moment and then I spoke to her more directly:

"You've only shared this knowledge with me for a brief time," I said. "And in the Divine Parents we both see great beauty. But Amadeo might well see something different. Remember what I've told you of the long centuries that lie behind me. The Divine Parents do not speak. The Divine Parents do not redeem. The Divine Parents ask for nothing."

"I understand," she said.

But she didn't. She had not spent enough years with the King and Queen. She couldn't possibly comprehend the full effect of their passivity. But I went on in a mild manner:

"Amadeo possesses a creed, and a seeming place in God's plan," I said. "He might well see our Mother and Father as an enigma belonging to a pagan era. That wouldn't warm his heart. That wouldn't give him the strength which he derives now from his flock, and believe you me, Bianca, he is the leader there. Our boy of long ago is old now; he is a sage of the Children of Darkness as they call themselves." I sighed.

A little flash of bitter memory came back to me, of Santino asking me when we met in Rome if Those Who Must Be Kept were holy or profane.

I told this to Bianca.

"Ah, then you spoke to this creature. You've never told me this."

"Oh, yes, I spoke to him and spurned him and insulted him. I did all of these foolish things when something more vicious was required. Indeed, when the very words 'Those Who Must Be Kept' had come from his lips, I should have put an end to him."

She nodded. "I come more and more to understand it. Yet still I hope in time that you will return to Paris, that you will at least reveal yourself to Amadeo. They are weak ones, are they not, and you could come upon him in some open place where you could—."

"I know well what you mean to say," I answered. "I wouldn't allow myself ever to be surrounded by torches. Perhaps I will do as you suggest. But I've heard Amadeo's voice, and I don't believe he can be changed now. And there is one thing more which is worth mentioning. Amadeo knows how to free himself from this coven."

"Are you sure?"

"Yes, I am. Amadeo knows how to live in the lighted world, and he is ten times stronger by virtue of my old blood than are those who listen to his commands. He could break away. He chooses not to do it."

"Marius," she said plaintively, "you know how much I love you and how loath I am to contradict you."

"No, say what you must say," I urged her at once.

"Think of what he suffered," she said. "He was but a child when it happened."

I agreed to all this. Then I spoke again:

"Well, he's no child now, Bianca. He may be as beautiful as he was when I made him through the Blood, but he is a patriarch in the dust. And all of Paris, the wondrous city of Paris, surrounds him. I watched him move through the city streets alone. There was no one there to restrict him. He might have sought the Evil Doer as we do. But he did not. He drank deep of innocent blood, not once but twice."

"Ah, I see. This is what has so embittered you."

I thought on it.

"Yes, you're right. It's what turned me away, though I didn't even know it. I thought it was the manner in which he spoke to his flock. But you are right. It was those two deaths, from which he drew his hot red feast, when Paris swarmed with mortals steeped in murder who might easily have been slain by him."

She laid her hand on mine.

"If I choose to snatch any one of these Children of Darkness from his lair," I said, "it is Santino."

"No, but you mustn't go to Rome. You don't know whether or not there are old ones among that coven."

"Some night," I said, "some night I shall go there. When I am more certain of immense power, and when I am more certain of the ruthless rage it requires to destroy many others."

"Be still now," she said. "Forgive me."

I was quiet for a moment.

She knew how many nights I had wandered alone. I had now to confess what I had been doing on those nights. I had now to begin my secret plan. I had now—for the first time in all our years together—to drive a wedge between her and me, while giving her precisely what she wanted.

"But let's leave talk of Amadeo," I said. "My mind is on happier things."

She was immediately interested. She reached out and stroked my face and hair as was her custom.

"Tell me."

"How long has it been since you asked me if we could have our own dwelling?"

"Oh, Marius, don't tease me on this account. Is it possible!"

"My darling, it's more than possible," I said, warmed by her beaming smile. "I have found a splendid place, a lovely little city on the Elbe River in Saxony."

For this I received the sweetest kiss.

"Now in these many nights when I have been off on my own, I have taken the liberty of acquiring a castle near the city, a much decayed place, and I hope you'll forgive me—."

"Marius, this is momentous news!" she said.

"I have already spent a considerable sum for the repairs—the new wooden floors and stairs, glass windows, and abundant furnishings."

"Oh, but this is wonderful," she said. She put her arms around me.

"I'm relieved that you're not angry with me," I said, "for moving so quickly without you. You might say I fell in love with the place, and taking several drapers and carpenters there I told them my dreams and now all is being done as I have directed."

"Oh, how could I be angry?" she said. "I want it more than anything in the world."

"There is one more aspect to this castle which I should disclose," I said. "Though the more modern building above is more like a palace than a castle, its foundations are quite old. Indeed, a major part of the foundations were built in early times. And there are huge crypts beneath it, and a true dungeon."

"You mean to move the Divine Parents?" she asked.

"I do. I think it's time for it. You know as well as I that there are small cities and towns springing up all around us. We aren't isolated here. Yes, I want to move the Divine Parents."

"If you say, of course, I go along with you." She was too happy to conceal it. "But is it safe there? Didn't you remove them to this remote place so that you never had to fear their discovery?"

I thought on this for a while before answering.

At last I said:

"It is safe there. And with the passing centuries, the world of the Undead changes around us. And I can't endure this place any longer. And so I take them to a new place. And there are no blood drinkers in it. I have searched far and wide for them. They aren't there. I hear no young ones. I hear no old ones. I believe it's safe. And perhaps the most true answer to that logic is this: I want to bring them there. I want a new place. I want new mountains and new forests."

"I understand," she said. "Oh, I do understand," she said again. "And more than ever, I believe that they can defend themselves. Oh, they need you, I don't doubt it, and that's why on that long ago night they opened the door for you and lighted the lamps. I can still remember it so vividly. But I spend long hours here simply gazing at them. And I have many thoughts during these hours. And I believe that they would defend themselves against any who sought to hurt them."

I didn't argue with her. I didn't bother to remind her that centuries ago they had allowed themselves to be placed in the sun. What was the purpose? And for all I knew she was right. They would crush anyone who tried to subject them to such injury.

"Come now," she said, seeing me fallen into a mood. "I'm too happy with this good news. Be happy with me."

She kissed me as if she couldn't stop herself. She was so innocent in those moments.

And I, I was lying to her, truly lying to her for the first time in all our years together.

I was lying because I hadn't told her a word of Pandora. I was lying because I didn't truly believe that she could harbor no jealousy of Pandora. And because I couldn't tell her that my love for Pandora lay at the very heart of what I did. What creature would want to reveal such a scheme to a lover?

I meant to place us in Dresden. I meant to remain in Dresden. I meant to be near Dresden at every sunset of my existence until such time as Pandora came again. And I could not tell this to Bianca.

And so I pretended that it was for her that I had chosen this beautiful home, and indeed it was for her, there is no doubt of it. It was for her to make her happy, yes. But that was not all of it.

Within the month, we began work on the new shrine, utterly transforming the castle dungeon in Saxony into a fit place for the King and Queen.

Goldsmiths and painters and stone masons were brought down the many flights of stone steps to enhance the dungeon until it was the most marvelous private chapel.

The throne was covered in gold leaf as was the dais.

And once again, the proper bronze lamps were found, fresh and new. And there were rich candelabra of gold and silver.

I alone labored on the heavy iron doors and their complex fastenings.

As for the castle, it was more of a palace than a castle, as I've said, having been rebuilt several times, and it was charming in its placement above the banks of the Elbe, and it had around it a lovely forest of beech, oak and birch trees. There was a terrace from which one could look down at the river, and from many large windows, one could see the distant city of Dresden.

Of course we would never hunt in Dresden or in the surrounding hamlets. We would go far afield as had always been our custom. And we would waylay the forest brigands, an activity which had become a regular sport for us.

Bianca had some concerns. And only reluctantly she confessed to me that she had some fear of living in a place where she could not hunt for herself without me.

"Dresden is big enough to serve your appetite," I said, "if I were not able to carry you elsewhere. You'll see. It's a beautiful city, a young city I should say, but under the Duke of Saxony it's coming along magnificently."

"You're sure of this," she asked.

"Oh, yes, I'm sure of it, and as I've told you, I'm also sure that the forests of Saxony and nearby Thuringia contain their number of murderous thieves who have always been such a special repast for us."

She thought on all this.

"Let me remind you, my darling," I said, "you can on any night cut your beautiful blond hair with the full confidence that it will grow back by day, and you can go out clothed as a man, traveling with preternatural speed and strength to hunt your victims. Perhaps we should play at this very soon after our arrival."

"Yes, would you allow me this?" she asked.

"Of course, I shall." I was astonished by her gratitude.

Again she showered me with grateful kisses.

"But I must caution you on something," I said. "The area to which we move has many small villages, and in these the belief in witchcraft and vampires is quite strong."

"Vampires," she said. "This is the word used by your friend in the Talamasca."

"Yes," I replied. "We must always cover the evidence of our feast, lest we become an immediate legend."

She laughed.

Finally the castle or schloss as they were called in that part of the world was ready, and it was time for us to make preparations.

But something else had come to my mind, and I was haunted by it.

Finally there came a night when as Bianca slept in her corner, I proposed to deal with this matter.

I knelt down on the bare marble and prayed to my motionless and beautiful Akasha and asked her in most specific words if she would allow Bianca to drink from her.

"This tender one has been your companion these many years," I said, "and she has loved you without reserve. I give her my strong blood over and over again. But what is my blood in comparison to yours? I fear for her, if ever we were to be separated. Please let her drink. Give her your precious strength."

Only the sweet silence followed, with the shimmering of so many tiny flames, with the scent of wax and oil, with the glitter of light in the Queen's eyes.

But I saw an image in answer to my prayer. I saw in my mind my lovely Bianca lying on the breast of the Queen. And for one divine instant we were not in the shrine but in a great garden. I felt the breeze sweeping through the trees. I smelled flowers.

Then I was in the shrine again, kneeling, with my arms out.

At once I whispered and gestured for Bianca to come to me. She obeyed, having no idea of what was in my mind, and I guided her up close to the throat of the Queen, covering her as I did so that if Enkil were to lift his arm I would feel it.

"Kiss her throat," I whispered.

Bianca was shivering. I think she was on the verge of tears, but she did as I told her to do, and then I saw her sink her small fang teeth into the skin of the Queen, and I felt her body become rigid beneath my embrace.

It was being accomplished.

For several long moments she drank, and it seemed I could hear their heartbeats struggling against each other, one great and one small, and then Bianca fell back, and I gathered her up in my arms, seeing the two tiny wounds heal in Akasha's throat.

It was finished.

Withdrawing to the corner, I held Bianca close to me.

She gave several sighs and undulated and turned towards me and snuggled against me. Then she held out her hand and looked at it, and we could both see that it was whiter now, though it still had the color of human flesh.

My soul was wondrously soothed by this event. I am only confessing now what it meant to me. For having lied to Bianca I lived with an unbearable guilt, and now, having given her this gift of the Mother's blood I felt a huge measure of relief from it.

It was my hope that the Mother would allow Bianca to drink again, and in fact this did happen. It happened often. And with every draught of the Divine Blood Bianca became immensely stronger.

But let me proceed with the tale in order.

The journey from the shrine was arduous. As in the past I had to rely on mortals to transport the Divine Parents in heavy coffins of stone, and I experienced some trepidation. But not as much as in former eras. I think I was convinced that Akasha and Enkil could protect themselves.

I don't know what gave me this impression. Perhaps it was that they had opened the shrine for me, and lighted the lamps when I had been so weak and miserable.

Whatever the case, they were carried to our new home without difficulty, and as Bianca gazed on in complete awe, I took them out of their coffins and placed them on the throne together.

Their slow obedient movements, their sluggish plasticity—these things faintly horrified her.

But as she had now drunk the Mother's blood, she was quick to join me in adjusting her fine spun dress and Enkil's kilt. She helped me to smooth the plaited hair. She helped me to adjust the Queen's bracelets.

When it was all done, I myself tended to the lamps and the candles.

Then we both knelt down to pray that the King and the Queen were content to be in this new place.

And after that we were off to find the brigands in the forest. We had already heard their voices. We quickly picked up their scent, and soon it was fine feasting in the woods, and a stash of stolen gold to make it all the more splendid.

We were back in the world, Bianca declared. She danced in circles in the great hall of the castle. She delighted in all the furnishings that crowded our new rooms. She delighted in our fancy coffered beds, and all the colored draperies.

I too delighted in it.

But we were in full agreement that we would not live in the world as I had lived in Venice. Such was simply too dangerous. And so having but few servants, we kept entirely to ourselves, and the rumors in Dresden were that our house belonged to a Lady and Lord who lived elsewhere.

When it pleased us to visit great cathedrals—and there were many—or great Royal Courts, we went some distance from our home—to other cities such as Weimar, or Eisenbach, or Leipzig— and cloaked ourselves in absurd wealth and mystery. It was all quite comforting after our barren life in the Alps. And we enjoyed it immensely.

But at every sunset my eyes were fixed on Dresden. At every sunset I listened for the sound of a powerful blood drinker—in Dresden.

And so the years passed.

With them came radical changes in clothes which greatly amused us. We were soon wearing elaborate wigs which we found ridiculous. And how I despised the pants which soon came into style, as well as the high-heeled shoes and white stockings which came into fashion with them.

We could not in our quiet seclusion include enough maids for Bianca, so it was I who laced up her tight corset. But what a vision she was in her low-breasted bodices and her broad swaying panniers.

During this time, I wrote many times to the Talamasca. Raymond died at the age of eighty-nine, but I soon established a connection there with a young woman named Elizabeth Nollis who had for her personal review my letters to Raymond.

She confirmed for me that Pandora was still seen with her Asian companion. She begged to know what I might tell of my own powers and habits, but on this I was not too revealing. I spoke of mind reading and the defiance of gravity. But I drove her to distraction with my lack of specifics.

The greatest and most mysterious success of these letters was that she told me much of the Talamasca. They were rich beyond anyone's dreams, she said, and this was the source of their immense freedom. They had recently set up a Motherhouse in Amsterdam, and also in the city of Rome.

I was quite surprised by all this, and warned her of Santino's "coven."

She then sent me a reply that astonished me.

"It seems now that those strange ladies and gentlemen of which we have written in the past are no longer within the city in which they dwelt with such obvious pleasure. Indeed it is very difficult for our Motherhouse there to find any reports of such activities as one might expect from these people."

What did this mean? Had Santino abandoned his coven? Had they gone on to Paris en masse? And if so, why?

Without explaining myself to my quiet Bianca—who was more and more hunting on her own—I went off to explore the Holy City myself, coming upon it for the first time in two hundred years.

I was wary, in fact, a good deal more wary, than I should want to admit to anyone. Indeed, the fear of fire gripped me so dreadfully that when I arrived I could do nothing but keep to the very top of St. Peter's Basilica and look out over Rome with cold, shame-filled eyes; unable for long moments to hear with my blood drinker's ears no matter how I struggled to gain control of myself.

But I soon satisfied myself, through the Mind Gift, that there were only a few blood drinkers to be found in Rome, and these were lone hunters without the consolation of companions. They were also weak. And as I raped their minds, I realized they knew little of Santino!

How had this come about? How had this one who had destroyed so much of my life freed himself from his own miserable existence?

Full of rage, I drew close to one of these lone blood drinkers, and soon accosted him, terrifying him and with reason.

"What of Santino and the Roman coven?" I demanded.

"Gone, all gone," he said, "years ago. Who are you that you know of such things?"

"Santino!" I said. "Where did he go! Tell me."

"But no one knows the answer," he said. "I never laid eyes on him."

"But someone made you," I said. "Tell me."

"My maker lives in the catacombs still where the coven used to gather. He's mad. He can't help you."

"Prepare to meet God or the Devil," I said. And just that quick I put an end to him. I did it as mercifully as I could. And then he was no more but a spot of grease in the dirt and in this I rubbed my foot before I moved towards the catacombs.

He had spoken the truth.

There was but one blood drinker in this place, but I found it full of skulls just as it had been over a thousand years ago.

The blood drinker was a babbling fool, and when he saw me in my fine gentleman's clothes, he stared at me and pointed his finger.

"The Devil comes in style," he said.

"No, death has come," I said. "Why did you make that other one whom I've destroyed this night?"

My confession made no impression on him.

"I make others to be my companions. But what good does it do? They turn on me."

"Where is Santino?" I demanded.

"Long gone," he said. "And who would have ever thought?"

I tried to read his mind, but he was too crazed and full of distracted thoughts. It was like chasing scattered mice.

"Look at me, when did you last see him!"

"Oh, decades ago," he said. "I don't know the year. What do years mean here?"

I could get nothing further from him. I looked about the miserable place with its few candles dripping wax upon yellowed skulls, and then turning on this creature I destroyed him with the Fire Gift as mercifully as I had destroyed the other. And I do think that it was truly a mercy.

There was but one left, and this one led a far better existence than the other two. I found him in handsome lodgings an hour before sunrise. With little difficulty I learnt that he kept a hiding place beneath the house, but that he spent his idle hours reading in his few well-appointed rooms, and that he dressed tolerably well.

I also learnt that he couldn't detect my presence. He cut the figure of a man of some thirty mortal years, and he had been in the Blood for some three hundred.

At last I opened his door, breaking the lock, and stepped before him as he stood up, in horror, from his writing desk.

"Santino," I said, "what became of him?"

Though he had fed like a glutton, he was gaunt with huge bones, and long black hair, and though he was very finely dressed in the style of the 1600s, his lace was soiled and dusty.

"In the name of Hell," he whispered, "who are you? Where do you come from?"

Again there came that terrific confusion of mind which defeated my ability to subtract thoughts or knowledge from it.

"I'll satisfy you on those points," I said, "but you must answer me first. Santino. What happened to him."

I took several deliberate steps towards him which put him into a paroxysm of terror.

"Be quiet now," I said. Again I tried to read his mind, but I failed. "Don't try to flee," I said. "You won't succeed with it. Answer my questions."

"I'll tell you what I know," he said, fearfully.

"That ought to be plenty."

He shook his head. "I came here from Paris," he said. He was quaking. "I was sent by a vampire named Armand who is the leader of that coven."

I nodded as though all this were quite intelligible to me, and as though I weren't experiencing agony.

"That was a hundred years ago, maybe more. Armand had heard no word from Rome in a long time. I came to see the where and why of it. I found the Roman coven in complete confusion."

He stopped, catching his breath, backing away from me.

"Speak quickly and tell me more," I said. "I'm impatient."

"Only if you swear on your honor that you won't harm me. I've done you no harm after all. I was no child of Santino."

"What makes you think I have honor?" I asked.

"I know you do," he said. "I can sense such things. Swear on your honor to me and I'll tell you everything."

"Very well, I swear. I'll leave you alive which is more than I've done with two others tonight who haunted the Roman streets like ghosts. Now talk to me."

"I came from Paris as I told you. The Roman coven was weak. All ceremony had fallen away. One or two of the old ones had deliberately gone into the fire. Others had simply run away, and Santino had made no move to catch them and punish them. Once it was known that such escape was possible many more fled, and the coven was in a state of disaster."

"Santino, did you see him?"

"Yes, I saw him. He had taken to dressing in fine clothes and jewels, and he received me in a palazzo much larger than this one. He told me strange things. I can't really remember all of them."

"You must remember."

"He said he had seen old ones, too many old ones, and his faith in Satan had been shaken. He spoke of creatures who seemed to be made of marble, though he knew they could burn. He said he could no longer lead. He told me not to return to Paris, to do as I pleased, and so I have."

"Old ones," I said, repeating his words. "Did he tell you nothing of these old ones?"

"He spoke of the great Marius, and of a creature named Mael. And he spoke of beautiful women."

"What were the names of these women?"

"He didn't say their names to me. He said only that one had come to the coven on the night of its ceremonial dance, a woman like a living statue, and she had walked through the fire to show that it was useless against her. She had destroyed many of the fledglings who attacked her.

"When Santino showed attention and patience, she talked with him for several nights, telling him of her wanderings. He had no taste for the coven after that . . .

". . . But it was the other woman who truly destroyed him."

"And who was this?" I demanded. "You can't speak fast enough for me."

"The other woman was of the world, dressing in high style, and traveling by coach in the company of a dark-skinned Asian."

I was dumbstruck, and maddened that he said nothing more.

"What happened with this other woman?" I finally asked, though a thousand other words flooded my mind.

"Santino wanted her love most desperately. Of course the Asian threatened him with pure destruction if he didn't give up this course, but it was the woman's condemnations that ruined him."

"What condemnations, what did she say and why?" I demanded.

"I'm not certain. Santino spoke to her of his old piety and his fervor in directing the coven. She condemned him. She said time would punish him for what he'd done to his own kind. She turned away from him in disgust with him."

I smiled, a bitter smile.

"Do you understand these things?" he asked. "Are they what you wanted?"

"Oh, yes, I understand them," I said.

I turned and went to the window. I unfastened the wooden shutter, and stood looking down into the street.

I saw nothing, but I couldn't reason.

"What became of the woman and her Asian companion?" I asked.

"I don't know. I have seen them in Rome since. Maybe it was fifty years ago. They are easy to recognize, for she is very pale and her companion has a creamy brown skin and while she dresses always as the great lady, he tends toward the exotic."

I took a deep easy breath.

"And Santino? Where did he go?" I demanded.

"That I can't tell you, except that he had no spirit for anything when I talked to him. He wanted her love, and nothing else. He said the ancient ones had ruined him for immortality and frightened him as to death. He had nothing."

I took another deep breath. Then I turned around and fixed this vampire in my gaze with all his considerable details.

"Listen to me," I said. "If you ever see this creature again, the great lady who travels by coach, you must tell her one thing for me and one thing alone."

"Very well."

"That Marius lives and Marius is searching for her."

"Marius!" he said with a gasp. He looked at me respectfully, though his eyes measured me from head to foot, and then hesitantly he said, "But Santino believes you to be dead. I think that this is what he told to the woman, that he had sent the coven members North to hurt you."

"I think it's what he told her too. Now you remember that you saw me alive and that I search for her."

"But where can she find you?"

"I can't entrust that knowledge to you," I said. "I would be foolish to do it. But remember what I have said. If you see her speak to her."

"Very well," he answered. "I hope that you find her."

With no further words, I left him.

I went out then into the night and for a long time I roamed the streets of Rome, taking stock of how it had changed with the centuries and how so much had remained the same.

I marveled at the relics from my time which were still standing. I treasured the few hours I had to make my way through the ruins of the Colosseum and the Forum. I climbed the hill where I had once lived. I found some blocks still from old walls of my house. I wandered in a daze, staring at things because my brain was in a fever.

In truth I could hardly contain my excitement on account of what I had heard, and yet I was miserable that Santino had escaped me.

But oh, what a rich irony it was that he had fallen in love with her! That she had denied him! And to think he had confessed to her his murderous deeds, how loathsome. Had he been boasting when he spoke with her?

Finally my heart was under my control. I could endure with what I had learnt from the young vampire. I would soon come upon Pandora, I knew it.

As for the other ancient one, she who had walked through the fire, I could not then imagine who it was though I think I know now. Indeed, I'm almost certain of it. I wonder what pulled her out of her secretive ways to visit some merciful release upon Santino's followers.

At last the night was almost spent, and I went home to be with my ever patient Bianca.

When I came down the stone steps of the cellar, I found her asleep against her coffin as if she'd been waiting for me. She was in a long nightgown of sheer white silk, tied at the wrists, and her hair was glossy and flowing.

I lifted her, kissed her closing eyes, and then put her down to her rest, and kissed her again as she lay there.

"Did you find Santino?" she asked in a drowsy voice. "Did you punish him?"

"No," I said. "But I will some night in the years to come. Only time itself can rob me of that special pleasure."

32

IT WAS BIANCA who gave me the news.

It was early evening, and I was writing a letter which I would later send to my latest confidante in the Talamasca. The windows were open to the breeze off the Elbe.

Bianca rushed into the room and told me immediately.

"It's Pandora. I know it. I've seen her."

I rose from the desk.

I took her in my arms.

"How do you know?" I asked.

"They're dancing now at the Court Ball, she and her Asian lover. Everyone was whispering about them, how beautiful they are. The Marquis and the Marquisa De Malvrier. I heard their heartbeats as soon as I entered the ballroom. I caught their strange vampiric scent. How can one describe it?"

"Did she see you?"

"Yes, and I put a portrait of you in my mind, my love," she said. "We locked eyes, she and I. Go to her. I know how much you want to see her."

I gazed down at Bianca for a long moment. I peered into her lovely oval eyes and then I kissed her. She was exquisitely dressed in a charming ball gown of violet silk and never had she looked more splendid. I kissed her as warmly as I have ever done.

After that, I went at once to my closets and dressed for the ball, putting on my finest crimson frock coat and all the requisite lace, and then the large curly wig which was the fashion then.

I hurried down the steps to my carriage. When I looked back I saw Bianca on the pavilion above gazing down at me. She lifted her hand to her lips, and blew a kiss to me.

As soon as I entered the Ducal Palace I sensed the presence of the Asian, and indeed before I ever reached the doors of the ballroom, he emerged from the shadows of an anteroom and put his hand on my arm.

Oh, for so long I had heard about this evil being, and now I confronted him. From India, yes, and most beautiful with large liquid black eyes, and a creamy brown skin that was flawless. He smiled at me with his smooth, enticing mouth.

His satin frock coat was a dark blue, and his lace was intricate and extravagant. It seemed he was studded with immense diamonds, diamonds from India where diamonds are worshiped. He had a fortune in rings on his hands. He wore a fortune in buckles and buttons.

"Marius," he said. He gave me a small formal bow, as though he were doffing his hat when in fact he wore none. "Of course," he said, "you are going to see Pandora."

"You mean to stop me?" I asked.

"No," he said with an idle shrug. "How could you imagine such a thing?" His tone was courteous. "Marius, I assure you, she has cast off many another." He seemed perfectly sincere.

"So I've been told," I said. "I must see her. You and I can speak later on. I must go to her."

"Very well," he said. "I am patient." He shrugged again. "I am always patient. My name is Arjun. I'm glad that we've finally come together. Even with the Roman rogue, Santino, who claimed to have annihilated you I was patient. She was so miserable then and I wanted to punish him. But I did not. I followed her wishes and left him unharmed. What a dejected creature he was. How he loved her. I followed her wishes as I've said. I'll follow her wishes tonight, as I always do."

"That's very good of you," I replied, my throat so tight I could scarcely utter the words. "Let me go now. I have waited longer than you can possibly imagine for this moment. I can't stand here and converse with you as though she weren't steps away from me."

"I can imagine how long you've waited," he said. "I am older than you think."

I nodded, and I slowly withdrew from him.

I couldn't bear it anymore.

Immediately I entered the immense ballroom.

The orchestra was playing one of the soft fluid dances so popular in those times, nothing as spirited as music would later become, and the lavish room was full of radiant faces and busy dancing figures, and myriad colors.

I peered through the happy crowd, moving slowly along one wall and then another.

Quite suddenly I saw her. She didn't know I was there. Her companion had sent her no mental warning.

She was sitting alone, artfully dressed in her fashionable clothes, her satin bodice very tight and graceful, her ornate skirts huge, and her lovely white face framed by her natural brown hair drawn back and up in a fancy style with rubies and diamonds.

I leant against the clavichord, smiling benevolently at the musician who played it with such skill, and then I turned to gaze at her.

How sad was her expression, how remote, how unutterably beautiful. Was she watching the colors of the room as I watched them? Did she feel the same gentle love for mortals which I felt? What would she do when she realized I was watching her?

I didn't know. I was afraid. I couldn't know anything until I heard the sound of her voice. I continued to look. I continued to savor this moment of bliss and safety.

Suddenly, she saw me. She picked me out of the hundreds of faces. Her eyes fixed on me, and I saw the blood rush into her beautiful cheeks and her mouth opened to speak the name Marius.

I heard it over the thin sweet music.

I raised my fingers to my lips, just as Bianca had done only a little while ago, and I blew a kiss to her.

How sad and happy at once she seemed, her mouth opened in a half smile as she gazed at me. She seemed as frozen in her place as I was.

But this was intolerable. What were these volumes of silence which divided us!

Quickly I crossed the dance floor and bowed before her. I lifted her cold white hand, and led her out and into the dance, and would take no resistance from her.

"No, you're mine, you're mine, do you hear?" I whispered. "Don't pull away from me."

"Marius, I fear him and he is strong," she whispered in my ear. "I must explain to him that we've found each other."

"I don't fear him. Besides he knows. What does it matter?"

We were dancing as if we said no such things to one another. I held her tight and kissed her cheeks. I didn't care what the mortals around us might think of this impropriety. How very absurd was the whole notion.

"Pandora, my blessed love, if only you could know how long I've waited. What use is it to tell you now that from the very beginning I have missed you in pure agony? Pandora, listen to me, don't close your eyes, don't look away. I knew within the year, the very year, that I had made a dreadful error!"

I realized that I was turning her too violently: I was pressing her hand too hard. I had lost the cadence of the dance. The music was a strange shrill noise in my ears. I had lost control of everything.

She pulled back to look into my eyes. "Take me out on the pavilion," she said. "We can talk in the river breeze. The music makes me dizzy."

Immediately I led her through a huge pair of doors and we found ourselves on a stone bench overlooking the river.

I shall never forget how clear it was that night, how much the stars seemed in my favor, and how brilliant the light of the moon on the Elbe. All around us were pots of flowers, and other couples or groups of mortals who had come to gain a little air before returning to the ballroom.

But in the main we had the shadows to ourselves and I gave way to kissing her. I felt her perfect cheeks beneath my lips. I kissed her throat. I felt her brown hair with its tight waves, which I had so often painted on my wild nymphs as they ran through my thick gardens. I wanted to pull it loose.

"Don't leave me again," I said. "No matter what is said between us tonight. Don't leave me."

"Marius, it was you who left me," she said, and I heard a tremor in her voice which frightened me. "Marius, that was so long ago," she said sadly. "Marius, I wandered so far and wide searching for you."

"Yes, yes, I admit to all," I said. "I admit to every error. How could I guess what it meant to break the tie? Pandora, I didn't know! Yea gods, I didn't know! Believe me, I didn't know. Tell me you will leave this creature, Arjun, and come back to me. Pandora, I want nothing short of this! I can't make pretty words. I can't recite old poems. Pandora, look at me."

"I am looking at you!" she declared. "Don't you see, you blind me! Marius, don't think I too haven't dreamt of this reunion. And now you see me in this shame, this weakness."

"What? I don't care! What shame and weakness?"

"That I'm a slave to my companion, Arjun, that I let him move me through the world, that on my own, I possess no will, no momentum. Marius, I am nothing now."

"No, that's not true, and besides it doesn't matter. I'll free you from Arjun. I have no fear of him whatsoever, and then you'll be with me and all your old spirit will come back to you."

"You dream," she said and the first coldness came into her face and into her voice. It was in her brown eyes, a coldness that comes from sorrow.

"Are you telling me," I demanded, "that you mean to leave me again for this creature? You think I will stand for it?"

"And what are you saying to me, Marius, that you will force me?" Her voice was low, distant.

"But you've told me you're weak, you've told me you're a slave. Is this not asking for me to force you?"

She shook her head. She was ready to weep. Again I wanted to pull down her hair, to see it loose, to take the jewels out of it. I wanted to take her face in my hands.

I did it. I held her face too roughly.

"Pandora, listen to me," I said. "One hundred years ago, I learnt from a strange mortal that in your wanderings with this creature you circled again and again the city of Dresden. And learning this, I moved myself to this city to wait for you. Not a night has passed that I have not awakened to look through Dresden to find you.

"Now that I have you in my arms I have no intention of abandoning you."

She shook her head. She seemed for a moment incapable of speech. I felt that she was imprisoned in her strange fashionable garments and lost in some painful reverie.

"But what can I give you, Marius, but what you've already learnt? The knowledge that I live still, that I endure, that I wander? With or without Arjun, what does it matter?"

She turned her eyes to me, wondering.

"And what do I learn from you except that you go on, and that you endure—that those demons in Rome did not destroy you as they claimed, that you were burnt, yes, I can see that in the color of your skin, but you survive. Marius, what more is there?"

"What on Earth are you saying!" I demanded. I was suddenly furious. "Pandora, we have each other! Good Lord. We have time. As we come together now, time begins for us all over again!"

"Does it, Marius? I don't know," she replied. "Marius, I'm not strong enough."

"Pandora, that's mad!" I said.

"Oh, you are so angry and it is so like our quarrels of old."

"No, it's not!" I declared. "It's nothing like our quarrels of old because it's about nothing. Now I'm taking you from here. I'm taking you to my palace, and I shall deal with Arjun as best as I can afterwards."

"You can't do such a thing," she said sharply. "Marius, I've been with him for hundreds of years. You think you can simply come between us?"

"I want you, Pandora. I shall settle for nothing else. And if such a time comes that you want to leave me—."

"Yes, and what if it does come," she said angrily, "then what shall I do when there is no Arjun on account of you!"

I fell silent. I was in a rage. She was staring at me intently. Her face was full of feeling. Her breast heaved under the tight satin.

"Do you love me?" I demanded.

"Completely," she said in her angry voice.

"Then you are coming with me!"

I took her by the hand.

No one moved to stop us as we left the palace.

As soon as I had her in the carriage, I kissed her wantonly as mortals kiss and wanted to sink my teeth into her throat but she forbade it.

"Let me have that intimacy!" I begged. "For the love of Heaven, Pandora, it's Marius who is speaking to you. Listen to me. Let us share blood and blood."

"Don't you think I want to?" she asked. "I'm afraid."

"Afraid of what?" I demanded. "Tell me what you fear. I'll make it vanish."

The carriage rolled on out of Dresden and through the forest towards my palace.

"Oh, but you won't," she replied. "You can't. Don't you understand, Marius, you're the same being you were in those times when we were first together. You're strong and spirited as you were then, and I'm not. Marius, he takes care of me."

"Takes care of you? Pandora, this is what you want! I'll do it. I shall take care of every tiny detail of your entire existence as though you were my daughter! Only give me the chance. Give me the chance to restore in love what was lost to us."

We had reached my gates, and my servants were opening them. We were about to enter when she signaled to me that I must hold the coach. She was looking out the window. She was looking up at the windows of the palace. Perhaps she could see the pavilion.

I did as she asked. I saw that she was paralyzed with fear. There was no disguising it. She stared at the palace as though it were full of menace.

"What in the name of Heaven can it be?" I asked. "Whatever it is that frightens you, tell me. Pandora, there is nothing that can't be changed. Tell me."

"Oh, you are so violent in your temper," she said in a whisper. "Can't you guess what reduces me to this abominable weakness?"

"No," I said. "I know only I love you with my whole heart. I've found you again and I'll do anything to keep you."

Her eyes remained fixed on the palace.

"Even give up the female companion," she asked, "who is inside this very house waiting for you?"

I didn't answer.

"I saw her at the ball," she said, her eyes glassy, her voice quivering. "I saw her and knew what she was, quite powerful, quite graceful. I never guessed she was your lover. But now I know that she is. I can hear her inside. I can hear her hopes and dreams and how they are pinned on you."

"Stop it, Pandora. It isn't necessary that I give her up. We are not mortals! We can live together."

I took her by the arms. I shook her. Her hair did come loose and then violently and cruelly I pulled at it, and I buried my face in her hair.

"Pandora, if you require this of me, I'll do it. Only give me time, give me time to make certain that Bianca is where she might survive well and happy. I'll do it for you, do you understand, if only you'll stop fighting me!"

I drew back. She appeared dazed and cold. Her lovely hair spilled down on her shoulders.

"What is it?" she asked in a low sluggish voice. "Why do you look at me this way?"

I was on the edge of tears, but I stopped them.

"Because I imagined," I said, "that this meeting would be so very different. And I did think that you would come with me willingly. And I did think that we two could live in harmony with Bianca. I believed these things. I believed them for a long time. And now I sit with you here and all is argument and torment."

"That's all it ever was, Marius," she replied in her low sad voice. "That's why you left me."

"No," I said. "That's not so. Pandora, ours was a great love. You must acknowledge it. There was a terrible parting, yes, but we had a great love, and we can have it again if we reach for it."

She gazed at the house, then back at me almost furtively. Something quickened in her and she suddenly gripped my arm with white knuckles. There came that look of terrible fear again.

"Come into the house with me," I said. "Meet Bianca. Take her hands in yours. Pandora, listen to me. Stay in the house while I go to settle things with Arjun. I won't be long, I promise you."

"No," she cried. "Don't you understand? I can't go into this house. It has nothing to do with your Bianca."

"What then? What now? What more!" I demanded.

"It's the sound I hear, the sound of their hearts beating!"

"The King and the Queen! Yes, they are inside. They are deep within the Earth, Pandora. They are as still and silent as always. You need not even see them."

A look of pure terror infected her features. I put my arms around her, but she only looked away.

"As still and silent as always," she gasped. "Surely that can't be. Not after all this time. Marius!"

"Oh, but it is," I said. "And to you it should be nothing. You needn't go down the steps to the shrine. It is my duty. Pandora, stop looking away."

"Don't hurt me, Marius," she cautioned. "You're rough with me as though I were a concubine. Treat me with grace." Her lips trembled. "Treat me with mercy," she said sadly.

I started to weep.

"Stay with me," I said. "Come inside. Talk to Bianca. Come to love us both. Let time begin from this moment."

"No, Marius," she said. "Take me away from that awful sound. Take me back to the place where I am living. Take me back, or I shall go on foot. I can't bear this."

I obeyed her commands. We were silent as she traveled to a large handsome house in Dresden whose many windows were dark, and there I held her still, kissing her, refusing to let her go.

Finally, I drew out my handkerchief and wiped my face. I drew in my breath and tried to speak calmly.

"You are frightened," I said, "and I must understand it and be patient with it."

She had that dazed cold look in her eyes, a look I had never seen in the early years, a look that now horrified me.

"Tomorrow night, we shall meet again," I said, "here perhaps in this house where you are dwelling, where you are safe from the sound of the Mother and the Father. Wherever you wish. But wherever you can get used to me."

She nodded. She lifted her hand and stroked my cheek with her fingers.

"How well you pretend," she whispered. "How very fine you are, and always were. And to think those demons in Rome thought they had put out your brilliant light. I should have laughed at them."

"Yes, and my light shines only for you," I said, "and it was of you I dreamt when I was burnt black by the fire sent from that demon blood drinker Santino. It was of you I dreamt as I drank from the Mother to regain my strength, as I searched for you through the countries of Europe."

"Oh, my love," she whispered. "My great love. If only I could be again the strong one whom you remember."

"But you will be," I insisted. "You are. I shall take care of you, yes, just as you wish. And you and Bianca and I—we shall all love one another. Tomorrow night, we'll talk. We'll make plans. We'll speak of all the great cathedrals we must see, the windows of colored glass, we'll speak of the painters whose fine work we have yet to study. We'll speak of the New World, of its forests and its rivers. Pandora, we will speak of everything."

I went on and on.

"And you will come to love Bianca," I said. "You will come to treasure her. I know Bianca's heart and soul as ever I knew yours, I swear to you. We will exist together in peace, believe me. You have no idea of the happiness that awaits you."

"Happiness?" she asked. She looked at me as though she hardly understood the words I had spoken. Then she said:

"Marius, I leave this city tonight. Nothing can stop it."

"No, no, you can't say this to me!" I declared. I grabbed her by the arms again.

"Don't hurt me, Marius. I leave this city tonight. I told you. Marius, you've waited for one hundred years to see one thing, and one thing only—that I live. Now leave me to the existence I've chosen."

"I won't. I won't have it."

"Yes, you will," she whispered. "Marius, don't you see what I'm trying to tell you. I haven't the courage to leave Arjun. I haven't the courage to see the Mother and the Father. Marius, I don't have the courage to love you anymore. The very sound of your angry voice frightens me. I don't have the courage to meet your Bianca. The very thought that you might love her more than me frightens me. I am frightened of it all, don't you see? And even now, I am desperate for Arjun that he may take me away from all of this. With Arjun there is for me a great simplicity! Marius, please let me go with your forgiveness."

"I don't believe you," I said. "I told you I will give up Bianca for you. Good God, Pandora, what more can I do? You can't be leaving me."

I turned my back on her. The expression on her face was too strange. I couldn't endure it.

And as I sat there in the darkness, I heard the door of the carriage open. I heard her quick step on the stones, and she was gone from me.

My Pandora, utterly gone from me.

I don't know how long I waited. It was not a full hour.

I was too distressed, too perfectly miserable. I didn't want to see her companion, and when I thought of banging on the doors of her house, I found it too utterly humiliating.

And in truth, in pure truth, she had convinced me. She wouldn't remain with me.

I was about to tell my driver to take us home when a sound came to me. It was of her howling and crying, and of objects within the house being broken.

It was all I needed to push me into action. I left the carriage and ran to her door. I shot an evil glance at her mortal servants, which rendered them virtually powerless, and threw open the doors for myself.

I rushed up the marble steps. I found her going madly along the walls, pounding the mirrors with her fists. I found her shedding blood tears and shivering. There was broken glass all around her.

I took her wrists. I took them tenderly.

"Stay with me," I said. "Stay with me!"

Quite suddenly behind me, I heard the presence of Arjun. I heard his unhurried step and then he entered the room.

She had collapsed against my chest. She was shaking.

"Don't worry," said Arjun in the same patient tone he had used with me in the Duke's palace. "We can talk of all these things in a courteous way. I am not a wild creature, given to acts of destruction."

He seemed the perfect gentleman with his lace handkerchief and high-heeled shoes. He looked about at the broken pieces of mirror which lay on the fine carpet, and he shook his head.

"Then leave me alone with her," I said.

"Is this what you wish, Pandora?" he asked.

She nodded. "For a little while, my darling," she said to him.

As soon as he had left the room, and shut the tall double doors behind him, I stroked her hair, and I kissed her again.

"I can't leave him," she confessed.

"And why not?" I asked.

"Because I made him," she answered. "He is my son, my spouse, and my guardian."

I was shocked.

I had never supposed such a thing!

In all these years I had thought him some dominating creature who kept her in his power.

"I made him so that he would take care of me," she said. "I took him from India where I was worshiped as a very goddess by those few who had set eyes upon me. I taught him European ways. I placed him in charge of me so that in my weakness and despair, he would control me. And it is his hunger for life which drives us both. Without it I might have languished in some deep tomb for centuries."

"Very well," I said, "he is your child. This I understand, but Pandora, you are mine! What of this! You are mine, and I have you in my possession again! Oh, forgive me, forgive that I speak so harshly, that I use words such as possession. What do I mean to say? I mean to say I can't lose you!"

"I know what you mean," she said, "but you see, I can't turn him away from me. He has done far too well in what I have asked of him, and he loves me. And he cannot live under your roof, Marius. I know you only too well. Where Marius lives, Marius rules. You will never suffer a male such as Arjun to dwell with you on my account or for any other reason."

I was so deeply wounded that for one moment I couldn't answer her. I shook my head as though to deny what she had said, but in truth I didn't know whether or not she was wrong. I had always, always thought only of destroying Arjun.

"You can't deny it," she said softly. "Arjun is too strong, too willful, and has been too long his own master."

"There must be some way," I pleaded.

"There will come a night, surely," she said, "when it is time for Arjun to part from me. The same may happen with you and your Bianca. But this is not the time. And so I beg you, let go of me, Marius, say farewell to me, and promise me that you will eternally persevere and I shall give you the same promise."

"This is your vengeance, isn't it?" I asked quietly. "You were my child and within two hundred years I left you. And so you tell me now that you won't do the same to him—."

"No, my beautiful Marius, it isn't vengeance, it is only the truth. Now, leave me." She smiled bitterly. "Oh, what a gift to me this night has been, that I have seen you alive, that I know the Roman blood drinker Santino was wrong. This night will carry me through centuries."

"It will carry you away from me," I said, nodding.

But then her lips caught me by surprise. It was she who kissed me ardently, and then I felt her tiny sharp teeth pierce my throat.

I stood rigid, eyes closed, letting her drink, feeling the inevitable pull on my heart, my head suddenly full of visions of the dark forest through which she and her companion so often rode and I couldn't know whether these were her visions or mine.

On and on she drank, as though she was starving, and deliberately I created for her the luscious garden of my most cherished dreams, and in it I envisioned the two of us together. My body was nothing but desire for her. Through every sinew I felt the pull of her drinking and I gave no resistance. I was her victim. I held to no caution.

It seemed I was not standing any longer. I must have fallen. I didn't care. Then I felt her hands on my arms, and I knew I was on my feet.

She drew back, and with blurred eyes I saw her gazing at me. All of her hair had spilled down on her shoulders.

"Such strong blood," she whispered. "My Child of the Millennia."

It was the first time I had heard such a name for those of us who have lived so long and I was faintly charmed by it.

I was groggy, so strong had she been, but what did it matter? I would have given her anything. I steadied myself. I tried to clear my vision.

She was far away across the room.

"What did you see in the blood?" I whispered.

"Your pure love," she answered.

"Was there any doubt?" I asked. I was growing stronger by the moment. Her face was radiant with the blood flush and her eyes were fierce as they had always been when we quarreled.

"No, no doubt," she said. "But you must leave me now."

I said nothing.

"Go on, Marius. If you don't, I can't bear it."

I stared at her as if I were staring at a wild thing of the wood, and so she seemed to be, this creature whom I had loved with all my heart.

And once again, I knew it to be finished.

I left the room.

In the grand hallway of the house, I stood stunned, and there Arjun was standing in the corner, staring at me.

"I am so sorry, Marius," he said, as if he meant it.

I looked at him, wondering if anything could work me into a rage to destroy him. Were I to do that, she would have to stay with me. And oh, how the thought of it blazed in my mind. Yet I knew she would utterly and completely hate me for it. And I would hate myself. For what did I have against this creature who wasn't her vile master as I'd always supposed, but her child!—a fledgling vampire of some five hundred years or less, young in the Blood and full of love for her.

I was far far from such a possibility. And what a sublime being he was as he surely read these thoughts in my desperate and unveiled mind and yet stood his ground with such poise, merely looking at me.

"Why must we part!" I whispered.

He shrugged. He gestured eloquently with his hands.

"I don't know," he said, "except she wants it so. It is she who wants ever to be on the move; it is she who draws designs upon the map. It is she who draws the circles in which we travel, now and then making Dresden the center of our roamings, now and then choosing some other city, such as Paris or Rome. It is she who says we must go on and on. It is she. And what can I say, Marius, except that it delights me."

I went towards him and for one moment he thought I meant to harm him and he stiffened.

I took his wrist before he could move. I studied him. What a noble being he was, his grand white wig in sharp contrast to his lustrous brown skin, his black eyes staring at me with such earnestness and seeming comprehension.

"Stay with me here," I said. "Both of you. Remain with me. Stay with me and my companion, Bianca."

He smiled and shook his head. There was no contempt in his eyes. We were male to male and there was no contempt. He told me only No.

"She will not have it," he said, his voice very placating and calm. "I know her. I know all her ways. She brought me to herself because I worshiped her. And once having her blood I have never ceased in that worship."

I stood there, clutching his wrist still, and staring about me as if I were ready to cry out to the gods. And it seemed my cry would break the very walls of this house if I let it loose.

"How can this be!" I whispered. "That I should find her and know her only for one night, one precious night of quarreling."

"You and she are equals," he said. "I am but an instrument."

I closed my eyes.

Quite suddenly I could hear her weeping, and when this sound came to my ears, Arjun gently freed himself from me and said in his soft gentle voice that he must go to her.

I walked slowly out of the hallway, and down the marble steps and into the night, ignoring my carriage.

I walked home through the forest.

When I reached my house, I went into my library, took off the wig which I had worn to the ball, threw it across the room and sat in a chair at my writing table.

I put my head down on my folded arms and silently wept as I had not wept since the death of Eudoxia. I wept. And the hours passed, and at last I realized that Bianca was standing beside me.

She was stroking my hair with her hand, and then I heard her whisper.

"Time to come down the steps to our cold grave, Marius. It is early for you, but I must go and I can't leave you this way."

I rose to my feet. I took her in my arms and gave way to the most awful tears, and all the while she held me silently and warmly.

And then we went down to our coffins together.

The following night, I went immediately to the house where I'd left Pandora.

I found it deserted and then I searched all of Dresden and the many palaces or schlosses around it.

She and Arjun were gone, there was no doubt of it. And going up to the Ducal Palace where there was a little concert in progress I soon learned the "official" news of it, of how the handsome black coach of the Marquis and the Marquisa De Malvrier had left before dawn for Russia.

Russia.

Being in no mood for the music, I soon made my apologies to those gathered in the salon and I went home again, as miserable as I have ever been in my existence. As heartbroken.

I sat down at my desk. I looked out over the river. I felt the warm spring breeze.

I thought of all the many things she and I should have said to each other, all the many things I might have said in a calmer spirit to persuade her. I told myself she wasn't gone beyond reach. I told myself that she knew where I was, and that she could write to me. I told myself anything I needed to keep my sanity.

And I did not hear it when Bianca came into the room. I did not hear it when she sat down in a large tapestried armchair quite near to me.

I saw her as if she were a vision when I looked up—a flawless young boy with porcelain cheeks, her blond hair pulled back in a black ribbon, her frock coat embroidered in gold, her shapely legs in spotless white hose, her feet in ruby buckled shoes.

Oh, what a divine guise it was—Bianca as the young nobleman, known to the few mortals who mattered as her own brother. And how sad were her peerless blue eyes, as she looked at me.

"I feel sorry for you," she said quietly.

"Do you?" I asked. I said these words with my broken heart. "I hope you do, my precious darling, because I love you, I love you more than I have ever loved you, and I need you."

"But that's just the point, you see," she said in a low compassionate voice. "I heard the things you said to her. And I'm leaving you."

33

FOR THREE LONG NIGHTS I pleaded with her not to go as she made her preparations. I went down on my knees. I swore to her that I had said only what needed to be said to make Pandora remain with me.

I told her in every way I knew how that I loved her, and would never have abandoned her.

I told her that she would never be able to survive alone, and that I feared for her.

But nothing would turn her from her decision.

Only on the beginning of the third night did I realize that she was really going. Up until then, I had thought that such was absolutely inconceivable. I couldn't lose her. No, such a thing could not happen.

At last, I begged her to sit down and listen to me as I poured out my honest heart, confessing every bad thing which I had said, every cheap denial of her which had come from my lips, every desperate foolish thing I'd said to Pandora.

"But what I want now is to talk of you and me," I said, "and how it's always been between us."

"Yes, you may do that if you wish," she said, "if it makes the pain less for you, but Marius, I am going."

"You know how it was with me and Amadeo," I said. "I took him into my house when he was very young and gave him the Blood when mortality gave me no quarter. We were Master and pupil always, and there was mockery and a dark division. Perhaps you never saw this, but it was there, I assure you."

"I saw it," she said. "But I knew your love was greater."

"And so it was," I said. "But he was a child, and my man's heart always knew there was something finer and greater. Much as I cherished him, much as the mere sight of him delighted me, I could not confide to him my worst fears or pains. I could not tell him the tales of my life. They were too big for him."

"I understand you, Marius," she said gently. "I always have."

"And Pandora. You saw it with your own eyes. The bitter quarrel again, just as it had been so many centuries ago, the bitter fighting in which no real truth can be discovered."

"I saw it," she said in her quiet way. "I follow your meaning."

"You saw her fear of the Mother and the Father," I pleaded. "You heard her say that she couldn't come into the house. You heard her speak of her fear of everything."

"I did," she answered.

"And what was this one night between me and Pandora but misery, as it had been long ago, misery and misunderstanding."

"I know, Marius," she answered.

"But Bianca, what has it always been with you and me but harmony? Think of our long years when we dwelt in the shrine, and went out on the night winds where I could carry us. Think of the quiet between us, or the long conversations in which I talked of so many things and you listened. Could two beings have been closer than we were?"

She bowed her head. She didn't answer.

"And these last years," I pleaded. "Think of all the pleasures we have shared, our secretive hunting in the forests, our visits to the country festivals, our quiet attendance in the great cathedrals when the candles burn and the choirs sing, our dancing at the Court Balls. Think of all of it."

"I know, Marius," she said. "But you lied to me. You didn't tell me why we were coming to Dresden."

"I confess, it's true. Tell me what I can do to make up for it?"

"Nothing, Marius," she answered. "I'm going."

"But how will you live? You can't live without me. This is madness."

"No, I shall live quite well," she said. "And I must go now. I must travel many miles before dawn."

"And where will you sleep?"

"That is my worry now."

I was almost on the point of frenzy.

"Don't follow me, Marius," she said, as if she could read my mind which she could not.

"I can't accept this," I responded.

A silence fell between us, and I realized she was looking at me, and I looked at her, unable to hide a particle of my unhappiness.

"Bianca, don't do this," I pleaded.

"I saw your passion for her," she whispered, "and I knew that in a moment you would cast me aside. Oh, don't deny it. I saw it. And something in me was crushed. I couldn't protect that thing. I couldn't prevent its destruction. We were too close, you and I. And though I have loved you with my whole soul, so I believed I knew you completely, I didn't know the being you were with her. I didn't know the being whom I saw in her eyes."

She rose from the chair and moved away from me. She looked out the window.

"I wish I had not heard all those many words," she said, "but we have such gifts, we blood drinkers. And do you think I don't realize that you would never have made me your child except for the fact that you needed me? Had you not been burnt and helpless, you would never have given me the Blood."

"Will you listen to me when I tell you that's not so? When first I saw you I loved you. It was only out of respect for your mortal life that I didn't share these cursed gifts with you! It was you who filled my eyes and heart before I ever found Amadeo. I swear this to you. Don't you remember the portraits I painted of you? Do you remember the hours I spent in your rooms? Think now on all that we've given each other."

"You deceived me," she said.

"Yes, I did," I said. "And I admit it, and I swear that I shall never do it again. Not for Pandora or for anyone."

On and on I pleaded.

"I can't stay with you," she said. "I must go now."

She turned around and looked at me. She seemed wrapped in quiet and resolution.

"I'm begging you," I said again. "Without pride, without reserve, I'm begging you, don't leave me."

"I must go," she said. "And now, please, let me go down to take my leave of the Mother and the Father. I would do this alone if you would allow it."

I nodded.

It was a long time before she came up from the shrine. She told me quietly that she would leave on the following sunset.

And true to her word, she did, her coach and four pulling out of the gates, as she began her journey.

I stood at the top of the stairs watching her go. I stood listening until the coach was deep into the forest. I stood unbelieving and unable to accept that she was gone from me.

How could this horrid disaster have occurred—that I lose Pandora and Bianca both? That I should be alone? And I was powerless to stop it.

For many months after that, I could scarcely believe what had befallen me.

I told myself that a letter would soon come from Pandora, or that she herself would return with Arjun, that Pandora would will it so.

I told myself that Bianca would realize that she could not exist without me. She would come home, eager to forgive me, or she would send some hasty letter asking me to come to her.

But these things did not happen.

A year passed and these things did not happen.

And another year and then fifty. And these things did not happen.

And all the while, though I moved deeper into the woods surrounding Dresden, in another more fortified castle, I remained near at hand in the hopes that one or both of my loves would come back to me.

For a half century I remained, waiting, not believing, and weighed down with a sorrow I couldn't share with anyone.

I think I had ceased to pray in the shrine though I tended it faithfully. And I had begun, in a confidential manner, to talk to Akasha. I had begun to tell her my woes in a more informal manner than before, to tell her of how I had failed with those whom I had loved.

"But I shall never fail with you, my Queen," I said, and I said it often.

And then as the 1700s commenced, I prepared to make a daring move to an island where I would rule supreme in the Aegean Sea, surrounded by mortals who would easily accept me as their lord, in a stone house which I had prepared for me by a host of mortal servants.

All who have read The Vampire Lestat's tale of his life know of this immense and unusual place because he vividly described it. It far exceeded in grandeur any other palace in which I had ever lived, and its remoteness was a challenge to my ingenuity.

But I was most purely alone now, alone as I had ever been before the love of Amadeo, or Bianca, and I had no hope of an immortal companion. And perhaps in truth I wanted none.

It had been centuries since I had heard of Mael. I knew nothing of Avicus or Zenobia. I knew nothing of any other Child of the Millennia.

I wanted only a great and gorgeous shrine for the Mother and Father, and as I have said, I spoke to Akasha constantly.

But before I go on to describe this last and most important of all my European dwellings, I must include one last tragic detail in the story of those who were lost to me.

As my many treasures were moved to this Aegean palace, as my books, my sculptures, my fine tapestries and rugs and other such were shipped and uncrated by unsuspecting mortals, there came to light one final piece of the story of my beloved Pandora.

In the bottom of a packing case, one of the workers discovered a letter, written on parchment, and folded in half, and addressed quite simply to Marius.

I was on the terrace of this new house, gazing out at the sea and over the many small islands that surrounded me, when the letter was brought to me.

The page of parchment was thick with dust, and as soon as I opened it, I read a date inscribed in old ink which affirmed that it had been written the night I parted with Pandora.

It was as if the fifty years separating me from that pain meant nothing.

My beloved Marius,

It is almost dawn and I have only a few moments in which to write to you. As we have told you, our coach will leave within the hour carrying us away and towards the eventual destination of Moscow.

Marius, I want nothing more than to come to you now, but I cannot do it. I cannot seek shelter in the same house with the Ancient Ones.

But I beg you, my beloved, please come to Moscow. Please come and help me to free myself from Arjun. Later you can judge me and condemn me.

I need you, Marius. I shall haunt the vicinity of the Czar's palace and the Great Cathedral until you come.

Marius, I know I ask of you that you make a great journey, but please come.

Whatever I have said of my love of Arjun, I am his slave now too completely, and I would be yours again.

Pandora.

For hours I sat with the letter in my hand, and then slowly I rose and went to my servants and asked them that they tell me where the letter had been found.

It had been in a packing case of books from my old library.

How had I failed to receive it? Had Bianca hidden this letter from me? That I couldn't believe. It seemed some simpler more haphazard cruelty had taken place—that a servant had laid it on my desk in the early hours, and I myself had swept it aside into a heap of books without ever seeing it.

But what did it matter?

The awful damage was done.

She had written to me, and I had not known it. She had begged me to come to Moscow and I, not knowing, had not gone. And I did not know where to find her. I had her avowal of love, but it was too late.

In the following months I searched the Russian capital. I searched in the hope that she and Arjun had for some reason made their home there.

But I found no trace of Pandora. The wide world had swallowed her as it had swallowed my Bianca.

What more can I say to reveal the anguish of these two losses—that of Pandora whom I'd sought for so long, and my sweet and lovely Bianca?

With these two losses my story comes to a close.

Or rather I should say we have come full circle.

We now return to the story of the Queen of the Damned and of The Vampire Lestat who waked her. And I shall be brief as I revisit that story. For I think I see most clearly what it is that would heal my miserable soul more than anything. But before I can move on to that, we must revisit Lestat's antics and the story of how I lost my last love, Akasha.

34

The Vampire Lestat

AS ALL KNOW, who follow our Chronicles, I was on the island in the Aegean Sea, ruling over a peaceful world of mortals when Lestat, a young vampire, no more than ten years in the Blood, began to call out to me.

Now I was most belligerent in my solitude. And not even the recent rise of Amadeo, out of the old coven in Paris, to become the Master of the new and bizarre Théâtre des Vampires, could lure me from my solitude.

For though I had spied upon Amadeo more than once, I saw nothing in him, but the same heartbreaking sadness that I had known in Venice. I preferred loneliness to courting him.

But when I heard the call of Lestat, I sensed in him a powerful and unfettered intelligence, and I went to him at once, rescuing him from his first true retreat as a blood drinker and I brought him to my house, revealing its location to him.

I felt a great outpouring of love for Lestat, and impetuously perhaps, I took him down to the shrine immediately. I watched transfixed as he drew close to the Mother, and then in amazement as he kissed her.

I don't know whether it was his boldness or her stillness which so mesmerized me. But you can be certain I was ready to intervene if Enkil should try to hurt him.

When Lestat drew back, when he told me that the Mother had confided to him her name, I was caught off guard and a sudden wave of terrible jealousy took hold of me.

But I denied this feeling. I was too in love with Lestat and I told myself that this seeming miracle in the shrine meant only good things—that this young blood drinker might somehow spark life in the two Parents.

And so I took him to my salon, as I have described—and as he has described—and I told him the long tale of my beginnings. I told him the tale of the Mother and Father and their unending quietude.

He seemed a splendid pupil during all the hours that we talked together. Indeed, I don't think I had ever felt closer in my life to anyone than I did to Lestat. I was never closer even to Bianca. Lestat had traveled the world in his ten years in the Blood; he had devoured the great literature of many nations; and he brought to our conversation a vigor I had never seen really in anyone I had loved, not even in Pandora.

But the following night, as I was out tending to affairs with my mortal subjects, of whom there were many, Lestat went down to the shrine, taking with him a violin which had once belonged to his friend and fellow blood drinker, Nicolas.

And mimicking the skill of his lost friend, Lestat played the violin passionately and wondrously for the Divine Parents.

Over the short miles I heard the music. And then I heard a high-pitched singing note such as no mortal could ever have made. Indeed, it seemed the song of the Sirens of Greek mythology, and as I stood wondering what this sound could be, it died away in silence.

I tried to bridge the gap which separated me from my house, and what I saw through the unveiled mind of Lestat defied my belief.

Akasha had risen from her throne, and held Lestat in her embrace, and as Lestat drank from Akasha, Akasha drank from Lestat.

I turned and sped back towards my house and towards the shrine. But even as I did so, the scene shifted fatally.

Enkil had risen and had ripped Lestat loose from the Mother and she stood screaming for Lestat in tones that could deafen any mortal.

Rushing down the stone steps I found the doors of the shrine deliberately shut against me. I commenced to pound on them with all my force. And all the while I could see within, through Lestat's eyes, that Enkil had forced Lestat down on the floor, and Enkil, despite Akasha's screams, meant to crush him.

Oh, how plaintive were her screams for all their volume.

Desperately, I called out to him:

"Enkil, if you harm Lestat, if you kill him, I shall take her away from you forever and she will help me to do it. My King, this is what she wants!"

I could scarcely believe that I had shouted these words, but they had come to my mind immediately and there was no time to ponder them.

The doors of the shrine were at once opened. What an impossible and terrifying sight it was, the two stark white creatures standing there, in their Egyptian raiment, she with her mouth dripping with blood, and Enkil, standing there, yet as though he were in deep slumber.

In horror, I saw that Enkil's foot was resting against Lestat's chest. But Lestat still lived. Lestat was unharmed. Beside him lay the violin, smashed to pieces. Akasha stared forward as though she had never waked, looking past me.

I moved quickly and put my hands on Enkil's shoulders.

"Go back, my King," I said. "Go back. You have accomplished your purpose. Please, do as I beg you. You know how I respect your power."

Slowly he removed his foot from Lestat's chest, his expression blank, his movements sluggish as they always were, and gradually I was able to move him to the steps of the dais. Slowly he turned to make the two steps, and slowly he sat down on his throne, and I with quick hands arranged his garments carefully.

"Lestat, run," I said firmly. "Don't for a moment question me. Run from here."

And as Lestat did as he was told, I turned to Akasha.

She was standing as if lost in a dream, and I put my hands very carefully on her arms.

"My beautiful one," I whispered, "my Sovereign. Let me return you to the throne."

As she had always done in the past, she obeyed me.

Within a few moments, they were as they had always been, as if it had been a delusion that Lestat had come, a delusion that his music had waked her.

But I knew it was no delusion, and as I stared at her, as I spoke to her in my intimate way, I was filled with a new fear that I did not express to her.

"You're beautiful and unchangeable," I said, "and the world is unworthy of you. It's unworthy of your power. You listen to so many prayers, don't you? And so you listened to this beautiful music and it delighted you. Perhaps I can some time bring music to you . . . bring those who can play it and believe that you and the King are but statues—."

I broke off this mad speech. What was I trying to do?

The truth is, I was terrified. Lestat had accomplished a breach of order of which I'd never dreamt, and I wondered what might lie ahead if anyone else attempted such!

But the main point, the point to which I clung in my anger, was this: I had restored the order. I had, by threats to my Royal Majesty, made him move back to the throne, and she, my beloved Queen, had followed him.

Lestat had done the unthinkable. But Marius had accomplished the remedy.

At last when my fear and my temper were better, I went down on the rocks by the sea to meet with Lestat and to chastise Lestat and I found myself more out of control than I imagined.

Who, but Marius, knew how long these Parents had sat in silence? And now this young one whom I had wanted so to love, so to instruct, so to enfold—this young one had brought out of them a movement which only further emboldened him.

Lestat wanted to free the Queen. Lestat thought we ought to imprison Enkil. I think I must have laughed. Surely I couldn't put into words how much I feared both of them.

Later that night, as Lestat hunted in the far islands, I heard strange sounds from the shrine.

I went down and discovered that various objects were shattered. Vases, lamps, lay broken or on their sides. Candles had been flung here and there. Which of the two Parents did these things? Neither moved. I couldn't know, and once again the fear in me increased.

For one desperate selfish moment, I looked at Akasha and I thought, I shall give you over to Lestat if that is what you wish! Only tell me how to do it. Rise against Enkil with me! But these words didn't really form in my mind.

In my soul I felt a cold jealousy. I felt a leaden sorrow.

But then I could tell myself it was the magic of the violin, was it not? For when in ancient times had such an instrument been heard? And he, a blood drinker, had come before her to perform, in all probability twisting and turning the music madly.

There was no consolation in this for me, however. She had waked for him!

And as I stood in the silence of the shrine, staring at all the broken objects, a thought came into my mind as though she had put it there.

I loved him as you loved him and would have him here as you would have him. But it cannot be.

I was transfixed.

But then I moved towards her as I had done a hundred times, advancing slowly so that she might refuse me if she wished, so that he might deny me with even the smallest show of power. And at last I drank from her, perhaps from the very same vein in her white throat, I didn't know, and then I moved back, my eyes on Enkil's face.

His cold features registered nothing but listlessness.

When I woke the following night I heard noises from the shrine. I found more of the many fine objects broken.

I felt I had no choice but to send Lestat away. I knew of no other remedy.

It was another bitter terrible parting—as miserable as my parting with Pandora, or my parting with Bianca.

I will never forget how comely he appeared, with his fabled yellow hair and his fathomless blue eyes, how eternally young, how full of frenetic hope and marvelous dreams, and how wounded and stricken he was to be sent away. And how my heart ached that I must do it. I wanted only to keep him close—my pupil, my lover, my rebel. I had so loved his rippling speech, his honest questions, his daring appeals for the Queen's heart and freedom. Could we not save her somehow from Enkil? Could we not somehow enliven her? But it was oh, so dangerous even to talk of such things, and Lestat could not grasp it.

And so this young one, this young one whom I had so loved, I had to forsake, no matter how broken my heart, no matter how lonely my soul, no matter how bruised my intellect and spirit.

But I was now truly afraid of what Akasha and Enkil might do if they were aroused again, and I could not share that fear with Lestat, lest I frighten him or even incite him further.

You see, I understood how restless he was even then, and how unhappy in the Blood, and how eager for a purpose in the mortal world, and keenly aware that he had none.

And I, alone in my Aegean paradise after he left, truly pondered whether I should destroy the Mother and Father.

All who have read our Chronicles know that the year in which this happened was 1794, and the world was rich in marvels.

How could I continue to harbor these beings who might menace it? But I didn't want to die. No, I have never really wanted to die. And so I did not destroy the King and the Queen. I continued to care for them, to shower them with the symbols of worship.

And as we moved into the multitudinous wonders of the modern world, I feared death more than ever.

35

The Rise and Fall of Akasha

I T WAS PERHAPS twenty years ago that I brought the Mother and
Father across the sea to America and to the frozen wastes in the
North where I created beneath the ice my fine technologically
splendid house described by Lestat in *The Queen of the Damned* and
from which the Queen rose.

Let me pass over quickly what has been mentioned here before—
that I made a great modern shrine for the King and Queen with a television screen that might bring them music and other forms of
entertainment and "news" from all over the planet.

As for me, I was living alone in this house, enjoying a whole string
of well-warmed rooms and libraries as I did my eternal reading and
writing, as I watched films and documentaries which intrigued me
mightily.

I had entered the mortal world once or twice as a filmmaker, but in
general I had lived a solitary life, and I knew little or nothing of the
other Children of the Millennia.

Until such time as Bianca or Pandora should want to join me again,
what did I care about others? And as for The Vampire Lestat, when he
came forth with his mighty rock music I thought it hysterically funny.
What more perfect guise for a vampire, I thought, than that of a rock
musician?

But as his many short rock video films appeared, I realized that he
was putting forth in that form the entire history which I had revealed
to him. And I realized as well that blood drinkers all over the world
were setting their cannons against him.

These were young beings of whom I had taken no notice, and I was quite amazed now to hear their voices lifted in the Mind Gift, searching diligently for others.

Nevertheless, I thought nothing of it. I did not dream his music could affect the world—not the world of mortals or our world—

—not until the very night that I came down to the underground shrine and discovered my King, Enkil, a hollow being, a mere husk, a creature drained of all blood, sitting so perilously on the throne that when I touched him with my fingers, he fell onto the marble floor, his black plaited hair breaking into tiny splinters.

In shock I stared at this spectacle! Who could have done such a thing, who could have drained him of every drop of blood, who could have destroyed him!

And where was my Queen, had she met the same fate, had the whole legend of Those Who Must Be Kept been a deception from the beginning?

I knew that it was not a lie, and I knew the one being who could have visited this fate upon Enkil, the only being in all the world who had such cunning, such intimacy, such knowledge and such power.

Within seconds, I turned from the fallen husk of Enkil to discover her standing not three inches from me. Her black eyes were narrowed and quickened with life. Her royal raiment was the clothing I had placed upon her. Her red lips formed a mocking smile, and then there came from her a wicked laughter.

I hated her for that laughter.

I feared her and hated her that she laughed at me.

All my sense of possession came to the fore, that she was mine and that she now dared to turn on me.

Where was the sweetness of which I had dreamt? I stood in the midst of a nightmare.

"My dear servant," she said, "you have never had the power to stop me!"

It was inconceivable that this creature whom I had so protected throughout time could turn on me. It was inconceivable that this one whom I so completely adored now taunted me.

Something hasty and pathetic came from my lips:

"But what do you want?" I asked, as I tried to grasp what was taking place. "What do you mean to do?"

It was a wonder that she even gave some mocking answer to me.

It was lost in the sound of the television screen exploding, in the sound of metal ripping, in the sound of the ice falling.

With incalculable power she rose from the depths of the house, sending its walls, its ceilings, and its surrounding ice down upon me.

I found myself buried, calling for help.

And the reign of the Queen of the Damned had commenced, though she had never taken that name for herself.

You saw her as she moved through the world. You saw her as she slew blood drinkers all around her, you saw her as she slew blood drinkers who would not serve her purpose.

Did you see her as she took Lestat as her lover? Did you see her as she sought to frighten mortals with her petty displays of old-fashioned power?

And all the while I lay crushed beneath the ice—spared for what purpose I could not imagine—sending out my warning to Lestat that he was in danger, sending out my warning to all that they were in danger. And pleading as well with any Child of the Millennia who might come to help me rise from the crevasse in which I'd been buried.

Even as I called in my powerful voice I healed. I began to move the ice around me.

But at last two blood drinkers came to assist me. I caught the image of one in the mind of the other. And it seemed impossible to me, but the one whom I saw so radiantly in the other's vision was none other than my Pandora.

At last, with their help, I broke the ice that kept me from the surface, and I climbed free under the arctic sky, taking Pandora's hand, and then gathering her in my arms, refusing for a moment to think of anything, even of my savage Queen and her deadly rampage.

There were no words now, no vows, no denials. I held Pandora in love and she knew it, and when I looked up, when I cleared my eyes of pain and love and fear, I realized that the blood drinker who had come North with her, he who had answered my summons, was none other than Santino.

For a moment, I was filled with such hatred I meant to destroy him completely.

"No," Pandora said, "Marius, you can't. All of us are needed now. And why do you think he has come if not to repay you?"

He stood there in the snow in his fine black garments, the wind whipping his black hair and I could see he was consumed with fear, but he would not confess it.

"This is no repayment for what you did to me," I said to him. "But I know Pandora is right, we're all needed, and for that reason, I spare you."

I looked at my beloved Pandora.

"There is a council forming now," I said. "It's in a great house in the coastal forest, a place of glass walls. We'll go there together."

You know of what happened then. We gathered at our great table in the redwood trees—as if we were a new and passionate Faithful of the Forest—and when the Queen came to us with her plan to bring harm to the great world, we all sought to reason with her.

It was her dream to be the Queen of Heaven to humankind, to slay male children by the billions, and make the world a "garden" of tender-spirited women. It was a horrific and impossible conception.

No one sought more diligently than your red-haired Maker Maharet to turn her from her goals, condemning her that she would dare to change the course of human history.

I myself, thinking bitterly of the beautiful gardens I'd seen when I had drunk her blood, risked her deadly power over and over by pleading with her to give the world time to follow its own destiny.

Oh, it was a chilling thing to see this living statue now speaking to me so coldly yet with such strong will and contemptuous temper. How grand and evil were her schemes, to slay male children, to gather women in a superstitious worship.

What gave us courage to fight her? I don't know except that we knew that we had to do it. And all along, as she threatened us repeatedly with death, I thought: I could have prevented this, I could have stopped it from ever happening had I put an end to her and to all of us.

As it is, she will destroy us and go on; and who will prevent her?

At one point she knocked me backwards with her arm, so quick was her rage at my words. And it was Santino who came to my assistance. I hated him for this but there was no time for hating him or anyone.

At last she laid her condemnation down on all of us. As we would not side with her, we would be destroyed, one after another. She would begin with Lestat, for she took his insult to her to be the greatest. And he had resisted her. Bravely he had sided with us, pleading with her for reason.

At this dreadful moment, the elders rose, the ones of the First Brood who had been made blood drinkers within her very lifetime, and those Children of the Millennia such as Pandora and myself and Mael and others.

But before the murderous little struggle could begin, there came another into our midst, approaching loudly up the iron steps of the forest compound where we met, until in the doorway we beheld the twin of Maharet: her mute sister, the sister from whom Akasha had torn the tongue: Mekare.

It was she who, snatching the long black hair of the Queen, bashed her head against the glass wall, breaking it, and severing the head from the body. It was she and her sister who dropped down on their knees, to retrieve from the decapitated Queen, the Sacred Core of all the vampires.

Whether that Sacred Core—that fatal root—was imbibed from heart or brain, I know not. I know only that the mute Mekare became its new tabernacle.

And after a few moments of sputtering darkness in which we all of us wondered whether or not death should take us now, we regained our strength and looked up to see the twins standing before us.

Maharet put her arm around Mekare's waist, and Mekare, come from brutal isolation I know not where, merely stared into space as though she knew some quiet peace but no more than that. And from Maharet's lips there came the words:

"Behold. The Queen of the Damned."

It was finished.

The reign of my beloved Akasha—with all its hopes and dreams— had come abruptly to an end.

And I carried through the world the burden of Those Who Must Be Kept no longer.

The End of the Story of Marius

THE LISTENER

36

MARIUS STOOD at the glass window looking out at the snow.

Thorne sat by the dying fire, merely looking at Marius.

"So you have woven for me a long, fine tale," said Thorne, "and I have found myself marvelously caught up in it."

"Have you?" said Marius quietly. "And perhaps I now find myself woven within my hatred of Santino."

"But Pandora was with you," said Thorne. "You were reunited with her again. Why is she not with you now? What's happened?"

"I was united with Pandora and Amadeo," said Marius. "It all came about in those nights. And I have seen them often since. But I am an injured creature. And it was I who left their company. I could go now to Lestat, and those who are with him. But I don't.

"My soul still aches over the losses I've suffered. I don't know which causes me the greater pain—the loss of my goddess, or my hatred of Santino. She is gone beyond my reach forever. But Santino still lives."

"Why don't you do away with him?" asked Thorne. "I'll help you find him."

"I can find him," said Marius. "But without her permission I can't do it."

"Maharet?" Thorne asked. "But why?"

"Because she's the eldest of us now, she and her mute twin, and we must have a leader. Mekare cannot speak and might not have wits to speak even if she could. And so it's Maharet. And even if she refuses to allow or judge, I must put the question to her."

"I understand," said Thorne. "In my time, we gathered to settle such questions, and a man might seek payment from one who had injured him."

Marius nodded.

"I think I must seek Santino's death," he whispered. "I am at peace with all others, but to him I would do violence."

"And very well you should," said Thorne, "from all that you've told me."

"I've called to Maharet," said Marius. "I've let her know that you are here and that you're seeking her. I've let her know that I must ask her about Santino. I'm hungry for her wise words. Perhaps I want to see her weary mortal eyes gazing on me with compassion.

"I remember her brilliant resistance of the Queen. I remember her strength and maybe now I need it. . . . Perhaps by now she's found the eyes of a blood drinker for herself, and need not suffer anymore with the eyes of her human victims."

Thorne sat thinking for a long moment. Then he rose from the couch. He drew close to the glass beside Marius.

"Can you hear her answer to you?" he asked. He couldn't disguise his emotion. "I want to go to her. I must go to her."

"Haven't I taught you anything?" Marius asked. He turned to Thorne. "Haven't I taught you to remember these tender complex creatures with love? Perhaps not. I thought that was the lesson of my stories."

"Oh, yes, you've taught me this," said Thorne, "and love her I do, in so far as she is tender and complex as you so delicately put it, but I'm a warrior, you see, and I was never fit for eternity. And the hatred you harbor for Santino is the same as the passion I harbor for her. And passion can be for evil or good. I can't help myself."

Marius shook his head.

"If she brings us to herself," he said, "I will only lose you. As I've told you before, you can't possibly harm her."

"Perhaps, perhaps not," said Thorne. "But whatever the truth, I must see her. And she knows why I've come, and she will have her will in the matter."

"Come now," Marius said, "it's time for us to go to our rest. I hear strange voices in the morning air. And I feel the need of sleep desperately."

. . .

WHEN THORNE AWOKE he found himself in a smooth wooden coffin.

Without fear, he easily lifted the lid, and then opened it to one side and sat up so that he might see the room around him.

It was a cave of sorts, and beyond he heard the loud chorus of a tropical forest.

All the fragrances of the green jungle assaulted his nostrils. He found it delicious and strange, and he knew it could only mean one thing: that Maharet had brought him to her hiding place.

He climbed from the coffin as gracefully as he could and he stepped out into a huge room full of scattered stone benches. On the three sides the jungle grew thick and lively against a fine wire mesh and through the mesh above a thin rain came down refreshing him.

Looking to his right and left, he saw entrances to other such open places. And following the sounds and scents as any blood drinker could do, he moved to his right until he entered a great room where his Maker sat as he had seen her at the very beginning of his long life, in a graceful gown of purple wool, pulling the red hairs from her head and weaving them into thread with her distaff and her spindle.

For many long moments he merely stared at her, as if he could not believe this vision.

And she in profile, surely knowing he was there, went on with her work, without speaking a word to him.

Across the room, he saw Marius seated on a bench and then he realized that a regal and beautiful woman sat beside him. Surely it was Pandora. Indeed, he knew her by her brown hair. And there on the other side of Marius was the auburn-haired boy he had described: Amadeo.

But there was also another creature in the room, and this without doubt was the black-haired Santino. He sat not far from Maharet, and when Thorne entered, he appeared to shrink away from Thorne, and then glancing at Marius to draw back again, and finally towards Maharet as if in desperation.

Coward, Thorne thought, but he said nothing.

Slowly Maharet turned her head until she could see Thorne, and so that he could see her eyes—human eyes—sad and full of blood, as always.

"What can I give you, Thorne?" she asked, "to make your soul quiet again?"

He shook his head. He motioned for silence, not to compel her but merely to plead with her.

And in the interval Marius rose to his feet, and at once Pandora and Amadeo on either side of him.

"I've thought long and hard on it," Marius said, his eyes on Santino. "And I can't destroy him if you forbid it. I won't break the peace with such an action. I believe too much that we must live by rules or we shall all perish."

"Then it is finished," said Maharet, her familiar voice bringing the chills to Thorne, "for I'll never grant you the right to destroy Santino. Yes, he injured you and it was a terrible thing, and I have heard you in the night describing your suffering to Thorne. I've listened to your words in sorrow. But you can't destroy him now. I forbid it. And if you go against me, then there is no one who can restrain anyone."

"That can't be," said Marius. His face was dark and miserable. He glared at Santino. "There must be someone to restrain others. Yet I can't bear it that he lives after what he's done to me."

To Thorne's amazement the youthful face of Amadeo appeared only puzzled.

As for Pandora, she seemed sad and anxious, as though she feared that Marius wouldn't keep to his word.

But Thorne knew otherwise.

And as he assessed this black-haired creature now, Santino rose from the bench and backed away from Thorne, pointing his finger at Thorne in terror.

But it was not quick enough.

Thorne sent all his strength at Santino and all Santino could do as he fell to his knees was cry out: "Thorne," over and over again, his body exploding, the blood flowing from every orifice, the fire finally erupting from his chest and head as he twisted and collapsed on the stone floor, the flames at last consuming him.

Maharet had let out a terrible wail of sorrow, and into the large room her twin had come, her blue eyes searching for the source of pain in her sister.

Maharet rose to her feet. She looked down on the grease and ash that lay before her.

Thorne looked at Marius. He saw a small bitter smile on Marius's lips, and then Marius looked to him and nodded.

"I need no thanks from you," Thorne said.

Then he looked to Maharet who was weeping, her sister now holding tight to her arms, and pleading mutely with her to explain herself.

"Wergeld, my Maker," said Thorne. "As it was in my time, I exact the wergeld or payment for my own life, which you took when you made me a blood drinker. I take it through Santino's life, which I take beneath your roof."

"Yes, and against my will," Maharet cried. "You have done this terrible thing! And Marius, your own friend, has told you that I must rule here."

"If you would rule here, do it on your own," said Thorne. "Don't look to Marius to tell you how to do it. Ah, look at your precious distaff and spindle. How will you protect the Sacred Core if you have no strength to fight those who oppose you?"

She couldn't answer him, and he could see that Marius was angered, and that Mekare looked at him with menace.

He came towards Maharet, staring intently at her, at her smooth face which now bore no trace whatever of human life, the florid human eyes seemingly set within a sculpture.

"Would I had a knife," he said, "would I had a sword, would I had any weapon I could use against you." And then he did the only thing which he could do. He took her by the throat with both his hands and tried to topple her.

It was like holding fast to marble.

At once there came a frantic cry from her. He couldn't understand the words, but when her sister drew him back gently he knew it had been a warning for his sake. He reached out still with both hands, struggling to be free, but it was useless.

These two were unconquerable, either divided or together, it did not matter.

"Put an end to this, Thorne," cried Marius. "It's enough. She knows what's in your heart. You can't ask for more than this."

Maharet collapsed to her bench and there she sat crying, her sister at her side, Mekare's eyes fixed on Thorne warily.

Thorne could see that all of them were afraid of Mekare, but he was not, and when he thought of Santino again, when he looked at the black stain on the stones, he felt a good deep pleasure.

Then moving swiftly, he accosted the mute twin and whispered something hurried in her ear, meant only for her, wondering if she would get the sense of it.

Within a second he knew that she had. As Maharet watched in wonder, Mekare forced him down on his knees. She clasped his face and turned it up. And then he felt her fingers plunge into the sockets of his eyes as she removed them.

"Yes, yes, this blessed darkness," he said, "and then the chains, I beg you, the chains. Otherwise do away with me."

Through Marius's mind, he could see the image of himself groping in blindness. He could see the blood flowing down his face. He could see Maharet as Mekare put the eyes into her head. He could see those two tall delicate women with their arms entangled, the one struggling but not enough and the other pressing for the deed to be accomplished.

Then he felt others gathered around him. He felt the fabric of their garments, he felt their smooth hands.

And only in the distance could he hear Maharet weeping.

The chains were being put around him. He felt their thick links and knew he could not break loose from them. And being dragged further away, he said nothing.

The blood flowed from his eye sockets. He knew it. And in some quiet empty place he was now bound exactly as he had dreamt of it. Only she wasn't close. She wasn't close at all. He heard the jungle sounds. And he longed for the winter cold, and this place was too warm and too full of the perfume of flowers.

But he would get used to the heat. He would get used to the rich fragrances.

"Maharet," he whispered.

He saw what they saw again, in another room, as they looked at each other, all of them talking in hushed voices of his fate and none fully understanding it. He knew that Marius was pleading for him, and he knew that Maharet whom he saw so vividly through their eyes was as beautiful now as she had been when she made him.

Suddenly she was gone from the group. And they talked in shadows without her.

Then he felt her hand on his cheek. He knew it. He knew the soft wool of her gown. He knew her lips when she kissed him.

"You do have my eyes," he said.

"Oh, yes," she said. "I see wondrously through them."

"And these chains, are they made of your hair?"

"Yes," she answered. "From hair to thread, from thread to rope, from rope to links, I have woven them."

"My weaving one," he said, smiling. "And when you weave them now," he asked, "will you keep me close to you?"

"Yes," she said. "Always."

9:20 p.m.
March 19, 2000